Dear Reader

Autumn is nearly upon us and with it the start of those longer evenings when you can curl up with the latest *Scarlet* novels. What a perfect way to spend an evening!

There are three fabulous titles this month for you to enjoy, including our second hardback *Finding Gold* by Golden Heart Award winner, Tammy Hilz: Jackson Dermont is on the trail of a thief and the mysterious Rachel Gold is high on his list of suspects. Is she guilty or innocent? In Kathryn Bellamy's novel, *A Woman Scorned*, we have a secret baby plot spiced up for the nineties, and in Vickie Moore's third Scarlet novel *Seared Satin*, security firm boss Tess Reynolds doesn't need any man's help until gorgeous Ethan Booker joins her to solve a deadly mystery.

By the way, is your collection of *Scarlet* novels complete, or are you longing for a certain title that sold out before you had chance to get hold of it? If so, feel free to drop me a line and I will ensure that your letter is passed on to the relevant department.

Till next month,

Sally Cooper

SALLY COOPER,
Editor-in-Chief – *Scarlet*

About the Author

Vickie Moore lives in Wichita, Kansas with her family and assorted pets. A full-time writer, she enjoys the enticing mixture of romance and suspense. Her family has become quite accustomed to finding references to homicidal intent jotted down anywhere . . . including on recipe cards!

When Vickie's not plotting love and murder, she enjoys being outdoors, gardening and painting.

Seared Satin is Vickie's third novel for *Scarlet*.

Other *Scarlet* titles available this month:

A WOMAN SCORNED – Kathryn Bellamy
FINDING GOLD – Tammy Hilz

VICKIE MOORE

SEARED SATIN

To Denise,
Thank you for being such a good friend. — Vickie Moore
11/98

Enquiries to:
Robinson Publishing Ltd
7 Kensington Church Court
London W8 4SP

First published in the UK by Scarlet, 1998

Copyright © Vickie Mohr 1998
Cover photography by J. Cat

The right of Vickie Mohr to be identified as author
of this work has been asserted by her in accordance
with the Copyright, Designs and Patents Act 1988.

All rights reserved. No part of this publication
may be reproduced in any form or by any means
without the prior written permission of the publisher.

This book is sold subject to the condition that it shall
not, by way of trade or otherwise, be lent, re-sold,
hired out or otherwise circulated in any form of binding
or cover other than that in which it is published and
without a similar condition including this condition being
imposed on the subsequent purchaser.

A copy of the British Library Cataloguing in
Publication data is available from the British Library

ISBN 1-85487-883-2

Printed and bound in the EC

10 9 8 7 6 5 4 3 2 1

To my good friend,
and sister, Linda Zimmerhanzel.
Thank you for so many things.

CHAPTER 1

7:05 a.m., December 22nd

He stood at the front of the crowds pressed against the chain link fence that cordoned off the perimeter around the once famous hotel. Thirty thousand people braved the frigid weather to watch a once-in-a-lifetime event: the implosion of the Worth Hotel.

Two ten-second blasts of the siren signaled the two-minute warning. The man casually lit a cigarette and took a long drag, making the tip glow cherry-red in the early morning dusk. The crowd's jubilant chatter silenced as a single ten-second siren announced the one-minute warning.

He turned to do a short study of the expectant faces surrounding him. Young and old alike practically stared at the carcass of the old hotel, as if they were afraid to blink, possibly missing the calculated implosion.

Three five-second sirens signaled the fifteen-second warning and the crowd hushed and became still. He turned back toward the Worth Hotel as the initial explosion in the southeast corner of the building shook unsuspecting pigeons into flight, away from the crumbling structure.

The first charge of the nitroglycerin-based explosive snapped support columns made of concrete and steel reinforcing bars in the southeast corner of the basement. Two seconds after the initial blast the cartridges exploded westward, across the floor plan of the once grand hotel. The east end of the seventeen-story building and the tower slid downward, as if greased with hot butter. A second later, cables in the lower part of the structure pulled the west wall of the hotel inward toward the falling tower. At four seconds, pre-cut columns in the basement tilted the west wall slightly toward the falling sections of the hotel. Parts of the building simply fell straight down as section after section collapsed. The last of the charges blasted columns in the west end of the basement, causing the wall to tumble inward on itself.

In six seconds the Worth Hotel and over eight decades of history disappeared into a billowing cloud of blue-gray dust, leaving only memories behind.

The crowd cheered at the phenomenon of modern explosive demolition while others remained quiet in reflection as they shuffled through the thick throng of people back toward their cars.

The man looked toward what was the last sunrise to warm the Worth Hotel. He noted the pink, red and orange hues of the sky as the morning sun filtered through the dispersing cloud of dust. His gaze shifted to the leveled structure of the old hotel, just starting to show through the cloud. He neither smiled nor frowned at the demise of the registered landmark as he flipped his cigarette to the pavement. He simply turned and walked away, leaving behind a small mountain of rubble.

And a body.

7:18 p.m., April 9th
'A couple of years ago, after a heavy rainstorm, an accident involving two cars was called in to the Sheriff's Patrol Department. The roads were slick and the visibility was low, which contributed considerably to the occurrence of the accident. A man in his late fifties driving a red Suburban pulled onto the highway, apparently not seeing the dark-colored Volkswagen Bug headed toward him. The twenty-nine-year-old driver of the Volkswagen, however, did see the Suburban, and made an effort to avoid the collision. Despite his best attempts, the Volkswagen clipped the rear-end of the Suburban, lurched through a ditch, glanced off a telephone pole, and rolled several times through a plowed field.

'The first officer on the scene, a young sheriff, reported to our office that the driver of the Volkswagen had been killed by decapitation. One of our representatives was dispatched to the scene immediately to recover the body after the report had been processed by the sheriff deputy.

'The field where the Volkswagen and the body were located had been tilled only the day before, and with the heavy rains it had turned the area into a huge mud puddle. The young officer offered to help our representative retrieve the body, since walking through the mud was almost next to impossible.

'Walking toward the Volkswagen, the sheriff officer pointed out the location of the head of the driver of the Volkswagen. Since the rest of the body was not to be found, they both assumed it was underneath the vehicle, which rested on its side close to the victim.

'It was now becoming very dark, and the sheriff officer turned on his flashlight to illuminate the victim's head for the coroner's representative to retrieve. As the young man bent over the head lying in the mud, the sheriff officer's beam lit the face up like a ghastly Hallowe'en specter. The eyes of the victim's head opened, much to the astonishment of the two men, and the head spoke to them in a whisper, asking for help . . .'

Ethan Booker, chief coroner-medical examiner, smiled as he paused to look at the grins of the officers at the fund-raiser, and the shocked, somewhat fearful looks of the civilians attending the event. The story was better than any fireside tale spun at summer camp, because this one was true.

Ethan could no longer contain his serious expression, and began to chuckle. He smoothed his hand over his tie as he continued. 'What neither of the men had realized was that the reason they could not see the rest of the victim's body was because it was submerged in the knee-deep mud they had been wading through. According to the victim, he had been fortunate enough to receive only minor injuries from the accident when the vehicle rolled over him, pushing him into the thick cushion of mud, in essence saving his life. However, it did take a while to convince the two men that the whole thing had not been staged as an elaborate practical joke on them.'

Chuckles from the audience had started when he'd explained the victim was submerged in the mud, and erupted into laughter as Ethan finished. He started laughing himself, and couldn't resist reaching below the podium for his own surprise.

'Those heroic and valiant officers are here with us today.' He paused as the laughter erupted yet again. 'Deputy Mike Taylor, and the medical investigator, Daniel James. They have been gracious enough to allow us to 'roast' them during this charity fundraiser. Gentlemen, on behalf of all those present, and a few others who would like to remain anonymous, a token of our esteem.'

With great fanfare Ethan presented each man with presents which they immediately opened. To the howls of delight from the diversified audience, the men lifted the lifelike miniature heads for everyone to see.

'Just in case you ever misplace your own, or that of someone else,' Booker laughed as he clapped Mike Taylor on the shoulder.

'One of these days, Booker,' Mike chuckled, lifting the miniature sunglasses from the box and placing it on the head. He lifted it again for everyone to see. 'One of these days.'

'Hey, he even looks like you, Mike,' a city police officer called out from the audience.

The officer curled his lip in a mock snarl. He turned toward Booker with a wink. 'Yup, you are definitely going to pay for this one.'

Booker's pager vibrated against his side. He checked his page, then frowned as he recognized the number from his office. 'Apparently not today, Mike.'

'Take care, Booker,' Mike called to him as Ethan made his way from the head table to a side door.

Ethan left the building through the back door, to avoid being waylaid by some of his friends, and walked to where his car was parked. He punched in the number on his cellular phone, then put the car into gear as it rang. His secretary Doris answered quickly.

'Doris, thank you,' he said. 'You saved me from the fund-raiser. By the way, what the hell are you still doing at the office?'

'Working, and don't thank me yet,' the matronly monarch of his office quipped. 'You might just think I've sent you straight from the frying pan to the fire.'

'What's going on?' Booker knew by her tone of voice that this was a business call.

He could hear papers shuffling in the background before she answered. 'Detective Roger Skinner from Homicide called. He has a body.' She paused for a moment. 'He specifically requested that you come out to check it. Twice so far.'

Booker pressed his lips together. The only time Detective Roger Skinner requested the chief coroner-medical examiner to come to the scene was when the case was an important one. 'Any idea what the story is?'

Doris let the answer float out on the exhalation of her breath. 'Something about the Worth Hotel; he didn't elaborate. He's not exactly the talkative type, you know.'

Booker did know. 'Okay, I'm not that far away. If he calls again, tell him I'll be there before he hangs up the phone.'

'The other line just lit up,' Doris muttered without enthusiasm, 'I wonder who that could be?'

Booker hung up from Doris, and at the same moment was waved through the barricade by a police officer to the vacant lot where construction crews were cleaning away the debris from the implosion of the Worth Hotel. As he'd expected, he found Roger Skinner just getting off his cellular phone with a sour look on his face.

Roger walked toward Ethan and met him at his car. Without any of his usual polite courtesies, he started right in on Booker. 'Why do you put up with that secretary of yours?'

'Because she knows how to handle people.' Ethan smiled as he closed the door to his car. 'What's going on?'

'That construction guy over there tossing his cookies found a surprise late this afternoon,' Roger stated, waving his hand toward a burly, barrel-chested worker flanked by a couple of his co-workers offering tentative support. 'They had decided to take advantage of the good weather and work late when he uncovered this sort of sheltered area. The guy saw clothes, and what looked like a shoe. He decided to investigate and found a body.'

'Your guys been through it yet?' Booker asked as they walked toward the taped-off area.

'Yeah, they're bagging up the last of it right now.' Roger lifted the yellow tape so they could duck under it. 'The problem is the media. When they imploded this thing a few months ago, it made national – hell, international news. Now they find a body? People are wondering if it was there before and they blew up the building on top of this guy. I think these guys have too much time on their hands, with no scandals going on at the moment, so they've decided to hound us for a while.'

'Aren't we the lucky ones?' Booker muttered, noting the number of news crews hovering outside the fences. 'So, based on the trickle down theory, the city council started making phone calls from one superior to another till it came down to me.'

'Makes you feel good to be bottom of the barrel, doesn't it, friend?' Roger offered, with his first genuine smile. 'Welcome to our version of a roast.'

'Yeah, well, it's my butt,' Booker said without enthusiasm.

'Better yours than mine, buddy,' Roger continued, smiling. 'Better yours than mine.'

Booker shook his finger at the detective. 'I will remember that, my friend.'

He turned away from the man and surveyed the obstacle course of construction he was going to have to complete just to view the body. When the Worth Hotel had been imploded, the demolition experts had arranged the explosives strategically so that the ruins would fall precisely where they had designed them to fall. Rubble, sometimes no bigger than a brick, was strewn everywhere. Small sections of the walls had remained intact, and had built up the original mound of debris to a height of approximately two stories. It had taken the clean-up crew several months to reach what used to be the basement area of the old hotel. The unfortunate construction worker had uncovered a cavity formed by a section of wall that had fallen onto another, leaving a triangular space just big

Booker nodded to the younger detective. 'Thanks, I'll get a sterile blanket – and, if you don't mind, I'll have you help me wrap it around him so we can put him in the bag.'

The officer swallowed uncomfortably, his voice edged with an almost pre-pubescent-sounding squeak. 'Sure, no problem.'

Booker made his way back to his car and retrieved the equipment he needed to transport the body. The young cop reluctantly helped him tilt the body first one way, then the other, so they could get the blanket under it. Carefully they lifted it and placed it in the body bag.

He murmured his thanks to the man as he knelt beside the bag and pulled a lock from his pocket. 'I assume you'll want to sit in on this one?' he asked Roger.

'Yeah. I'm going to have to if I plan on getting any rest from those vultures in the next few days,' Roger said, stepping beside Booker to watch him lock the zipper of the body bag. 'When are you going to do it?'

Booker shrugged. 'I'll call you tomorrow when I'm ready.'

'That can't be soon enough,' the detective said, then turned back to his notes to scribble something.

'They're really giving you a hard time, aren't they? The news guys, I mean?' Booker eyed the man he had known and admired for several years.

Roger nodded, returning his look. His gaze flicked past Booker's shoulder and his lips tightened into a grim line. 'And it looks like it's about to get worse.'

Booker followed his gaze, his jaw tightening in response. 'Great.'

'You're on your own,' Roger said, patting Booker quickly on the back before he escaped into a literal cloud of dust.

Booker turned to follow, never too egotistical to hide his tail and run. He thought he had almost made it when a voice called out from behind him, stopping him immediately in his tracks.

'Dr Booker, may I speak to you for a moment?'

Though stated as a question, Booker knew better than to mistake it for anything but an expected command performance by their town leader. Mayor Daisy 'the dowager duchess' Mayhill was petite and fragile-looking, but that was as close as she came to her floral namesake. Booker fought the urge to groan as he turned toward their city's esteemed mayor. He'd always thought, to himself of course, that the woman's name had been her mother's own form of a bad joke on the world at large.

'Mayor Mayhill, what can I do for you?'

'You could start by telling me that the unfortunate individual found here tonight was a homeless man who ignored the "No Trespassing" signs and died from natural causes,' she shrilled, her voice ringing with quiet authority. After all, they both knew they didn't want others hearing their conversation.

'I wish it were that easy,' Booker started, attempting to give her a disarming smile, 'but you know I really cannot speculate on anything till I've had a chance to thoroughly examine the body.'

'Poppycock,' she snorted.

He should have known she would be immune. Who knew when was the last time she had succumbed to a man's smile? Rumor had it her husband had died just to get away from her. Personally, Booker couldn't blame him.

'You listen to me, young man.' Daisy shook a bony finger at him, her lips thinning into a line till she noticed the lenses of several cameras focused on her and forced a somewhat concerned expression onto her face. 'Don't jerk me around, Booker.'

'I don't have any idea what you're talking about,' he muttered with a frown.

'This whole . . . mess could turn into a volatile problem for all those involved, especially under the ever-watchful eye of the public,' she said, with a meaningful nod to the media swarming beyond the fence. 'I need you to keep me abreast of the situation so I can run damage control as needed.'

Booker studied the woman before him as he tried to assess her statement. 'I hope you are not suggesting a cover-up, Mayor Mayhill.'

'Of course not,' the mayor responded quickly. She folded her arms across her chest, looking almost like a petulant child. Almost, but not quite. After a moment, most of the peevishness slipped from her expression. She glanced toward the news crews, then turned her back to them as she leaned closer to Booker. 'Look, I'll be honest with you, this thing has put my butt a sling with all the damn coverage they're giving it.'

'I don't understand. Why would this cause such a problem for you?' Booker eyed her speculatively. 'You didn't put the body down there, did you?'

Mayhill had the decency to look offended, but only for a moment. Then she smiled. 'That would've really given them fodder for their fiction, wouldn't it?'

The mayor started cackling. The noise coming from her could not be called anything else. She patted him on the arm. 'You are such a character, Booker. Who would've thought? A coroner with a sense of humor? That's rich.'

'It was in my job description,' he stated dryly.

She calmed down to an occasional chuckle before becoming somewhat serious. 'When will you be doing the autopsy?'

'Tomorrow morning.'

'Good. Let me know what you come up with.' The mayor gave him a half-wave as she turned away from him. The diminutive woman made her way back to her car, skillfully avoiding the press, Booker noticed.

He gave the forensic technician transporting the body a few instructions, then headed toward his car, ignoring the reporters calling out to him. Talking to the media was one of the last things he wanted to do. What he was going to do was go home, take a shower to wash off the coat of construction dust he'd accumulated, and hit the sack. Today might have ended on a bad note, but tomorrow already promised to start out on another one.

'Today's your lucky day, Booker.'

Booker lifted his head from his work. He was finishing up the autopsy on the body found in the rubble of the Worth Hotel. Giving his assistant Julie Williams his full attention, he gave her a dry look. 'Don't tell me. They made a mistake and my lottery ticket really did hit the jackpot?'

'Yeah, and now you can leave all this,' she chuckled, holding her hands out and looking around the room.

'Never,' he said, letting Smitty, his technician, finish the closing. 'I love my job.'

Smitty snorted. 'And I'm sure the Porsche has nothing to do with it.'

'Don't knock my car. At least it runs,' Booker reminded him. The lift of his brow revealed his humor, though he appeared stern.

Smitty continued to grin good-naturedly, ignoring Booker's comment and directing his observations to Julie. 'You know what they say about a man and his car. The more powerful the car, the more the man feels he has to make up for, if you know what I mean. In my case, however, my car lets a woman know that I do not suffer from any inadequacies or feelings of failure.'

'That, or I'd say it's more like it screams to a woman to "watch out, man looking for replacement for his mother",' she said. Ignoring Smitty's playful glare, she moved to stand beside Booker, where he was washing his hands at the sink, and held a plastic bag up for him to see. 'Joe's already processed this if you want to take a look. We think it might be the guy's wallet.'

'Was there a name in it?' he asked, turning the handle off with his elbow and grabbing a towel.

Julie flipped the bag over and looked at the label on the back. 'Identification from the driver's license, credit cards, et cetera, all say it belongs to a Gare Harolds.'

'What do the police have on this guy?'

'I knew you'd ask that.' She smiled, pulling her notebook from under the bag. 'Gare Harolds was reported missing back in December by his wife. No one has seen or heard from him since. Apparently they found out later that he had been kidnapped.'

'Did they have any –?' Booker started, but his ever-efficient assistant cut him off.

'Yes, they did,' she finished, pulling her last surprise out and handing it him. 'His dentist's office sent these over for you to take a look at.'

'Thanks,' he murmured, turning his attention to the envelope. 'Is John here?'

'No, but he will be in about five minutes.' Julie turned to leave the autopsy suite. Booker called to her, and she stopped and looked back at him.

'You've done good work here, and saved us all a lot of time.' He nodded toward the chrome table where Smitty was finishing closing the autopsy incision. 'We all appreciate it.'

'Remember that when it comes time for my raise,' she laughed, then continued on her way.

Booker watched Julie's growing confidence as it showed in her walk. There had been a time when that wasn't so. He moved to the X-ray light and flipped it on, then slipped the victim's dental X-rays into the holder.

'He must have had good hygiene – not much dental work.'

Booker looked at his odontologist over his shoulder. John Sanderson was like a ghost, slipping in and out of a room without being noticed. At times it could be irritating.

'So, what do you think?' Booker asked.

'I think we jack him open and take a gander,' John stated, popping his ever-present wad of bubble gum. Since he had decided to quit smoking, he'd been driving the office crazy with his cigarette substitute. 'Are there any dental charts with those X-rays?'

Booker looked in the envelope and pulled the sheets out. Handing the papers to John, he pulled the X-rays they had taken earlier as part of the autopsy and placed them beneath those from the dentist's office. John impressively popped his gum to the rhythm of an old nursery rhyme here – 'Mary had a little lamb' – as he studied the charts. 'Okay, let's start checking these puppies.'

John meticulously compared the work depicted on the charts with the two sets of X-rays, pointing it out to Booker. One of the things Booker admired about the man was his almost anally retentive need to examine each and every aspect of a victim's dental work. After almost two hours, the gum popped one last time before he started gathering the dentist's information to place back in the envelope.

'I think we have a dead ringer here.'

Booker eyed John as he shook his head at the man's terrible pun. Fortunately Julie chose to walk in at that time and save them from John's bad monologue of jokes. 'Would you call Skinner for me and tell him we've confirmed the victim's identity through the dental charts?'

'The wallet?' she asked.

'Yes. Gare Harolds. All the information you'll need is in the wallet,' he answered, then thanked her. Booker helped John and Smitty finish the last of the examination before he started gathering the paperwork together. When they were done, Smitty wheeled the gurney across the tiled floor to the cooler.

Booker left the autopsy suite, closing the door behind him. He nodded hello to a couple of detectives talking to Bill, their firearms expert, as he made his way down the hall to his office. As soon as he sat in his chair, his intercom buzzed.

'Dr Booker, I have a visitor for you.' Doris only used her 'formal' tone when it was the press, one of the city council, or the victim's family. He had to assume it was one of the latter, since he had already dealt with everyone else.

'Thank you,' he said over the intercom, and wondered what Doris was up to. Usually she gave him at least a clue to the person he would be dealing with.

Booker stepped out of his office and went down the small corridor that led to Doris's desk and the reception area. A woman stood looking at the painting on the wall, her back to him. He was taken by surprise at the height of the woman. She appeared to be almost as tall as he was, and slimly built, though there was no mistaking the curves beneath the modest dress she wore.

She turned toward him at the sound of his steps and Booker was struck by the contrast of her flaming red hair and the creamy smoothness of her fair complexion. She held out a slim hand to him and gave his a firm shake. 'Dr Booker, I appreciate you taking the time to see me without an appointment.'

'Not a problem. How may I help you?' he asked, finding himself unable to look away from the sea-green of the woman's eyes.

'I'm Elaine Harolds,' she stated, clearing her throat. 'You have . . . my husband, Gare.'

'Oh.' Booker frowned. Surely Skinner hadn't talked to the wife that quickly. 'I'm sorry, Mrs Harolds, for your loss,' he said simply, leading her toward his office. 'Please come with me.'

Booker led her back through the corridor and stopped at the door of his office to allow her to go ahead of him.

'Please, have a seat,' he said, waiting for her to sit before he took his own. He leaned forward and rested his forearms on his desk as he waited for her to speak. The soft scent of her filled his office and he inhaled it slowly, letting the fragrance wash over him. He didn't know why it should surprise him that the beautiful woman seated before him was Gare Harolds' wife. It was not unusual for an older man to have a much younger wife, and he had never claimed to be a matchmaker. Still, he would not have imagined her with the stocky, almost pit-bull-like man he had just finished doing an autopsy on.

Mrs Harolds pulled a tissue from her purse and began to worry it between her fingers. 'You, uh . . . have identified the person . . . found, as my husband?'

'Yes, ma'am,' he answered, without elaborating.

'How was he killed?'

Booker's brow rose. The woman's nervousness had seemed to evaporate before his eyes. Her gaze was direct. 'I apologize, Mrs Harolds, but at this time I cannot discuss that with you. Perhaps you can talk with Detective Skinner, the man handling your husband's death.'

'Of – of course,' she stammered, as she looked to her hands for a moment. 'I understand.'

Booker found himself watching her long fingers as they moved restlessly over the tissue she held.

'Had he been . . . dead long?'

His gaze flicked back to her eyes and he studied her. The question was really not an unusual one, but the look in the woman's sea-green eyes was. She seemed to be searching for answers, though not out of grief, or trying to comfort herself. 'It appears he may have been dead for a few months.'

'Was he dead before the explosion?' she asked quickly, leaning slightly forward in her seat.

Booker's brow rose as he continued to study her. The woman ducked her head and appeared to be fighting for control of her misery. 'Again, I apologize, I must also refer that question to the detective handling the case.'

'I see,' she said, her voice holding a hint of irritation. 'Can you at least tell me whether he was killed there at the hotel or elsewhere?'

'I did not say he had been killed, Mrs Harolds, and I must again refer you to the detective working this case.' Booker had started to pick up his pen to write the detective's phone number down when a thought suddenly occurred to him. 'I'm sure he gave you as much information as he possibly could when he notified you of your husband's death, did he not?'

Mrs Harolds' red head flicked up quickly to meet his gaze. 'Of course he did. I only wanted to see what your office had to say about . . . regarding my husband's death.'

Booker eyed her speculatively. Something didn't quite feel right about the bereaved widow's direct questions. 'Mrs Harolds, I was wondering if I could ask you for your –'

'I'm sorry I disturbed you, Doctor,' she broke in. The woman rose suddenly from her chair and blew her nose loudly. Her pouty frown remained on her face. 'If you'll excuse me, I'm not feeling the best in the world right now. Thank you for your help, Doctor. I truly appreciate it.'

Booker started to rise, but the nervous widow practically flew from his office. He stared at the emptiness in the doorway after her quick departure. Very quick, he thought to himself. He had been about to ask for her identification when the woman had fled from the room. His mind went over the encounter as he tried to put his finger on what exactly had bothered him. He couldn't come up with any one thing that had made him suspicious of the woman, but there had been something.

Booker shrugged. Fortunately it was not up to him to worry about such things, he thought, Roger could do that very easily. Who knew? Maybe the young and beautiful Mrs Harolds had the pool boy on the side, and had not exactly missed her husband when he disappeared.

Man, he needed a vacation if he was starting to come up with scenarios like that, he thought, turning to his computer. Right now, however, he had paperwork to finish. It was amazing how much paperwork murder caused . . .

Several hours later, Booker munched on the half-eaten sandwich as he proof-read his report. The intercom buzzed and he distractedly pushed the button, his eyes never leaving the paper. 'Yeah.'

'Detective Skinner is here.'

'Would you send him in, please?' he mumbled thickly as he took his last bite and threw the rest of the sandwich in the trash.

Moments later Skinner stood in the doorway and knocked on the doorjamb. 'Hey, Booker, I was wondering if you could take a couple of moments to answer a few questions for me and Mrs Harolds.'

Booker frowned as he stood, rubbing distractedly at his chin. 'Again?'

'Yeah,' the detective answered, eyeing him strangely as he motioned to someone standing in the hallway to enter the room. A short, attractive pudgy woman in her early forties stepped into his office. The red-rimmed lids of her grief-stricken eyes matched the color of her hair and Booker's mouth fell open.

Now Skinner was definitely eyeing the medical examiner strangely as he watched him stare at the woman standing uncertainly in his office. 'Dr Booker, I would like to introduce you to Mrs Elaine Harolds.'

CHAPTER 2

'Damn it,' Quintessa Reynolds muttered, pulling the horrid red wig from her head and tossing it none too gently to the seat beside her. 'I can't believe you did that.'

Tess fumed and ranted at herself all the way to her house outside of town. Pulling her car into the garage, she got out and entered the kitchen through the side door. She muttered a few more oaths at herself as she threw her keys on the kitchen counter.

Never had she let someone get her so rattled. Never. And never should she have let a man rattle her like that, but rattle her he had. Going on a tip from a friend, Tess had disguised herself as Harolds' wife and made the trip to the coroner's office to see what information she could glean before the real Mrs Gare Harolds had a chance to make an appearance. Tess might not have had a whole lot of time lately to cultivate any male relationships, but the reaction she'd had when she turned toward Dr Ethan Booker had shocked her. It had shocked her right into silence, then completely thrown off her equilibrium, forcing her to stumble her way through what should have been a productive fact-finding situation.

Tess shook her head as she remembered how she had practically run from the man's office. She knew her attempts to cull information from the doctor had made him suspicious. Suspicious enough to start to ask for her identification. The only saving grace was that she had known he was going to do it and she had escaped before he could. If he'd got those words out, the situation could have been worse.

It would have been disastrous.

If he'd asked for identification that she could not have produced, there would have been a lot of explaining to do. Now the real Mrs Gare Harolds most surely had been notified, and that particular avenue of information was no longer available to her.

'Damn it, Tess,' she muttered out loud to herself. What had it been about the man that had thrown her so off balance? she wondered. Yes, he had been gorgeous, she had to give him that, but that alone had not been it. She knew, worked with, had even dated several very good-looking men, but this one was different. He had been taller than she, with wide, well-built shoulders and short dark hair, peppered with a touch of gray. Somehow, though, she doubted he was a day over thirty-five. The slate-blue of his eyes had been direct, probing, yet sensitive as he had studied her. The moment she had met his gaze it was as if every fiber of her being, her soul, had simply said *there he is*.

There he is? Nothing was *ever* that simple, she reminded herself. Besides, she did not have the time, let alone *want* to find out the why or the what he was 'there' for.

Pulling a soda from the refrigerator, Tess headed toward her bedroom at the back of the house. She stripped out of the frumpy dress and pulled on a pair of shorts, then a shirt, before heading to her office, sipping at her drink as she went. She dropped into her chair and frowned at the e-mail message flashing on her screen. Whoever said cyberspace was a time-saver was full of it as far as she was concerned. Yes, it had been helpful in keeping in touch with colleagues across the nation, but it had also proven to be a time-drain if she did not watch herself.

Tess reached to her mouse and double-clicked on the e-mail icon to check her messages. Scrolling through the menu, she scanned the titles to see if any needed her immediate attention. Her gaze moved down the menu and caught immediately on one screen name.

Badger.

Icy tension stabbed through her and she unconsciously looked over her shoulder to the doorway behind her, then stopped herself. She was alone in her house, which was equipped with the security system she herself had designed. She was safe in her own home. Or was she? The mere sight of the screen name before her had instinctively caused her to tense up, her 'fight or run' reflex going into overtime. The thought that a faceless individual disguised behind such an obscure name could enter her own home through the internet caused chills to dimple her skin. Badger's physical being might not be standing before her, but the black and white of the words written by the individual were. For some reason Tess could not fathom, that terrified her even more.

She double-clicked on the name, and Badger's message flashed before her. She knew what it was going to say, Badger's message never deviated much, still . . .

Saw you today. Hated the dress.
They are dead. You are next.

Tess forced herself to relax. She had unconsciously balled her hands into fists so tight her knuckles were white with the effort. She stretched her shoulders to force the tension from between them, then returned her gaze back to the message. Juvenile, simple – almost like a really bad children's verse. Though the last line was always the same. *They are dead. You are next.*

She searched her mind for a clue, just as she had been doing for the past three months, since the messages had started coming. Badger seemed to enjoy following her around and letting her know he was doing it. Tess had been in the security business for ten years now and she had never been able to place him. Or her. That was one thing she had learned a long time ago. The bad guys aren't always guys.

They are dead. Tess wondered, yet again, if the faceless Badger was referring to the deaths of two of her most prominent clients, Gare Harolds and Ken Torkelson, former executives of RexComp Inc. Both men had helped build RexComp into an industry leader in computer products, then they had simply disappeared. Ken Torkelson's body had been found in a shallow forest grave approximately two months later. Gare Harolds had not been seen or heard of since, and his body had remained unfound.

Till a construction crew had started clearing away the debris of the Worth Hotel.

Tess rubbed at the headache starting to throb behind her forehead. There had been a few death threats directed at the men before they had disappeared. Her security firm specialized in the protection of high-profile corporate executives. She had taken every precaution to protect their lives, and that of their families. She had used every bit of her experience to work with the men, and still, for some reason, she felt she could have done more. She reminded herself that the men had *chosen* to take off on their own to a secluded cabin without letting anyone know, to do – well, one could only shudder to imagine what. The rumors of wild romps with silicon-enhanced women were legendary. Still, no one knew for sure what, if anything, had happened while they were there. The two men had simply disappeared.

Tess shook her head and turned her thoughts back to the computer screen. The child-like threatening message remained before her. Though every part of her wanted to simply turn off the computer and eliminate the message, despite what it could do to the hard drive, Tess forced herself to print the message out. Once the paper slid out of the laser printer, she opened her file cabinet and placed the message in the folder with the others. She backed out of the system and shut it off.

Picking her soda up, she headed back toward the kitchen. She needed a few crackers to ease the burning the tension had caused in her stomach. She needed more information about the finding of Gare Harolds' body. If, in fact, it even *was* his body. But how was she going to do that?

As she stepped into the kitchen her gaze fell on the morning newspaper and the headline at the lower right of the page. The police commissioner's ball was tonight, and local law enforcement heads were going to be present for the charity event. The ball had become an annual event for the community, giving the whole population, from the very wealthy to the blue-collar worker, the opportunity to enjoy an evening with the city's leaders.

Tess smiled as a thought worked its way into her mind. Yes, it would definitely be an opportunity, she thought. She glanced at her watch. Snatching her purse, shoes and car keys, she headed to the door. She had just enough time to go get a dress.

Tess leaned down and traced her fingers down the seam of her pantyhose along her calf. Damn the sales girl for talking her into these stupid, confounding pantyhose. It had taken her five minutes trying to get the seams at least somewhat straight. Oh, well, she doubted any of the engineers attending tonight would be bringing their rulers.

Sighing in resignation at the slightly crooked seams, she straightened, her gaze immediately meeting a trio of men watching her. Slack-jawed.

Men.

Narrowing her eyes, she controlled the urge to snap at them. Straightening her shoulders, she walked past them, their mouths still open, to the doors of the ballroom. She nodded her head to the man who had recovered enough to open the door for her.

Entering the room, she instinctively stopped to scan the crowd. A couple of hundred of the city's music lovers had turned out for the gala for charity. The cause was a worthy one, and Tess was more than happy to pay for the buffet dinner ticket to attend. In fact she contributed to it regularly. A band played masterfully at the back of the ballroom. Tables were situated to the sides, leaving the center of the room open for the more courageous, or vibrant, to dance.

Tess moved through the throngs of people toward the champagne fountain to get a drink. Though she was dressed to kill, Tess had no intention of harming her victim. No, on the contrary, she planned to seduce him.

Booker stuck his finger into the collar of his tuxedo and tugged. Discreetly. He returned his attention to the blonde standing in front of him. He smiled at her and nodded at a comment she'd made, realizing he hadn't missed anything during his inattention.

'Well, I told Dirk that the rules are the rules, and if Miss Mohaney continued not to observe the hemline length requirement for the golf course, we would have to review it before the board. Of course, Josie Crawford-McHughes agreed with me completely.' Meredith Thomas-Combs nodded with self-righteous indignation as she crossed her arms over her broad bosom.

Booker wisely chose not to make a comment. He hadn't met Miss Mohaney, but he could assume right away that she was probably twenty pounds lighter than Meredith and was, therefore, unquestionably not what Meredith would deem acceptable. Booker glanced around him, searching for a means of escape. He couldn't believe the wealthy still continued to stick their children with names like Meredith, or Dirk. And this hyphen thing with the last names? Booker shook his head. He needed out of this conversation quickly, before his brain congealed from all the status quo.

His mother had always told him that women loved a man in a tuxedo. If that were the case, he probably wouldn't mind wearing one so much. But if the woman standing in front of him cooing and preening was any example of what he was in for, he should have worn an old pair of blue jeans. With frayed hems.

'Don't you agree, Dr Booker?' The recently divorced Meredith had apparently finally noticed that he wasn't paying as much attention as she had originally thought, so she prompted him with her question.

Booker shrugged. 'I don't know. Does she have great legs?'

He enjoyed watching the woman blink, several times, as she seemed to digest his comment. She placed her jeweled hand to her breast. 'Whatever do you mean?'

'Never mind,' he murmured. Obviously the highbrows couldn't take a joke either. 'Please excuse me, Mrs Combs.'

Booker stepped away from her into the throng of people and made his way around the dance floor. The wide glass doors stood open to the cool evening air and the sheer panels of the drapes moved with ethereal ease in the gentle roll of the wind. Fresh air sounded good, and he walked toward the brief escape the night offered on the balcony. He nodded and murmured hello to acquaintances as he headed toward the doors.

Pausing to acknowledge a city councilman who'd been particularly supportive of the forensic science center, Booker held a brief conversation. With a wave, he turned away and his gaze met the sea-green eyes of a woman with a beautiful mane of red-gold hair sculpted into an elegant French twist. She wore a black sleeveless full-length evening gown that draped her tall form beautifully.

Beautiful. It was the only word he seemed able to describe her with. She started to step forward, drawing attention to the slim shape of her leg as the masterful cut of the slit from the hem to her thigh showcased her movement. She was beautiful.

The woman stopped, and Booker saw the hesitancy in her eyes. He strode to her, his gaze holding her till he stood before her. Those around them thought he was being so gallant when he took her hand and brought it to his lips, then held it to his chest. The truth was he took her by the hand to keep her from bolting, if the hesitancy in her eyes was any indication of her intention.

He stood in front of her, so close he could smell the enticing pull of her perfume. She remained quiet, not attempting to move away from him as her gaze continued to meet his. Booker quirked his lip as he leaned closer to her.

'I assume introductions are in order, considering you are *not* the Mrs Harolds I spoke with this afternoon. She had identification.' Booker's gaze moved over her golden hair pulled back from her face. With his free hand, he took one of the wispy strands that had escaped into his fingers. The tips of his fingers barely brushed against her throat as he lifted the strand of hair and admired it. 'And I can also assume you were having a bad hair day and chose to wear a wig.'

'I can explain why I came to your office.' The woman's voice was soft, almost a whisper as she looked away. She shifted nervously before him.

'That . . . is something I cannot wait to hear,' he assured her as he leaned yet closer to her to force her gaze back to his. 'Again, I must assume it has to be one hell of a good reason to pull such an asinine and . . . juvenile stunt.'

Her mouth fell open and her eyes turned forest-green with her anger. She stammered for a brief moment, looking a little strangled. She looked as if she dearly wanted to do something, and he had a feeling it was not to tell him how wonderful he looked in a tux. The way her hand stiffened in his own, he had an idea what she wanted to do was more along the line of throwing him bodily to the floor and stomping on him.

'Juvenile?' she croaked through gritted teeth. She tried to pull her hand discreetly from his, without success, then allowed it to remain as she stepped into his face. 'Are you trying to tell me that so many people put on disguises and waltz into your office it's become mundane enough to require an elaborate scheme just to catch your attention?'

Booker let his gaze move purposefully down the front of the halter neckline of her evening gown to the curve of her thigh, peeking through the slit in her skirt, then back to her face. 'I must say I like this look a lot better than the one you had on earlier today.'

'How dare you –'

Booker's gaze hardened, cutting her words of protest off. 'What I'm trying to tell you, lady . . .' He paused, the anger in his eyes cooling that in hers. 'Marching in looking like a bad female impersonator could get you thrown in jail. I don't know if that's how you get your kicks, and with your looks I could suggest a few more pleasurable options for you, but you could have seriously jeopardized a homicide investigation.'

'I knew exactly what I was doing, Dr Booker,' she returned haughtily. 'I did not wear that ridiculous outfit just to get my "kicks", as you so eloquently put it, and I couldn't care less what you have to suggest for alternatives. Obviously you met the real Mrs Gare Harolds, and obviously you saw that I did my research very well with the disguise I wore. I wore that hideous outfit only to get the information I needed. I'm very cognizant of police procedures, and I would have done nothing to impede the investigation into Gare Harolds' death.'

The woman's quiet tirade came to a close, her chest heaving slightly with the exertion of her anger. They stood there, toe to toe, her height almost matching his, but not quite. She was still forced to look up into his face, as he was to look down to her. Booker suddenly realized that her hand was still held in his, and that their heated emotions had them practically clutching at each other. The feel of her warm skin pressed against the sensitive flesh of his palm evoked a quiver of reaction within him. He still didn't even know the beautiful impostor's name, he reminded himself.

Releasing her hand, he stepped back from her and narrowed his eyes as he studied her. 'Why did you come into my office?'

She licked her lips nervously as she distractedly ran the hand he had released slowly down the front of her dress, as if smoothing away the feel of him. Gripping her purse, she tilted her head to eye him. 'Don't you want to know my name?'

Booker laughed, putting his hands on his hips as he shook his head. Looking back to her, he gave her his first genuine smile. 'And at this point I'm supposed to believe you would actually tell me your real name?'

'I have identification,' she returned, frowning at his disbelief.

'I'm sure you do,' he chuckled.

It was the golden-haired woman's turn to narrow her green eyes at him. 'You are so cynical, Dr Booker.'

'See, that's not fair, sweetheart,' Booker stated, winking at her. 'You know my real name.'

'I'm trying to give you my real name,' she reminded him slowly through clenched teeth, as if speaking to an obstinate child.

Booker crossed his arms over his chest and tilted his head as he gave her his full attention. 'Okay, let's have it. What is your real name?'

The woman's lips thinned into a straight line as she took a slow breath. She looked away for a moment, as if coming to a decision, then back to him. 'My name is Quintessa Reynolds.'

'Quintessa,' Booker repeated, shaking his head. 'Now I really believe you.'

'Look, Booker, I did not pick out the name, my mother did,' the woman said, rolling her shoulders, as if to ease the tension pooling between them. 'Obviously she suffers from delusions of grandeur and decided to take it out on me.'

'Obviously,' he murmured, his smile dimming as he focused back on the main thrust of their conversation. 'So, Quintessa, why did you come to my office?'

'Call me Tess,' she said automatically, looking away as she fidgeted nervously with the clasp of her handbag.

Booker remained silent as he awaited her answer. She licked her lips and glanced around them. They were standing immediately in front of the ballroom doors that led to the romantic shadows of the night. Tess quickly dismissed that notion. She didn't want to be in any sort of romantic setting with the doctor. The conversation so far was definitely not swinging her way, and she needed to get the upper hand if she was going to get any co-operation from the man. She continued to look around them till her gaze focused on the dance floor. The tide of people was moving gracefully around the floor as a waltz was being played.

Tess grabbed Booker's hand and started toward the dance floor. 'Come on, let's dance.'

She pulled him somewhat reluctantly to the dance floor and turned toward him. For a moment they awkwardly faced each other as they both realized that the waltz would force them to touch each other.

Booker made the first move, and, placing his hand on her hip, took her hand in his own as he started to lead them through the time-tested moves of the waltz. The moment she felt the heat of his touch through the thin fabric of her dress she knew that dancing with the doctor was going to be a mistake. She could all too easily imagine his hand searing through the satin of her evening gown and branding her skin beneath. Her traitorous mind taunted her with thoughts of the sensitive flesh of his palm smoothing across her stomach.

Tess closed her eyes for a brief moment, forcing herself to go mentally through the motions of giving her cat Sabrina a bath. The thought of the cat's fur, spiked from water and clinging to the feline's form, making her look like a rat, helped. Briefly. Till she took a deep breath in relief and again caught the masculine fragrance of Dr Booker.

'Is something wrong?' the man disturbing her had the audacity to ask.

Tess' eyes flew open. 'No, I'm fine. Just fine.'

He continued to study her as if he didn't believe that either. The waltz ended and segued into a slow, sensual love song. Booker looked away from her for a moment. His attention returned to her quickly and directly. 'Impersonating a dead man's wife is not only illegal, it's downright morbid. What is it you were looking for?'

Tess mulled her answer over for a moment, wondering how she should best describe her situation to him. Noticing the restless movements of her fingers, she realized with a start she had been caressing his collar while her thoughts were spinning. Clearing her throat, Tess met his gaze determinedly, pointedly ignoring what her naughty fingers had been doing. Thankfully Booker seemed prepared to let her get away with it.

'I'm the senior officer and co-founder of Millennium Securities,' she started, deciding the truth was her best option. At the moment, anyway. 'We are a private security consulting firm specializing in the security of executives of large corporations. These individuals usually inquire about our services after threats have been made to their company, or directly to a specific individual.'

'A bodyguard service?' Booker asked.

'Not exactly.' She shook her head, searching for the words to explain the complexities of her job. 'We do provide physical protection, but it's more than that. Say, for instance, a conglomerate is experiencing leaks in security. We would come in and help them not only to find the individual responsible, but also to help design a customized security protection package specifically for their needs. This could include security mechanisms for the building, security for the computer systems from hackers, and protection for the people being threatened. The CEO, for instance.'

'Why would anyone want to threaten an executive officer?'

Tess shrugged. 'For more reasons than you and I can fathom. Sometimes it's a special awareness group threatening a manufacturing firm. If the individual in charge is high-profile, wealthy and powerful, there is always the danger of kidnapping. Or, in this day and age, it may simply be a stalker or a lunatic. Then there's international terrorism. I won't even go there.'

'So what does this have to do with Gare Harolds?'

Booker asked the question, his words low and soft like the music around them. A couple bumped into them on the crowded dance floor, causing Booker to pull her closer, his hand resting just above where the fabric scooped from her deep open-backed gown.

Tess jolted at the feel of his fingers on her skin. No, two fingers and a thumb, she thought with a moment of panic. That was definitely a thumb resting along with the rest of his hand at the small of her back. The accidental touch was minimal, to say the least, but oh, so erotic to her senses.

She swallowed, trying to remember when was the last time she had been with a man. The fact that she couldn't even remember should tell her how long it had been, and must be the only sane, logical reason for her reaction to the touch of this tall, handsome man.

Nothing more. Right?

He rubbed his thumb across the ridge of her spine and spoke softly in her ear. Tess jumped at the intrusion of his words? 'What?'

Booker pulled back to frown at her. 'I asked what Gare Harolds had to do with your firm?'

'Oh,' she said simply. *Simply?* What the hell was wrong with her? She was the head of an internationally recognized and highly respected security firm, yet she didn't seem to be able to think, much less talk in full sentences. She felt as if she was experiencing the gangly awkwardness of a teenager on her first date. Shouldn't going through that particularly bad experience once in a lifetime be enough for a person to have to endure?

'Oh,' she repeated. Guess not.

Tess firmly shook thoughts of Jimmy Rodgers, tall, lean and an idiot, from her thoughts. Booker's question had been simple enough. That damn word again, she thought to herself.

'Gare Harolds is one of . . .' Tess hesitated, remembering the television images of the body being removed from the rubble in a black plastic bag. '*Was* one of my top clients. He was the CEO of a computer products company – one of the leaders in the business. He hired my firm to find the technology leaks in his company that were costing them literally millions of dollars of lost competitive edge. As we started the investigation, undercover, we discovered the individual that appeared to be behind the espionage. Two days later, she disappeared. The company started receiving threats against Gare Harolds' life, and that of his vice-president, Ken Torkelson. I tightened security around them, but the two men took off one day to a remote mountain-top cabin to . . .'

Her voice drifted off as her lips primly drew together. What the two men had gone to the cabin to do, incognito, was something that she didn't really care to discuss with the already very physically distracting doctor before her. The rumors had been wild and varied, but the common theme through them all was sex. Those close to the men had said they'd brought their special 'lady-friends' to spend the weekend with them, though the women had not been either of the men's wives. One individual had even suggested that Torkelson and Harolds had been closet gays, carrying on an affair with each other at the luxurious company-owned cabin. Tess really couldn't care less which of the rumors were actually true. The prude in her, however, kept her from discussing it with her colleagues. And especially with the man whose hand on her back was driving her to distraction.

'What did they go to the cabin to do?' Booker prompted.

'To, uh, have a meeting.' Fortunately the dance came to an end, saving her from answering the speculation in his eyes. She stepped thankfully out of his embrace and looked around them. She was relieved to see no one appeared to be watching them. The flashing red of her hormones made her feel self-conscious, as if anyone looking could see her reaction like a beacon.

Tess licked her lips nervously and looked back to him. 'Look, I realize you have no reason to believe a shred of anything I've told you. I came to your office today to try to confirm the identification of Gare Harolds and to see if I could learn anything about the cause and manner of his death. For whatever reason, I blundered that whole situation. I never act that unprofessionally. Still, the fact remains that I feel the people who planned the espionage may also be responsible for Torkelson's and Harolds' kidnapping and murder.'

Booker held his hand up to stop her. 'If what you say is true, I can understand why you would need the information, but there is nothing I can do to help you in this. I cannot divulge information that could be imperative to the investigation of these murders. Not only is it illegal for me to do so, it's unethical. I can only give you the same answer as I did when you came into my office today, looking so becoming.'

Tess tilted her head and gave him a mild glare at the mention of her 'becoming' appearance earlier. 'What is that?'

'Obviously my words impressed you greatly,' Booker said dryly. 'I believe I suggested to you that you should contact the detective investigating Harolds' death.'

Tess shook her head. 'I understand police procedure perfectly, Dr Booker. And I could probably very easily obtain the reports regarding their investigation. What I need is *your* expertise.'

'And what, may I ask,' Booker started, leaning toward her till their faces were only inches apart, and giving her a suggestive small smile, 'is my expertise?'

She crossed her arms over her chest. 'Dead bodies.'

Her answer caused him to straighten as he frowned in confusion. Obviously he hadn't expected that particular response.

'I guess I was hoping it had something more to do with live bodies.'

'Ha-ha,' she retorted, not wanting to admit to the slight thrill the suggestion had caused within her. She uncrossed her arms and looked around them, then lowered her voice as much as she dared, considering the noise level of the room. 'Can we go somewhere where we can talk?'

He leaned toward her. 'Talk about what?'

She took a slow, steadying breath, then shook her head slightly. Already she could tell he was going to be difficult. But, difficult or not, she needed to talk him into co-operating with her. 'About Gare Harolds' death.'

Before he could disagree with her, she raised her hand to stop his protest. 'I realize you can't talk about the case. We can at least talk about the case before you were involved, right?'

He thought about it for a moment. The moment stretched into several moments, filled with silence. He put his hands on his hips, appearing to be lost in thought as he stared at a spot on the floor. At last he let his hands drop to his sides, as if coming to a decision. 'Okay, we can talk about the case.'

He pointed a finger in her face, almost touching her nose. 'But . . . we do not talk, at all, about the case being handled within my jurisdiction. Agreed?'

'Deal,' Tess said quickly. She smiled as she sealed their agreement with a handshake.

At the electric feel of his hand on the sensitive flesh of her palm she pulled her hand away as discreetly as possible. 'Great. Where would you like to go?'

His brow rose and his lip quirked. Tess interrupted before he could give his suggestion. No doubt it had something to do with cherry gelatin and peanut butter. 'How about we go have a cup of coffee at this nice little place I know?'

Booker shrugged, teasing her as he acted disappointed. 'If that's what you want?'

Tess eyed him. 'Are you ever serious?'

'Only if I have to be,' he answered quickly. His gaze suddenly focused on a point behind her, and his expression became serious. His hand went automatically to the small of her back as he started propelling her in the opposite direction. 'How about that cup of coffee you promised me.'

His words were a statement, not a question, Tess noticed. She started to turn, to see what had caught Booker's attention and changed his demeanor so suddenly. He gave her a none too gentle push toward the door as he followed behind her.

'Is there something wrong?' she asked, trying to twist her body enough to catch a glimpse of his face. She found it extremely hard to do as he continued to shepherd her toward the door.

'Not really,' he stated, his voice low and quiet as he spoke in her ear. He was so close behind her now, as they navigated through the crowd, that she could feel the heat of him through the thin fabric of her dress, and the light breath of his words on her ear. 'Of course, I'm completely contradicting my advice to you.'

'How's that?' she asked, frowning at his cryptic statement.

'Well, if I don't get you out of here quick,' he said calmly, 'I'll be introducing you not only to the detective working Harolds' case, Roger Skinner, but also our esteemed mayor. Now wouldn't *that* be a fun situation to explain?'

'That cup of coffee is sounding better all the time.'

'That's what I thought too,' Booker said without humor as he steered her toward the front door.

Booker moved her toward the exit. This evening definitely had not turned out as he had expected. Not that he had expected much of anything. The woman beside him remained silent as he opened the door for them. The cool night air hit his face and he welcomed the slight chill of it.

What was he doing? he wondered. The story she had spun for him was of a world he was not familiar with. The only time he ever moved in the same circles as the powerful élite was when one of them died from foul play. Or, she could just be a nut who got her thrills by dressing up in disguises and pretending she was Miss Marple.

Booker studied her face out of the corner of his eye. She didn't look like any Miss Marple he'd ever known. He noticed the goosebumps of her chill on the exposed flesh of her slim arms. Automatically he removed his jacket and placed it over her shoulders.

Pulled from her silence by his gesture, Tess looked at him with a puzzled expression. 'What are you doing?'

He held up his hands, as if to ward off her words. 'You're cold. I was simply offering you my jacket, that's all.'

'Oh.' Her elegant brows drew together in a frown. 'I'm sorry. I didn't mean to snap at you. I just didn't expect . . .'

'Chivalry?' he finished, his lips twitching in amusement. 'With your looks, I would think men would be stampeding to perform a chivalrous act for you.'

'You got the "perform" right,' Tess answered dryly. 'However, I don't think chivalry was what they had in mind.'

'Are you a prude, Tess?' he teased.

'No, I—' She snapped her mouth shut. Waving her hand in dismissal, she abruptly changed the subject. 'Where are you parked, Dr Booker? My truck is over here.'

They stopped in a pool of light under a streetlamp. Tess nodded toward a dark green Explorer parked at the end of the row. 'I'll follow you to a coffee shop.'

Booker's brow rose. 'This is your idea remember, sweetheart? I'll follow you, or, better yet, you can ride with me.'

'I bet,' she said, shrugging out of his jacket. Murmuring her thanks, she left him to retrieve his car.

Booker did not feel comfortable allowing her to walk alone to her vehicle. It was not that they were in a bad neighborhood. On the contrary, the club was nestled in an exclusive suburb of the city. But it was dark, and she was wearing an evening gown that made her look too good to pass up.

He watched as she pulled her keys from her evening purse. He started after her to walk with her. She could at least give him a ride to where his car was parked, and he would know that she wasn't alone. He raised his hand, his mouth opening to call out to her to wait for him. Tess extended her arm, holding the remote for her truck in her hand. Booker called out to her, the sound of his voice causing her to turn toward him even as she pushed the button to unlock the doors of her Explorer.

The explosion rocked the vehicle from side to side, making it hop like a wild cat. Red and yellow fire billowed within the interior, then balled from the truck. The impact shattered the windows of the cars parked to either side of the Explorer. The force of the explosion lifted Tess, throwing her back to collide with Booker, where he'd been coming up behind her. They fell in a heap into the thorny cushion of the shrubs lining the parking lot.

Booker felt hot and cold. Tiny pinpoints of pain tingled all over him, not yet pulling together to cause one big ache. He remembered thinking he was going to start hurting any minute, that the pain would probably be intense. He turned to find Tess's head nestled against his shoulder as softly as if she had just cuddled up to him to go to sleep. Blood flowed in droplets across the creamy smoothness of her skin, which was marred with black smudges from the explosion. Her hair had fallen from its pins and a thick, glossy red strand fell across her cheek.

He reached to smooth away her hair and check her pupils. Already he could hear the sirens, signaling help was on the way. Thank goodness, he thought. His lips and tongue seemed too dry for him to speak. He could hear the pounding of feet as people rushed to their aid.

Booker's hand shook as if weighted with fatigue when he tried to reach her face to check on her. He could feel the buffering blackness of unconsciousness overtaking him. Still, he fought it in his effort to check the woman beside him. He started slipping slowly into enveloping depths of unconsciousness. The last image he recalled was the memory of Tess's face when he had called to her. She had turned toward him with an indulgent, eager half-smile.

Booker tried to swallow. The effort was too much as his eyes closed. He hoped she wasn't dead.

CHAPTER 3

Ethan Booker opened his eyes, then immediately shut them again when the blinding light of the overhead fluorescents seemed to stab through the center of his brain. He groaned as the throbbing seemed to increase with each degree he became more aware of his surroundings. Carefully this time, he opened his eyes to look around him. He found a nurse, a friend of his, grinning at him. He decided that if she was grinning he couldn't be too bad, so he started to sit up. Gingerly he raised himself to a sitting position, then slowly eased his legs over the edge of the examination table.

That small amount of movement had cost him, and he stopped to let the pounding within his skull subside. He caught the movement of the nurse, Jenny, as she came to stand in front of him.

'I can't tell you how long I've dreamed of seeing your naked chest, Ethan,' she chuckled, crossing her arms over her breasts as she eyed him appreciatively. 'Believe me, I took my time examining you, babe.'

'I'm glad I could be of service,' he croaked, his voice rough from his parched mouth. He moved his hand to start buttoning his shirt when a sharp pain shot through his side. He winced, but kept buttoning. 'What did you do to me, Jenny? I feel like hell.'

'I didn't do anything to you, sugar. If I did, it sure wouldn't require a hospital visit,' Jenny said.

'That's not what's written on the bathroom wall,' Booker retorted, without his usual energy. His body just wasn't up to much of anything. Usually he enjoyed sparring with the voluptuous nurse. Tall, blonde and striking, Jenny was the object of more than one of the staff members' fantasies. Though they teased each other, Ethan had not felt attracted to her other than just as a friend. Jenny must have felt the same, since she had never appeared to be much interested in anything more than their banter.

'Well, we figured your girlfriend did this to you,' she quipped good-naturedly at his comment. She stopped, giving him a questioning look. 'She *is* your girlfriend, isn't she?'

Booker winced at that thought. 'No, she's my wife.'

Jenny cackled loudly at his statement, the sound spiking jagged shards of pain into his head. He automatically reached for his forehead as he groaned.

'Oh, sorry,' she said softly, covering her mouth to stifle her giggles. It was a big joke around the hospitals that one of the most eligible bachelors in the city just also happened to be a medical examiner. Though the nurses morbidly joked about what kind of a 'stiff' date Booker would turn out to be, considering his occupation, more than one nurse had been willing to sacrifice herself to find out.

Booker was reluctant to admit the immense relief he had felt at Jenny's question. It was obvious that

Tess was all right, otherwise she wouldn't be teasing him about her.

'Where is she?' he asked quietly, not wanting to jolt his own head.

Jenny eyed him curiously. 'She's down the hall. They wanted to take some X-rays to make sure she didn't have a concussion.'

'Is she awake?' Booker avoided looking at her after he noticed the twitching of her lips in amusement.

'Not yet,' Jenny answered, tilting her head to study him. She reached over and placed her hand on his arm in a sincere gesture of comfort, her expression softening. 'Hey, Ethan, don't worry. She'll be just fine.'

He was deciding how to respond to the insinuation of that particular can of worms when the entrance of his friend and fellow colleague, Will Turner, saved him from having to say anything.

'Booker, don't you know how to have a normal date?' his friend quipped as he picked up his chart and started looking it over.

'She wasn't my date,' he stated.

Will and Jenny both looked at each other, then away as they fought to smother their smiles. 'Sure, Booker. I understand. We won't tell.'

He started to shake his head in exasperation, but caught himself before he could perform the painful act. Instead he rubbed distractedly at his forehead. 'Am I dead?'

Will chuckled as he flipped through the pages. 'Not yet. But I'd say by the look on Skinner's face you might want to be.'

'Great,' Booker muttered. 'Where is he?'

'He's in the waiting room,' Will replied, handing the chart to Jenny. He stood in front of Ethan and checked his pupils again. 'I think he wanted to storm in here and shake you awake to find out what the hell happened, but I told him to keep his hind end out of here till I said he could come in, or I'd kick his law enforcement butt.'

'Thanks, Will.' Booker pressed gingerly at his ribs as he examined himself.

Will noticed the movement and smiled. 'Nothing's broken, if that's what you were wondering. You were pretty damn lucky, I'd say, considering your girlfriend's truck blew up in your face.'

Booker started to open his mouth to protest when Will cut him off. 'I know. She's not your girlfriend.'

'Where is she?' he asked again, wishing like hell he could just go home, take some aspirin, and fall into a deep sleep till he felt better.

The two attending him seemed to find his question highly amusing, though they didn't laugh. Will wiped his smile away before he answered. 'She just got out of X-ray. We decided to admit her for observation, so I imagine she's on her way up to a room by now.'

'How is she?' Booker asked.

Will apparently noticed something in his expression, and his own softened as his voice lost its teasing tone. 'She does have a slight concussion and several abrasions, but she'll be fine. I imagine she'll be just as sore as you are in the morning.'

Booker didn't even want to contemplate the pain he was going to face in the next couples of days as his muscles protested loudly against their abuse. He slid to his feet, then clutched at the edge of the table as the room swam before him.

Will rushed to grab his arm, concern causing him to frown. 'Hey, don't rush it, Ethan. I think you need to spend a night here too.'

Booker shook his head slowly. 'I can't. I need to talk to Tess.'

'Skinner isn't going to let you go anywhere till he talks to you first,' Will reminded him.

'Look, Will,' Booker started, waving his hand in a gesture of frustration, 'I don't know what to tell him. I practically just met her, and I was walking her to her car when it blew up. There's really nothing more to tell.'

Except the parts about Tess, her security firm, the death threats and two missing executives. He looked at Will. 'I just want to talk to her and make sure she's okay.'

Will looked at him for a long moment, then nodded, as if he had come to a decision. He wrote something on a piece of paper and handed it to him. 'Okay. Here's the number of the room they're taking her to. We'll keep Skinner busy so you can sneak up there and see her, then you're on your own. Got it?'

Booker nodded as he smiled. 'I owe you, Will.'

Jenny snorted behind him. 'Don't forget the other witness, James Bond.'

'You too,' he added, giving her arm a gentle squeeze.

Jenny walked to the door and pretended to finish putting something on his chart as she discreetly checked the hallway for him. She bit her lip as she looked, then nodded at him and waved him out of the room.

Booker moved as quickly as he could, murmuring his thanks to them as he made his way down the hallway, away from the lounge where the detective waited. As he turned the corner toward the elevators, he couldn't say why he was avoiding Roger. Only that he wouldn't be able to think straight till he saw Tess for himself and knew that she was all right. The story she had been telling him about powerful executives, high-tech security and kidnappings was a fantastic one. One that he would have had a hard time believing. At least till the bomb had gone off. Now the implications of what she had been trying to get him to listen to had suddenly become very realistic.

And very dangerous.

Someone wanted Quintessa Reynolds dead. That much was very painfully obvious, he thought as he moved his stiffening body toward the elevator. He pushed the button, then waited with his hands on his hips for it to arrive. He was going to make sure Tess was all right.

Then he was going to get some answers.

At the sixth floor the elevator door opened with a soft chime. Booker stepped out into the hallway and glanced at signs on the walls to see which way he needed to head to get to Tess's room. A nurse walked by, giving him a curious look as she continued on her way.

Damn Jenny for calling him James Bond, he thought. Glancing down at his tuxedo, he realized why the nurse had been looking at him so funny. He was covered with smears of dirt and grass, his jacket sleeve was torn, and it looked as if a few sparks from the fire had seared through the fabric of his trousers. Booker doubted James Bond had ever looked this bad after an explosion. Though he did have to admit he felt somewhat like the infamous British agent as he carefully made his way to Tess's room.

Turning the corner, Booker was surprised to find no one guarding Tess's door. He frowned at this lack of protection for her. Then again, the police might have someone stationed in her room.

He opened her door and peered into her room. He breathed a short sigh of relief when he found her room empty of officers. Moving beside the bed, Booker paused to look at her for a moment. Her eyes were closed, her thick lashes resting against her pale skin. Her hair was loose, falling in ringlets around her face. The vivid white of a bandage stood out in a stark contrast to her hair. It covered most of her forehead and part of one eye. A dark bruise that in a couple of days would be really ugly masked the slight swelling of her right cheek.

Ethan's hand seemed to move with a will of its own as he reached to trail his fingers in a soft caress down her uninjured cheek. Tess murmured his name as she unconsciously nuzzled against the warmth of his hand. He felt his heart constrict with a feeling he didn't care to decipher. He whispered her name, the sound of his voice causing her to stir. She moaned, and her brows drew together in a frown as she turned her head toward him.

Tess's eyes fluttered, then opened. The sea-green color caught his attention and he found he could not look away. She licked her lips, then tried to smile. She winced in pain and took a slow, ragged breath. 'I guess seeing you means we made it.'

'I don't know,' he said, as he reached for a strand of her hair, unable to resist touching her again. 'I've been called an angel a time or two in my life.'

'More like a devil, I suspect,' Tess said, her voice hoarse. She swallowed, then tried to lift her arm till she felt the tug of the cord on the IV. Booker untangled her and she reached to her forehead, tentatively exploring the length of the bandage covering her skin.

'What happened?'

'That's what I came to see you about,' he stated, his lips thinning into a grim line. 'Your vehicle blew up when you pushed the remote to unlock the doors.'

'That was pretty sloppy work,' she murmured. Her lids kept drooping as she fought the heavy veil of sleep.

Booker frowned at her comment. 'Well, there's a big mess in the parking lot. And your truck, or what's left of it, is sitting in the middle of it. Do you have an idea who might have tried to do this?'

'I can think of a few people,' she answered sleepily, no concern in her voice.

He felt anger stirring within him. He couldn't believe this woman's reaction. Someone had tried to blow her up, not to mention him, into little jagged pieces of body parts, and she was practically drifting off to sleep.

He gripped her arm gently. Leaning toward her, he spoke quietly in her ear. 'I can't help you, Tess, if you won't give me some names to work with.'

'I don't need your help,' she murmured, her lids

closing as her face relaxed into sleep. 'I take care of myself. Always have. Better that way.'

Booker shook his head as she drifted off to sleep. There would be no answers coming from her now. '*I take care of myself. Always have.*' What had she meant by that? Probably emotional baggage he should avoid.

Looking into her sleeping face, he found he couldn't just walk away from her. Where had she come from? he wondered. So many questions that could not be answered till she was awake and co-operating. He had to smile at that thought. He hardly knew her, but he would bet just about anything that she was not the type of person to just co-operate. Unless it benefited her to do so.

He brushed a strand of her hair out of her face, then turned quickly to leave. They had both been lucky tonight. *She* had been lucky, he corrected himself. Another foot or two closer, and she would be in a lot more serious trouble at the moment. He refused to think about that.

Booker spoke briefly with Tess's nurses, giving them his pager number, which caused more than a few smiles. He gave the grinning nurse taking his instructions a dry look. Couldn't a person care about a human being without it becoming news? The woman's grin widened. Guess not.

Fatigue weighed heavily on him as he made his way down the hall. Skinner was going to have his hide for leaving the hospital without talking to him, but the only thing he wanted at the moment was to go to sleep. Looking down at his clothes, he amended that thought. Take a shower, then go to sleep.

He yawned as he pushed the button for the elevator. After he'd got some rest, he planned to be back at the hospital in the morning. He wanted the opportunity to talk with Quintessa Reynolds before she left. It went without saying that she would chafing at the bit to get out of there once she woke up.

The elevator doors slid open and Booker stepped in. He pushed the button for the bottom floor and leaned tiredly against the wall. It suddenly occurred to him that he didn't have a vehicle to get home in. He'd obviously ridden with Tess in an ambulance to the hospital. He rubbed at his forehead, wondering how he was going to get out of this place without asking Skinner for a ride, when he realized he could simply walk across the parking lot to his office and ask one of his people to give him a lift home.

Exiting the elevator, he headed out the back door of the hospital. The night was cool, a welcome relief to his tired body. The slight bite of the wind helped revive his senses. The walk across the parking lot wasn't long by any means, only a block or so, but to his weary eyes it looked and felt like a couple of miles. With another wide yawn, he headed toward his office across the darkened and deserted parking lot.

When the lights from the science center appeared through the trees, Booker could have smiled with relief. If he'd had the energy. As it was, he had little left when he stepped over the curb to cut across the tree-lined grass that landscaped the area around his office. Moving through the night-darkened shadows of the trees, Booker could see through the windows Ernest, their evening security guard, walking through the waiting area on one of his rounds for the night.

His gaze tiredly set on the windows, Booker stepped onto the sidewalk and headed toward the door.

Out of nowhere, two men fell into step with him. In the only second he had to think about his situation, he realized what an idiot he had been. Walking alone in this neighborhood in a darkened area of the parking lot was asking for trouble. He started to turn toward one of the two thugs, his fist raised to fight, when the pain at the back of his head hit him first. Then the blackness.

Tess stirred from the heavy, drugged feeling of her sleep. Her mouth was dry, cottony, and her head . . . Her head was killing her. She started to lift her hand toward her head and gasped at the sharp protests of her body. It felt as if her entire body had been flattened by a steamroller, then reinflated.

Slowly she opened her eyes, feeling woozy and disoriented. Looking at the ceiling, she suddenly found a possible explanation for her disorientation. She had some idea where she was. She searched her fragmented memory and recalled the explosion. How could she have forgotten that one?

Wincing as she lifted her head, Tess let her gaze move around the room and confirmed she was indeed in the hospital. Her gaze stopped on the tight-lipped figure of a man sitting in a chair studying her. She could tell by his attitude he was a cop. A cop who was going to want some answers. Answers that even she would have a hard time giving.

'Good morning, Miss Reynolds,' he said. He stood and moved to the side of her bed. 'I trust you're feeling better.'

At her dry look, he smiled knowingly. He had had a few aching muscles in his time. 'Or worse, depending on how you look at it?'

'I'm fine,' she answered. His tall frame towering over her prone form bothered her more than she would have cared to admit to him. She pushed the button on the controls to raise the head of the bed, till she was in a sitting position and not forced to look up at him. 'I assume you're here about the incident last night.'

'If you want to call your truck exploding into a fireball an "incident",' he started, leaning against the edge of the bed and crossing his arms over his chest, 'then, yeah, that's one of the reasons I'm here.'

'One of the reasons,' Tess frowned, a feeling of foreboding coming over her. She looked around her frantically as she tried to recall if Booker had been with her or not. She remembered that he had walked with her part of the way, but nothing more. She couldn't remember if he had already left to get his car. She glanced back to the officer. 'Is Booker, I mean, Dr Booker all right?'

The man's brow raised in mild surprise. 'From what I've been told, Booker is fine.'

'Who are you,' she asked, suddenly wary. Perhaps her initial perception had been wrong.

'I'm Detective Roger Skinner,' he answered. 'I'm with the homicide department. I've worked with Booker more times than I care to remember. He's also a friend of mine.'

Tess's mind had stopped at the word 'homicide'. What would a homicide detective want with her? She knew it could not have anything to do with Harolds' case. That involvement was in another jurisdiction. Biting her lip, she hoped frantically that Booker was all right, and that no one had been hurt, or worse, in the explosion meant for her.

She looked back at the detective, unable to resist asking. 'If you're Homicide, why are you here?'

'As I said, Booker is a friend of mine,' Skinner stated.

Tess's frown deepened, and she shook her head. 'I'm sorry. I realize I'm not feeling the best at the moment, but I don't understand what you're getting at. I thought you said Dr Booker was okay.'

'I said I *heard* he was okay,' Skinner added. His lips flattened with his irritation. 'Apparently Booker decided to leave the hospital without talking to me, and now he's apparently missing.'

'What?' Tess said quietly, a chill moving over her. She ignored the pain as she leaned forward. 'What do you mean he's missing?'

'As in gone, Miss Reynolds,' Skinner replied. He rubbed distractedly at his forehead as his irritation glimmered with his concern for his friend. 'He was seen coming out of an elevator and heading toward the back door. His offices are located just across the parking lot, so we assumed he had headed over there to catch a ride, but he never made it.'

'And you have reason to suspect that something more than catching a taxi ride happened to him?' she asked, trying to not let her fear creep into her voice. The detective met her gaze, and for a moment they remained silent, studying each other.

He nodded slowly. 'I won't beat around the bush, Miss Reynolds. I've checked your background. Your firm is highly respected and highly recognized. I don't know what exactly happened to your truck last night, but I do think what happened to Booker is connected with you. And the Gare Harolds case.'

She held his gaze, then nodded slightly. 'Then you know Gare Harolds was a client of mine?'

'Yes.' He moved to stand at the foot of her bed. 'And he was murdered. What do you have to add to that?'

Tess shrugged. She knew what the detective was trying to do, but she refused to give in to the guilt he was trying to place on her shoulders about Booker. She could do that well enough by herself. Still, she respected the man – as she respected any law enforcement officer.

'I'm sure you have the reports from Colorado, where Harolds disappeared. I had been hired by his company to find and seal a security leak. Also to protect him and the vice-president, both of whom had received several death threats and attempts on their lives.'

By the detective's expression, and his stance, Tess knew he had read the reports and anything she could say would be nothing new to him. Still, it was procedure. 'Harolds and his vice-president made an unexpected and private trip to a cabin.'

'And disappeared,' Skinner finished, his expression masking anything he might be wondering about the 'unexpected' trip.

Tess shook her head as the futility of it all filled her again. She had told Harolds time and time again that she could not protect him if he continued to disappear. 'The vice-president's, Ken Torkelson's, body was found not too long after. Since Harolds had not been found, we assumed that maybe it had been a kidnapping gone bad. We never received a ransom request and, until now, we never had a body.'

'Who were your suspects?' he asked.

Tess held her hands up in front of her in an empty gesture. 'The one suspect we had also disappeared. And at the time we only suspected her. We hadn't had time to determine what, if any, her participation was.'

'Why would they now want to try to kill you?' Skinner asked, tilting his head as he effectively changed his tactics.

If the good detective thought he was going to scare her by using the word 'kill' he had thought wrong. She smiled at his question, a small, feline smile. The Harolds case was not the first she had worked on, and in her business it sometimes got tough. There was also the possibility of her computer stalker, but the different possibilities were not something she was going to discuss with the detective.

'Just lucky, I guess.'

Skinner's gaze became hard and direct as he placed his hands on the end of the bed. He leaned forward, his stance nonchalant, but his expression anything but disinterested. 'Smartass remarks probably caused your participation in that little "incident" last night. I personally couldn't care less if someone blew your truck up every night of the week, but Ethan Booker is a friend and something has happened to him. And, it only happened because of his association with you.'

Skinner's statement wiped the smile off her face. 'If I knew where he was, I would tell you immediately. The last thing I want is for Booker to be caught up in this. Or hurt. But I didn't take him. You need to realize that and concentrate on finding him.'

Skinner's expression became thunderous. Tess met his hard gaze with one of her own. The door to her room opened and a young nurse walked in carrying a tray. She smiled brightly as she greeted them both and moved to Tess's beside. The nurse looked up, caught the man's dark expression and her own became uncertain.

'I'm sorry, did I interrupt something?' she asked innocently.

'No,' Skinner barked, turning on his heel to head to the door. He put his hand on the knob, then turned briefly back to Tess. 'You are not an officer of the law, Miss Reynolds, and I would remember that. I will find Booker – and as far as the Harolds case goes, stay out of my way.'

The detective opened the door and left. Silently it closed, the click of the handle audible in the quiet of the room. The nurse turned to Tess, her eyes wide with exaggerated innocence. 'Boy, you ticked him off, didn't you?'

'I'd call that an underestimate.' Tess gritted her teeth as she moved her body as quickly as she could to get off the bed. Fortunately she remembered the gown, and grabbed the back before she exposed her rear end to the nurse.

The young bubbly 'nurse' was actually none other than her assistant and right hand, Janet Evans. Janet also happened to love her job and take it very seriously. Glancing at the fictitious nurse's uniform Janet wore, Tess sometimes wondered if she took it a tad bit too seriously.

They were close to the same age, but that was where the similarities stopped. Where Tess was tall, with what could loosely be called auburn hair, Janet's African American heritage from her mother's side gave her features an elegant, exotic flair. She had her mother's dark complexion, her father's green eyes, and a petite frame which made people, especially men, want to take care of her.

Tess almost snorted at that idea. Janet was more than just an assistant to her. She was a friend, and someone she trusted unquestioningly. If anyone needed to be taken care of, Janet would be the one to do it.

Janet frowned as she watched Tess's painful jerky movements. 'What do you think you're doing?'

'Something's happened to Booker. I know it,' she muttered through her teeth as she searched through the closet for her clothes.

'I hope you're not going to do what I think you're going to do.' Janet's statement ended sounding more like a question. She bit her lip as she put her hands on her hips. 'I don't think I need to remind you that you've been admitted to the hospital for a reason. It's called concussion. You do remember what that is, don't you, Tess? You've only had it happen to you two or three times.'

'This makes four.' Tess glared at Janet as she pulled the remains of her evening gown from the closet. Frustrated, she inspected the dress. It didn't matter to her one bit that the gown was ruined. What bugged her was that she doubted there was enough of it left for her to put back on to get out of this place. 'And now I'm checking myself out.'

'In that?' Janet asked. Tess could not mistake the humor in the woman's voice.

'No, damn it, not in this,' she retorted as she threw the dress somewhere in the general vicinity of the trash can. She critically scanned the room, looking for a suitable replacement. Her gaze stopped on the woman wearing the nice nurse's uniform in front of her.

Janet raised her brows knowingly at Tess's look and she shook her head. 'I know what you're thinking and you can just forget it.'

With that statement, Janet turned and left the room. Tess muttered a few oaths. Janet was probably getting back-up, or hospital staff with a syringe, to try to keep her there. She moved as quickly as she could to go through the drawers and the closet to try to find something, anything to put on.

The door to her room opened. Tess turned to the door, half expecting a pair of cops with handcuffs or a huge male nurse, a real one, to come walking in. What she did not expect was her wonderful friend waltzing back into her room carrying a set of blue scrubs for her to wear.

Janet tossed them toward her, making her move painfully fast to catch them. 'Here, put these on,' she suggested.

Tess frowned as her gaze met Janet's questioningly. 'Where did you get these?'

Janet just smiled as she shrugged her shoulders. 'I improvised.'

Tess decided to skip a comment on Janet's 'improvising.' She untied her gown and started stepping into the scrubs. Janet watched her, her humor having melted into concern. 'What's the rush, Tess?'

'The man you so graciously chased out of here was a detective,' Tess answered, tying the strings of the shapeless surgical pants. 'He said Booker left the hospital last night and no one has seen him since.'

Janet's brows rose in surprise. 'You mean the really cute doctor?'

'I mean the doctor who works on dead bodies, Janet,' Tess stated dryly. She pulled the shirt over her head, stifling part of her groan at the movement. 'Skinner thinks it's related to the explosion last night.'

'Do you?' Janet asked, helping Tess get her sore arms awkwardly through the holes.

Tess pulled the shirt down, then lifted her hair out of the neckline. Having nothing else, she was forced to wear her black high heels with her newly acquired outfit. She stopped for a moment as she pondered Janet's question. Slowly she released her breath as she shook her head, her voice low with guilt. 'I'm almost certain it is. And Skinner was right. If something happened to Booker, then it's happened because of me.'

Janet leaned against the side of the bed as she stubbornly crossed her arms over her chest. 'Wallowing in self-pity and guilt is not going to change anything. And it certainly won't help that gorgeous doctor, will it?'

Tess tilted her head to give her friend a direct look. Her brow rose. 'Then what do you suggest I do, Miss Marple?'

Janet grinned easily. She personally loved the fictitious Miss Marple, and owned a complete collection of all of Agatha Christie's work. 'I highly recommend you go kick somebody's butt.'

'Sounds like a plan to me.' Tess chuckled as she motioned for Janet to follow her.

Leave it to her good friend to help her thoughts back in focus. Skinner's statement about the disappearance had upset her more than she cared to admit. She did not know Ethan Booker well, but his impression on her had been unusually strong. Now he might be facing possible danger because of her, and it upset her. But Janet was right. Sitting around whining about it was not going to help him in the least. She'd always been an action-oriented person, which had led her toward the career she had fallen in love with. Having focus helped her put aside her doubts and take care of the situations that unexpectedly but usually came up.

Like Booker's disappearance.

Skinner said he had been seen headed toward the parking lot. It had been assumed he was headed to his office to catch a ride from one of his employees. What had happened to him once he'd stepped outside the hospital doors? That was exactly what Tess planned to find out. Before anything happened to him.

Going to the door, Tess opened it a little to check the hallway. Looking back over her shoulder to Janet, her expression had already become direct, as had her thoughts. It was time to get to business.

'We better go help Booker before he gets himself into any more trouble.'

Joe patted the unconscious form of the man lying on the bare floor of the 'borrowed' cargo van. His name wasn't really Joe, but it didn't hurt in his profession to go by a nickname. It was easier that way, and he had specifically picked Joe because of its generic quality. Very few people knew his real name, and he preferred it that way. At least with the bland name he had picked he didn't have to worry if one of his occasional partners accidentally said his name at the wrong time. Or, if a disgruntled client decided to turn on him, Joe could usually just fade away till he rectified the situation. One way or another.

He pulled a wallet out of the man's pocket and started to open it as he glanced at the man lying before him. He frowned, slightly curious at the man's crumpled look and the fact that he was wearing a tuxedo. Opening the wallet, he ignored the money and credit cards in his search for the man's identification. They had been told to pick up the man who had been taken to the hospital with the woman named Reynolds. Their boss had not given them the man's name, and Joe didn't like such vague orders. Vague orders usually meant trouble.

And trouble was now what they had, in the biggest way. He found the man's driver's license and muttered an oath under his breath. 'Damn it.'

'What's wrong, man?' Dennis asked, glancing uneasily back at him. His jerky movements caused the gold hoop ring in his ear to swing wildly back and forth. Joe didn't like working with the young idiot, but at the time hadn't had a lot of choice, since he had been called in from out of town to take care of the Reynolds woman. Idiots like Dennis hadn't realized that one of the tricks to not getting caught was to blend in. Not dress yourself up in such a way that everyone and their dog would remember your distinctiveness, complete with multi-colored hair.

Joe shook his head as he closed his eyes, then pinched the bridge of his nose to release some of the pressure starting to throb there. Dennis eyed him nervously in quick little peeks as he kept driving. 'What's the deal, man? Did we grab the wrong guy?'

'No, we did not grab the wrong guy.' He scanned again the identified man's credentials in his wallet. 'He's the one we wanted. He's also a medical examiner.'

Dennis frowned, still not quite catching on. 'Medical examiner? What the hell is that?'

'A coroner,' Joe replied, trying to get a bell to ring in Dennis's head. When he saw the kid's perplexed look, he rolled his eyes. 'A medical doctor who performs autopsies.'

'You mean a guy who cuts up dead people to see what killed them?' Dennis asked, his lip curling in distaste.

Joe started to open his mouth, then wisely thought better of it. Fortunately for Dennis he was a moron, otherwise Joe might have had to kill him to make sure he didn't get in the way. There was no use trying to explain the complexities of the situation to him.

Dennis took Joe's silence as a form of agreement and turned his attention back to the road ahead of him. 'That's gross, I tell you.'

'Well, we all have to make a living,' Joe replied in his usual noncommittal fashion. He hadn't expected that his orders were to pick up a county medical examiner. That created a situation which he strictly avoided. It was extremely unwise ever to become involved in a predicament in which an individual, any individual, was connected with law enforcement. Never did a person in Joe's profession want to do something that would cause the whole of the law enforcement community to hunt him down.

Not even for the hefty fee he had been given to carry out his orders tonight.

'So where are we going to dump him, man?' Dennis asked as he rounded a corner a little too quickly.

Joe glanced back to the man's wallet. 'It says here that he lives on Timberline Road.'

'Dump him back at his house? I didn't think that was what we were supposed to do.' Disbelief and nerves filled Dennis's whiny little voice. 'I thought we were going to . . . well, you know.'

'Well, you thought wrong.' Joe's hard gaze leveled on the kid in front of him.

Dennis flinched and decided to keep his eyes on the road. He hadn't liked the feeling the man's eyes had given him. It had given him the willies, and for the first time he wondered whether the money he had been given was worth it.

'I'll give you a free piece of advice, kid,' Joe said in his monotone voice. 'No amount of money is worth messing with the police. We take this guy back to his house and we dump him on his lawn. Safe and sound. The last thing you or I need is for every cop in the vicinity to be looking for us. You got that?'

Dennis nodded, keeping his eyes forward. He blinked away the tears threatening him. The skin on the back of his neck felt as if it was crawling, and Dennis knew without a doubt he was in trouble. The first chance he got, he was getting away from the stranger as fast as he could and disappearing for a while. He didn't know the guy, but he did know the guy was from out of town and would have to leave some time.

The drive to Timberline Road was quiet, heavy with tense silence. In front of Booker's house, Joe opened the panel door and grabbed the man under the arms, then slid him out onto the lawn. Quickly, yet easily, Joe hopped back in and shut the door as the van moved down the road in the early-morning hours.

Glancing at his watch, Joe estimated, all total, they'd been on the man's street less than two minutes. Scanning the darkened houses of the upscale neighborhood, he figured everyone was asleep, getting their good night's rest before hitting the office grind in the morning.

Slipping into the bucket seat beside the now quiet Dennis, Joe leaned casually back in his chair as he thought about the note he would return with the money he had been given for tonight's excursion. Minus a handling fee, of course. Then his thoughts turned to the unexpected vacation he would have to take.

It would have briefly upset Joe, who prided himself on his quiet intelligence, to realize that he and the punk kid beside him had both reviewed their shared problem and came to the same conclusion. It was time to disappear for a while. Something was definitely going to hit the fan.

And, by the looks of it, it was going to hit soon.

CHAPTER 4

Skinner paced back and forth in Booker's living room, muttering something unintelligible below his breath. Ethan watched his friend's movements as he prodded the bump on the back of his head with gentle fingers. Being knocked unconscious twice in less than twenty-four hours could not be good for his head, he thought. Let alone the incredible headache he was experiencing.

Eyeing Skinner's angry pacing, Booker was thankful the detective was not ranting and raving in his usual booming voice. That would have been the death of him.

'I don't understand this,' Roger said, talking to no one in particular. 'I just do not understand this. You go to a simple charity ball and your girlfriend's truck is blown up.'

Booker had started to raise his hand to correct Roger's assumption about Tess being his girlfriend when the detective cut him off with a shake of his finger. 'I don't want to hear it, Booker.'

Roger resumed his authoritative pacing. 'I hear you've been taken to the hospital, unconscious, after an explosion. I arrive in the emergency room and they tell me I'm going to have to wait to see you. It finally occurred to me, after a while, that they were stalling me, and I made them let me in the room. You weren't there.'

'I can explain, Roger,' Booker started. It was obvious that Roger had shown up at the emergency room as a friend, not as a detective. Booker felt guilty for having tried to avoid him in the first place. 'I really am sorry. At the time, I just did not want to have to explain what had happened. I don't even really *know* what happened. I just didn't feel up to hearing a lot of questions that I wouldn't have been able to give you the answers to anyway.'

'Well, now you have even more answers to cough up, don't you?' Roger glared back at him. He had finally quit pacing and now stood leaning against the fireplace with his hands jammed stubbornly in his pockets. 'You could start with what happened after you left the hospital.'

Booker shrugged as he mulled over what little he could remember had happened. 'I just wanted to go home and get some sleep. So, I decided to walk across the parking lot to the office and get a ride. When I stepped out from the trees onto the sidewalk, two guys grabbed me, hit me, then I was out. I woke up on the lawn in my front yard, staring up at my neighbor, Mrs Sanderson, bending over me with all those green curlers in her hair.'

'That's it?' Roger demanded.

'Yeah, that's it. What the hell did you expect? Me to put up an incredible fist fight like in the movies?' Booker asked, irritated at Roger's response. The detective was acting as if he had fallen off his chair rather than being knocked unconscious, kidnapped, then dumped, very unceremoniously, on his front lawn. All for no apparent reason. It was enough to fluster any man's ego.

'You didn't get a look at either one of the guys who took you?' the detective asked patiently.

Booker shook his head, feeling sheepish. 'I did actually start to have it out with one of them, but then the other guy came up behind me and whacked me before I even had a chance to do anything. It was embarrassingly uneventful.'

Roger's lips twisted into something that might loosely resemble a smile. Booker frowned at the movement, then they both started laughing at the absurdity of it.

Roger chuckled as he rubbed distractedly at his forehead. 'It really would not have been funny if you'd been hurt.'

'I know, but I wasn't,' Booker reminded him, holding the aching pain of his ribs. Laughter was definitely not the best medicine when your ribs were bruised and sore.

'Any idea why someone wanted to take you for a ride?' Roger continued. Though he might now be smiling, Booker wasn't fooled. Skinner was still a detective.

Again, he shook his head. Since waking up to the rather unlovely sight of his next door neighbor staring him in the face, Booker had racked his brains to try to figure out why he had been taken for such an unusual ride. The only thing he could come up with was Tess Reynolds. For some reason, however, he was reluctant to share that thought with Roger. Not just yet, anyway.

'What about your girlfriend?' Roger asked. The man was a detective for a reason, and one reason was his incredible intuitive ability.

Booker leveled his gaze on him. 'She's not my girlfriend. And I don't know what, if anything, she has to do with this whole mess.'

'Well, she must have something to do with this mess, Booker,' Roger stated, his lips thinning into a grim line. 'First you disappear and now she does.'

'What?' Booker's gaze flew to him. He was on his feet before he knew it, and before the pain hit him. He held his side with his hand as he directed all of his attention on the man in front of him. He gritted his teeth against the pounding all over his body. 'What do you mean, she's disappeared?'

'I mean, Booker,' the detective stated, the man's expression as serious as his own. 'that, like you, she was at the hospital, last I knew. Now she's gone. They did not release her. She did not check out, and now no one knows where she is.'

Booker might have been surprised by his reaction to the woman's disappearance had he not been so stunned at the vanishing act itself. Tess was missing. What if the two men who had nabbed him had accidentally grabbed him instead of her? Once they'd figured out they had the wrong person, who was also an elected officer, they'd probably dumped him to keep themselves from getting into any more trouble than they needed. Unconsciously he rubbed at the swelling at the base of his skull, and he did something he had not done in a long time.

He worried.

'Tell me again what we are doing?' Janet whispered as they drove slowly along the dirt road. They were in one of the company cars, it was running, and they were on a deserted road, but Tess's assistant apparently still felt the need to whisper.

Tess leaned forward as she peered over the steering wheel at the row of houses behind the wall that was across a plowed field. She refused to lower her voice as Janet had, and instead spoke in a normal tone, the sound filling the silence of the car. She nodded toward the field. 'Across that field is where Booker lives.'

'Oh,' Janet said, sounding suddenly more interested as she craned her neck to look at the tastefully situated homes. 'Good neighborhood. I bet he makes a nice annual salary.'

'And probably has the ego to match it,' Tess stated primly. She pulled the car into a farmer's drive that was sheltered from view by a row of trees. She put the car in 'park', and turned off the engine. 'All we have to do is go across the field and hop the wall into his yard.'

'What if he has a big dog?' Janet asked quickly, biting her lip nervously.

'He does not have a big dog.' Tess leveled her gaze on Janet.

'How do you know?'

Tess gave her a dry look. 'Does he look like the type to dote on anything?'

Janet's lips widened into a mischievous grin. 'He can dote on me any time.'

Tess rolled her eyes and shook her head. 'Figures I would hire a hormone-driven assistant.'

Tess opened her car door and stepped out. Shutting it quietly behind her, she had started to move away from the car when she noticed Janet was still sitting inside, a look of uncertainty on her face.

She moved to the passenger door and opened it. 'Why don't you stay here? I can take care of this by myself and be back in time for us to go have dinner, okay? My treat.'

Janet chewed her lip as she looked up at Tess. 'It's still daylight, Tess. You're taking a big chance doing this, aren't you? I mean, isn't this breaking and entering?'

'Technically speaking, probably it is,' Tess answered truthfully. It bothered her to see the worry in her friend's eyes. She lowered her voice. 'We're not here to steal anything from Booker. I just want to take a look at his place. Maybe the people who took him have been there and left something behind. We aren't breaking into his house to case it, but to see if there is anything there that can help us find him before something happens to him. We're here to help him.'

Janet nodded. 'You're right.'

'Stay here. I'll be back in a little while,' she said, starting to shut the car door.

Janet stopped it, and got out of the car. Concern still showed in her eyes, but she smiled at her friend. 'I'm not leaving you alone after what happened last night. I'll go with you. Somebody has to keep you out of trouble.'

'Okay, let's go,' Tess said.

The two women walked along the row of trees surrounding the field. Farmers planted the tree rows to help shelter the fields and keep the rich topsoil from eroding away in the wind. The darkening evening shadows helped the two women dressed in black to blend in with the dark green of the trees. They quickly made their way to the wall that set the neighborhood away from the farm fields and traveled part of the way down till Tess nodded her head toward the house on the other side.

'That should be his house,' she whispered.

'Should be?' Janet asked quickly, her voice barely audible above the wind. 'You mean you don't know?'

Tess gave her friend a hard look. 'Yes, I do know, and yes, this is his house. Does that make you feel better?'

'Yes,' Janet answered, sighing with visible relief. 'Uncertainty scares the hell out of me at the moment.'

Tess scaled the wall easily, pulling her athletic form to the top and glancing quickly around to make sure no one was outside enjoying the evening air. So far so good, she thought, seeing no one around. Looking back at her friend, she realized the petite Janet might have a problem. She'd put her hand down to help pull her up when Janet surprised her by scaling the wall as quickly as she had. Tess looked at her friend with new-found admiration.

Jumping from the wall, they remained crouched on the lawn as they scanned the back yard of Dr Ethan Booker's home. A six-foot privacy fence shielded his yard from neighbors and the noise of the street, as did the neatly trimmed lilacs and privets that lined the fence. Beautifully tended gardens landscaped the back yard, complete with a fish pond and a statue of a Greek woman pouring water rhythmically among the water lilies. Tess had to admit she was highly impressed with the scenic, yet peaceful atmosphere he had created to escape from the morbid realities of his job. Sometimes a person's yard and home could tell a lot about an individual. What she saw before her was a person who faced the black and white reality of death on a daily basis and chose to surround himself with the color of life when he came home.

'Are you still with me?' Tess whispered as she turned back to her partner in crime. At Janet's nod, Tess motioned for her to follow.

Polly Sanderson took a sip of tea from her cup while standing at the window of her upstairs office. She was a writer, though no one knew it yet, because she didn't want the pressure that 'coming out of the closet' would bring. Once a person admitted to actually suffering from such an unusual illness, people, normal people that was, would want to know if she was still working on her book. Was it done yet? Was she published yet? How many books had she published? And the embarrassing questions were more than she wanted to deal with at the moment. At the moment she chose to simply lose herself in her story.

Retired, widowed, and with no family living close by, Polly found writing an enjoyable experience. One that fitted her secluded lifestyle well. Lately, though, her characters had been giving her a little problem, and so she had chosen to take a little time away from the computer. It seemed to help to let her mind wander to something else for a while.

Since yesterday, when she had found her young, good looking neighbor unconscious on his own front lawn, Polly had taken to standing at her office window whenever the words would not seem to come. In the three years young Dr Booker had been her next-door neighbor, he had never given her a moment's trouble. He had been kind, helpful, courteous, and oh, so nice to look at. And his voice – oh, how she loved a smooth, sexy voice. If she had been about twenty years younger she would have enjoyed her neighbor much more.

It had worried Polly that perhaps his life was too uneventful. She had been excited for him when he had got his new little sports car. Maybe he would pick up a few chicks, or whatever the current term was now. But he hadn't, as far as she knew. Still, finding him on his lawn had encouraged her. When she had first seen him lying out on the lawn, wearing a tuxedo, she had thought he had passed out from too much liquor. She had gone outside to check on him, but when she'd got closer she'd realized that his jacket was torn and his face looked as if he had been beaten. It had concerned her to see him in such a condition and she had called the emergency crews immediately.

Then to find out he had been kidnapped – it was all too exciting, she thought. So romantic, like one of her novels, she thought wryly.

Now she found herself once again standing at the window, watching young Booker's house, since his life had taken such an exciting turn.

Polly was raising her cup of tea to her lips when she stopped. It hadn't taken long for the excitement to continue. She smiled as she watched the two attractive women scaling the wall to the back yard. Booker was home; that much she knew for sure. Polly chuckled to herself as she thought of the surprise waiting for the good young doctor.

If for one moment she'd truly believed he was in danger, she would have called the police and hightailed it over there with her shotgun, but she knew he wasn't. She had a good feeling about those girls, and she'd never been wrong before. No, Booker was not in any danger. Not physically anyway.

At that thought, Polly let her creativity run away with her. Glancing to see the two women at the back door of his garage, Polly smiled as she simply turned away and went to her computer. Her neighbor had no idea how much he was helping her . . .

Tess and Janet moved quickly in a low crouch across the length of the back yard, making sure to keep close to the protective cover of the hedge. At the back of the house, Tess flattened herself against the side of the building. Standing at the back door of the garage, Tess scanned the area around them. The back door where they stood was situated in a tree-lined alcove, conveniently shielding them from the view of most of the neighbors who might just happen to look out of their windows toward Booker's yard. Tess turned her attention to the small box housing the security system. She took the tools she would need and placed them in her mouth before she started working to remove the cover from the box. It took her only a few short moments to work the wiring and disable the system.

Once the system was turned off, she switched her tools and started to turn her attention to the lock of the back door. When she could no longer handle the constant movement beside her she turned toward Janet and put her hands on her hips as she simply watched the woman shuffle nervously and impatiently from foot to foot.

'What are you doing?' she asked quietly.

'I'm nervous, okay?' Janet whispered back defensively. 'You may have done this kind of thing before, but I haven't.'

'Well, quit hopping. You're distracting me.' Tess shook her head as she turned back to the lock of the door. She pulled the slim picks she needed from the tiny case she held and popped the lock in less than thirty seconds. Opening the door, she cautiously stuck her head in to check the garage out. The fading evening light illuminated the two cars inside just enough for her to make out what they were.

'Wow,' she murmured softly as she stepped in the door and admired one of the cars, a sleek red Porsche, parked inside. She was not a car buff, but she admired beauty when she saw it. She continued to eye the car as she walked past it to the door leading into the house, then, just as quickly, her thoughts returned to the task at hand. The door to the house took even less time, and she eased it open slowly, just in case it made any noise as she did it. Luck remained with her as it opened silently and she stepped into the house.

Waiting for Janet to move past her, Tess shut the door, though not all the way, so it wouldn't latch.

They found themselves standing in the kitchen. The lights were off, but there was just enough light from the setting sun to illuminate the room. Just as she had thought how a person's yard or home told a lot about an individual, Tess was surprised by how truly interested she was in finding out more about Ethan Booker.

Her eyes moved over the room and she took in every detail. Pots hung from a decorative rack above the kitchen island, the copper and cast-iron a complementary contrast to the dark blue tile of the kitchen counters. Oak cabinets with glass doors showcased Booker's stoneware and china. Somehow it didn't surprise Tess that Ethan Booker liked to cook. The very vivid image of him standing in bare feet, jeans and an unbuttoned shirt as he cooked them dinner filled her thoughts, and her mouth began to water. There was more to an appetite than just hunger, and Ethan Booker somehow had become something she did not want to admit that she craved. But crave she did. Though, it would all mean nothing if she couldn't find him, she reminded herself.

Tess shook herself from her thoughts and moved through the kitchen to peek through an entryway. She found his front room. Again, it did not surprise her that she should find his house neat. Booker had probably been a bachelor for a long time and, though he probably had a housekeeper come in, he would be the kind of individual to pick up after himself. He seemed the type of person who didn't expect someone else to take care of him.

Pictures sitting on the fireplace mantel caught her attention, and she moved to look at them before she could question herself as to what her true motive was for wanting to see them. Several were obviously from his childhood – black and white photographs of chubby babies, continuing with lanky, long-legged kids grinning to show a lost tooth. One photo caused her to pick it up for a closer look before she realized what she was doing. It was obviously Booker when he was about six or seven – first grade, perhaps. He wore a striped shirt, blue jeans with a hole in the knee, and no shoes. He smiled brightly at the camera, complete with a missing front tooth, as he held a baseball bat in one-hand. The other rested on the top of a huge Great Dane dog, and a girl with braids and freckles sat cross-legged beside them. Tess smiled at the innocence of Booker as a child represented in the photograph she held in her hands.

'Cute little thing, wasn't he?' Janet said.

Her friend's voice startled her. She hadn't realized that Janet had walked up beside her. She cleared her throat as she worked for a serious expression. 'I guess he was.'

'Hello,' Janet said softly, her attention arrowing to another picture. She picked it up and looked at it with interest. 'I wonder who this is?'

Tess frowned at the beautiful woman with dark hair and blue eyes smiling back at them from the photo. It was obviously a recent photo, and judging by its location – with the rest of the important photos – it was someone he knew quite well. Someone he probably cared a lot for. Tess recognized the stab of jealousy that moved quickly through her and was surprised. Never had a woman's photo caused such a reaction in her. There were men she had known a lot better than Booker, men she'd had a relationship with, who had tried to make her jealous with photos of another woman. All to no avail. There had even been one instance when an old boyfriend had decided to use the real thing. When Tess had seen the two of them together, she had shaken his hand and wished him the best of luck. She then had surprised the 'other' woman by turning to her and thanking her. Yet here she was, in the house of a man she barely knew, wishing she knew what the hell this woman's picture was doing on his mantel.

This isn't getting us anywhere, she reprimanded herself. She turned away from the photos and began to take in the details of the room. As she had noted earlier, it was obvious that the house had not been disturbed – so what was she still doing here? she asked herself. She stood in the middle of the room and shook her head as she pursed her lips in concentration. There would be no information gathered from his house.

'It's obvious they didn't come here, Janet,' she said, keeping her voice low. 'We aren't going to learn anything here. The next step will have to be talking to some of our cop friends. Or, as much as I'd hate to do it, talk to Booker's friend. That detective.'

'So you don't want to snoop?' Janet asked casually, leaning over to lift the lid of a decorative jar on the end-table. 'Maybe go check out his underwear drawer and see whether he's a boxer or a brief kind of guy?'

Tess barely caught herself from letting her jaw drop open at the question. She couldn't think of even one appropriate response to that question. She simply stared at the woman in front of her.

Finally noticing her silence, Janet looked back to Tess with a wicked gleam of humor in her eyes. 'Oh, come on. I was just kidding, Tess. Don't be such a prude.'

Tess just shook her head in exaggerated wonder. 'Remind me to add psychological testing to my employers' requirements. And I'm not a prude.'

She'd started walking back through the hallway toward the kitchen when a noise from upstairs caused her to freeze in her tracks. She held her hand up to silence anything Janet might try to say. Her muscles, though sore, had been somewhat limbered by their excursion over the wall, but now they seemed to return to a tense state and she stood still, her gaze directed toward the stairway leading to the second floor.

There was the sound again. A sliding noise, as if someone was opening, then closing a drawer upstairs. Tess turned to Janet. She mouthed instructions for her friend to stay where she was while she herself went upstairs to investigate. At the sign of reluctance visible in Janet's face, Tess frowned at her and motioned sternly with her hand for her to stay. Janet's expression registered her hurt feelings, something Tess would worry about later. Right now she was more concerned with the woman's safety.

She needed to go upstairs to see who was searching through Booker's things. It was obvious it wasn't a cop, so that left only one other interested party. The people who had taken Booker in the first place.

Tess moved slowly up the stairs, testing each step carefully before she-put her full weight on it. She was more than halfway up when she could see a light coming on in what looked like the bathroom. Frowning, she continued up the stairs, pulling her shock gun from the catch on the back of her belt loop. At this point she didn't want to pull her other gun. If this guy knew where Booker was being held, she wanted to talk to him.

The light went off and a shadow passed briefly in the hallway, heading away from her. At the top of the stairs, Tess kept the wall to her back. As she passed each room, she would glance inside to make sure there were no other surprises.

She moved toward the room in which the lights had been turned on so briefly. Glancing inside, Tess confirmed that it was a bathroom. A shadow moved across the wall in front of her and Tess flattened against the door. The person was walking into the bedroom beyond the adjoining bathroom.

Tess had stepped slowly, carefully toward the bedroom when an ominous hiss caused her to stop. Her gaze darted toward the sound to find a huge cat staring at her. Thank goodness it wasn't a dog, she thought, or Janet would kill her. She stuck her foot toward the feline to edge it on its way. The cat obviously thought she meant to play, and it batted at her playfully with its paws. Tess ignored the signs of the animal's good nature and nudged it with her foot. The creature didn't like being told to go, and hissed at her one last time before it rose regally, then walked stiffly away.

The light in the bedroom went out, effectively catching Tess's attention. She moved cautiously through the bathroom toward the intruder. The door to what she believed to be Booker's bedroom unfortunately opened inward, blocking part of the darkened room from her view. Peeking through the door, she held her shock gun in front of her as she scanned the room. Unable to see anyone, Tess reasoned that the individual now stood in the area behind the door.

Taking a deep, slow, quiet breath, Tess worked to ease the tension filling her as her heart pounded with adrenaline. She moved quietly through the doorway, keeping her mind and body focused toward the area that she had not been able to see. Fully expecting to confront the intruder in the darkened area of the room, Tess shrieked when an arm came from behind and wrapped tightly around her. She struggled against the man holding her, unable to bend her arm to tag him with the shock gun. She strained, trying to twist the six inches she needed to hit him.

The man grabbed her and roughly threw them both to the bed. He took her wrists in his hands and held them above her head. Tess growled at him as she twisted and bucked wildly under him. He hit the arm holding the shock gun against the mattress, forcing it out of her grasp. Tess started to move her leg to knee him in the groin but the man obviously anticipated her move. He shoved his legs roughly between hers, and their bodies pressed intimately together as he used his body to keep her legs from hurting him.

'Damn you,' she gasped at him, twisting her head to try and bite him.

'Freeze, jerk.'

Janet's voice boomed behind them from where she stood in the bedroom doorway. The darkened room kept them from seeing what she held in her hand, but neither Tess or the stranger wanted to take a wild guess. Or the chance. Their movements stilled; the only sound in the room was the rush of their combined labored breathing. Janet's silhouette moved and Tess watched proudly as she boldly moved toward the light switch and flipped it on.

For a brief moment the brightness of the light caused Tess to squint and turn away. She forced herself to look toward the man still holding her and she gasped as she recognized the face. Her lips twitched somewhere between a smile and relief from the fear that she had experienced while wrestling with him on the bed.

'Booker,' she said simply, unable to form any other words.

'Miss Reynolds,' he answered. Tension seeped from the body still covering hers. Now she felt the weight of him covering her. Pressing against her. He seemed to suddenly enjoy the position he had her in. He lifted his head slightly to look at the length of their bodies locked together on the now rumpled covers, her legs still pressed wide around him.

'So good of you to drop in,' he said casually, teasingly, the energy of his eyes still vibrant, but now playful. 'If you'd wanted to wrestle with me, all you had to do was call. And I would have let you win.'

Tess gave him a dry look, her smile disappearing as she reminded herself she was not that glad to see him. She had been concerned about his well-being, just as she would have been for any other citizen. That was all.

'Would you mind getting off of me?' she suggested through tight lips.

He grinned mischievously, looking relaxed and ready to spend the rest of the evening just where he was. 'This was your idea, not mine, remember?'

'He can stay there all evening if he wants, Tess,' Janet chuckled wickedly behind them. Tess glanced toward her ally in crime and found her petite friend leaning casually against the wall holding a butcher's knife. 'I'm really enjoying the view.'

Booker frowned, suddenly remembering the other woman. And the fact that he was wearing only a towel. He cleared his throat as he shifted modestly away from Tess. 'Next time let me know if you decide to bring company. I, myself, usually like to play one-on-one, but I've never been one to disappoint a lady. Or ladies,' he said, with a nod toward Janet.

Janet only grinned and gave him a bold wink.

'Ha. Ha. Ha,' she said, with no humor. Tess rolled her eyes. How did she get herself into such weird situations anyway? She turned back to Booker with an accusing glare. 'What the hell are you doing here?'

Booker gave her a pointed look. 'I live here.'

'Really?' she retorted, rolling from the bed to stand. She started straightening her clothes, her hands moving in jerky strokes from the anger mixed with relief at seeing him safe. She turned away from Janet and his too watchful eyes as she fought to get her emotions under control.

Damn the man, she thought. When the light had come on, and she had seen his face above hers, Tess had smiled with pure joy at seeing him alive and well. All the anger had instantly dissipated from her and she had had an overwhelming urge to hug him fiercely to her, to kiss him just so her body would know he was actually there with her. It had more than surprised her that her reaction of relief and joy had been so strong. It had scared her.

Tess did not like to be scared.

She frowned angrily toward him. 'Skinner showed up in my hospital room, saying you had disappeared. What happened?'

Booker shrugged, studying her face. He spoke slowly, softly, as his eyes continued to hold hers. 'I was walking over to my office and two guys hit me on the back of my head. It must have been a case of mistaken identity, as far as we can tell, since they did nothing but dump me on my front lawn.'

Tess's frown deepened as she mulled over his words. She put her hands on her hips and chewed her lip in thought as she tried to decipher why someone had gone to so much trouble to do nothing. Nabbing a coroner, an appointed official, even if it was a mistake was asking for trouble. The individuals had either known who he was when they'd grabbed him, then changed their minds. Or they had made a mistake, and when they'd found out who he was tossed him out on his lawn so as not to stir up any more trouble. Either scenario was risky. Why would anyone want to kidnap Booker?

Doubt and guilt filled her mind. She looked back toward him. 'Could there be anyone who is holding a grudge against you?'

Booker's brow rose. 'Professionally speaking, my patients are already dead by the time they get to me. How could I upset them?'

Her eyes narrowed at his humor. 'What about an old girlfriend? Or somebody's husband?'

'No.' Booker's gaze darkened at the last of her questions. 'And no.'

Tess studied him for a moment, then looked away. There could have been only one reason he had been abducted. And she was it.

Seeing Booker safe and alive had given her a tremendous feeling of relief, followed by shock. Now that the shock was wearing off, the pounding of her injured head resumed and her muscles began to feel as if they were stiffening. Her aching body suddenly seemed drained of all its energy. Guilt weighed heavily on her. Somehow she had messed up the case with Gare Harolds, and now she had pulled two other people in with her.

Tess wrapped her arms around herself. Bowing her head, she pinched her nose between her fingers as she tried to relieve the pain and pressure from the thunderous pounding. She was tired and needed relief from the pain booming in her head.

She'd started toward the bedroom door to leave when her feet weaved unsteadily beneath her. Automatically she put her arms out to balance herself, only to find that Booker had beat her to it. Janet had started to advance forward her, then stopped, apparently realizing she still held the butcher's knife in her hand.

Tess narrowed her eyes at the object her friend held. 'What is that?'

'Uh . . .' Janet stumbled, then chuckled nervously. 'I couldn't think of anything else.'

Booker's deep chuckle so close behind her caused Tess to frown, and the rumble of his humor sparked tingles to shoot through her body. Her eyes drooped tiredly and she barely caught his comment. Something about carving up a rump roast.

She looked down at his strong hands and long fingers as he gripped her waist. She could feel the heat of him as he stood only inches behind her. Wickedly her thoughts conjured the image of his broad chest as he sat on the edge of the bed wearing only a towel. The vivid pleasure that speared through her body caused her to smile softly.

'Uh oh,' Janet murmured, watching Tess's face intently.

'What is it,' Booker asked, concern softening his voice.

'I think we're about to lose her,' Janet stated.

Tess had silently agreed with the accuracy of her friend's statement. The doctor had given her a prescription for pain killers to use when he released her from the hospital. She, of course, had not had the time nor any intention of filling the prescription. Now it seemed nature had decided to ignore her stubbornness and take over.

Tess felt herself falling to sleep. At the time she thought it seemed strange that they called it 'falling' to sleep when she felt herself being picked up. She snuggled against the warmth that held her and murmured her pleasure.

And slept.

CHAPTER 5

Tess awoke. She opened her eyes, finding herself in her usual morning position. She was on her stomach, legs sprawled out, tangled in the covers, and her hair nested heavily on her face. She blinked, then narrowed her eyes as she became aware of her surroundings through the thick cloud of hair. She started to lift her head, then gasped at the sharp protest of her muscles. She'd always heard the second day was worse than the first and she'd experienced it enough times to know it was true. Didn't mean she had to like it, though.

Still . . . where the heck was she?

Tess rolled slowly, painfully over onto her back, and met the yellow gaze studying her. She blinked, then frowned at her observer. She was being studied by a pair of vivid yellow eyes belonging to what had to be the ugliest cat she had ever seen.

The cat was the usual gray-brown with black tabby markings, except for its feet, which were pure white like tiny little snow boots. Its coloring and silky fur would have made it a fine specimen had it not been for the shape of the poor animal's head. The dog-shaped head of the cat wildly contradicted the feline's beautiful body. Its eyes, beautiful, vivid, yellow, were rimmed with white, as was its mouth. Though the rest of its face was typically tabby, the unusual and somewhat mystical shape of a diamond was perched on the canine length of the animal's nose. The fringe of dark tabby hair mixed with white protruding from his narrow cheeks completed the almost werewolfish look of the cat.

Though the cat was definitely the oddest Tess had ever seen, the feline continued to study her as if she was the most uninteresting thing it had ever seen. It had always amazed her how accurately and easily a cat could let it be known what it thought of you as a mere human.

'The genetic pool was not nice to you, huh?' she stated to the cat.

If the cat had had eyebrows it would have raised one at her comment. Instead, the feline simply stood, turned, and hiked its hind end in the air right in front of her face as it sashayed away. It was clearly letting her know in no uncertain terms exactly what it thought of her comment. Of course, the view the animal so thoughtfully provided let her observe that 'it' was no longer appropriate, because 'it' was definitely a he.

'Well, I see you've already made one friend today.'

At the sound of Booker's voice, Tess swallowed the moan in her throat and pulled herself stiffly to a sitting position. She had never liked talking to a man while she was in a prone position.

'Obviously he's too sensitive,' Tess said, her gaze, and her stomach, directed to the tray he carried. 'Typical male.'

Booker chuckled as he put the tray on her lap in front of her. 'Nah, he's just playing hard to get.

That's all. If you ignore him long enough he'll be rubbing himself all over you, trying to win you over.'

'Like I need another man in my life right now,' she retorted, buttering the wonderfully large blueberry muffins Booker had provided.

'Just lining up, are they?'

At her pointed look, Booker laughed, and he held his hands up in mock surrender. 'Just thought I would ask. I wanted to see how much competition I had.'

Tess gave a very unladylike snort as she finished her first bite of the muffin. She was buttering another piece of the huge muffin when with a guilty start she realized that she didn't know where her friend was. 'Where's Janet?'

Booker picked up a small carafe and poured her a glass of orange juice. 'After you fell asleep – literally – she hopped the fence and took the car home. Has anyone ever told you that you're not a very lively escort?'

At her miffed glare, he smiled innocently. 'No? I didn't think so. How are you feeling this morning? Better?'

'I feel much better, thank you,' Tess replied automatically. Booker's mention of morning had suddenly made her aware of time. She glanced toward the window and thought the sun looked too bright. She turned back to him. 'Is it still morning?'

'Late morning anyway.' He smiled casually, picking up the piece of muffin she had forgotten and buttering it. He popped it into his mouth as he studied her face with those gray-blue eyes. 'Don't worry, I'm sure you're an early riser. At least when you don't have concussion.'

Tess could tell by his point-by-point assessment as he watched her that he was mentally examining her condition without actually having to touch her. For his own safety, he had probably realized that she'd bite his hand if he actually tried to touch her.

He picked up another piece and buttered it. He went about it casually, innocently Occasionally he would glance at her, his head tilted, and smiling that truly disarming innocent little boy smile. After a moment, he raised an eyebrow questioningly. 'What? You look like you would just love to kiss me.'

'Yeah, right,' Tess said, flustered, looking away, anywhere but at him. Her cheeks flamed with her embarrassment. Damn, how that man could push her buttons. The very enticing and all too real thought of kissing him had been exactly what she had had in her mind. Watching him masterfully spread the butter onto the muffin, then watching those long tapered fingers carry it to his mouth had been more erotic than eating a muffin should be allowed to be.

He chuckled, pleased with himself. He ate the bite of muffin, letting the silence stretch between them. Tess pleated the fabric of the comforter between her fingers as she became all too aware of his close proximity to her. Her gaze moved nervously about the room, down to the spread in front of her, to her shirt – then stopped. She was not wearing the dark shirt she had been wearing last night. Taking a quick, discreet peek beneath the covers, she realized her legs were bare.

She turned, glaring at him, enunciating every word with full Victorian emphasis. 'How did I get into this? I don't remember changing into these clothes.'

Booker laughed, his charismatic smile contrasting against the bruises and scratches evident on his face. 'I would think our focus should be on the fact that we never did get to have that all-important conversation about the Gare Harolds case. Remember that? You were going to enlighten me.'

'The hell I was,' Tess retorted, her cheeks burning with the thought of him undressing her last night. 'You took my clothes off. That is what we should be focusing on.'

'I'm a doctor. It's not like I've never seen a naked woman before,' he returned easily.

'The only difference is they're usually dead,' she snapped, her voice raising slightly. She clutched the covers in front of her. 'In case you haven't noticed, I'm not dead.'

'No, you're not,' he said softly, his voice low, like a sweet caress. The corners of his lips turned up in a small smile as he studied her. The dark, sooty fringe of his lashes framed his steel-blue eyes as he held her gaze. The steady, soft look he gave her hypnotized her, and Tess suddenly realized that the focus of their conversation had completely slipped from her thoughts.

Booker scooted the tray toward her knees, then put his arm on the other side of her legs as he leaned toward her. His gaze never left hers, and she could feel the heat of him, the pull of him as he brought his lips to hers. She had known he was going to kiss her, probably should have stopped it, but she could not.

Did not want to. She had never been one to lie to herself, and she would have been lying to say she hadn't wanted to kiss him. To touch him.

Touch him she did, as she slid her hand into his hair and opened her mouth to him. His kiss deepened and he lifted his free hand to smooth the tumble of hair from her face. His lips felt firm, yet soft as he moved over the curves of her lips with devilish torture. She imagined what it would be like with him if he were to touch her with his lips, his hand, his body. It would be torture, the sweetest, most exquisite form, as he pushed her and pushed her till she spiraled with pleasure.

She imagined, wondered what it would be like with him. Then the ability to form coherent thoughts was lost to her as he gently skimmed the tips of his fingers along the ridge of her cheek. He trailed them lightly, slowly, like his kiss, till he reached the sensitive skin of her throat and he cupped her head.

His lips left hers as he traced the ridge of her jaw with the tip of his tongue. He shifted closer to her to press her to him. He started to wrap his arm around her to bring her more fully against him when his back protested sharply, making him wince. At the same moment Tess lifted her arms to circle his neck, and her ribs spiked her heightened senses with a quick pain. They both caught their breath quickly as their bodies protested, forcing them back to reality.

Booker chuckled as he leaned his forehead against hers. 'Getting old is a bitch.'

Tess smiled, turning to press her lips against his throat. 'It's not that we're old, it's the fact we got beat up.'

'More like blown up, in case you don't remember,' he reminded her.

Booker leaned away from her and helped pull the pillows up behind her so she could lean against the headboard. He moved the tray back, motioning for her to continue her breakfast. Picking up part of a muffin, he fixed it, then handed it to her. 'Now, why don't you tell me the tale of Gare Harolds' disappearance and subsequent discovery?'

The word 'discovery' brought a grisly image to mind of what Gare Harolds might have looked like at the time of his discovery. She eyed the once irresistible muffin, then carefully placed it back on the plate.

'Well, I guess it would depend on your findings in his autopsy. If he died at, or during, the implosion of the Worth Hotel, then what I have might not be of too much help,' Tess stated. She picked up her glass of orange juice and took a small sip as she mulled her thoughts over, trying to switch gears from the achingly sweet kiss he had just given her to murder. The transition was not easy, and her brain felt as if it were clogged with rusty gears being forced into motion. 'However, if your findings showed that he was killed at some other location, then placed into the Worth Hotel, well, then maybe I have something that could help us.'

'I assume this "other location" is out of my jurisdiction?' Booker asked.

Tess nodded, beginning to feel more confident with their conversation. 'Law enforcement and Harolds' company security have already processed the scene, and it has been released back to the family.

Fortunately, I was able to convince Mrs Harolds to seal the cabin till I could bring in an expert for our own investigation.'

'I assume that's where I come in?' he stated, his brow raised, giving her a slight smile.

Tess shook her head and chuckled softly. 'Are you ever in a bad mood?'

'Frequently.'

She didn't believe it. She didn't believe it for a minute. Even after the explosion he had been cracking jokes. It felt good, right to be talking with him this way. Too good, she thought, the smile fading away. Tess's light mood started to slip away as she looked at her hands. A feeling of melancholy was drifting quietly over her. Booker's kiss had been unexpected, perhaps inappropriate, but goodness forgive her for relishing the feel of it. She picked unconsciously at the comforter covering her while her thoughts mulled around madly in her head. Booker seemed like a good man, solid, caring and sincere, despite his wicked sense of humor. And it scared her. Hadn't she learned the hard way that falling in love was sweet . . . wonderful? It was the relationship part after that that lacked considerably.

Right now she was scared. Scared of the powerful response that this man seemed to be able to spark in her. Tess closed her eyes against the rush of thoughts washed in by the melancholy. It was simply better, easier, never to start than to try to pick up the pieces afterward.

Booker watched the smile fade from Tess's face. She had been in a light mood after sparring with him, but now he could feel her withdrawal from him. From the slight frown on her brow, he could tell that her thoughts were not pleasant, maybe somewhat sad. He suddenly realized that he had stopped what he was doing and was studying her, trying to figure out the change in her. Had it been their conversation? He had no idea, but he would guess that there was a lot more below the surface of Tess Reynolds than she liked to let show.

And what about that kiss?

Booker had to shake his head in wonder on that one. Quintessa Reynolds had the ability to shake his world. His life had been simple. A simple routine and uneventful relationships. Work provided more than enough emotion for him in his life without complicating it with a serious relationship. Then Quintessa Reynolds had walked into his office wearing that flaming red wig, the memory of which caused his lips to quirk in a small smile. He hadn't known her more than a couple of days. In that short span of time they had already been involved in a vehicle explosion and he had been kidnapped.

And that kiss.

It was completely unlike him to just lean over and kiss a woman. A virtual stranger. But . . . there was something about her. The range of emotions that moved easily back and forth through her, the sparkle in her eye, and the small spattering of freckles across the bridge of her pretty nose drew him to her like the proverbial moth to a flame.

Damn, he needed to get out more often, he thought. Somehow he had a feeling that nothing would be normal or easy with Quintessa Reynolds.

It was a feeling that he did not want to deal with at the moment, maybe not even later. They didn't seem to be able to have a normal conversation like normal people, let alone behave like normal adults while they were around each other.

Booker rose, clearing his throat as he walked toward the door of the guest bedroom. 'I'll let you finish your breakfast. I laid your clothes out for you on the chair. You can change into them when you finish eating. I'll be downstairs when you're ready to discuss the case.'

He closed the door behind him as he left. Tess breathed a deep sigh of relief and let her head rest against the headboard. This case was already threatening to consume her. She'd never lost a client before, and to have two go directly against her wishes only to be kidnapped and killed had hit her hard. Tess might not have ever had much going for her in the emotional department, but she had had just about everything going right for her professionally. Torkelson's and Harolds' disappearances and deaths had affected her a lot. Not only had she lost two clients she had respected, but two families had lost a father and a husband.

The case was a hard one, a complicated one, and the last thing she needed was a hormonal surge screwing up her thought process. Life truly enjoyed dumping on her, never did things seem to go easy for her, but she did take pride in the work it had taken for her to accomplish what she had. She had to shake her head at the irony of it. To solve the most difficult case of her career she needed to put aside her personal feelings and find the best people to work with her in piecing together the very few parts of the puzzle she had.

And the one person who came highly recommended was the very same man who had the uncanny ability to evoke those 'personal feelings.'

Polly stood at her window again. She had stayed up late last night finishing a scene, after her neighbor had so fortunately provided her with fodder for fiction. Being old and retired had its advantages. She had been able to sleep in to make up for her long night. Now she was back at it again, though right now Polly had decided to take a short break. She wanted to check to see if anything new was going on next door.

After watching the two women scale the wall and enter Booker's house last night, she had heard the Coopers' dog barking. The ignorant little beast lived on the other side of Booker and barked at pretty much everything. Still, she had decided to get up and check what the commotion was anyway and she had seen a stealthy movement in Booker's back yard. When the petite form of one of the women had paused briefly under a light, she had smiled to herself. Obviously the tall redhead was staying.

Polly's attention now returned to her neighbor's house as he finally made an appearance that morning. Wearing an old shirt and a pair of jeans, he walked to the driveway to retrieve his daily paper. He leaned over to pick it up, briefly giving her a nice view of his rear end before he turned back toward the house. The old woman chuckled at the scowl on his handsome features. She'd bet just about anything that that redhead had put it there.

A new idea gripped her and she turned back toward the computer. Whoever the tall beauty was, she was exactly what both she and her young neighbor had needed.

Tess pulled her black sweatshirt over her head, then pulled her hair out of the neckline. The jeans were loose, but thankfully not that loose. She pulled her black sports shoes on, then tried to act casual as she inspected herself in the mirror.

She tilted her face, first one way then the other, as she inspected the purple bruises starting to turn yellow on her forehead. She had taken a hot shower after Booker left and it had helped loosen up the tight soreness of her muscles. When she had first crawled out of bed, literally, she had silently cursed her stiff body and made a straight line for the therapeutic heat of the shower.

Besides her clothes, Booker had thoughtfully provided a hair brush and a toothbrush for her use. He was probably used to unexpected overnight guests, she thought without humor. Where had that come from? Tess growled to herself. It didn't matter to her one bit what Dr Booker chose to do in his spare time. She said the words silently to herself even as her traitorous mind first conjured up images of the picture of the beautiful brunette downstairs, then moved to the kiss they had experienced earlier.

Experienced. 'Experienced' seemed like a woefully inadequate word to use to try and describe what she had felt. Maybe he was used to kissing women who were practically strangers, but she wasn't. Used to kissing strange men, that is. Tess shook her head at her sense of humor, which seemed to snake in at the most inopportune times.

Her thoughts returned to what had happened that morning as she stood there in front of the bathroom mirror. The memory of the kiss fogged out the reality around her and her body reacted just as boldly as it had before. Her lips missed the feel of his against her own, the heat of him, as he caressed the curves of her mouth with the tip of his tongue. The chill of arousal swept over her and she started when she found that the mere thought of his touching her could cause such a strong reaction.

What had come over her? she wondered with a frown. When she'd seen the picture downstairs she had felt a stab of envy, jealousy, that the woman was so close to Booker that he kept a picture of her on his fireplace. Though Tess did have green eyes, she had never been one to experience that *feeling* before.

'Come on, Tess, get a grip,' she said softly to herself as she quickly brushed her hair. 'You don't have time for this.'

Tess had left the bedroom to head toward the stairs when a feeling of uneasiness washed over her. After that . . . that kiss, Booker had simply walked out of the room and she hadn't seen him since. She didn't know exactly how she was going to go about facing him after the way he had touched her. Correction, she thought, trying to remain fair. How they had touched each other. She had been just as much involved in the episode as he had.

She pulled at the hem of the sweatshirt she wore to straighten it, just as she straightened her shoulders and forced herself to move on. This is ridiculous, she thought, I'm a grown woman, not a simpering teenager. She had faced much more harrowing experiences in her lifetime than just a kiss.

Despite her forced bravado, Tess's steps were reluctant as she slowly made her way down the stairs, telling herself she was just being casual. The cat ran up the stairs and met her halfway, expertly weaving his body around her as she continued to descend. Tess had to smile at the feline. He was working very hard to get her attention, which wasn't difficult, considering that if she did not pay attention to his movements she would soon be tripping over him and falling flat on her face all the way down the stairs.

She stopped, still smiling at his antics. She leaned over and picked him up. It was easier to carry the animal than try to avoid stepping on him. She rubbed her face against his fur, thinking of her own cat. 'For such an ugly little guy, you sure are sweet.'

As she stepped from the bottom of the stairs, Tess looked up to find Booker standing in front of the fireplace watching her. His gaze was solemn, somewhat leery. She swallowed, looking away. Okay, so scaling a cliff would be easier than this conversation was going to be.

She nervously chewed at her lip as she warily circled the room to finally settle in an overstuffed easy chair. She continued stroking the cat's silky fur, then darted her eyes toward Booker. 'Um, what's his name?'

'Sylvester,' he replied, his voice almost a monotone. He moved away from the fireplace to the opposite end of the couch from her and sat on the armrest.

Tess couldn't suppress her smile. 'As in the cat?'

'Yeah, something like that,' he answered simply, crossing his arms over his chest.

This is a crock, she thought. She didn't have time for this uneasy pussyfooting they were doing around each other. She was going to have to put away the sophomoric feelings that were running rampant between them and get to work. Obviously whoever had been connected with Gare Harolds' death was worried about her involvement in the investigation. There just simply was not any room for hesitancy between them.

Tess put Sylvester down and stood. She walked to the fireplace, her gaze moving against her will to the picture of the beautiful woman on the mantel. Suppressing the urge to stick her tongue out at the image, she pivoted toward Booker. The only way to get this . . . this mess all out in the open was to confront it. And confront it – or, more accurately, him – was exactly what she was going to do. She stood with her hands on her hips, her feet slightly apart, her face expressionless. Every nuance of her stance was confrontational.

Tess waited till his gaze met hers. 'Booker, I'm not good at beating around the bush or small talk, so I'll just get right to the point.'

His brow rose – his only response to her direct conversation. Thankful for no resistance on his part, she pressed on. 'I don't know exactly what happened up there earlier. I'm not saying that I regret what happened, but, considering our current circumstances, I think it would be a good idea if we just put all this behind us.'

'What exactly is the problem?' he asked, his voice irritatingly nonchalant.

Okay, so he was going to be somewhat obstinate, she thought. As usual, she wasn't that good with dealing with people's feelings. Being sensitive meant being hurt. She had learned that the hard way, and the best way to deal with it was not to be sensitive at all. Period.

Tess prided herself on being able to take care of herself. Both physically and emotionally. It hadn't taken her long to figure out that if the door kept slamming in your face, you didn't open the door any more. At Booker's question, she started pacing.

'We had this . . .' Her voice trailed off. She was reluctant to say the words that seemed to understate what had happened, even though that was exactly what was needed at this point in their conversation. 'This kiss,' she said at last. 'And now we're edging around each other in circles like two dogs circling a bone.'

Booker chuckled as he visibly began to relax, and he ran his hand through his hair. 'You definitely have a way with words.'

She gave him a dry look accompanied with an arched eyebrow, thankful that he was returning to his typical teasing nature. 'Don't interrupt me when I'm preaching.'

'Oh, sorry,' he said with mock contrition, and he slid onto the couch to sit in a more comfortable position. 'Please continue.'

'As I was saying,' she stated, her jitters dissipating as she felt the tension slip from the room. From between them. 'We can't be pussyfooting around each other.'

Booker looked to Sylvester, who was now sitting beside him, licking his paw to clean his face. 'I don't think she meant that to be offensive, buddy.'

'You are such a nut, Booker.' Tess laughed, stopping her pacing to put her hands back on her hips. 'Aren't you ever serious?'

'Be careful,' he stated with an innocent smile. 'I believe that question was exactly what got us in trouble the last time.'

'Well, we're in enough trouble as it is,' she reminded him. She walked back to the easy chair and sat down. Now the tension was gone and they could talk. Her smile softened but did not fade, even as her tone became businesslike and serious. 'It's obvious that the individuals involved in Harold's death are worried that we may be getting too close.'

Booker leaned forward, resting his forearms on his knees. 'Any idea who these "individuals" might be?'

Tess frowned as she shook her head, lifting her empty palms face up. 'I have no idea at all. As I mentioned before, the one suspect we had disappeared before we had a chance to talk with her. Or to find out about her involvement in the security leaks.'

Booker put his hands together and propped his chin on his fingers. He tilted his head as he looked at her. 'I'm kind of new to this sort of game, so I guess I need you to explain the rules to me. If you don't have any idea who might have killed Harolds, how do you expect to figure it out now?'

Tess shrugged, not at all put out by his question. This was an area she was comfortable with. An area where she was an expert. 'They blew up my truck, hoping I would be in it, and they kidnapped you. Obviously they're not going to take a "wait and see" attitude about this case. Either they think I've got something or I'm getting close to something that may lead us straight to them.'

'That's a lot of maybes to be taking such risks,' he said.

'I know,' Tess answered thoughtfully. Her brows furrowed into a frown as she rose and began pacing in a slow circle around the room, lost in thought. She walked with her hands clasped behind her back as she mulled through the different speculations, then shook her head as she flipped through them, dismissing the thoughts as she went. 'You are right, though, Booker. Just exactly why are they taking such elaborate risks to get us out of the way? I can understand why they want to get rid of me, because of my obvious prior involvement with the case, but why did they kidnap you?'

'Good question,' he murmured, leaning back against the couch. He lazily stretched his legs out in front of him to rest them on the coffee table. He let his head fall back against the soft pillow of the couch and put his hands behind his head. He too stared ahead of him as he tried to come up with an idea. Tess noted that though his posture was once again relaxed, his eyes were anything but. That mind of his was buzzing with thoughts.

'It could very simply have been a case of mistaken identity,' he stated. At Tess's silence and her look of 'yeah, right' he smiled and continued on. 'But it seems more likely that I was abducted merely because of my being hauled to the hospital with you.'

Guilt shimmered through her expression before she quickly suppressed it. 'Was your wallet missing?'

Booker shook his head, 'No, in fact it was lying on top of me when I came to.'

Tess nodded. That made perfect sense. 'Obviously they took one look at who you were and dumped you.'

Booker smiled a lop-sided grin. 'Boy, you sure know how to make a man feel wanted, sweetheart.'

'Get real, Booker,' she sniffed, ignoring his pointed teasing. Tess stood and started her pacing again. She ended up standing in front of the fireplace with her hands on her hips as she continued to mull things through. She spoke out loud, though she was mostly talking to herself. 'Harolds' company was large, a leader in the industry. During my investigation, I narrowed down the suspects to two of his competing companies who would benefit the most from his death.'

'How would his death affect the company?' Booker asked.

She turned her head to look at him over her shoulder. 'He was CEO *and* chairman of the board. He basically founded and built that company from scratch. He *was* RexComp Incorporated. His death would affect the entire internal structure of the company. Who's to say a new chair wouldn't revamp the company, altering its structure to fulfill the new chair's own direction for the company? Such an unexpected turnaround could severely affect the company's public image, its stability and, most importantly, the value of the company's stock.'

Tess finished, her words hanging between them for a few moments. With a start, she found herself staring at the picture of the beautiful brunette. Something she did not care to be doing, so she turned quickly to look at Booker. She frowned as she recalled how Harolds had continually ignored the security precautions that had been taken for his safety.

'A man like that doesn't become the chairman of the board without making a few enemies,' she explained. 'Unfortunately, Harolds also basically lacked a heart, or compassion for his own employees, which helped make that enemies list even longer. When Gare Harolds disappeared, there were a lot of people in the industry, and in his own company, who were more than ready to dance on his grave if they ever found his body.'

'Nice guy, I take it,' Booker said without humor.

Tess chuckled humorously as she thought of the alleged happenings at the infamous mountain cabin Harolds had in Colorado. 'Oh, yeah, definitely a man loved by the masses.'

Booker watched her as she walked back to the chair to perch once again on the edge of the seat. 'What did they find at his cabin after he and the vice-president disappeared?'

'Nothing,' Tess answered, running her hand through her hair in frustration. But the entire case had continued to grow, till now she had people trying to blow her up, and there wasn't a damn bit of evidence to help her start anywhere. 'They processed the cabin, and the entire area within at least a half-mile of the cabin, yet they still found nothing.'

'No fingerprints? Evidence of burglary or breaking and entry?' Booker frowned at her answer. He'd given up his relaxed pose and was now leaning forward, studying her with an earnest expression.

'The only fingerprints were those of Harolds and Torkelson,' Tess said, then almost stammered when she suddenly remembered the identity of a third and fourth set of prints which had also been found. The unidentified pair had turned out to be pair of hookers invited to spend a 'working' weekend with the two executives. Booker's gaze narrowed and Tess realized he had seen her hesitancy and was wondering what exactly she was holding back.

She licked her lips and decided it would be best to just get that last little piece of torrid information out. 'There were another two sets of prints found, but they were identified as belonging to guests of the two men.'

Okay, so she had relayed the information as blandly as possible. Maybe she would luck out and Booker would be happy with that.

'Who were they?' he asked.

Figures, she thought. The way her luck ran, she never bothered to buy a lottery ticket. Why waste the money.

'Two, uh, ladies,' she answered, cagily avoiding the truth.

Booker studied her for a moment, then glanced down to his hands clasped in front of him as his lips quirked momentarily. She could tell he understood why she was being so hesitant. 'I see.'

'Yeah,' she said, taking a slow breath. She let that particular topic just slide on by. Instead she zeroed in on another thought and fixed her gaze on Booker. 'I realize that you cannot discuss certain aspects of the case, but can you at least tell me if you've determined whether Harolds was killed at the scene where his body was found?'

Booker shook his head. The question was straightforward and would not jeopardize the case in the least. 'No, I don't think he was.'

Tess thought about that for a moment. 'Which means he probably was alive when he was taken from the cabin.'

He frowned, then nodded as he followed her reasoning. 'It would have been pretty useless to haul a body across the state line. They could have just dumped it along with Torkelson's body.'

'Exactly.' Tess smiled, enjoying brainstorming with him more than she cared to admit to herself. So she didn't. 'So, something must have happened along the way and they decided to put his body in the hotel before it was imploded, hoping the blast would cover their tracks.'

'I wonder if they still have their fiber and hair samples,' Booker mused, his brow furrowed in concentration.

Tess started to feel a glimmer of excitement. His adrenaline was starting to flow too. An idea sparked in her mind and grew till she smiled at the sheer ingenuity of it. 'Would it help if you saw the scene yourself?'

'The cabin?' Booker asked, his gaze moving to hers.

She nodded. 'Like I explained earlier, it's been sealed since the disappearance. You could process the scene for anything that would help you to determine the actual scene of Harolds' death.'

Booker started to shake his head. Tess raised her hand to stop him before he answered. 'At least think about it. It would serve both our purposes. I could hire you as a forensic expert to process the scene for my firm's investigation and we would take care of all your expenses. It would save your jurisdiction a lot of money, and give your investigation additional information that might help you determine if he was killed in this state or back in Colorado.'

'I don't know, Tess,' he stated. 'My schedule is already full as it is, without trying to go above and beyond on just one case. Not to mention the ethical issues of conflict of interest.'

'Gare Harolds was kidnapped in Colorado and his body dumped here,' she reminded him. 'You're talking multi-jurisdiction anyway.'

The doorbell rang before Booker had a chance to respond to Tess. With an exasperated look he stood and walked quickly to the door. Opening it, he found Roger, looking mean-tempered and aggravated. Booker could tell immediately that something had happened.

'What is it?' he asked without preamble.

'We found your girlfriend's car about an hour ago,' he stated as he walked past Booker into the living room. His gaze fell on Tess, now standing in front of Booker's fireplace, and he stopped short, his face registering his surprise. 'What the hell are you doing here?'

Tess didn't even bother to answer his question, nor to respond to his sarcastic reference to her as Booker's girlfriend. She was anything but. Skinner's question had obviously been asked more out of reaction than thought. With a growing sense of foreboding she ignored it, frowning as she brought him back to his original statement. 'What do you mean you found my car?'

'Just what I said,' he stated. Though they stood several feet apart, the two had immediately taken a defensive position against each other. Skinner stood with his feet slightly apart and his fists balled on his hips. The stance pulled open his suit jacket, easily exposing the lower part of the shoulder holster and gun he carried. He focused his gaze on her, his expression stern. 'They found it abandoned about a half-mile from here on a dirt road.'

'Oh, no,' Tess murmured, feeling the icy tingle of fear shimmer over her. The car had been found abandoned. The realization of the implication hit her hard, momentarily stunning her thoughts. It seemed as if her mind, which had been working so smoothly, now skittered for a moment, then she forced it to start moving again.

Without a word she shouldered past Skinner and headed straight to the front door. Booker, who had been watching her carefully, grabbed her arm as she walked by him.

'Where are you going?' he asked, his voice holding just an edge of hardness. She could feel his gaze on her face till she was forced to look at him.

She didn't have time to acknowledge the fear or worry that was growing within her. She didn't have time to pussyfoot around surly detectives or sexy coroners. She met his questioning gaze with a hard one of her own. She was surprised to hear her voice sound so calm, controlled, though every part of her screamed for frantic action.

'The guys who blew up my truck and kidnapped you,' she bit out angrily, her words coldly reminding him of their situation. 'They now have Janet.'

CHAPTER 6

They drove in silence. Booker had more or less forced her into his car, then drove in fuming silence as they followed Roger to where Tess's car had been found. Tess sat in the passenger seat with her arms crossed over her chest, pointedly looking out of the window, ignoring the man beside her as they bumped along the dirt road.

When the two cars parked alongside the road, behind two police cars, Tess opened the door and got out, then slammed it shut behind her before Booker even had a chance to turn the engine off.

She stalked away from his car to head straight toward hers, ignoring the curious stares of the uniformed officers and the stern expression of Skinner. Pushing her fear and emotions away, she focused on the vehicle. Slowly, methodically, she went over the exterior of the car, then opened the door and started on the interior.

She slid in behind the steering wheel awkwardly. Janet had moved the seat forward and lowered the steering wheel to accommodate her petite form. Scrunching over, she let her legs hang out the door as she checked first under the seat, then ran her hand

121

along underneath the dashboard. Opening the glovebox, she rifled through the papers and found nothing new or out of the ordinary. Looking over her shoulder, she took a cursory glance behind her to the back seat, and again found nothing.

Turning back toward the steering wheel, Tess frowned, her hand resting on it as she thought about what she had found in her search – which was nothing. She let her hand fall to the seat beside her as she lost herself in her thoughts. The tips of her fingers touched paper, and she turned to look. The corners of a folded paper that looked a lot like a map stuck out between the seats. With a casual glance around her, Tess made sure no one was watching her. She pretended to be once again examining the company car as she carefully slid the paper out to take a quick look. It was a map, and once she looked at it, she knew it had been placed there for her to find. She slipped it discreetly under her shirt and tucked it in the waistband of her jeans.

Several moments later, she stoodup from the car, and her eyes immediately met with Booker's dark gaze. She ignored the feelings that his look evoked and moved past the two men to head back toward Booker's car. Tess opened the car door and got in. After she'd shut the door she simply sat, staring straight ahead, determinedly waiting for him to return to the car.

She watched as he and Skinner had a brief conversation, then he headed back toward her. Opening the door, he too got in. For a brief moment after the soft sound of the door latching they both remained silent, both avoided looking at each other.

'Did you find anything?' he asked, without looking at her.

'No,' she stated, her voice flat and emotionless, knowing it was a lie. For her own good, and his protection, it was what needed to be done.

At his silence, Tess sneaked a quick look at his profile. He looked as if he wanted to say something, then his lips pressed together in a firm line. He turned the key and the engine roared to life.

'Fine,' he said in the same tone. 'I'll take you home.'

They remained silent during their drive to her house; she only occasionally broke it when she gave him directions. They heavy silence and tension had returned between them. Tess was thankful for it as she rested her head against the headrest and closed her eyes for a moment. Their awareness of each other was humming yet again. Not the physical awareness between a man and a woman, like it had been before, but an emotional awareness. Tess was plagued with an overwhelming sense of guilt, frustration, and a frightening sensation of helplessness. Janet's life was in danger and it was her fault. Tess knew it without a doubt, just as she knew Booker sensed her anger at herself.

Part of her wanted to reach out to him and explain why she was so angry, but she knew better than to do something like that. Instead she rode in uncomfortable silence, her arms wrapped around her providing the only warmth against the cold that had settled over her like a blanket of dull gray clouds.

Her mind tortured her with the memory of the warmth of the embrace of this man sitting beside her.

The feel of his skin against hers. The sense that for that one moment in time she'd been content.

Tears brimmed in her eyes and Tess bit at her lip. She nipped it hard, relishing the pain as it drove away the tears. Damn it, she wasn't going to allow this to happen, she thought to herself. She had always taken care of herself before and she would continue doing it now. She had to keep her mind clear, her thoughts decisive and precise. Janet's life depended on her keeping her head level.

Booker pulled into her driveway. She didn't even look toward him as she rose from the car to get out. 'Thanks for the ride.'

Tess's expression was solemn, stoic, as she made her way up the sidewalk toward her house. She heard him cut the engine, but refused to acknowledge it as she climbed the short steps to her front porch. She pulled her key from her small waist pack, no wider than a normal belt, and opened her front door. Stepping inside, she punched the code on her alarm, then headed into the house.

At the sound of her arrival, Tess heard her cat Sabrina call to her from within the house. The Siamese trotted quickly around the corner and headed straight toward her. Forgetting the door behind her, Tess knelt as the cat got closer. Siamese cats were cats with strong personalities. Sabrina would not like the idea that she had been left alone for a couple of days with no one for company except when Janet had stopped by to feed her. Sabrina had quickly trained Tess to her desired routine, and when Tess dared to deviate the cat let her know immediately. Still, Tess loved the cat dearly, and knew that they would both be so happy to see each other. Sabrina would 'climb' her legs to get to her. Even with the denim material of her jeans, Tess didn't relish the idea of Sabrina's claws digging into her skin, so she knelt to pick up her spoiled cat.

She nuzzled the cat, and Sabrina returned her love as she purred like a motor. Tess tensed when she heard Booker walk into the house behind her. She lifted her head as Sabrina seemed to notice her sudden change and notice the stranger at the same time. Her traitorous cat squirmed from her hold and leaped to the floor to head straight for Booker.

Tess let her breath out slowly, then turned to face him. She found him cradling her swine of a cat. Sabrina's eyes were half closed in feline ecstasy and she was purring like a madman. She frowned at the spectacle and her lips thinned into a line of disapproval.

'I didn't realize you had a cat also,' Booker said as he scratched the animal behind the ears. Sabrina twisted in his grasp as she worked herself against his hands like an erotic snake dancer.

'I would say it is more accurate that Sabrina has me,' Tess stated, shaking her head. 'And obviously she doesn't have the morals of an alley –'

She let the cliché remain unfinished. After all, Sabrina *was* a cat. Booker chuckled at her statement.

Tess watched them for a moment, then felt a surge of nerves move through her. The sight of Ethan Booker scratching her cat's ears, causing the animal to succumb to feline ecstasy, was more than she wanted to endure at the moment.

She didn't want to admit that having him standing in her house was like a double-edged sword. Part of her wanted him there, actually liked him there. His personality was such that she found herself naturally at ease with him. But it was because of that natural feeling that she wanted him out of her house. Earlier she had wanted him to go with her to Harolds' cabin for his expert opinion, but now she just wanted him gone. There was too much at stake. The pleasure he had distracted her with had already cost her. Perhaps if she hadn't been so wrapped up in the attraction of this man she might have been able to avoid Janet's kidnapping.

Tess turned toward him, her folded across her chest. 'Booker, why are you still here?'

His slate-blue eyes darkened as he studied her expression. He ignored her question, bypassing it with the same cool tone. 'Let the police handle this, Tess.'

'That's what I plan on doing,' she snapped, turning on her heel and walking away from him.

Booker followed her leisurely. 'Where are you going?'

'To the kitchen for some aspirin,' she snapped, rubbing at her temples. 'My head is killing me.'

'Concussions have a tendency to cause that.' He leaned casually against the counter, still cradling her cat as he scratched the animal behind the ears.

Tess opened the cabinet and searched through her meager supply of over-the-counter remedies till she found the treasured bottle of aspirin. She blatantly ignored Booker's presence as she pulled a glass from another cabinet and poured herself some water.

She tossed the aspirin in her mouth and drank the water. The cool chill of the liquid quenched the parched dryness of her mouth, immediately making her feel slightly better. Her head was waiting rather impatiently for the aspirin to kick in.

She put the glass down, then placed her hands on the counter as she simply stared out through the kitchen window. So many thoughts, so many emotions were crowding her mind. She closed her eyes, letting her mind go blank as she tried to ease the tension in her neck and head. It would be hard enough for the aspirin to tackle her monster headache without having to overcome the obstacles of her nerves.

A pair of hands slid to her shoulders, startling her. Fears and doubts had plagued her so completely that she momentarily forgotten Booker's presence. She started to open her mouth to protest, her lips parting, only to have a sigh of pleasure softly escape. Her objections were lost as his long fingers skillfully kneaded the aching knots of tension from her shoulders. He smoothed her hair from her neck to allow access to his hands. A new sensation sparked through her the moment his skin touched hers.

His fingers were heated by the friction of his touch moving against her skin. The warmth softened the tightened sinew of her muscles and her shoulders began to visibly slump as she relaxed against his massage.

Her headache was forgotten. Her nerves forgotten as his strong fingers moved upward. Tess let her head fall forward as she murmured a soft moan of pleasure. He continued to touch her, knead her with his strong hands. The feel of his male touch against her soft skin caused an even more disturbing sensation deep within her. His hands stopped to cup her shoulders and Tess's eyes opened dreamily. Slowly he turned her toward him, his eyes darkened to a smoky blue. He pulled her to him, his hands holding her hips as he pressed her to him. Instinctively her hands gripped his arms, the bulges beneath his sleeves surprising her with his strength, a contradiction of the gentle, firm caress of his hands. Her own slid over his wide shoulders to circle his neck as he lowered his mouth to hers. She opened herself to him as if it were the most natural thing to do, despite the fact they had only known each other a few short days.

His lips were firm but gentle as he lightly touched her lips till she parted under him in a woman's instinctive invitation. He continued to touch her lightly, softly, as he traced the curves of her mouth with the tip of his tongue. Tess groaned in frustration and she stood on tiptoe, pressing herself against him as she tried to capture the rapture of his kiss. His tantalizing, teasing touch had caused the spark within her to flare and grow till she thought she would die wanting him. She slid her hand into his hair as finally he took her, his tongue moving swiftly to plunder her still straining need.

The pleasure shot through her, melting her urgency as she settled into his embrace. His hands moved from her hips to slip under her shirt and caress the heated skin of her back. Her breasts ached for his touch and she pressed herself against the solid-muscled ridges of his chest, partially filling her need for him.

His fingers caressed her ribcage, moving teasingly close to her breasts, but never quite touching them. Tess felt herself getting lost easily in the taste of him, the touch of him, the need for him. Too easily, she suddenly thought. It was the first cognitive movement of her brain since he had first touched her.

She pulled away from him, her cheeks burning at her reaction to him, to the wild beating of her heart that he seemed to be able to evoke in the span of a second. She cleared her throat as she unwound herself from him. She backed away from the heat of his decisively male body till her hips bumped into the edge of the counter. Unable to back any further, or move around him, she crossed her arms over her chest. The only way she was going to be able to escape the intoxicating proximity of him would be to ask him to move, or make him.

His sultry gaze was hooded as he studied her. She licked her lips nervously. 'Don't you have something to do, Booker? A body to work on, perhaps?'

His brow raised, and she remembered too vividly what body he had been working only moments before.

'Never mind,' she muttered, shouldering her way past him. 'Thanks for the ride.'

Tess strode away from him and headed toward the stairs to go to her room. She had plans to make, arrangements to start and calls to place, she reminded herself as she mulled over her strategy. She decided she was going to will – no, force that damn man out of her mind.

Hearing the click of the front door, Tess stopped, her hand on the rail as she blew out her breath in relief. That man was too damn sexy for his own good, she thought. And what had she been doing, clinging to him like that? Like a drowning man gasping for air.

Oh, now she knew things were bad. Poetry. Poetry was always a bad sign. When she started thinking of things in terms of poetic expression, it was getting dire.

Turning, she headed back down the stairs. She needed to ground her traitorous, poetically bad thoughts. Walking into her office, she went to her desk and sat. Picking up the phone receiver, Tess stopped when she saw the e-mail message flashing on her screen. An uncanny sense of foreboding moved through her as she replaced the phone back on the hook.

Jiggling the mouse to interrupt her screensaver, she clicked on the e-mail icon to retrieve her messages. Her lips thinned as she waited for the modern to hook up to the server. She clicked her mail box and her messages flashed on to the screen. As had become her habit lately, she immediately scanned for one name.

Skimming down the list, she caught it, her gaze focusing on it as her hand tightened on the mouse.

Badger.

Tess doubled-clicked on the message and his words filled the screen.

I have what you want.
Come get it, if you can . . .
<LOL>

Instinctively she noted the change in his style. Badger

had quit using his bad rhyming. It meant the game had changed. Now it was getting serious.

Deadly serious.

The airline stewardess picked up the microphone and announced to those waiting to board the plane which rows could start seating. Tess glanced at her ticket, noting her number as she blended into the line waiting to be processed and seated. Somehow she had lost the map, but she had seen enough of it to know where she needed to go.

She gave a polite smile to the stewardess greeting them as they stepped into the plane. She found her seat first, then loaded her carry-on luggage in the storage bay overhead before she ducked her head to take her seat by the window. She had kept her briefcase with her so she could use the precious time it was going to take to get to her destination to study the area she was headed to. She pulled a map out to study. Tess had had one of the research techs send it to her.

She was unfolding it when someone took a seat beside her. Automatically she turned her head slightly, to give her fellow passenger the usual cursory airplane smile. Something that was neither friendly, nor rude, and did not invite discussions about trip plans, kids, or work. Her polite smile froze as she met Booker's amused gaze.

Her eyes narrowed icily. 'What the hell are you doing here?'

He didn't bother to answer her, instead he reached into his jacket and pulled a folded paper out to toss on her lap. Tess's eyes widened, first in bewilderment as she recognized the map she had retrieved from her car after Janet's disappearance, then in anger when she realized just how he had got it.

She had had it tucked into the waistband of her jeans when he had taken her to her house.

Her cheeks burned, her ears scorched. Her expression was furious as she turned on him. 'Why, you –'

'Now, now,' he calmly cautioned her. 'Remember you wanted my expert opinion on this case. Forensically speaking, that is.'

The jerk, she thought.

'What about that line about ethical reasoning you were trying to palm off on me?' she demanded with a hiss, trying to keep her voice down, though everything about the man at the moment made her hands itch to close around his throat and squeeze. 'You remember—conflict of interest?'

Booker's gaze became solemn. 'Obviously that has changed, hasn't it?'

It was not spoken as a question, but as a fact. A harsh one.

The anger within her dimmed, though she was not pleased at the idea of his joining her. His presence, his expertise, could prove invaluable. His presence, his expertise, could prove disastrous to her, she thought. With a shiver she remembered the kiss they had shared in her kitchen earlier that day. It had been . . . Words failed her. It had been nothing less than wonderful, she thought ruefully, which was exactly why it disturbed her so deeply that he was joining her.

Janet's life was at stake. That simple statement alone made her protests seem insignificant. Tess resigned herself to the situation and reminded herself that she should be thankful for Booker's help. She settled back in her seat and crossed her arms over her chest as she looked out of the window so she wouldn't have to talk to him.

'Where are we going?' he asked.

She didn't bother to turn toward him. 'You're here. Obviously you've figured it out for yourself.'

Tess could actually feel the man smiling beside her. 'After I found the map I knew the general direction you would be heading. And I knew you wouldn't just leave this to the police, so I decided to come with you. After all, my forensic expertise would serve both our purposes . . . give my investigation additional valuable information.'

She detested having her own arguments used against her. She turned toward him. 'If you only knew the "general direction" of where I was headed, how did you know to take this flight?'

Booker smiled like a Cheshire cat. 'I followed you.'

'You followed me?' she squeaked, trying to swallow her laughter.

Booker looked offended. 'I do have other talents besides being a forensic pathologist, you know.

'Well, I figured that,' she chuckled. 'But following me. Come on, tell me the truth. You called someone and had them look up the information.'

Shaking his head, he simply smiled as he waited for her to quiet down. 'After I dropped you off, I went home and packed a bag, because I knew you would take the first flight available. I did call a travel agency, to see what flights were available heading to Colorado, but there were a couple and I didn't know exactly which area you were headed to. So I went to the airport and waited for you. I saw which ticket counter you went to and figured out which flight you were taking. That easy.'

It *was* easy, she realized, and she frowned. And logical. She reluctantly had to admit he had done a pretty good job of deductive reasoning. 'That was pretty good thinking.'

He leaned toward her, his gaze holding hers. For a brief moment she was horrified and thrilled at the thought he might kiss her. Instead he gently tapped her on the end of her nose with his finger. 'And I'm efficient too.'

Booker settled back in his seat, leaving Tess in a mess of jumbled thoughts. For a second she had actually hoped he was going to kiss her, in front of the stewardess and the other passengers.

His voice pulled her from her thoughts. 'If I were to continue along the logic of reasoning line, I assume we're headed to Harolds' cabin?'

She turned and studied him. He was sitting in the seat with his large frame slumped casually in a relaxed pose. His head was leaning against the headrest as he tilted to look at her. Her gaze fell to his lips, and for a wild moment her mouth watered to taste him again.

'Uh . . .' she started, turning away from him and the hunger he seemed able to initiate within her. She opened her briefcase and pulled the file of information she had requested from her research associate. Shutting the briefcase, she used it as a table and opened the file to go over the contents with him.

'Harolds' cabin is in a remote, very secluded area,' she explained, pointing to the map that showed the acres of forest land in relief.

'No doubt for his female "guests",' Booker stated without humor.

Tess turned quickly to see if his comment was meant to be funny or as disgusted as he sounded. 'Yes, I'm sure that was a consideration when he bought the place. Anyway, it is accessible by two roads, one of which is maintained, the other is not. There is also a clearing where a plane, a small one, could land.'

Booker nodded, mulling it over. 'Did he have a pilot's license?'

Tess shook her head. 'He didn't, but Torkelson did.'

'Did the police investigate that area of possibility?'

She shrugged. 'As far as the kidnappers escaping, I don't think so. There really wouldn't be that much to look into. It would be exceedingly hard for a plane, even a small one, to not be picked up by radar.'

'Just a thought,' he said easily.

'A good one, though,' she found herself saying. She'd never been one to work with a partner. Didn't really want the responsibility. But working with Booker was different. For the moment, Tess was content not to try to decipher why.

'So you think they are headed to the cabin?' he asked, his gaze flicking to hers.

'I don't know.' Though she knew the map had been left for her to find, a sort of treasure map, with Janet as the big red X. However, it was only a gut feeling. Intuition. Nothing based on hard facts. She knew, without a doubt, that the map had not been in her car before. Someone had placed it there for her to find.

She had always been a woman of action, and she had to do something to help her friend. Sitting aside and letting the police handle it was completely against her character. Still, she was loath to admit to him that she didn't really have anything concrete to go on.

'But the possibility is more than likely, isn't it?' he continued.

Tess nodded. 'Yes, it is. I think they left the map for me to find. I've never carried a Colorado map in my car, and Harolds' cabin just happens to be in that state. It would be one heck of a coincidence, and I don't believe in coincidences.'

'I don't either,' Booker agreed. His gaze dropped to the map she held on the briefcase. 'When we get to the cabin we can process it for any additional information, and I assume we also look for something indicate Janet's whereabouts.'

'I don't really have too much of anything to go on at the moment,' Tess stated, quelling her nerves and her fears for her friend's life. 'But . . . I think we'll find something when we get there.'

He studied her, the slate-blue of his eyes darkening with concern. He lifted his hand to trace a gentle finger over her lips before he let it fall back to his lap.

'Let's hope so, sweetheart.'

Sylvester dived greedily into his cat food, causing Polly to smile. Really, she thought, the cat acted as if he'd never been fed, and she knew without a doubt that Ethan Booker took good care of his pet. Polly chuckled at the feline's half-closed eyes. Probably experiencing nirvana, she thought wryly. If there was one thing Sylvester enjoyed, it was eating. Suddenly thinking of the litter of kittens the Masons' cat had had, she shook her head.

Well, there was *one* other thing Sylvester truly enjoyed.

Young Ethan had asked her to take care of his cat while he went on an unexpected trip. Polly had agreed to take care of him, of course, though she'd done it for purely selfish reasons. She just knew he had to be leaving on some adventure with that tall, beautiful redhead of his who'd spent the night the other evening.

She stroked the cat's back as he ate. Sylvester was torn between rubbing against her caress and ravishing his 'kitty vittles'. Finally he decided to continue plundering his food, then worry about a little love. Polly smiled at the indecision evident in the cat's actions and smiled. Sylvester had such a unique personality; he would make a good character in her book.

Inspiration struck, and she felt like giving him a big hug. Knowing he wouldn't want to be disturbed, she instead gave him a pinch more of food. She stood and walked to Ethan's phone. She borrowed a pen and a piece of paper to quickly scribble a note to herself.

One never knew when inspiration was going to hit.

Tess turned the overhead light on to read the map. Booker was frowning, concentrating on navigating the winding back roads as they traveled deeper into the dark wooded area. At least they were paved, he thought. Rain beat down on them and the wipers were going at full speed.

They had slowed to a crawl, the road too narrow and dangerous to pull over and wait it out. It was not quite dark, but still they had their lights on as an added precaution in driving in the heavy rain.

'There should be a crossroad up ahead,' Tess stated, following the line on the map which she hoped represented the road they were on.

'Where?' Booker asked, his voice slightly edgy.

'I don't know,' Tess answered, her eyes narrowing as she tried to see through the rain for any road markers. The windows were fogging up, making it hard to see. 'Can't you turn the defroster on?'

Booker switched it on without a word, his mouth tight as he peered through the storm. 'I still don't see a road.'

Tess didn't either. She continued to search the crowd of trees lining the road, praying the whole time that she had not got them lost. The last person in the world she wanted to admit she was lost to was Ethan Booker. Not to mention the thought of being *alone* and lost in the woods with him. Her eyes moved methodically along the road edge, then she spotted something.

She pointed at it quickly, keeping her enthusiasm down. 'There. I think that's the road.'

'You think?' Booker asked tightly, doubting her instructions.

'There,' she stated, excited, but remaining quiet about it. Thank goodness they weren't lost. She had only been out to the cabin once, but she recognized the old dilapidated fence with the sign stating the grandiose name of 'Wintergreen', a hunting lodge that had used to cater to the rich. That was before the ecologically and politically correct had made the hunting of big game unfashionable. Tess was glad people were starting to be less barbaric. She never had understood the sport of hunting.

Booker stopped their four-wheel drive and eyed their destination speculatively. 'That is not a road. That is two ruts close together.'

'It's the road, Booker,' she retorted, fixing him with a look of impatience. 'I've been here before. I recognize that run-down old fence and that ugly sign. I'm telling you this is the right way.'

'If you say so, sweetheart,' he answered, moving the vehicle slowly through a deep puddle.

'Quit calling me sweetheart,' Tess muttered as she studied the map. Even though they had found the turn-off, there were still several miles to travel ahead of them. Harolds had liked his privacy, of that there was no doubt.

'Sure, sugar,' he replied smoothly, squinting to see through the rain-drenched windshield.

Tess looked up from the map, 'You know, if you keep calling me stuff like that, I will have to break several bones in your body.'

'The thought of your hands on my body is an enticing image,' he said with a mischievous smile, obviously unaffected by her threats.

Perhaps he thought she was joking.

'Booker, just keep your mind on your driving,' she said without humor.

'Spoilsport.'

They bumped and splashed along the road that Tess did have to admit was more of a trail than anything. The trees, thick and lush with new spring growth, edged toward the road to form an imposing wall on either side. There were, in fact, two ruts, braving through the middle of the trees and grass. They were following those ruts, now filled with water from the spring rain, through the dense curtain of the storm.

Tess was thankful she had her seat belt on as they hit a series of rough holes. It was the only thing that kept her in her seat and not bouncing off the cab of the four-wheel drive they had rented at the airport. She gripped the dashboard, only sparing a glance at Booker as she spoke through clenched teeth. 'Geez, Booker, I think you missed a few back there.'

'You are more than welcome to drive if you're dissatisfied,' he stated, his tone tight, matching that of his white-knuckled grip on the steering wheel.

Tess ignored his barb and continued to peer through the darkness and the rain. 'We should be running into it pretty quick now.'

And they almost did run into it.

Fortunately the storm and the close proximity of the trees had forced them to slow to a snail's pace as they made a sharp turn that dead-ended at the back of the cabin. Booker jerked to a stop, and for a moment the two of them peered at the cabin through the constant swish of the windshield wipers. In the black of the night and the heavy rain, the two story cabin looked formidable. Lightning illuminated the stark image of the building against a tree, making it look more like a summer house for Bela Lugosi than a luxurious mountain cabin.

'Nice-looking place,' Booker said.

Tess didn't bother to glance in his direction. From the lack of his enthusiasm in his voice, he sounded about as excited as she was about running through the driving rain to walk into a pitch-black house in the middle of the night. For all they knew the storm could have already knocked out the electricity in the area, and with the cabin being so remote, it could be a while before it was turned back on.

'Believe it or not, it actually is a pretty nice place,' she said, leaning forward to dig the keys out of her purse. 'At least when all hell isn't breaking loose.'

She pulled the keys from her bag and gave them a small toss as she took a deep breath. She met Booker's gaze and grinned. 'Are you ready for this?'

'I almost believe you're excited about this,' he murmured. 'Okay, on the count of three. One –'

'Three,' she blurted out, pulling the catch and throwing the door open wide. She quickly grabbed her bag out of the back seat of the four-wheel drive and ran for the cover of the porch. She carefully hurried up the steps and let her breath out in a rush as she shook the drench of water from her hair and shoulders.

She turned and laughed as she watched Booker slip through the mud and grass to follow her. He tromped up the steps to stand next to her. He shook his wide shoulders, spraying her with a fine mist of water.

She dodged the spray. 'Hey, that's not fair.'

'That's what you get for laughing at me,' he stated, grinning at her as he took the keys from her hands. He moved to the door and worked to try to open it. With no porch light, it took several moments for him to get the key inserted correctly. Once in, it turned easily, and Booker pushed the door open.

Booker moved inside and felt around the wall for a light switch. As luck would have it, he found it and switched it on. The entryway was immediately bathed in light, and Booker stepped out of the way to let Tess in. After he'd shut the door, he moved past her and set his duffel bag on the polished wood of what could informally be called the foyer.

'I think the first order of business would be to look for candles or flashlights, in case the storm does knock the power out,' he said.

Tess nodded. 'Good idea. I did bring a couple of flashlights, but they aren't as good as candles if it does go out.'

'I'll go with you, just in case there are any boogie men,' Booker said, grinning.

Tess had to return his smile. Obviously he wasn't concerned about boogie men of the supernatural kind, but more of the kind that blew your truck up in the parking lot and kidnapped you, then dumped your unconscious body on your own front lawn.

They started with the kitchen, looking quickly through the cabinets and countertops, then continued on to the mud room. Tess stood on tiptoe, peering over the edge of a tall shelf as she ran her hand over the surface. She was smoothing her hand against the wood covering when she bumped into something fuzzy. The something fuzzy promptly crawled, rather quickly, onto her hand. The sensation stabbed through her already alert thoughts. Her mind snagged on one piece of information and threw the rest out. The something fuzzy that had crawled onto her hand was also multi-legged.

A spider.

Tess screamed as she yanked her hand out and shook it wildly. The sudden movement dislodged the furry creature with a thump to the floor and it started to scurry away.

Booker gripped her arm in reassurance as he spoke to her in a low, humorous tone. 'Tess, it's only a spider.'

'Spider,' she shrieked. 'That isn't a spider, it's an eight-legged monster.'

Booker chuckled as he found an old grocery sack and nudged it under the critter. Stepping to the back door, he opened it and turned the creature loose to find his own way through the storm.

Tess shivered uncontrollably. One of her earliest childhood memories was waking up to her mother's nervous voice as she coaxed her to slip out of bed calmly. Once she'd slid slowly out of the covers, wondering why her mother wanted her to get out of bed so early, she had turned around to see why. A brown recluse, in fact, two of them, had been crouched on top of the comforter where she had been sleeping. At the time she had only thought of them as big, ugly brown spiders, till she had become old enough to understand why her mother had been so insistent and scared.

With a toxicity rating of four, the brown recluse's venom was more deadly than most poisonous snakes. One bite from a brown recluse and within eight hours the victim would be in agony. Tess had known a girl who had been bitten. The girl still carried the scars where the spider had bitten her, and the skin around the bite had died, then rotted.

She didn't care if the fuzzy creature Booker had just put outside was not a brown recluse; it still had eight legs and was a spider. Yuck.

Apparently seeing her expression of rapt fear, Booker put his arm comfortingly around her shoulders and led her away from the mud room. He sat her at the table, then looked into the pantry and found a bottle of whiskey. He rummaged through the cabinets till he found a clean glass, then poured her a shot.

He put it in front of her as he spoke to her gently. 'Drink this.'

Tess frowned at the amber liquid in the tiny glass. 'What is it?'

'Scotch,' he answered.

She shook her head. 'I don't like hard liquor.'

'Just drink it and it will help you quit shivering,' he said, then added, 'Doctor's orders.'

She stared at it for a moment. A chill racked through her again, possibly brought on by the chill of the rain and the close encounter with the huge arachnid fiend. Tess picked up the shot glass and downed it in one gulp that any Texan would have been proud of.

The liquid burned deliciously down her throat even as the bitter aftertaste caused her to scrunch her face up. 'That is disgusting.'

'I know. I've never particularly cared for Scotch either,' Booker chuckled as he gave her a pat on the shoulder. 'Stay here while I'll find those candles. Okay?'

Tess nodded, barely acknowledging his statement as he left the room. A shadow caught her eye in the mud room and she wondered if it was yet another spider. Picking up the bottle of whiskey, she poured another splash into the little glass. She lifted it to her lips as she tossed her head back and swallowed.

Setting her glass down with a light tap on the table, she let the liquid warm through her, burying the chills under a hazy blanket of alcohol.

Booker wasn't really that bad a man, she thought with a dreamy smile as she recalled the touch, the taste of his lips against hers. A shiver passed through her. Not from the thought of evil little creatures scurrying around them, but from the thought of the handsome man she was alone in the cabin with.

Then the lights went out.

CHAPTER 7

Tess stiffened. For a second, only a second, she allowed herself to sit quietly as her eyes adjusted to the blackness. The lights could have been knocked out by the thunderstorm. Tess knew that was a plausible enough explanation, considering they had been traveling in it for over an hour.

Or there could be a more destructive reason behind the black-out.

Slowly, quietly, she bent over to touch her right ankle. Pulling the leg of her jeans up slightly, she nudged the small ankle belt a little lower till she could retrieve the small gun. She palmed the small derringer, a gun her grandpa would have called a peashooter. It was really not a very effective gun, one that would require her to be at close range to hit her target, but at least it provided a modicum of defense.

Tess stood, making sure she didn't nudge the chair back and cause it to scrape against the wood and make a noise. Booker had gone to look for candles, heading through the door of the kitchen toward the main part of the luxury cabin. He had not called out to her, nor had she heard any noise. That could be good . . . or it could be bad.

Holding the gun up in her right hand, she proceeded through the door, keeping her back to the wall till she could scan the darkened room. Lightning flashed from the storm, briefly illuminating the quiet living area. The quick flash allowed her to quickly assess the general layout of the room. Carefully she made her way around the overstuffed sofa, then between the coffee table and a bearskin rug complete with head. Tess cringed at the loss of such a beautiful animal, but shelved the thought away to deal with later. Stepping one foot carefully in front of the other, she made her way across the spacious openness of the room toward the split wood railing of the stairway.

A feeling of *déjàvu* washed over her as she recalled the night she had entered Booker's house, only to be tackled by him. She frowned at the memory as she started to lift her foot to make her way up the stairs. From behind her, a hand grabbed the wrist holding the gun, and another arm wrapped around her, pinning her free hand to her chest. Tess drew her breath in sharply, squelching the urge to scream as she stiffened in her captor's embrace, then relaxed. Her non-confrontation move put her captor off guard, just as she'd suspected it would and she whirled around as she drew her fist back to hit.

Instead she was blinded in the face with the stark beam of a flashlight. The beam then moved to the face of her captor. Her intended target.

'Tess, it's me, Booker,' he said quickly, grabbing her wrist again. 'The storm knocked the lights out. Everything is all right.'

Tess simply stared at him for a moment as his words registered, then she let her breath out in a rush as the tension drained from her body. Giddy relief filled her and she started to chuckle. 'I was about to hit you.'

'More like knock my block off, sweetheart,' he muttered, as he released the hold on her arm. 'Come on, I found a box of candles and matches. We can light a few and start a fire in the fireplace to warm this place up a little.'

She nodded, following behind him as he moved to the fireplace. Booker lit one candle, the shimmering flame illuminating a circle around them. He held it up slightly to look over the mantel. Obviously Harolds had been used to the power being knocked out, as there were several decorative candle-holders arranged on the fireplace. Or–Tess's thoughts recalled the man's extracurricular activities – he probably used them to set the mood.

Booker lit the candles in the holders; the arrangement lit the room nicely. Tess's nerves had relaxed, and the Scotch Booker had given her once again settled over her. She walked over to the couch and rearranged a couple of the throw pillows to make a comfortable backrest.

Sitting down, she stretched out on the couch, propping her head and back against the pillows. Suddenly she felt so tired, her nerves and the tension of the past several days catching up with her. Sleepily she watched Booker arrange the logs in the fireplace, then work to start the fire. Though her eyes felt heavy, exhausted, desire stirred within her as the flickering candles illuminated the hard muscles of his arms and shoulders shifting beneath his shirt as he went about lighting the fire.

She let her eyes drift shut, a soft smile on her face. For just a moment, a brief moment, she would allow herself to think about that man. Fantasize about what it would be like to let him kiss her again. To touch her.

'What are you doing?'

Booker's voice startled her from what had promised to be a very tantalizing dream. She shook herself as she raised her head to look at him. 'I'm sitting on the couch.'

'Looks more like you're lying on it and getting ready to go to sleep,' he said, his back toward the fire. The starting flames of the fire grew behind him, his tall body silhouetted against the yellow-white fingers shooting from the wood.

'I just might,' she said easily, lying back down. She smiled good-naturedly at him as her eyes blinked slower, heavier each time.

He shook his head as he stood with his hands on his hips. 'I thought you wanted me to come down here and process the house for you. A cooperative venture and all that. Retrieve additional information for my investigation into the cause and manner of Gare Harolds' death.'

'I do,' she murmured sleepily. She frowned at the tone of his voice. If he kept it up, he wouldn't be starring in any more of her fantasies. Then she smiled again. Closing her eyes, she thought of the six-foot-three blondish-brown-haired actor who played the half-mortal, half-god in a mythological show that she tried to watch every weekend. Now there was a man with muscles, blue eyes, and a voice. What a voice, she thought. She could listen to the silky maleness of his voice day in and day out. There was a man she could play with.

She'd settled easily into that entertaining scenario when Booker's nagging voice once again broke into her thoughts.

'I hate to disturb your sweet dreams, angel,' Booker said, his voice suddenly closer to her, 'but you are sleeping on one of the pieces of evidence you wanted me to process.'

Now that got her attention. Tess's eyes snapped open and she started as she found herself looking directly into his face, which was only about eight inches from her own. Booker was squatting, his forearms across his knees as he met her gaze.

'Oh.' She lifted her head, putting her hand in front of her to push herself up. 'I didn't even think about that.'

He stilled her movements by putting his hand on her shoulder. He smiled, a humorous glint in the dark grayish blue of his eyes. 'Don't worry about it. I talked to the officials down here after you first told me about this place. They had already processed the couch and the living room. In fact, they had done an excellent job on processing the entire house for trace evidence. They're going to send me reports on their findings, and if I need anything more, then they will cooperate.'

Tess frowned at him, a little miffed at his statement. 'Then why are you here?'

He grinned. 'To take care of you.'

She snorted inelegantly as she returned her attention back to the pillows beneath her. She punched and fluffed them as she rearranged herself. Like a cat, she had to have everything just right again before she settled back down. Tess snuggled back into the pillows and blatantly ignored the man chuckling softly in front of her.

'Go away,' she ordered him, without any real vehemence in her voice.

'I'm crushed,' he laughed.

'I'm sure you are,' Tess said with a sigh. She nuzzled against her pillow and her eyes drifted closed. Tomorrow would be a hard day. The individuals who had taken Janet had left that map in her car for a reason. Though there had not been any identifying marks on the map, it had been folded a certain way, leaving the section where Harolds' cabin was located folded to the front. Tomorrow she could start meticulously searching the cabin room by room till she found what they had left for her.

Still, something about what Booker had said wormed its way into her thoughts, and she frowned. His presence was not really required, forensically speaking, so why was he here? She opened her eyes and met his gaze. His gaze was hooded, unreadable.

'Why are you here, Booker?' she asked again, softly.

He studied her, his face cast in dancing shadows from the fire behind him. Slowly he reached his hand to her face and stroked her cheek with his fingers. 'I really have no idea why I'm here.'

In truth, he didn't. He had a backlog of cases at work. He had shocked Doris when he'd called in to take some of the personal time he had accrued. She had been nagging him for a year to use it, then had sputtered helplessly when he had done so. He had not known Tess Reynolds very long, had even met her under false pretenses. Yet since he had met her he had been involved in an explosion and been kidnapped. That was more history than some couples shared in a decade. Tess Reynolds was a woman who took care of herself and those around her. Yet for all the toughness of her exterior he could look at her as he did now and see the softer side of her. The sensitivity in the green of her eyes that she kept at bay, or that people did not take the time to see.

Booker looked at her, eyes fringed with dark lashes, as she waited for his answer. He traced the sprinkle of freckles across her cheeks and nose. The little girl look softened the stark beauty of her face. She bit at her lush lips. Perhaps, he thought, her uncertainty was weighing on her. The movement pronounced her dimples, provoking the memory of her laughter, her wild sense of humor.

He didn't know why he had followed her to Harolds' cabin on what could prove to be a dangerous trip, but he had. He only knew he wanted to be with her, and get to know the exciting multi-faceted creature in front of him.

'Will you stop looking at me like that?' she whispered, her dimples deepening. 'I feel like you're dissecting me with that mind of yours.'

His brows rose as he chuckled wickedly. 'Now there is a thought. Why don't you take your clothes off and let the good doctor examine you?'

Tess burst into a fit of laughter. 'That has never actually worked for you, has it?'

Booker shrugged, pretending to be embarrassed. 'I figure one of these days the odds have to be in my favor.'

'I doubt a man who looks like you ever has a problem getting a date,' Tess stated, with assurance. 'You look like you could be a regular Casanova.'

'What?' Booker was shocked.

'Oh, come on,' Tess touched his arm. 'Surely someone has told you that before?'

'No, they never have,' he stated indignantly.

'Don't act so puritan,' she laughed. 'There are worse things in life than being compared to a gorgeous Casanova, you know.'

'Oh,' Booker said. He sat on the floor in front of the couch, leaning on his elbow, his head resting on his fist in front of her. His face was no more than inches from her own. 'Do I take it you think I'm gorgeous?'

Tess tensed, her lips thinning into a prim line. She leaned away from him, pressing herself against the pillows in an effort to put distance between them. 'I didn't say that, exactly. What I meant was –'

'That you find me wildly attractive?' he offered sweetly.

'I don't th-think so,' she stammered, her eyes roaming, lighting everywhere, anywhere but on him.

Booker pressed his advantage and leaned closer to her. Tess continued to lean away from him till she was practically looking down her nose at him, because she was pushing up and over her nest of pillows. His gaze centered on her lips, full and curvaceous. Inviting.

'I guess there's only one way to find out, huh?' he said, his voice low, husky with the thought, the want of tasting her.

Tess drew a sharp breath, her eyes widening as she licked her lips nervously. 'How will you know I'm not fantasizing about Casanova?'

'I'll just have to take my chances, won't I?' he assured her, though he didn't appear worried in the least.

He touched his lips to hers for a moment. It was a simple touch. A lingering second that the soft flesh of her lips were pressed against him. Then she melted. It wasn't so much a movement on her part, but a feeling from her. Booker tilted his head as he parted her lips and deepened his kiss. He touched her, tasted her, as he raised his hand to skim his fingers along her cheek, then to sink them into the silky depths of her hair. She sighed with pleasure into his kiss, her arms skimming up his biceps to his neck. A slow caress till she circled him within her embrace. Booker rose to his knees, his lips never leaving hers as he partially shifted his large frame over hers. Her hands slid into his hair as she hungrily pressed herself to him. He kissed her, his hands moving over her from the gentle swell of her hips to the firm contours of her stomach, till he cupped them underneath her breasts.

Booker teased her parted lips with the tip of his tongue, then moved achingly slowly across her cheek till he could nuzzle the silky cream of her neck. He held her breast, reveling in her fullness filling his hand. She arched against him, her breast pleading for his touch, her neck inviting his lips.

Booker sought the quickened pulse of her heart, beating erotically within her neck. His tongue traced the firm ridge of her throat. He smoothed his thumb across the hardening pebble of her breast.

Tess turned her head to capture the sensitive tip of his ear, and she traced it first with her tongue, evoking a moan of pleasure from him, then nibbling lightly on the edge. Her breath vibrated in his ear as she spoke softly, her voice husky with her desire for him. 'Oh, Casanova, you're so sexy.'

Booker stiffened at the strange name, then Tess giggled under him as she bit lightly on his ear. He raised his head slightly, till he could meet the mischievous humor of her gaze.

'You are not funny,' he reminded her, though he couldn't quite stop himself from smiling.

'I'm laughing,' she pointed out.

'So you are.'

He peered down at her, as if he were contemplating her humor. He stopped, then frowned as he focused at a point on her neck.

'What is it?' she asked, watching him intently.

His frown deepened as he peered closer. Tess tilted her head to feel the spot where he was staring, dutifully exposing her neck to him. Booker dived at her, nipping her sensitive skin playfully into his mouth.

Tess laughed as she pushed against him. 'Booker, stop. You're tickling me, and I don't think Casanova would have wanted to be known for *tickling* women.'

He raised his head to grin wickedly at her. 'How do you know he wouldn't?'

'How do you know?' she returned, wiping at her neck.

'I don't,' he answered easily, tapping the end of her cute little nose with his finger. 'And neither do you, sweetheart.'

Tess giggled, her gaze fixed on him. Just looking at him caused the desire to flare within her once again. Her expression mirrored his own feelings as her smile softened and her eyes met his.

His gaze fell to her lips. Though the feel of them flashed vividly in his mind, he still hungered for more of her. He started to lean toward her when the lights of the cabin suddenly came on. Tess closed her eyes automatically against the sudden brightness in the room. Obviously they had been turning the lights on as they'd tested the switches.

Booker leaned back, blinking as his eyes became adjusted to the sudden glare. 'As usual, the timing is impeccable,' he muttered.

His gaze moved back to Tess. Once again her reserved nature had slipped back into place as they were faced with the reality the light had startled them with. Booker touched her cheek, already missing that responsive side of Tess as he shifted away from her. Tess sat up, covering her awkwardness by rearranging the pillows around her.

She cleared her throat, then glanced at her watch. 'I guess it's time to call it a night.'

'I suppose so,' he agreed, watching her steadily.

She rose, pulling at the hem of her loosened shirt nervously. She stepped away as she motioned with her hand toward the stairway. 'Uh, I guess I'll go ahead and find a room. Goodnight, Booker.'

'Goodnight,' he said, feeling as if he would like to growl at something small and defenseless. Maybe cut down a tree to release some of his pent up frustration.

He settled back against the overstuffed couch, letting his head fall back against a cushion as he released a low groan. Booker doubted like hell that Casanova had ever had to worry about a beautiful woman walking away from him and a romantic roaring fire.

Damn it.

'Would you say Gare Harolds was killed at the site of the Worth Hotel before it was imploded?' Tess asked.

She stood in Harolds' library, or den, meticulously flipping through the books to see if anything had been placed between the pages. They had both risen early, then had eaten an awkward and quiet breakfast. At least Tess had felt awkward, like the-morning-after awkward, and they'd been overly polite with each other. Then they had started with the upstairs, searching each room, going through every drawer, checking in every conceivable place for a clue as to where the kidnappers might have taken Janet.

Booker had followed her sullen form down the stairs and informed her he would help her search Harolds' den. He now sat in the large leather chair behind the massive desk, going through drawers and scanning papers. He continued to go through stacks of paperwork even as he answered her question.

'It's really hard to tell,' he started. 'Obviously they wanted to dispose of the body in the hotel, thinking that the implosion would effectively eliminate the evidence. If the corpse hadn't been sheltered as it was, within a cement slab lean-to, it probably would have been severely destroyed by the blast. And, being lost within the debris, it would have been very easy to overlook. They really had covered their tracks well; they couldn't have possibly counted on the body being so well preserved.'

Tess pulled a book out, then flipped through the pages. 'So the blast destroyed the trace evidence?'

'Pretty much,' he answered. He was frowning as he looked through a stack of bills. 'Geez, this guy spent more in a day than I make in a year.'

'Considering you drive a Porsche, I don't see where you have the room to complain,' Tess pointed out to him. She shoved the book back into its place and started on the next row.

'That was a gift,' he said distractedly.

Tess's brow rose as she turned to look back at him. 'A gift? Hell of a friend.'

Booker shook his head, as if finally hearing her words. He flipped through the last of the statements and pushed them back into their respective drawer. 'Not a friend, a relative.'

So, Booker had a wealthy relative who cared enough about him to give him a Porsche? Interesting, she thought, shelving the idea away till she had a private moment to mull that one over. She turned her attention back to the problem at hand. 'Will any of the samples you've taken from here help you with your investigation?'

'Every little bit helps.' He shrugged, leaning over to pull out the bottom drawer. He scooted the chair over so he was straddling the drawer and started going through the hanging files it contained. 'The trace evidence found in the area around the body, and to an extent even on the body, cannot be considered too reliable. There was a blast, the building fell, and for the next several months it was pretty much a garbage heap. However, if we could match anything from the cabin to what was found on or in the clothing, it would prove helpful to the detectives' investigation.'

Tess smirked at the title of the book in her hand. It looked as if Harolds had also had a taste for exotic literature. 'How was he killed?'

'He was shot in the back of the head, execution style.'

'How could you tell?' she asked, turning to study him.

'When I first saw him we hadn't moved the body or turned him over,' he explained. 'We used a special blanket to preserve any trace evidence and transferred him to a body bag. When I got him back to the lab, we started the post-mortem and found an entrance wound at the back of the head in the occipital area.'

'No exit wound?' she asked.

Booker shook his head. 'That and the tattooing around the wound led us to believe that it was a small-caliber weapon shot at close range. Probably a .22 fired about six to eight inches from the target.'

'You mean Harolds' head,' she stated, her lip curling with the image of that fine thought. 'I assume "tattooing" has something to do with the gunpowder marks around the wound?'

He nodded, pulling out another file to glance through it. 'You will never find gunpowder smudging and tattooing at the same time, which helps us differentiate the distance of the blast. Harolds' wound had gunpowder particles embedded in the skin in a "tattoo" around the wound which could not be wiped off. If it had been closer, the soot would have been easy to wipe away. If there is no soot, or embedding of gunpowder, then the blast has been fired from a greater distance.'

'Gee, I'm ready for lunch.' She stopped what she was doing for a moment as she chewed her lip. 'So he *could* have been killed at the site of the Worth Hotel?'

'Yeah,' he answered. He leaned back in the chair as he returned her gaze. 'There will be no way of telling for sure or not. Any shell casings or other items would have been destroyed in the implosion. I do believe the body had at least been moved. There was very little blood on his clothes and, though it's sometimes hard to tell with mummification, the lividity was "fixed" differently from the placement of the body. Again, the implosion could have altered that fact.'

Tess's brow rose at his explanation. She was almost afraid to ask, but, like a moth drawn to a flame, she couldn't resist. Her voice reflected her disbelief. 'He was mummified?'

'I'm not talking about the King Tut kind of mummification, Tess.' Booker chuckled at her reaction. 'It's a very natural occurrence when a body decomposes in a dry climate, like the basement of a house. Or the basement of an imploded hotel.'

Tess stared at him for a moment. She couldn't think of one thing to say, so she turned back to the books and blindly pulled one out. Skimming through it, she realized it was one she had already looked at.

Booker closed a drawer behind her. 'There's nothing here. I've looked through every single drawer, file, piece of paper, and I cannot find a thing.'

'I know.' Tess put the book back and turned toward him as she put her hands on her hips. 'What do you think we should do now?'

'I was hoping you had an idea,' he said, without enthusiasm.

He leaned back in the chair, putting his hands behind his head as he slumped in the seat. His gaze roamed over the room as he searched his thoughts for their next plan of action. His gaze drifted to the picture window in Harolds' office, and for a brief moment he allowed himself to admire the scenic view on display outside.

He smiled as he watched a pair of squirrels playing in a tree beginning to bud with flowers. 'What about outside?'

Tess followed his gaze, her brows furrowing with her seriousness. 'We don't have time to go frolicking outside.'

Booker tilted his head toward her. Speaking slowly, as if dealing with a stubborn child, he said, 'I meant take a look outside, sweetheart.'

She straightened at the obviousness of his statement. Okay, so she had misunderstood his meaning. However, she refused to let him know that. 'Uh . . . that sounds like a good idea.'

They headed to the closet, to retrieve their jackets, then went outside. The cabin was a large one, nestled within a clearing of trees. A large pole barn stood on the edge of the clearing. Together they made their way to it, since Tess figured it would be a good place to start.

Once they got there, they found the doors locked with a hanging combination padlock. After nosing around a while, Booker found a set of bolt cutters and went to work on cutting the lock from the doors. Silently Tess reveled in watching him when he removed his jacket and she could see the bulges of his muscles at work beneath his shirt. Standing behind him with her hands jammed in her jacket pockets, she swallowed several times and simply watched in fascination. The man had a fine set of biceps, wide muscled shoulders, and a tight little rear end; she did have to give him that.

After several entertaining moments, Booker was able to cut through the lock. He released his breath in a rush and let the bolt cutters fall to the ground beside him. He worked the lock back through the loops and discarded it beside the bolt cutter, then pushed at the door and slid it open.

Tess picked up his jacket and handed it to him as she walked past him. The barn was huge and crowded full of machinery, including a small forklift. They had to pick their way through.

She nudged what looked like an old leather horse collar hanging from a low beam out of her way as she stepped into a stall. 'There might have been horses in here at one time, when the previous owners had this place. I seriously doubt, however, that Harolds would have gone to that much trouble.'

'Not much of an animal-lover, huh?' Booker said. He stood at the other side of the barn, sifting carefully through an assortment of items, then moved to check out another stall.

'No,' she answered. For a moment she was distracted as she caught sight of a spider. It was little, and didn't scare her, not that much anyway, so she edged it toward the wall with the toe of her boot. 'Harolds just considered himself a lover. Period.'

Booker looked over his shoulder at her, his gaze studying her for a moment. He turned and moved toward her till he stood behind her.

Tess had looked away once he started walking toward her. She could now sense him standing behind her. Waiting. She didn't turn back toward him, but continued looking through the shelves against the wall.

Harolds had been the kind of man who considered himself to be built to please women. He had been handsome, and had worked out religiously to maintain his well-built body. Women had enjoyed loving him and he'd known it.

Though he'd had a wife, and a couple of children, Gare Harolds had never let that stop him in his pursuit of women. For some odd reason that Tess had never understood, Gare Harolds had steadfastly refused to leave his wife, even though a few of his mistresses had tried to get him to.

Tess had had the unpleasant job of interviewing one of the unfortunate females who had fallen under the spell of the impressive Gare Harolds. Marcy was a normal female, one whom Tess would have liked in any other kind of circumstance. She had been young when she had first started working for Harolds, and had worked for him for some time. She had believed him in the beginning, when he had told her about the 'unfortunate' circumstances of his marriage. He'd told her he felt he'd been meant to raise his children in an unbroken home, that it was his wife who didn't understand him. They still loved each other, were still friends, but that was it. They rarely had sex any more, and he was a man built to have sex. Needed it as a physical confirmation of his identity.

He had poured his story out to the young office worker, and she had bought it, hook, line and sinker.

They had carried on their affair for more than two years. During that time his wife had given birth to their youngest child. Marcy had felt bad about their relationship, but unfortunately had fallen in love with the man. She had been able to convince herself that their relationship was meant to be. Was right.

Then Marcy had started hearing the rumors.

Harolds had taken a sales trip to Vegas with a female co-worker. The co-worker had been supposedly staying in a hotel room with another female employee. When they had returned to work the next week, it had been all over the company. The female co-worker who had traveled with Harolds had not returned to her room till five o'clock in the morning one night.

Marcy had been devastated. She had confronted Harolds, and of course he had denied everything. But Marcy had known him too well. She'd known Gare Harolds' greatest fulfillment was giving women their ultimate pleasure. Though he'd been a careful man, discreet, Marcy had figured he would jump to take advantage of any opportunity presented to him.

Tess shook her head as she remembered the determined young woman. Marcy had broken off the affair with Gare Harolds, but had refused to be driven away from her job when he'd become upset. She had stayed, and Harolds had learned to tolerate her presence. The only positive aspect of their affair had been that Marcy was not afraid to stand up to Harolds. They had butted heads on more than one occasion and grudgingly he had come to respect her ability. Marcy might have slept with the boss, but she had worked her way up to the supervisory position she held because of her ability alone.

Tess leaned over and picked up a shovel to lean it back against the wall. She didn't know why Harolds' extra-marital activities bothered her so much, but they had. Perhaps it was because a small part of her had been attracted to him, and the thought had repulsed her after she'd found out what kind of man he was.

She heard Booker shift behind her and she was glad he couldn't see her face. It wasn't that she was ashamed of the attraction she had felt for Harolds; it was more complex than that. More complex than she wanted to think about at the moment.

'Sounds like you didn't like him that well,' Booker said softly.

'I didn't,' she answered truthfully. She picked up a strand of straw and began braiding it in her hands as she turned to face him. 'He was a bastard without a heart.'

'Then why did you do work for him?' Booker studied her, his gaze hooded. 'Money?'

'No,' Tess chuckled without humor. 'Money has never been a motivating factor for me. I didn't agree with what Harolds did in his private life, but it wasn't my place to judge his actions either.'

Booker nodded. 'That's very admirable. Probably more admirable than I could have been.'

She shrugged. 'There was nothing admirable about it. My firm was hired to control his security leaks. Nothing more.'

'Then why is all of this hitting you so hard?' he asked quietly.

Tess's gaze flew to him. She hadn't realized that he read her so well. She returned his gaze for a moment, unsure what to say. 'It's not,' she said simply.

Booker stepped forward, raising his hand to cup her chin. He tilted her face up to his till she met his gaze. 'Did you have an affair with him?'

Her gaze hardened. She looked into the slate color of his eyes, expecting to find him mocking her. Or judgement. She found neither, instead she found concern and understanding. At that moment, her heart softened toward him a little more. 'No, I did not have an affair with that pitiful excuse for a man.'

He smiled, his gaze dropping to her lips as he ran his thumb over the ridge. 'So you feel responsible for his kidnapping and death?'

Tess was surprised by his sudden change in tactic. His insight into her thoughts. She stammered for an answer. 'My firm was responsible for his and Torkelson's safety.'

'But they failed to follow your directions, is that right?' he asked.

She nodded. She had not personally liked Gare Harolds, in fact she had considered him no better than the slime on a slug's belly, even in the midst of his incredible sexuality. He had used people, bullied them, then tossed them aside without a care when they were no longer useful. Tess had wondered many times if her intense dislike for the man had shadowed her reasoning. Perhaps if she had been more professional and put her feelings of dislike aside, she would have pushed him harder to follow the necessary precautions that might have saved his life.

'Tess, he chose to ignore the security precautions,' Booker reminded her. 'He hired your firm in the first place, obviously he knew the consequences.'

'I should have pressed him harder. Yelled at him, or something, to get him to listen to me,' Tess snapped at him. She closed her mouth tightly, jerking her face away from his hands as she turned away. Tears welled in her eyes. Not for Gare Harolds – no, she had not shed a tear for him at all. The tears threatening to spill were for the loss of life. Two lives, as a matter of fact, that had been placed in *her* hands to protect. And they were gone.

Torkelson and Harolds might have deserved to be divorced, sued, and their egos cut down to size, but not to be killed. Not to be kidnapped, then shot execution style. If she couldn't be trusted to protect two men who were hardly worth protecting, how could she be trusted to protect anyone?

'The only way you could have pressed harder for him to take your precautions seriously would have been to sleep with him,' Booker stated, his voice hard.

Tess whirled toward him, her face flushed with anger. 'Go to hell, Booker.'

He was leaning casually against the wall of the old horse stall, his arms folded over his chest. His gaze was direct and ungiving. This was a side of Ethan Booker Tess had not been faced with. His manner was callused, leaving no tolerance for self-pity. 'How could you have saved him, Quintessa? Tell me that.

You seem to be perfect and invincible. How does Miss Invincible save the world?'

Her hands clenched into fists, her knuckles turning white as she seethed. Her lips were pressed into thin, hard lines as she fought through the haze of anger to reply to his insensitive statement. 'I never said I could save the world.'

'And neither are you responsible for the death of those two men,' he stated in a low voice, his gaze softening. He let his arms fall to his sides as he moved to stand in front of her. He touched her face. 'You failed no one. You did the best you could. You gave them the best protection within your power. They chose to take off on their own. They made their own decisions; they faced their own consequences.'

'I know.' Tess sniffed, gripping the hard warmth of his hand as he touched her. It felt good, so good to touch him, to talk to him. 'I guess I had become so smug over the fact that I had never lost a client. Then finally one day it happened. And I didn't like how it made me feel.'

'It won't feel good. You wouldn't be human if it did,' he whispered, pulling her into his arms. He wrapped her within his embrace, nestling her head against his shoulder. He rested his chin on her head, inhaling the fragrance of her. 'And it never will.'

'Booker, I didn't know you were such a philosopher.' She chuckled softly against his chest as she sniffed.

'I'm not.' He gave her a gentle hug, then planted a quick kiss on her cheek. He swatted her on the rear end as he released her and walked off. 'Now, get your butt in gear.'

Tess laughed. 'You're a good man, Ethan Booker.'

'My mother would be glad to hear that,' he threw over his shoulder, and started working his way through the barn. He found the door of an old tack room. It took him a few moments till he was finally able to wrench it open on its rusted hinges. What he found inside caused to him to freeze.

'Tess, come here.'

She paused. The tone of his voice instantly dispelled the warm feelings that had filled her and forced a chill to move over her. She moved quickly till she pushed beside him. She stopped to see the tight look of anger and fear on his face before she turned to follow his gaze. The tack room was empty except for a chair. A length of rope was thrown haphazardly beside it. What drew her attention was the photograph propped against the back of the old wooden chair.

It was an instant picture of Janet. Tied up in the chair with a length of rope. A gray bandanna stuck in her mouth and tied around her head to keep her from talking. She still wore the black outfit she'd had on the night they broke into Booker's house.

Tess started to reach toward the picture, then withdrew her hand in fear. Janet's fear stricken eyes bored into her, and Tess felt her heart start to pound. It hurt her deeply to think of the terror her friend must be experiencing.

Booker leaned over and withdrew a scrap of paper that rested under the picture. 'I think they left us a note.'

Tess finally found the courage to pick up the picture of her friend. Her hands shook as she studied the picture, willing every detail to be seared into her memory. 'I'll get the bastards for doing this to her.' Her voice caught as she spat the words out.

Booker gripped her shoulder. 'Get in line, sweetheart.'

His brows furrowed deeply and his lips thinned into a hard line. He gently took the photo from her and placed it in his pocket, then showed her the note, with its awkwardly squared letters, from the kidnapper. 'Tess, you need to see this.'

Tess's eyes moved over the note. The message hit her and she started shaking, both with fear and anger. A moment before she had only thought she was scared. Now she was terrified. Her gaze darted toward Booker, instinctively seeking the comfort his presence naturally gave to her. His look was hard and menacing, something she never would have expected from her humorous coroner.

'I guess they want to play games now,' he said, without any emotion. That only showed Tess how dangerous Ethan Booker could be when forced.

She looked back to the note and its message.

Glad to see you do have a brain in that lovely head.
You have forty-eight hours to find our next clue or your sweet friend will suffer from a sore throat.
This time you won't have to go so far.
Badger

Tess ran her hand through her hair as her thoughts raced and whirled in her mind. Badger had raised the stakes, using Janet's life as if it were worth no more than a plastic poker chip. As if that alone would not pressure Tess to perform, he had now forced her into a game she had to play. Her opponent was time itself.

The prize . . . was Janet's life.

CHAPTER 8

Janet was blindfolded. The material covering her eyes was thick, so thick she couldn't tell if there was even a light on in the room she was being held in. The rough, callused hand of one of the kidnappers skimmed across her face to touch her lips. Instinctively she bit the roughened fingers of the man, relishing the howl of pain her action evoked.

The man yanked his hand from her mouth, almost dragging her teeth with him. She couldn't see anything, couldn't enjoy watching the pain she had inflicted. Still, she smiled when she heard the needling whining of the injured man as he complained to the other faceless captor in the room.

'The bitch bit me,' he whined. By the movement of the sound of his voice, she knew he must be pacing back and forth in front of her. 'I can't believe the bitch bit me. I ought to slap her for doing that.'

'No, you will not.'

It was the voice of the third man. Janet only occasionally heard this man, so she assumed that he was not staying where they were. He was the leader; that much she was sure of. Whenever she heard his voice, the other men immediately responded with deference to him. She also knew the other men feared him.

They weren't alone.

The men had kept her blindfolded from the moment they had taken her from Tess's car after they'd forced it from the road. Only at night was she allowed to take it off. In the morning she was usually awakened by a bright light being shone directly into her eyes, temporarily blinding her till they could put the blindfold back on.

'I'm sorry, sir,' the ape she'd bitten said, his voice still holding a thin thread of his whining. 'But she bit me.'

'What were you doing to cause her to bite you?'

Each word was pronounced with emphasis in a cultured low voice. The very smoothness of the man's soft tones caused fear to tingle through her. She had no doubt that although the man speaking had a very civilized tone, his demeanor was anything but.

Janet swallowed nervously, and she imagined the ape did too. The silence that hung in the room radiated with tension, suppressed anger and fear. The fear was her own, and that of the big ape standing quietly in front of her. For the tiniest moment she almost felt sorry for the ape, having to face the displeasure of the man with the sinister voice. Then again, as far as she was concerned they all deserved to experience a little fear for what they were doing to her.

'I only touched her,' the ape stammered unconvincingly. 'That's all. I didn't do nothing, I swear.'

Again there was silence. Janet tensed, and forced herself to take slow, easy breaths when she found she had been holding it. Her heart pounded within her chest, the noise of it audible in her ears. The blackness that filled her vision heightened her fear. She was unable to see what sort of exchange was going on between the two men.

She heard the click of one of the men's shoes against the cement of the floor as he walked slowly toward them. It must be the mean one, she thought, unable to think of any other appropriate name for the individual. The steps stopped directly in front of her and she slowly drew in her breath. What was he going to do to her?

'Apologize to her.'

'What?' By the ape's reaction, he was probably as shocked as Janet was to hear the mean one say it.

'Do I need to repeat myself?' he said slowly, softly, as if dealing with a difficult child.

'No, sir,' the ape said quickly. The large individual drew in a shaky breath. 'I apologize, miss, for touching you.'

Janet did not know how to respond. Her upbringing prompted her to reply to the apology, but, considering the circumstances under which it had been given, she was sure societal decorum would understand if she remained silent.

She heard the slow slide of a foot against the smooth, hard surface of the cement floor. She flinched at the unexpected touch of the mean one's finger against her cheek.

'My employee obviously took liberties that were not granted to him, my dear. Rest assured that neither of these gentlemen will ever harm you again,' he said soothingly.

Janet fought the shiver that the chill of his voice caused within her. His fingers skimmed down her cheek to stroke her throat with the palm of his hand. He continued to speak to her as his hand boldly caressed her body. Janet's breath came in short gasps of fear as his hand smoothed down her collarbone. She pressed herself against the back of the chair as she tried to move away from him. She remained silent, refusing to cry out in protest. Instinctively she knew that her fear would flare his passion and spur him on. She bit her lip, thankful for the blindfold to hide the tears welling in her eyes as his hand slid to her breast and cupped her fullness.

He gave her breast a gentle squeeze. 'You are our guest and will be treated accordingly.'

Then his hand was gone.

She heard the slow tread of the vile man as he left. The metallic click of the door signaled his exit. Janet let her breath rush from her as she let her head fall forward. Oblivious to the two men remaining in the room with her, she gulped air as she fought back the nausea and fear.

'Damn,' the ape said. The man's shaking voice broke into her thoughts, reminding her of the men's presence in the room.

He walked slowly back to the table where he had originally been sitting. With relief, Janet heard the scrape of his chair as he drew it back to take a seat. The two men remained quiet, and she wondered for a moment if they were as shellshocked as she was.

If the truth were to be told, she didn't really care what they thought. She was just glad the vile one had left. She could handle the presence of these two; at least they didn't scare her. Not any more, she thought. Their presence was almost comforting compared to the other man's.

Janet concentrated on her breathing as she drew breath in, feeling it pull the tension up from her body. She held it for a moment, then released it, letting it take the tension with it. Rhythmically she continued the pattern as she felt the nervous energy ease from her body.

The fear was another matter. Something about the mean one charged the air, or the atmosphere, with a threatening charge. Janet could almost feel the tingling of tiny pin-pricks of pain moving over her where he had touched her. By his voice, his actions, she could tell nothing about him. She had no idea how tall he was, couldn't even guess as to his age from the sound of his voice. But something about him struck fear in her as easily as it had the mountain of an ape that had been left to guard her.

Tess, please hurry and find me, she prayed silently. Before that monster comes back.

Booker watched Tess's face intently as he walked with her to her car. Since they had found the photo, she had not said a word, had only headed back into the cabin, then come back out a few short moments later to go to the car. With a doctor's critical eye, he'd noted the pale complexion of her face and the jerky movements of her body as she strode to the car. She was fighting the shock and fear that the photo of Janet had evoked within her with action. From the tight anger of her expression, he could only assume it would involve violence.

Tess fitted her key into the lock of the four-wheel drive and turned it. The lock popped up easily and she reached in and retrieved a shiny metal chrome suitcase. She turned slightly, and her expression showed a hint of surprise, as if she hadn't even known he'd been with her the past few moments. Without a word she shoved the suitcase into his arms and turned back to the car. Reaching in, she grabbed a second case and yanked it out.

She shut the door and started toward the cabin. 'Come on.'

Booker frowned at her terse tone as he followed her back to the cabin. They took the cases into Harolds' den and placed them on the polished wood of his massive desk. Tess quickly and expertly unlocked the cases, then flipped the lids open.

He gave a slow whistle at the assortment of armament. 'Damn, Tess. Going a little light on the hardware, aren't you?'

She leveled a look at him. 'I prefer to be prepared.'

Booker leaned over and pulled a 9 mm pistol from its slot in the fitted gun case. A magazine was nestled next to it in its own compartment, which he scooped out with his other hand. Tess turned quickly toward him, her eyes widening as she saw him handling the firearms. Her mouth started to open in protest and she reached toward the gun in his hand.

Booker slipped the magazine easily into the grip of the gun and slapped it into place with the palm of his hand. The clip locked in with a resounding snap. He watched with amusement as her fear turned to disbelief as he handled the gun so deftly.

Her gaze moved slowly from the pistol in his hand to his face. He gave her a half-smile. '9 mm, semi-automatic Glock pistol, model 17 with a seventeen magazine.'

Tess shook her head. Finally her brain seemed to get past its mental roadblock. 'You're a coroner; how did you do that?'

He started chuckling. 'I work with law enforcement on an everyday basis; I can't help but learn a few things. My office also happens to be known for its firearms laboratory. However, my knowledge originally came from a stint in the Army. I also worked with central intelligence at one point. Occasionally I carried a gun.'

'You're just full of surprises, aren't you?' she said, with a look of amused awe.

His smile softened as he lifted his hand to stroke the soft curve of her cheek. 'And I would love to share every one of them with you, Tess.'

Clearing her throat, she pressed her lips primly together. 'Unfortunately, we've been pressured into a deadline.'

Letting his hand drop, he nodded. He had learned a few things about Tess Reynolds. She was a loyal friend. That loyalty was what drove her to take care of those around her. She would do what it took to find her friend Janet, despite any danger she would personally be facing. In a short period of time his life had become accustomed to Tess Reynolds. In a few short days he had started getting used to the roller coaster ride he'd been on from the first moment he saw her. The maniac calling himself Badger was pushing her into a cat and mouse game, using as bait something that he knew she would not turn her back on. Her friend Janet.

Booker gave silent thanks that he was there to help her. To be with her so that he could personally see that she was safe.

He pulled the note out of his shirt pocket and put it on the table beside one of the cases. 'The note says we have to look for the next clue,' he said, purposely avoiding a reference to the time frame they were being forced to work within. 'It also says that this time we won't have to go so far. I assume that since she was kidnapped and brought here, they are referring to our flight here. If this time we don't have to go so far, then the next item has to be close by. I'd say at least within hiking distance.'

Tess's gaze remained on the note as she mulled his words over. 'That makes sense. This cabin is very secluded. Even that blacktop road is a fairly significant distance from here, as you may recall.' She shrugged as her mind raced through the possibilities. 'But where? Where would that bastard be keeping her?'

'Where's your map of this area that you had on the plane?' he asked.

Tess turned and headed toward the door. 'It's in my bag upstairs. I'll go get it.'

Her heart raced as she made her way up the stairs toward the room she had taken over as her own. She had a feeling, a gut instinct, that Booker's observation was heading them in the right direction.

At the head of the stairs she walked down the short hallway to her room. Her bag was on the floor beside the bed. She picked it up and dropped it on the bed to retrieve the map. It, along with a few other items she had brought, were in a folder, tucked in her bag. Unzipping the case, she flipped the lid open to retrieve the folder. Her brow furrowed as she stared blankly for a moment at the contents of the suitcase. Everything was as she had left it, except for one thing. The file with the important map was missing.

Now her heart pounded with fear. A shower of nerves cascaded over her as the meaning of the disappearance dawned on her. The back of her neck prickled with her apprehension as she backed slowly away from the suitcase. Slowly, meticulously, she scanned the room to see what else had been disturbed. As far as she could tell nothing else had been taken or moved, only the file with the map. A part of her truly wished she had brought one of her guns up with her. There was a whole floor between her and Booker.

Keeping her back close to the wall, she moved cautiously to the hallway and peeked her head carefully out the door of the bedroom to check the area first. Was it Badger who had taken the file from her baggage? Could he still be in the cabin, waiting to ambush them? Thoughts rushed through her mind, her fear muddling the process even more till her stubborn anger flared. Tess's jaw tightened as she clenched her teeth. Anger at the faceless individual filled her with a brief sense of desperation. Badger was trying to fix the game by stacking the deck against her.

Without even knowing it, the sadist had probably made his first mistake. Quintessa Reynolds did not like to lose, and she sure as hell did not like being set up. The downward shape of her lips twisted upward in an expression that no one would mistake for a smile. Badger might have thought he could hinder her by taking the map and the other tools of information she had brought with her, but that was where he was wrong. Fortunately her security firm was one of the best in the country, and she could get the information she needed immediately.

The nameless, faceless individual who had dubbed himself as Badger might have thought to scare her off with this juvenile stunt, but it wouldn't work. The most it would achieve would be to slow her down, but not for long. She would search this section of the surrounding forest with or without a map. She would find Badger's next idiotic clue, and eventually she would find him.

If Badger wanted to play games, she would gladly play with him. Except now it was the game of life, and he was about to win the prize. Tess was going to make sure he didn't enjoy it either.

Quickly she descended the stairs and forced her hands to relax from the fists her nerves had balled her hands into. She walked quickly toward the den. Walking through the door, she started to tell Booker about the file when the sight of him leaning over the unfolded map on the study table stopped her.

'You've got the map,' she stated, without preamble.

'Yeah, it was sitting on top of the desk. I found it under one of the gun cases after I moved it,' he said, without looking up. His gaze was intently studying the layout around the cabin.

Her silence must have finally registered on him and he glanced up to her. His eyes almost did a double take as he noted the look in her face. 'What is it, Tess?'

She pointed to the map he was leaning on with one elbow. 'I did not leave that map on Harolds' desk. I distinctly remember folding it and putting away in the folder I had brought. That folder was in my bag the last time I saw it. I did not leave it down here.'

Booker's gaze held hers as he registered what she was saying. He calmly picked up the Glock he had loaded earlier and cocked it. 'I'll check the house.'

'It will be quicker if I help you secure the house,' she pointed out as she pulled her Colt semi-automatic out of its case.

His eyes held hers, and she could see the reluctance held within them. He didn't like the idea of her placing herself in such a situation. To his credit, he said nothing, simply nodded. 'You take the upstairs and I'll take the downstairs.'

She murmured her agreement as she cocked her gun. They followed each other single file out the door of the study, then separated. Tess fought the urge to look back over her shoulder for one more look at the reassurance that Booker's presence gave her. She knew there should be some significance to that urge, but chose not to explore it. The house had been breached while they were out searching the barn. The very thought of Badger or one of his men entering the cabin in their absence was more disturbing than Tess cared to admit. She forced her thoughts to focus instead on the stairway in front of her and the rooms at the top of it.

It angered her that they were having to use precious time to search the house so they could feel safe enough to begin their search for Janet. She used that anger to carry her past the fear she was feeling, and to help her concentrate on putting one foot in front of the other as she made her way up the stairs. Quickly and quietly she moved up them, then stopped as she paused at the top of the stairs. She listened for a moment and heard nothing. Her instincts had been honed over the years and she trusted them; they now told her there were no other presence upstairs with her. Still she carefully searched each room, checking closets, making sure windows were locked and looking under beds. She was not familiar with the decor of the rooms, but could see by the fine layer of dust on the surface of the furniture that nothing had been moved recently in any of the other bedrooms.

She finished the upstairs with the room Booker was staying in. She could smell his cologne and immediately her body responded to its scent. He'd left the bed unmade, and her gaze lingered on the rumpled sheets where his body had been. Tess swallowed, forcing her gaze away as she advanced on the closet. Opening it, she flipped the overhead light on and inspected the floor, still finding nothing.

As she turned back toward the bed, her traitorous mind evoked the image of what Booker would be like sleeping within those sheets. She could imagine one of his legs kicked out from under the covers. The thought of his masculine muscled leg exposed to her view, his thigh partially revealed, teasing her from under the covers, hinting at what was beneath, caused a ripple of arousal to move through her.

Tess shook her head at her pitiful state. She had a job to do, so much riding on the line and she was being turned on by rumpled sheets. Empty rumpled sheets at that.

She stepped to the bed and knelt beside it to look under it. Peering under the frame, she found what she'd expected to find. Nothing.

Tess stood and headed back toward the staircase. She kept her gun ready, though she had a pretty good idea that they had already found what Badger had wanted them to find. He'd moved the map and the folder because he had logically assumed that was where they would start. Removing the folder and map from her suitcase to place it in Harolds' study was not meant to be anything more than it was. It was a simple gesture to let them know he was in the area, that he was watching them, and that he had access to their information.

As she was descending the stairs, she looked up as Booker walked in from the front room. He stopped when he saw her and waited for her to join him.

'I'll assume that you came up with nothing also,' he said.

Tess nodded. 'Nothing missing. Nothing moved. Only the folder with the map.'

Together they walked back into the study. Tess moved behind the study table to return her attention to the map. 'I figure it was his way of letting us know he's keeping tabs on what we're doing.'

'I agree,' Booker said, rubbing thoughtfully at his chin. He walked around the table, perching his hip on the edge as he folded his arms over his chest. She could feel his gaze on her. 'Tess, have you ever thought about who this Badger might be?'

'Of course I have,' she answered, a little more sharply than she had intended to. His question hadn't disturbed her, but his presence had. His bent knee almost touched her where she stood, he was so close that the heat of his presence warmed her. It unnerved her. A woman who had depended on herself for so long, who had become used to being alone, she had slipped so easily into the companionship that Booker had given her. It seemed so easy to be with him, feel safe with him, secure with him, to just talk to him as she was now. She had built so many walls around herself, and somehow he had leaped them.

Usually she was cautious in her dealings with anyone, but with Booker it was different. It had surprised her when she'd realized that her guard had slipped with him and she'd found herself discussing her thoughts freely with him, without fear of his disapproval or judgement. It was his physical presence that unnerved her. She had only to look at him and the needs she had suppressed for so long rose up within her. The contradiction within herself had her on edge.

Taking a deep breath, she turned her thoughts back to the question at hand. More than ever, it was imperative that she be able to focus on the task that had been forced upon them. 'The messages from Badger started showing up a couple of months before Harolds' body was found. I had just finished a leg of my investigation into the two men's deaths when I received the first message.'

'Wait a minute.' Booker held his hand up to stop her for a moment. 'You've been receiving messages from this individual for a while now?'

Tess nodded. 'At first I thought they were from a prankster. Maybe a kind of computer stalker, or something. It wasn't till we found the note the other day that I connected Badger with the kidnapping of Janet. I assume he also had something to do with the explosion of my truck and your attempted kidnapping.'

'You've received other messages from him?' Booker barked. He rubbed his hands over his eyes, then let his fingers move through his hair till his hands gripped behind his head. He looked toward the ceiling, and Tess could see by the expression on his face that he was fighting for control of his anger.

'Okay.' He exhaled, rubbing distractedly at his forehead. She could tell by the frown marring his handsome features that he was disturbed by what she was telling him. 'Let's start from the beginning. What was your investigation pertaining to?'

'I was interviewing family, friends and acquaintances of Harolds and Torkelson. I had finished that particular leg of the investigation with one of Harolds' mistresses, a woman by the name of Marcy. I had also been following the paper trail left by the two men before their deaths. Things like credit card purchases, checks, cash receipts, dentist's bills and so on. I had also received communication logs from the men's phone lines, detailing personal and business calls.'

Booker nodded as he listened. 'Did anything pan out?'

Tess could see where his line of reasoning was headed. 'Not particularly. I couldn't find anything out of the ordinary, or relevant to their murders. I had pretty much marked that leg of the investigation as a dead end. No pun intended.'

'Then you received the first message?' he prompted, his eyes studying her.

'Yes, just a few lines of taunting bad rhymes,' she answered.

'As opposed to a few lines of taunting good rhymes,' he countered, his statement an automatic stab of humor that she had become accustomed to expect from him. He was frowning as he processed what she said. 'What was the gist of the other messages that he sent to you?'

Tess shrugged as she recalled the messages. 'Something along the lines of "they are dead and you are next."'

Booker's look became thunderous, and his lips tightened with his anger. 'I would assume that you contacted the police once you started receiving death threats?'

She shook her head, raising her hand to stop him before he launched his verbal tirade at her. 'What could I have taken to them? Sure, I printed out all the messages. I even had my computer guys try to follow the cyber trail, but, as knowledgeable as my guys are, Badger apparently is just as good, and he covered his tracks even better. I had nothing more than paper with threats written by a psychotic poet. The police have got better things to do than to try to follow up on something like that. If my firm, which is equipped with the latest technology, couldn't track this guy down, how could I expect the police to, with their more limited capabilities and budget?'

She could see by his expression that he had to accept her point. Didn't look as if he enjoyed it, though.

'When did you connect him with Janet's kidnapping?' he asked.

Booker was watching her intently, his brows furrowing into a frown as his jaws clenched. He had his arms resting on the table at either side of him. Except for the dark look of his expression, and the white-knuckled grip he had on the edge of the table, his voice and his stance were casual, almost nonchalant. Tess studied him for a moment, wondering what was racing through his thoughts.

Finally she forced her gaze away. 'After you dropped me off.' Her cheeks warmed as she recalled what had happened when he had dropped her off, and how he had retrieved the map from her. It still unnerved her to think he had affected her so intensely she hadn't noticed his clever fingers sliding the map from her waistband. Her gaze fell to those clever fingers and she stammered for a moment, then forced her mind to get back to the business at hand. 'I checked my e-mail, and that's when he left a message saying that he had what I wanted. He taunted me to come get it.'

'Or she,' Booker added.

Tess nodded in agreement. Hadn't she thought the same thing before? 'It's like this Badger just appeared one day. I sort of wondered if the messages were connected with Torkelson's and Harolds' death. Now I know they are. But I have no idea who or why.'

'And Harolds' sterling character just adds more and more people to the list,' Booker said in a low voice. His gaze dropped to the floor as he was lost in thought. Tess was studying the features of his face when suddenly his eyes focused back on her. Her eyes widened, as if she had been caught, the movement causing his lips to quirk in a small smile. 'What about the mistress? The one you interviewed?'

Tess frowned for a moment, not following where he was going. 'The mistress? What about her?'

'Harolds' mistress,' Booker said, his slate-blue eyes softening as his gaze drifted to her mouth. 'Did she ever come with Harolds out here?'

'I assume she probably did,' she answered quietly. Tess licked her lips unconsciously as a shiver of awareness moved through her. It startled her to see how easily the man before her could distract her. She cleared her throat as she walked away and put the table between them. With the width of the piece of furniture safely between them, she turned back to him. Now her thoughts seemed to slip back into the groove of reasoning that she needed at the moment. 'Why do you ask?'

Booker tilted his head as he looked at her. He smiled a lop-sided grin, as if he knew where her thoughts had been going and why she had moved away from him. 'Obviously she might be able to help us find the next step. *We* didn't find anything in the house; maybe there's something around here that she can tell us about.'

He laced his fingers together around his knee as he leaned back. 'How far did the police search around the cabin?'

'If I remember correctly, it was about three acres' radius.' She shrugged, but she pursed her lips in thought as she mulled his question over. He was on to something, though. Marcy might be able to tell them if there were any other structures within hiking distance of the cabin. She returned her gaze to Booker and offered him a brilliant smile. Now they were headed somewhere; she could feel it. 'You're pretty good at this, Dr Booker.'

'You can thank me later,' he said softly, his gaze dropping to her lips.

The heavy-lidded look on his face shot bolts of awareness through her. All too easily her mind conjured the memory of his lips on hers as he masterfully caressed her. She backed away from him, the awareness of him, then jumped when her hip bumped into a leather wing-backed chair.

'Uh,' she stammered, feeling helplessly like a hormone-driven teenager, 'I think that's an incredible idea, Ethan. I mean, Booker. I'll just give her a call right now.'

She turned quickly away and moved to sit behind Harolds' massive desk. She flipped through her data organizer till she found Marcy's phone number. She punched the number in and impatiently counted the rings as she waited for the woman to answer. At the same moment her cellphone rang.

She put her hand on the mouthpiece of the phone and looked up at Booker. 'Would you get that for me, please?'

He smiled a smile full of mischief, full of magic that promised more things than she wanted to think about. He nodded, then reached over to pick up the phone. Pushing the button, he greeted the caller as he walked out of the room, so their separate conversations wouldn't disturb each other. Tess was thankful for his thoughtfulness. It was bad enough trying to get her mind to slog past his incredible presence without trying to carry on an intelligent conversation with a potential informant.

Harolds' former mistress' phone finally picked up. Tess took a breath to talk, then groaned when she realized it was the answering machine picking up instead of Marcy. She listened to the message, then left her cellphone number and her name for the woman to call her back. Replacing the phone in the cradle, she frowned. They could still search the surrounding area. It would be better than sitting around waiting for Marcy to call back, only to find that she might have no idea of any structures near by.

Booker walked back into the room and put her cellphone back down on the table by the map. 'Were you able to get a hold of her?'

Tess shook her head. 'I left a message for her. With any luck we'll hear from her soon. Who was on the cellphone?'

'Your neighbor – the one taking care of your cat,' he answered, smiling. 'She's had an unexpected family emergency and needed to leave town for a few days. She didn't know what to do with your cat.'

Tess stiffened. 'She didn't put Sabrina in a kennel, did she?'

Booker chuckled as he shook his head. 'No, she did not. She knew how you felt about that. I had her take your cat to my neighbor, Polly. She loves cats, and takes care of mine when I have to leave town for business.'

Tess titled her head as she looked at him. 'What would a coroner go out of town on business for? Excuse the pun, but isn't your kind of business sort of dead?'

'Workshops, consultations – it's really not that different from other medical fields,' he said with a grin, obviously amused by her bad pun. 'The forensic field is constantly being upgraded, changed, just like your high-tech industry.'

'You have a point, and I appreciate your neighbor taking care of Sabrina,' she returned as she started gathering her things. 'I just don't like the thought of her being stuck in a cage.'

His gaze followed her movements as she strapped on a holster belt fitted with pouches for two magazines for her gun. She picked up a Colt Combat Elite 38 Super and snapped in a nine-round magazine, then holstered it.

'Expecting someone?' he asked.

Tess looked up to study his hooded expression. She didn't know if she sensed disapproval in his voice or not. Right now she couldn't worry about hurt feelings, his or her own. 'We don't know what to expect, do we?'

Booker nodded. Pulling the other case from the floor, he set it on the table and popped the lid. He pulled a shoulder holster out and readjusted it for his own wide frame. He loaded the Glock and holstered it, then checked each magazine before he slipped them into the fitted pouches.

'For lack of any better ideas, I think we should start

with the path I found cut into the brush behind the barn.' He picked up the map and refolded it. Tess's eyebrow rose in admiration as he folded it back to its original state, unlike the haphazard fashion she had finally managed.

He turned back to her. 'Come on, sweetheart. We're burning daylight.'

CHAPTER 9

The sun was climbing higher in the sky, burning the morning mist and making the spring day unusually humid and hot. Tess stopped briefly to remove her jacket and tie it around her waist before she started forward to follow Booker. She trudged through the undergrowth in the forest as she wiped the sweat from her brow.

'How far do you think we've walked today?' she asked tiredly, her feet feeling heavier and clumsier by the moment.

'More miles than I want to think about,' he threw over his broad shoulders at her.

Booker had pulled off his jacket and tied it around his waist an hour before she had. Since that moment she had been forced to watch the steady movement of his muscles beneath his close fitting dark T-shirt as she followed him. The spring day had surprised them with its heat, and she had been forced to turn her gaze away from the tantalizing width of his shoulders. Then she had, unfortunately, found the equally enticing view of his jeans. Finally she had resigned herself to simply watching the hypnotic movement of placing one foot in front of the other. Her own feet that was.

For the past three hours they had been making a systematic search of the forest surrounding Harolds' cabin, and so far had found nothing but an abundance of trees, bushes and an occasional critter skittering away from them into the undergrowth. They had searched far past where the police had after the kidnapping of Harolds and Torkelson, yet still continued for lack of a better lead. The cryptic note had said they would not have to go far to find the next item from Badger, so they continued searching. Anything to find Janet.

Tess's cellphone hung from her belt, but so far had not rung with the expected phone call from Harolds' former mistress Marcy. She wiped the sweat from her brow with the back of her hand as she took a deep breath. She was tired, hot, and her stomach was joining in with its own complaints.

She had always prided herself on being physically fit. Not only did she jog each day, but she kept up with her weight training as well.

But Booker.

Booker the coroner, who worked in an office all day, was walking her feet right into the ground. Obviously, from the size of his build, he enjoyed the weights more than she did, but for his size he was surprisingly graceful. She had been forced to acknowledge that particular observation while she gritted her teeth and tried to think of anything besides the man walking in front of her.

For the past hour she had made a challenge to herself. If he could keep this kind of pace up then she could as well. Now her feet ached dully; the burning sensation along the sides had subsided long ago. Later she would probably find out that that was not a good sign.

Tess had given up any kind of conversation, and simply cajoled, bargained, reasoned until finally she was threatening herself into continuing behind Booker. Her brows were furrowed into a deep scowl as she continued to watch her feet moving. Booker stopped in the path in front of her, and she barreled into him before she realized what had happened.

Startled, she stepped back and tiredly looked up at him. 'What's wrong?'

His gaze held hers, and he lifted his hand to her cheek to skim his fingertips across the ridge of her face. 'We've been walking for hours now. We need to rest.'

'Thank you,' she breathed on a sigh. Her lids drifted heavily closed as she took a moment to just enjoy not walking another step.

Booker rubbed the pad of his thumb across her chin. 'If you're up to it, it sounds like there's a stream up ahead. We could rest and have a drink at the same time.'

'Oh, Booker, don't tease me,' she said quietly, so tired she felt like whining. He chuckled as he turned to continue down the path and she followed behind him. Silently she assured herself that she only needed to take one more step, just one more step . . .

'I wouldn't tease you, sugar,' he assured her smoothly. Though she could see only his back – and what a nice backside it was too – she could hear the smile in his voice. The corners of her lips twisted upward in response to his usual humor. 'Unless you wanted me to.'

That statement caused instant searing images to fill her thoughts. His hands, his lips, his body moving against hers. Her smile was replaced with a frown.

The unwanted awareness and desire she felt for this man made her edgy and irritable. She glared at his back as she wondered how the hell a man with such a morbid job could have such a bright and witty sense of humor.

As if sensing her thoughts, he suddenly stopped and turned to face her. His gaze met hers briefly, then moved to her lips. He lowered his lips to her and Tess let herself savor the taste of him, the feel of his warm hands lightly gripping her arms, if only for a tiny moment. Then, just as quickly, he released her with a smile and turned back to the path.

'You better not be joking about this stream, Booker. I would hate to have to shoot you,' she quipped between her teeth, still feeling the tingle of his kiss. The man truly baffled her. She had refrained from repeating the word 'teasing' because it provoked too many vivid images in her mind. Images that were all too real and all too warm. His kiss, though brief and undemanding, had stirred so many things within her.

Tess continued following behind him down the wooded path, and after a few moments began to seriously wonder whether she was actually going to have to shoot him or not. She was about to question him when she too heard the rippling a steam ahead of him. Suddenly her exhausted mind perked up and she felt a small surge of energy. She didn't have to chant to her feet any more.

No, she was going to soak them.

Booker turned away from the path and started moving through the trees. Tess was forced to watch his movements through the brush, if only to keep her from being hit by a tree branch whipping back at her. To his credit, as Booker pushed through the low branches he would hesitate and look back, to make sure he didn't whip her with one of the limbs.

It was a good thing they weren't trying to sneak up on anyone, Tess mused. They were making enough noise as they trudged through the curled brown leaves and small twigs to alert anyone to their presence. At the moment she didn't care. The small murmuring of the stream had grown to a low, purring roar.

Tess could feel the heat seem to dissipate as her eyes caught sight of the beautiful rippled surface of the stream in front of them. She smiled, her eyes fixed on the object of her desire. To hell with Booker. She would toss him aside in a minute just to feel the cold dampness of the water as it drove away the parched dryness of her throat. To feel the caress of the water against her aching and burning feet. At the moment, only heaven could be more enticing.

Tess did not hesitate for a moment. She walked straight to the water's edge and sank to her knees. She cupped her hands to fill them with water and drank the cool liquid, then dipped her hands again for another taste. Booker was kneeling beside her as he repeated her actions.

After she had drunk her fill, she sat back on her bottom and stretched her feet in front of her as she leaned back on her arms. Tilting her head toward the sun, she closed her eyes as a small smile of pleasure relaxed her face.

'We'll take a few moments to rest before we head out again,' Booker said, making a stab at conversation.

'Hmm,' she murmured. The warm caress of the sun as it filtered through the towering trees was relaxing to her tired and aching body. She felt herself sway as a nap beckoned to her. As much as she would have loved to take a quick nap, Tess would feel too guilty to enjoy it.

Opening her eyes, she sat up and started unlacing her hiking boots. She glanced up momentarily, to find Booker watching her with an amused smile. Yeah, she could probably guess what was going through that gorgeous head of his, all right. She twisted her lip in a smirk as she shook her head at him.

She first pulled one boot and sock off, then took a brief moment to massage her foot. She had been right about the burning sensation going away not being good, because the blisters were going to be huge. She started working on the other boot, not relishing what she was going to find on that foot either.

Once both her boots and socks were off, and she had massaged the soles of her feet till she felt as if she could walk reasonably well again, she scooted toward the stream. Tess sucked in her breath as she gingerly put her feet in the icy cold water.

'Damn, that's cold,' she said, as she readjusted her legs till she could roll up her jeans. She smoothed her feet along the slick green rocks on the bottom of the stream till they were submerged to above her ankle.

She sighed with pleasure as the cold drove away the burning ache and replaced it with an invigorating tingle.

Booker moved beside her and Tess found that he too had removed his socks and boots, to soak his feet in the cool water. She smiled with amusement as the large man timidly stuck a toe in to test the temperature. Her smile spread to a grin as he gritted his teeth and plunged his feet in.

'For a moment there I thought you'd had a good idea,' he said between clenched teeth, then quickly yanked his feet back out. He scooted away from the water till he sat on a green spongy bed of grass.

Tess turned to look at him over her shoulder as she laughed. 'It is a good idea. My feet feel better already.'

Booker's brow rose skeptically. 'Mine are now frozen.'

'I can't help it if you're a wimp,' she laughed. The cold of the water was starting to sting at her feet, so she stood up and stepped carefully back onto the bank. She walked to where he had now sprawled out on the grass and sat down beside him.

Tess wrapped her arms around her knees as she listened to the relaxing gurgle of the stream accompanying the soft swish of the trees in the wind. She took a deep breath, filling her lungs with the fresh mountain air, then exhaled, feeling part of the tension leave her body.

Out of the corner of her eye she saw Booker roll to his side beside her. Her gaze fastened on his toes. They were long and slim, with black tufts of hair on his big toes. Tess had never experienced a foot fetish, but for some reason even this man's toes seemed to draw her attention.

Mentally shaking herself, Tess darted her gaze to his face. Her cheeks warmed with embarrassment at the knowing smile on his face. His head rested on his fist as he looked up at her.

'Just can't get enough of me, can you?'

Tess narrowed her eyes at the audacity of the man. 'You are truly a swine, Booker.'

Damn the man for correctly figuring out what was on her mind. She had to force herself to admit it, but, yes, she did enjoy looking at him. But he didn't have to say it out loud, did he?

Booker lifted his free hand to brush a strand of her hair behind her ear. At the warm touch of his fingers against the sensitive skin behind her ear, she jumped. He sat up, then surprised her as he moved to take her foot into his capable hands and began massaging her aching feet. Slowly his skilled hands began working their magic on the tortured arches.

Tess's mouth fell open with a moan of pleasure as she closed her eyes and gave herself up to the pleasure of the massage. His strong fingers stroked and kneaded the pain from her feet, leaving in its wake a shiver of anticipation as other parts of her body became aware of him.

His hands gently lowered one foot, then lifted the other. Only briefly did Tess open her eyes as he switched, then she closed them again as he started on the other foot. Slowly he worked the soreness out. Tess found herself lost in the rhythm of his hands. So much so, it took a moment to realize he had stopped. She opened her eyes to find him studying her. He again moved beside her, his gaze never leaving hers. Fraction by fraction he closed the distance between them till he'd dipped his mouth to meet hers, his arms gently pulling her within his embrace. Tess sighed into his kiss, only slightly aware that their bodies had lowered to the cool blanket of grass beneath them. The heat and strength of his arms encircled her, leaving her breathless with the feel of him.

The heat, the feel, the scent of him enveloped her, wrapping her within the awareness of him. The strong need she had for him was uncustomary for her, and scared her, making her want to get away from him till she could collect her thoughts. Sort things out in her own time as she normally did.

But with Booker nothing seemed normal any more.

Her body melted under the heat of him pressing against the length of her. She licked her lips nervously, before nerves too slipped easily away from her. The tension, the stream, everything slipped from her thoughts, leaving only Ethan Booker. He held her gaze, the gray-blue of his eyes soft as he looked at her. Only her.

Tess bit the inside of her lip as she looked up at him. Something inside her, a small seed of something, opened within her. She pushed it back before it had a chance to grow. She didn't need hope. Hope for something that could never be.

She swallowed as tears threatened, tightening her throat. She couldn't even allow herself a moment to just savor being with Ethan. It would only make things harder on herself.

Her voice caught as she spoke to him. 'This is not a good idea, Ethan.'

'You're right. It's not,' he whispered. His gaze moved over her face in a slow caress. A part of her womanhood she had never allowed to grow started blooming beneath his gaze. He reached to caress her face, his touch reverent as he traced the ridge of her cheek. His lidded gaze focused on her mouth, and for a moment her heart started to pound in anticipation. 'We need to keep going. We still have a lot of ground to cover before the sun goes down.'

Ethan lowered his lips to hers for one last taste and Tess rose to meet his touch. Her eyes drifted closed on a sigh, his touch dispelling her worries. Tess sighed as his lips left hers, never quite leaving her skin as he trailed small nips across her cheek. He nuzzled her throat, caressing her skin with the ridges of his mouth as he touched her. He slid lower, till he caught the erratic beat of her heart in his kiss as his tongue traced the sweet dip of her throat.

Ethan groaned, letting his forehead rest against her skin. 'I need a cold shower.'

'There's always the stream,' she offered, with a giggle.

The shrill ringing of her cellphone jarred her ruthlessly from the dream-pillowed lightness that he had created with her. Her breath caught and her eyes flew to his, to stare dumbfounded into his gaze. She swallowed, the tension and the nerves back in full force. And then some.

His gaze became reluctantly distant as he moved off her to give her room to sit up. Instinctively he knew she would want to deal with this problem with as much presence as she could muster.

Tess rose to stand as she punched the button to answer the phone, then cradled it on her shoulder before she answered.

Though she felt somewhat breathless, she was relieved to hear the normal and professional tone of her voice. 'Reynolds, here.'

'Tess?'

She rubbed her arms, her hands stopping when she heard Janet's voice. She swung around to Booker, her frantic gaze locking with his. 'Janet, are you all right? where are you?'

'I'm fine, Tess.' Janet's voice was strong. Calm. If she hadn't known her, Tess would have thought she was calling to pass the time of day. Her heart pounded, because she *did* know Janet and she could hear her friend's fear threaded in her voice. 'Listen, Tess, they wanted me to call you to give you a message. It's more of a clue, I guess. Kind of like 'I'll give you three guesses' sort of thing. I really can't tell you what it means –'

'What kind of clue?' Tess interrupted, straining to hear anything that might help her. Booker had moved to stand close beside her. Oddly, his presence was not distracting, but comforting as she listened to her friend.

They were obviously both talking on cellphones, and the line became full of static for a moment. Tess frowned, gripping the phone tighter as she fervently willed the line to clear. As if answering her prayer, Janet's voice came back strong, this time a little hurried.

'Listen carefully, Tess. You're supposed to look for something ordinary, but out of the ordinary. It's about an hour away from the cabin. The note says it's due east from it.'

'Out of the ordinary?' Tess shook her head, wishing desperately she could make some sense of the nonsensical directions. 'Janet, I don't understand. What do they mean by "out of the ordinary"?'

'Tess, I don't –'

The line clicked and went dead. Tess pulled the phone from her ear and held it out in front of her for a moment as she simply stared at it. She bit at her lip, and her heart took over her mind at the sound of fear in Janet's voice. Tears burned at the back of her throat, but she refused to give the bastards who had taken Janet the pleasure of making her cry.

Swallowing the turmoil of her emotions was hard, and it was a few minutes before she could trust her voice. She bent her head, letting her hair swing forward to hide her face as she clipped the small phone to her belt. Her gaze fixed on the grass still clinging to her clothes. Guilt and anger speared through her, causing her to grit her teeth.

How could she have allowed herself to do such a stupid thing?

She stepped over to her boots and sat on the ground to put her socks on. Out of the corner of her eye she was thankful to see Booker doing the same thing. He deftly laced his boots with swift tapered fingers. Suddenly Tess found herself meeting his gaze, and she quickly looked away.

In the brief moment that she had met his gaze she had seen the regret held within them. She had also seen the understanding. She swallowed, suddenly feeling nervous. The silence that stretched between them was tense filled with things that perhaps she should say or explain, but did not have the courage to. He understood her anger; that much she had seen in his expression. For whatever reason, it unnerved her. Somehow he had looked past the barriers she had built long ago, which time had reinforced again and again over the years. Somehow he had looked past them and seen a part of her that she very rarely showed anyone.

And he understood.

Her cheeks burned with her unease. She refused to look at him. Afraid to see what his expression would reflect once he had seen that part buried deep within her.

She finished tying her boots and stood. Running a quick hand through her hair, she called to him over her shoulder. 'Are you ready to head out?'

'Yes,' he answered, politely remote.

Tess started heading toward the underbrush to get back on the path they had been following before they had been . . . sidetracked. It took her a moment before the realization broke through her muddled thoughts that Booker was not following her. She stopped and turned quickly back toward him, afraid to find that maybe they had been ambushed.

Relief flooded her quickly when she saw him standing exactly where she had left him, with his arms folded across his chest. Irritation quickly followed in its wake as she turned back to him.

'We don't have time to be pussyfooting around, Booker,' she stated, letting her displeasure fill her voice.

'You're right. We don't,' he agreed easily.

Tess was somewhat taken a back by his ready agreement. She frowned as she looked around them, as if she could find an answer to what was unspoken between them. Her gaze flicked back to him. 'We need to get busy.'

His gaze hardened and he held hers for a long, tension-filled moment. When he finally spoke his voice was low and edgy. 'And that's it?'

Tess shrugged as she let her breath out in exasperation. 'What else is there supposed to be, Booker? Janet's been kidnapped and I have got to find her.'

'You mean "we," don't you? There are two of us here, Tess,' he said. He shifted, balling his hands on his hips, and for the first time Tess could see anger in his expression. So the humorous coroner could get mad, she thought, without amusement. 'We're wasting time by not working together on this.'

'I made this mess,' Tess said through clenched teeth, horrified and angered when her voice caught with the emotion threatening to overtake her. 'And I'll take care of it. I didn't ask you along, at least not after the circumstances changed. This is a whole new game, and I don't have time to waste babysitting you.'

Booker stepped toward her till he was nose to nose with her. 'No, you would rather waste time feeling sorry for yourself than try to find Janet.'

Tess's mouth flew open. 'How dare you? Damn it, Booker, I am thinking of her. We're not playing a game here, though that sicko who has her would like to think he is. He's making me play his game, using his rules, and he's not giving me much time to get it done.'

He lowered his head as he took a deep breath. He tapped a rock in front of him with the toe of his boot, then looked back at her. 'Tess, we both know that we're dealing with a dangerous individual. Look at it this way: if we combine our expertise it will help us to better evaluate the different facets of the investigation. You said it yourself, when you were trying to get me to come here in the first place. Not to mention that the two of us working together can cover more ground than just one person.'

Tess sighed. There was no arguing with his logic; it was too intelligent and reasonable. It was probably what she would have thought, had their positions been reversed and they'd been searching for *his* friend. She looked away as she bit on the inside of her lip and contemplated what he'd said.

She looked at him and found no 'I told you so' expression, but, then again, she guessed she knew him well enough to know that he would never do that. She ran her hand through her hair, then nodded. 'Okay, you're right. What do you suggest we do?'

Booker gave her a devastating grin that made her almost glad that she had conceded his point. 'I think it's time to map out our plan of action, sweetheart.'

Janet shivered as she tried to follow the conversation going on behind her. The room was cool, but not cold by any means. It was the cruel man's voice that filled her veins with the icy rush of fear. There was a subtle difference, something she could not explain, but it was there all the same. Something about the man had changed, maybe hardened. She had only thought him cruel before, but now she realized that there were different levels of cruelty.

After she had made the phone call he had removed her blindfold, yet had kept her under the pool of a light, like in an old spy movie. Her chair faced the wall and her back was kept to them. Had she dared to turn around and try to look at them she still would not have seen anything, because the men remained in the black shadows beyond the reach of the light they were blinding her with. So far she had *not* dared to turn around to look, because she somehow instinctively knew the cruel one would just use it as an excuse. An invitation to do who knew what to hurt her. She remembered the way he had touched her and did not want to provoke him in any way.

Janet knew the cruel one was a sick bastard by the mind games he enjoyed playing with her, and even with the two apes he had left to guard her. He had removed the blindfold only to taunt her. Taunt her with the most basic of human cravings – to become aware of her surroundings. He was toying with her. Making her captivity a game, one which would advance to a new level if she turned her head toward him. If she turned around now, she would be expendable. That much she knew.

Janet drew in a shaky breath. She did not want to become expendable.

She chose not to give him the satisfaction and instead closed her eyes, to pretend that she was still blindfolded, therefore removing the continuing urge to turn around. She took a slow, steadying breath as she fought the shivers of apprehension shimmering through her. She concentrated instead on the conversation of the men behind her.

'I'll be back tomorrow,' the cruel one said. Janet could hear a rustling noise, as if he were packing something into a bag, then she heard him zip it closed. 'If I have any further instructions, I'll call them to you later.'

'Aren't you afraid that chick will walk back in on you?' Janet recognized this man's voice as belonging to the more intelligent of the two apes guarding her. He was the one who had not touched her.

'Our guest has made certain that Miss Reynolds and her companion will be busy for a while.' He chuckled, the lifeless sound of it grating against her nerves like fingernails on a chalkboard and causing goosebumps to rise on Janet's skin.

Janet's heart started to pound. Had she been an unknowing part of setting them up? she wondered.

'Once they find my little surprise,' he went on, as if discussing a favorite baseball game, 'then we'll have a couple of days, two at the max, to find what I need.'

'What are you looking for?' the stupid one of the apes asked.

The silence was thick, pregnant with fear. Though Janet couldn't see a thing, she knew without a doubt that the stupid idiot had realized his mistake once the words had left his mouth. The tension, the silence, stretched for what seemed an eternity. Janet could almost hear the two men's fearful heartbeats beat along with hers.

'Do you really want to know?' the cruel one asked, his voice low and amused, its soft humor filled with menace.

'No . . . no, sir. It's really none of my business,' the big ape sputtered. Janet heard the scrape of a chair, apparently jostled in the quick retreat of the large man. 'Have a good trip. Here, let me take your bag out.'

Janet had to smile. He was obviously just as much in hurry as she was to get rid of the cruel one. Then the smile froze on her face as her mind focused on one all-important question.

What the hell have I done? she berated herself.

The cruel one was obviously planning something for Tess and Booker, and she had been manipulated into setting them up to walk right into it. She swallowed fearfully, biting her lip as she prayed for their safety.

What have I done? she thought.

CHAPTER 10

'Okay. Now, I've not known Janet for all that long, but she seems like a pretty feisty girl, am I right?' Booker asked with a devilish grin.

Tess appreciated his effort to try to raise her spirits. 'Yes, she is that. I've always admired how open and flamboyant she is.'

Booker raised his brow as if to say, *And you're not?* Tess ignored it, and thankfully he let her. 'Good, then she also seems like the kind of woman who would try to get a message to you when she's in trouble. So why don't you tell me exactly what she said, or as best as you can remember.'

She gave him a pointed look. 'As best as I can remember is very good, Dr Booker. She said, and I quote, "It's more of a clue, I guess. Kind of like 'I'll give you three guesses' sort of thing. I really can't tell you what it means."'

He paused, as if waiting for her to say something else. Finally he shrugged his shoulders. 'So what do you think she meant by it?'

'I think she meant she was giving us the message they had given her to tell us,' she said, looking at him strangely.

Booker chuckled as he shook his head. 'Obviously you've never played Clue or Charades, huh?'

Tess ran her hand through her hair. 'Booker, what does this have to do with anything? She called to give us the message. She was probably reading it from a cue card.'

'Do you think she was?' he asked, watching her expression.

She didn't know where he was going with this line of reasoning, but she knew he must be headed somewhere. A man didn't reach his position by playing games. She pushed aside her exasperation and decided to try to follow him. She mulled over what Janet had said in her mind. She frowned at her lack of clues, but conceded he might have a point. 'No, I guess you're right. I don't think she was reading from a cue card.'

'Exactly,' he said, and he snapped his fingers. 'Janet's a pretty smart little cookie. She's going to help you as much as she can so you can help her. She said something about it's kind of like playing three guesses.'

'Okay, and that's supposed to mean . . . ?' Tess asked, trying to urge on his reasoning. She felt as if they were heading on the right track, and that surprisingly Booker just might be the one to get them headed in the correct direction.

'It seems awfully out of the ordinary, considering she's been kidnapped, don't you think?' he asked, then waited for her agreement. 'Three guesses . . . I think she's trying to tell us something, but what?'

'Three streets, three stops, three houses,' Tess offered, then shook her head. It didn't make sense.

She finally shrugged her shoulders. 'I don't know. What do you think it means?'

Booker started pacing. He frowned as that incredible mind of his started to work. Tess could almost lose herself in just watching him think. He was an animated man normally, but when he was pondering a potentially serious problem he became vibrant. She smiled as she watched him pace within the confines of the narrow path between the trees.

'Now, remember the psycho said we wouldn't have to go so far this time? So I think they're somewhere out here. Obviously three trees, three squirrels, or even three holes wouldn't mean much of anything,' he offered quietly. 'No, I think she was trying to tell us something more important.'

Tess nodded absently as she replayed Janet's words again and again in her mind. Then it hit her. Her gaze darted back to him, the swift movement catching his own attention. She smiled brilliantly at him, barely able to control herself from flinging herself in his arms to kiss him. At that thought her smile dimmed a little, and she primly clasped her hands in front of her.

'What?' he asked, turning fully back toward her as he stopped his pacing. 'You've thought of something, Tess. Spill it before I throw you in the stream and make you tell me.'

She gave him a 'yeah, right' look, then shook those playful thoughts away. 'You said you thought they were keeping her close around here because of what the psycho said, right? Well, it makes sense about what you said she *wouldn't* be telling us. I think what she *is* trying to tell us is there are three people holding her.'

She looked at him so expectantly and so hopefully Booker felt like taking her in his arms. Considering what had happened last time, he chose not to. He did allow himself to give in to the urge to clasp her by the shoulders. 'As usual, Sherlock, your deductive reasoning is brilliant.'

Tess felt her cheeks warm under the glow of his praise. She looked away as she smiled. It took her a moment to realize that she was grinning like an overwhelmed little schoolgirl, and she quickly tempered her expression. 'I don't know if that's what she's trying to tell us or not, Booker. It's just a thought.'

'It's a damn fine thought, Tess, and you know it,' he stated. 'It makes perfect sense. But what about the part when she said she didn't know what it means?'

Tess chewed the inside of her lip for a moment as she mulled that thought over. So far he had been right; she could feel that deep within her gut instinct. She put her hands on her hips and stared thoughtfully at the clod and leaf-covered path they had been following. Could the last part of what Janet said about not knowing what it meant relate to the part about the three guesses? Tess met Booker's gaze. 'She said she didn't know what it meant. If it's related to the message, then it means nothing to us. If she meant it to relate to the three guesses, maybe she's telling us she doesn't know where she's being held.'

'That would be a given, wouldn't it?' Booker said. He shook his head after a moment. 'They wouldn't want her to know where she was anyway, and you said you thought she wasn't reading from a card. Why not?'

It took her a moment for her racing thoughts to stop and focus on the question he'd thrown out at the end. She tilted her head as she studied him. 'Why not, what? Why wasn't she reading from a card?'

'Exactly,' he smiled. 'Let's just say she wasn't reading from a card, but she knew there were three people with her. How did she know that? More than likely they're keeping her blindfolded, so that means she would be relying on her ears to decipher what's going on around her.'

Tess picked up where he left off. Her adrenaline started pumping. She touched his arm and she practically started laughing. 'Booker, you are incredible. In fact, you are a genius.'

He raised an eyebrow at her warily. 'Thank you . . . I think.'

'No, I'm serious,' she laughed, taking his hands in hers. 'She said she didn't know what it means because she *is* blindfolded, more than likely. That means she's not seen them and can't identify them, which protects her somewhat from them.'

Booker caressed her knuckles with his thumbs as he held her hands. The relief in her expression changed with that simple touch. His gaze warmed as he continued to look at her. Tess couldn't put her finger on it, but something had shifted. Something had changed. And now the atmosphere was charged with the intensity she always felt when she was close to him.

She looked away, clearing her throat as she casually stepped away from him. She tried to lessen the awareness by turning away and scanning the forest around them. 'Janet said we needed to head due east of the cabin.'

'Yes, she did,' he agreed quietly. Booker moved to stand beside her, but kept his distance from her. He pointed toward another natural path, widening beneath a cluster of trees not too far from them. 'If it's about an hour from the cabin, due east, then we'll need to travel southeast for a while to intercept that area. We've been criss-crossing as we made our circular search so we wouldn't miss anything. Apparently we made our search pattern too wide and missed it. We'll start at that area and expand our search from that point, leaving everything else out.'

Tess nodded. For a coroner, he'd made a good plan. It was logical and concise. Exactly what they needed, considering their time constraints. 'Okay, let's get started. Like you said, we're burning daylight.'

During their hike for the next hour, Tess was thankful that Booker seemed content to keep communication between them to a minimum. As much as she needed the silence to regroup her thoughts, it also gave her active mind way too much time to think about other things.

Like the wide set of his shoulders that her gaze tended to continually drift to as she followed him through the never-ending trees.

Finally he stopped, and Tess took the blessed opportunity to drop her hands to her knees as she leaned forward to pant while closing her eyes. Her lungs ached, her feet hurt, and she'd been fantasizing about a juicy steak for the past twenty minutes till she had almost convinced herself that she could smell it.

She looked up to see Booker peering at something through the trees. 'What is it?'

Her voice sounded hoarse and hollow, even to her own tired ears. If Booker noticed her exhaustion he didn't let on, but simply raised his hand to point at a spot on the next ridge. 'It's the cabin. I was checking to make sure that we are due east of it, as given to us in the message.'

Tess took one final gulp of air and straightened. She stepped beside him to search the hills till she too saw the cabin nestled within the foliage. The cabin didn't appear that far, but the depth of the trees hid the fact that there was a small valley between them and the cabin which would make the hike almost an hour long.

'Okay,' she started, feeling some of her energy returning. Now they were at least getting somewhere. Getting closer to finding Janet. 'Last time we went through this area we traveled together, and obviously missed a lot of things. This time I suggest that we split up. Between the two of us, we could effectively cover more space.'

Booker's gaze had darkened the moment she suggested they should split up. He held up his hand to stop her even as he shook his head. 'We do not split up, Tess. That's too risky. What if they're out here waiting for us?'

She tilted her head as she studied him. She hated to admit that he did have a point. 'You're right. How about we split up, but stay close enough that we can either see each other or be within shouting distance?'

Booker frowned as he considered it. Finally he

blew his breath out in exasperation. 'All right. I guess we don't really have much choice, do we?'

Tess shook her head. 'No, we don't. We didn't make the rules, remember?'

'Remind me to give this guy what he deserves when we finally find him,' Booker muttered, his anger hardening his features.

Tess's brow rose at the ruthlessness she was seeing in his face. 'You'll have to get in line, Booker.'

He gave her a dry look, then lifted his hand to point toward a path that looked as if it might turn and parallel the one they were following. 'I'll follow that path and you can stay on this one. I want us to call to each other every four minutes to check in. If one of us doesn't call or doesn't answer then we need to head to the last place of contact and continue our search from there.'

'Sounds like a plan.' She nodded as she stood on the path, raising her hand to rub at the back of her neck. She peered down the path she would be heading down with a certain amount of fear. She'd be damned if she was going to admit it to him, though.

'Tess,' Booker said quietly, his soft voice pulling her from her thoughts.

'What?' she answered automatically, and turned back toward him. Her eyes widened when she found him standing so close to her. It unnerved her that he had moved beside her without her being aware of it. She frowned as her gaze moved from the eye level position at his chest, which she had focused on, till she reached his face.

He hooked his finger under her chin and held her as he lowered his lips to hers. His kiss was soft, reassuring at first, but it quickly deepened to something more needy. Something filled with a hunger they mutually shared.

Booker pulled back just enough to meet her gaze. His voice was as much a physical caress as the touch of his fingers on her chin. 'Be careful.'

Tess nodded, unable to respond verbally. Not after that brief, shattering kiss. She blinked, then frowned as she nodded again and started to head down the path he had designated for her to take. Whew! Did that man know how to rock her world . . .

Booker eyed the narrowing path before him. All too quickly it was going to end in a nice abundance of poison ivy, something he did not relish walking through. He stopped for a moment as he eyed his options, then decided to take the harder of the two paths. It had more obstacles to get over, but it returned more quickly to the original path that stayed parallel with Tess's.

He glanced at his watch, knowing it was time for her to check in. He smiled when Tess, as punctual as he had come to expect from her, called out to him. What he had not expected was her calling out a variety of different foods. They were keeping their communication to a minimum, so the only words exchanged between them to keep track of each other were progressively becoming more enticing. Booker had only thought he was hungry before, but after Tess's one-word meals he was starting to become absolutely ravenous.

He wondered if voraciousness was grounds for justifiable homicide? If he ever found the psycho who had them running around in circles in the middle of the forest, he might consider it.

The wind picked up around him, the rushing push through the long needles of the pines creating a low roar. Booker kept glancing up till he could see through the treetops, and frowned once he spotted the building clouds of a storm. It wouldn't be too much longer before they would be forced to quit, or risk being caught out in the woods during a storm which might produce deadly lightning.

As the sun dipped lower in the sky, the sounds of the night started waking around him. The symphony of the evening in any other circumstances might have sounded relaxing, perhaps while sitting in the comfort of his own living room and listening to them on a compact disc, but listening to it while being in it? It reminded him too much of childhood camp stories about Big Foot.

The path he had been following had pretty much disappeared, leaving him picking his way through the trees and occasional underbrush. He eased himself through the soft whisper of pine needles as he pushed between the two trees. As he stepped into a small clearing something skittered through the low branches of the bordering trees, and as far as Booker could tell it was about the size of a pot-bellied pig. He didn't get a good look at it, and at the moment didn't really care to have a close encounter to find out what it was.

He would have missed it completely if he hadn't been eyeing the foliage where the small animal had disappeared as he'd walked by.

Not sure what it had been, Booker wanted to keep alert, so he wouldn't be surprised by fangs, teeth or claws. Whatever it might have. If he hadn't been watching for the little critter he would have missed the angular walls of the shelter, cutting barely above the forest floor.

'What the hell is that?' he said softly.

Moving cautiously toward it, he tilted his head as he studied it. '*You're supposed to look for something ordinary, but out of the ordinary,*' he had heard Janet say before she'd been disconnected. An underground shelter was ordinary enough and definitely 'out of the ordinary' located in the middle of nowhere with the closest place being a cabin that was an hour's walk away.

Booker rejected the idea of calling out to Tess. Instead he pulled his own cellphone from his pocket and dialed the number he had taken the liberty of memorizing from the 'numbers' sheet that hung on her refrigerator in her house. He circled cautiously around the small structure as he waited for her to answer.

When he heard her pick up, he stopped. 'Tess, I found something.'

'What is it?' she asked breathlessly. Even now he could hear in the background on the phone that she was moving swiftly toward him.

'It's an underground shelter,' he answered grimly. He had seen too many times what a twisted mind could do to torture those still alive. For Tess's sake, and most of all Janet's, he hoped they found nothing in it.

'What?' she asked. He knew by listening to the phone that she had stopped in her tracks at the unexpected answer. He could almost see the perplexed look on her beautiful face.

'Remember—something ordinary, but out of the ordinary,' he prompted in a low voice.

'I guess that fits the bill,' Tess said on a sigh. He could almost envision her running her hand through the golden auburn of her hair as she frowned. 'Look, don't do anything till I get there to help you.'

'Don't worry, I have no great desire to stumble over any booby traps in an effort to beat you to the glory, sweetheart,' he said, as he scanned the area to try and spot her. Her voice had never been that far from him, so he knew it wouldn't be long before she joined him. 'I agree with you that we should exercise great caution before we open this little surprise package.'

She paused for a moment, and Booker wondered if she had already disconnected. Finally she spoke, her voice tight with emotion. 'Thanks, Booker.'

'Not a problem, sugar,' he assured her in a smooth voice. He knew how much it had taken for her to say those simple words, and he didn't want to make at any harder for her. 'I'll be waiting for you.'

He disconnected, pausing for a moment as he simply looked at the phone. Tess Reynolds might not want to admit it, but she was one hell of a woman.

Replacing his phone on his belt, he started walking a careful circumference around the small shelter. It appeared to be an approximate ten-foot-square structure, made of cement that was buried almost completely underground. The roof of the structure slanted in a gentle slope upward to accommodate a thick steel door. The shelter rested in the middle of a small clearing that had probably been made to house it. The foliage of the underbrush pushed close to the walls, giving him just enough room to walk cautiously around it.

He shook his head again as he thought about the fact that he could so easily have just walked past it without ever seeing it. Truly it was a very clever place to hide such a structure, but for what reason?

Booker heard Tess's approach as she walked through the thin layer of leaves and needles that covered the forest floor. By the look of the thick walls and the steel door, if there was anyone inside, he doubted they would have been able to hear them approach.

Standing with his hands on his hips, he turned to look over his shoulder at her. 'So what do you think?'

She strode to his side, already frowning with concentration. Tess said nothing, only shook her head as she started walking around the structure in a slow inspection for herself. As she moved around the structure she would pause every so often, to bend over and look at something, occasionally to move an item aside with the toe of her boot as she studied the shelter.

'I don't see any little surprises around the edge,' she said, her voice distant and distracted. She stepped past Booker, and methodically went over every inch of the door, running her fingers over seams and testing the hinges.

She finished her inspection and knelt in front of the door. Sitting back, she put her forearm across her knee. 'I don't understand it, Booker. What's this thing doing out here?'

'I don't know,' he answered truthfully as he came up behind her to crouch beside her. 'Although from what you've told me about Gare Harolds, I guess it shouldn't be too much of a surprise.'

'I guess it shouldn't be,' she agreed, as she reached out to run her finger along a hinge as she studied it. 'But it is. I know what a bastard he was, and I still can't think of one thing he would have had this for. He wasn't into guns or drugs, and why would anyone build a hide-away next to their hide-away?'

'With Harolds dead, we will probably never know the answer to that one,' Booker said off-handedly. He turned his head to look at her. 'Do you think you can open it?'

She met his gaze. Booker watched the doubt, the humor, her pride, all flicker briefly across her beautiful face before she smiled her answer to his challenge. 'If I open it, are you going to treat me to a steak?'

'If you can open that damn door, you're on, sweetheart.' He grinned at her as he gave her a mischievous wink.

Booker rose to step out of her way as Tess started to work. The steel door of the shelter was bolted shut with a large hanging clasp lock. She reached into her back pocket to retrieve a small leather wallet and opened it. Booker's eyes had followed her movement, then lingered on her derrière for a moment. He smiled good-naturedly, then reminded himself what he was supposed to be doing.

She pulled two slim picks from the wallet and inserted them into the keyhole at the bottom of the lock. Her face was a study in concentration as she maneuvered the internal works of the lock.

After a few moments of silence he heard a small click, then Tess's self-satisfied chuckle. She turned back to him with a devastating smile. 'Open sesame.'

A rising gust of wind blew a scattering of leaves over them. Booker reached over to Tess's curls and removed a couple of leaves. 'Another storm's headed our way; we'll need to hurry.'

Tess's smile softened. 'You're right. Let's get this over with.'

She removed the clasp lock from the loop and pulled the flap back. She slid the lock back into the loop and briefly met his gaze before she nodded, then turned back to her task. He pulled his flashlight from his belt and flipped it on as Tess slowly pulled the door open. Surprisingly, the heavy door swung open easily and quietly.

He moved in close behind Tess, lifting the beam of the flashlight to shine over her shoulder into the dark opening of the underground shelter. As the light moved through the interior of the shelter he gave a low whistle. 'Damn, wasn't expecting any company, was he?'

The room was sparse. It held what looked like an Army issue bunk bed against one wall, and a large metal trunk that probably held flimsy mattresses and rough wool blankets for the bed. At one end of the cement room the wall was completely covered with wood-planked shelves full of bottled water and canned food of many varieties.

Booker lifted one of the cans, a generic brand of green beans, and turned toward Tess. 'Didn't you say you were hungry?'

She frowned at the can in his hand, her lip curled up in distaste. 'No, thanks. I think I've lost my appetite.'

'Me too,' he said.

Booker turned to study the rest of the room, letting his flashlight move across the other wall. A table with three chairs rested against the wall. On its surface was a kerosene lantern and a couple of small metal boxes that probably contained other supplies as well.

He frowned as the beam flashed on a Polaroid picture. He moved quickly to the table and picked it up, heedless of any fingerprints it might hold. His lips thinned into an angry line.

'Tess,' he called softly, his voice flat and emotionless.

Though he didn't look, he could feel her as she moved to stand beside him. He heard the quick intake of her breath, then saw the shaking of her fingers as she reached to take the photograph from him.

Once again it showed Janet tied to a chair, presumably one of the three sitting around the table. She was blindfolded, the set of her jaw grim and angry. Beside her on the table was a large clock, its electronic face showing the time. Instinctively, Booker looked at his own watch. The clock in the picture showed the time as one o'clock in the early afternoon, and it was now after five.

'They've obviously had plenty of time to move her,' he stated matter-of-factly.

Tess remained silent beside him. She leaned forward to peer at a small object resting on the surface of the table close to where the picture had been.

'What's that?' she asked quietly as she pointed with her finger.

Booker had been so intent on the photograph that he hadn't seen the object lying beside it. It was an hourglass about seven inches tall. The intricate engraved woodwork with gold inlay was richly polished, the smooth glass reflecting the beam of the flashlight. The hourglass was obviously a pricey item, more suited to the luxury of the secluded cabin than the rugged confines of the underground shelter.

Tess muttered an oath as they both watched the movement of the sand in the hourglass. Neither was able to look away. Booker clenched his teeth in anger and his hands instinctively curled into fists as frustration seemed to overwhelm him.

Frustration they both shared as they watched the last few grains of sand trickle through the tiny middle of the hourglass to fall on the peak that had been built in the bottom. Then nothing.

Time had run out.

Janet continued to pretend she was asleep and slowly let her head fall forward. As her hair swung forward, she turned her head ever so slightly to scan her surroundings through the filtering curtain of her hair.

Damn it. Wouldn't you know she'd been blessed with thick hair, and it was making it very hard for her to observe her surroundings.

A little while after the cruel one had left, the two men had taken her picture again. They had then shuffled her outside down a trail, while still keeping her blindfolded. It had been not only terrifying to walk the path without being able to see, but extremely difficult. She had kept stumbling till she finally fell. With her hands tied behind her back she had been unable to protect herself from the fall, and had landed on her face, scratching the side of her cheek against the rough texture of the forest floor.

The ape who had been so severely reprimanded by the cruel one for trying to touch her had apparently taken pity on her and picked her up to carry her over his shoulder. Janet had gritted her teeth at the thought of the man touching her. Her head had swayed from side to side as he'd continued in his long gait down the path. With her arms still tied behind her, she'd been unable to do anything more than just hang over his shoulder.

Too bad she didn't suffer from motion sickness, she'd thought dryly. It would have served the ape right if she'd vomited all over his backside.

The man was muscled, that much she had been able to feel pressed against her legs and stomach in her precarious position. Still, he had occasionally grunted with the effort of having to carry her extra weight as he'd traversed the obstacles of the path they were following. For the first time in her life she'd been glad that she had gained those five pesky little extra pounds. The thought had caused her to chuckle.

'Damn it, Joe, she's laughing,' he'd whined to the guy in front of them.

'So?' he answered tersely. 'Is there a law against her laughing?'

'Well, no,' he said. His deep voice sounded offended. 'It's just that she's laughing at me. I know she is.'

'Shut up, Barney. We still have a long way to go and I don't want to listen to your whining,' the guy said on an exasperated sigh.

'Barney?' Janet couldn't help but shrill his name. How incredibly fitting, she thought, and the more she thought about it, the more she found it hilarious. At first she tried to quell her reaction, afraid of what the big ape would do to her, but soon she could no longer hold it. Janet started laughing, deep, belly-crunching laughter. She laughed so hard she almost choked from the effort because of her upside down position.

'Aw, damn it, Joe,' the ape whined, even louder. He had to, Janet was laughing so hard he could barely hear himself. 'Now look what you did.'

Janet bit her lip as she tried to quiet her laughter. She was finally able to quiet herself to snickering, with an occasional loud chuckle.

'I said, shut up, Barney.'

That did it. Janet broke out into laughter again. The hilarity of it was just too much for her warped sense of humor. This time she wasn't alone, as Joe laughed with her, their combined humor filling the open area around them.

'Barney' suddenly picked up his pace, and the movement stilled her momentarily. He effortlessly hoisted her off his shoulder, and for a brief, terror-filled moment she wondered if he was going to throw her on the ground. Or, worse yet, off a cliff.

Janet almost sighed with relief when she felt Joe's arms catch her form. Barney had thrown her off onto her new-found partner in a stand-up comedy routine.

'Fine, you carry her, then,' Barney pouted. With a huff, he stomped off ahead of them.

Joe continued chuckling under his breath as he spoke to her, 'I think you made him mad.'

Janet had decided at the time it would be more prudent not to say anything. The smaller, more compact Joe had carried her the rest of the long walk without grunting even once. After depositing her somewhat gently in the back seat of a vehicle, he had driven for a long time. Without being able to see anything, she had lost her perception of time, so she was unable to determine just how long they had been on the road.

Now, at their new location, Janet had once again been allowed to remove the blindfold. They were in a house, that much she could tell. She could hear the faint rumble of thunder in the distance. A storm. Tilting her head slightly, she could see the lengthening shadow of a lamp as the sun began to set.

Since the cruel one had left, and in her new-found friendship with Joe, Janet had been as cooperative as possible with the two men holding her. Since they'd been 'nice' enough to let her remove the blindfold, maybe their generosity would include her being allowed to sleep without her hands being tied. Or, at the very least, without them being tied behind her back.

She smiled at the possibilities, then stopped when she caught the movement of one of the two men walking toward her. Quickly Janet closed her eyes and allowed herself to look relaxed. Taking a quick peek, she could tell it was Joe walking to stand beside her.

He shook her shoulder gently, though his voice retained its normal gruff tone. 'Wake up, doll. It's time to go to bed.'

Instinctively her head snapped up, and her eyes widened in fear as she looked at him, seeing his face for the first time. Joe returned her look with a pointed one of his own. 'To sleep, little girl.'

Joe took her arm to help her stand and led her to a bedroom. It was a dingy little house, more suited for big, burly hunters to stay on weekend excursions than to live in on a regular basis.

He stopped at a door and swung it open, waving his hand for her to enter. Janet let her gaze roam around the sparse room. There was an old bed that had seen better days against one wall, covered with a threadbare comforter. The rest of the room sported a window, with the thick, shapeless curtains closed, and an old rickety chair. Nothing more.

'In case you're wondering,' Joe started, his rough voice breaking into her thoughts, 'the window has been nailed and painted shut. Not to mention it's double-paned. It would make a lot of noise if someone tried to break it.'

'What would make you think I was curious about that?' Janet said off-handedly.

Joe chuckled good-naturedly at her quip. Janet let her breath out in frustration at this little bombshell of news. So much for that idea. She started when she felt a tug on the ropes binding her wrists together.

'Kind of jumpy, aren't you?' he asked softly behind her. 'Don't worry, I just thought you might sleep better with your hands untied.'

'Thank you, Joe,' she said sincerely.

Before she could turn back toward him, she heard the door close behind her. There was the soft click of a lock on the outside, then nothing.

Her heart felt heavy as she realized just how alone she truly was.

CHAPTER 11

The man Janet had named the cruel one opened the remote cabin's door with a key. He knew his hired gun Joe wondered why he just didn't take out the woman and the man causing them so much trouble and simply get it over with. There was only one reason why he didn't.

If he killed her first, without finding out where she had put the item he needed, then he could be endangering himself even further.

He had already been in the cabin once to move the map. He grinned at the memory of that. He knew that the almost insignificant act would serve to continue to rattle Tess Reynolds' thoughts. He had learned a long time ago that the best way to stay one step ahead of your competition was to keep them unsettled. Kidnapping Reynolds' pretty friend, moving small items, the notes, the pictures; he had thoroughly planned everything to shake Tess Reynolds' world. Eventually he would be able to work through that meticulous methodical mind of hers till she slipped. That one slip would allow him to figure out where the damning piece of evidence was.

Insignificant as it was, that one piece of information could destroy everything for him. Years of planning and months of effort would be shot, and he would either be dead or facing a minimum sentence of life in prison.

That was not a risk he was willing to take.

The afternoon sun was slipping into the horizon, causing the shadows to lengthen in the room. He pulled out a small penlight and turned it on. There was still enough light to see, but not enough to search effectively for what he was looking for.

He moved quietly through the front room and headed straight to the stairs. He would start with her room first. He stepped quickly up the stairs, ducking his head to dart a short glance out the window, checking for their return. He eased down the hallway and entered the room Tess Reynolds had chosen to stay in.

Going through the drawers one by one, he sifted through the contents. He smiled to himself when he opened the drawer containing her undergarments and sleepwear. Having followed the conservative Quintessa for a couple of months now, he was not surprised by the flannel nightshirt that had to reach well past her knees. He was surprised, however, by the satin thong panties in the drawer. He would never have figured the Reynolds woman as anything more than a prude.

Obviously there was more to Tess Reynolds than met the eye.

Finding nothing in the drawer, he closed it and turned to scan the room. He'd already been through her duffel bag the last time, but he inspected it again anyway. Just in case.

Nothing.

He stood for a moment with his hands on his hips as he looked at the bag. Where would she have put it? he wondered. Had she even brought it with her? Glancing around the room he had searched extensively, he now doubted that she had. Tess Reynolds was a cautious individual. She had probably secured it before she left.

'Well, Miss Reynolds,' he said out loud in the empty room, enjoying the sound of his voice ringing in the silence. 'You're going to get a brief reprieve.'

Striding from the room, he pulled his cellular phone out of his pocket and punched the number in quickly. His man answered after the first ring, as he had expected him to.

'Keep an eye on our guest; we may still need her,' he said into the phone. 'I'm headed back to town to check on a few things. I want one of you to come back to the cabin and keep an eye on what they're doing. I'll be back tomorrow morning. Late.'

Disconnecting the line, he walked boldly out the front door. Not bothering to lock or even shut it, he stepped quickly down the front steps. He started the hike toward his vehicle to make the drive to the private airstrip where a plane was waiting for him.

He strode down the path, his brow furrowed in a frown as he mulled things over in his mind. Damn it, he thought. What had she done with it?

'The note said we had forty-eight hours,' Tess fumed as she snatched up the ornate hourglass. 'Why is the damn thing running out now?'

Booker knew she did not expect an answer. He gently retrieved the hourglass from her before she threw it and shattered it against the wall. 'I don't think it matters, Tess. This nutcase is messing with us. Nothing more than that.'

She put her hands on her hips, frowning as she contemplated what he'd said. Finally she let her breath out on a sigh as she nodded. 'You're right. He's just trying to pull the strings tighter and tighter on us, isn't he?'

He stepped in front of her, put his hands on her shoulders and began kneading the tension he found knotted below his fingers. 'That's exactly what I think. He may or may not be coming back here to check to see if we found anything during the allotted time, but I don't really think that's the point, do you?'

Tess murmured her agreement, closing her eyes as he massaged her shoulders. For a moment she allowed herself to relax under his touch. To feel the warmth of his skin against hers penetrate and release the tension that was tightening around her.

Booker watched her expression visibly relax as he moved his hands over her shoulders to the creamy softness of her neck. Instinctively she let her head fall forward to give him access to the back of her neck. Her body gently swayed with the massaging movements of his hands, slowly rocking toward him. She was close enough that he could smell the hint of her perfume. Close enough that he could feel the heat of her through the fabric of his shirt.

Booker cleared his throat and released her suddenly as he stepped back from her. He turned to retrieve a few items, to give himself time to calm the reaction she seemed to evoke in him all too easily.

Tess's eyes fluttered open and she blinked as she pulled herself back into awareness of her surroundings. Frowning, she too began to concentrate her efforts on getting ready to leave the underground shelter.

What had she been doing? she berated herself. The man only had to touch her and she melted like butter, she continued. Damn that man. He could drive her to distraction with only a look from those sexy boy-next-door eyes that could charm . . . well, probably charm more than just her socks off if she wasn't careful.

Booker strode to the door without a backward glance in her direction. 'We better hit it hard if we want to make it back to the cabin before dark.'

Her mouth fell open slightly, before she remembered to shut it. Then again, maybe she didn't have to worry about it so much.

The hike back to the cabin didn't take long, but they still had to walk the last stretch of it in the fading light. The tall trees shadowing the path made the trail dark. Once again, Tess found herself picking up her pace to keep up with Booker's broad back. Badger liked to play games way too much to plan something for them on their way back, but still . . . Something about walking through the forest in the dark brought back childhood memories of bears. And Big Foot.

Tess shrugged that thought off, refusing to let her mind wander in that direction. In her mind she began to make a list of what she needed to do once they got back to the cabin. She was relieved more than she cared to admit when she saw it appearing through the foliage ahead of them. At that moment, nothing looked safer to her.

Her smile widened as they walked around a bend in the path to break into the clearing that the house sat in. Her smile faded as she noticed the front door of the cabin.

'Booker?' She called quietly to the man who had not said a word to her since he had touched her in the shelter.

'What?' he asked, without looking back at her.

'The front door of the cabin is standing wide open,' she said.

Booker stopped in his tracks. His sudden halt almost caused her to bump into his wide back. 'We locked it when we left.'

'Yes, we did,' she answered, though she knew he had not been asking her a question.

They both pulled their guns out and cocked them. Carefully they wound their way around the house to ease up the front steps. Booker led the way and they sprinted quickly across the expanse of the front porch to settle at each side of the door. They both pressed themselves against the wall. Tess tilted her head to listen, then shook her head when she heard nothing coming from inside the house.

She pointed for him to back her up, then slipped quickly in the door before he could argue with her. Booker tightened his lips as he muttered a few oaths under his breath. He pushed through the narrow opening of the door and slid along the foyer wall as he stayed behind Tess.

Methodically they moved from room to room of the first floor as they searched for the intruder. This time

Booker beat her to the staircase and headed silently up the stairs, forcing Tess to follow him as they worked to secure the second floor.

Coming out of the last bedroom, Booker relaxed his stance as he walked back to Tess's room. He spoke quietly, not so much for fear of someone overhearing them, but in concern. 'Whoever it was, he's gone.'

Tess nodded as she stood in the middle of her room, looking at the contents of her duffel bag strewn about. 'I think we both know who it was.'

'Yeah,' he said. He uncocked his gun and placed it back in the holster. 'We'll go back through and check all the locks, though we have to assume now that he must have a key, since there was no sign of a forced entry.'

'I agree, but this time we'll set up a few surprises for him,' she added, with a wicked gleam in her eye as she smiled. 'Then we won't have to worry about his sneaking up on us while we're sleeping tonight.'

Booker arched an eyebrow at her expression. 'Remind me never to make you mad.'

Quickly they re-checked the windows and the doors, finding them as they had left them. It seemed only the front door had been opened. After securing the locks, they began to brainstorm ways of protecting the first floor. Doors were easy, as they moved pieces of heavy furniture in front of them. Windows were a little more difficult. Tess giggled at some of Booker's more elaborate suggestions, but had to admit he had a devious mind when it came to plotting. They finally settled on breaking lightbulbs in a towel, then shaking the sharp fragments below each window. The shards wouldn't stop an intruder, especially if he was wearing shoes, but at least they would hear the crunching of the glass if anyone came in.

Tess stood back to admire their handiwork. 'It's a good thing we aren't planning on leaving this evening. It will be impossible to get in the cabin, let alone try to get out.'

Booker chuckled. 'It will at least give us time to work on sorting a few things out tonight. Come help me scope the kitchen out to see if we can find something to eat. I'm starving.'

' "Starving" doesn't even begin to describe what I want,' Tess sighed as she followed him toward the kitchen.

She had been tiredly looking at the floor as she walked, and had missed Booker stopping in front of her. She bounced off his chest and he steadied her, his hands settling easily on her hips.

Tess looked up at him. 'What are you doing?'

His gaze moved up. Those soft, vulnerable eyes met his. His lips lifted in a small smile that reached to his own eyes. 'Maybe you would like to describe what you want. Maybe I can help you have it, Quintessa,' he said softly, as he tilted his head and his gaze slid like a slow caress to settle on her lips.

She swallowed, her mouth drying as she watched him, unable to look away. Unable to make a smart retort. Unable to deny him anything.

Her gaze never left the curve of his lips as he slowly lowered his mouth to hers. Tess closed her eyes on a sigh as she slid her arms around his neck, the movement natural to her. Like coming home, she thought.

He caressed her lips with the tip of his tongue before he explored the velvet contours of her mouth. Tess opened herself up to him as she pressed her body against his. Ethan's hand slid heatedly up her spine till he found the soft curls of her hair. He kissed her till she thought she would lose herself in the taste of him. Lose herself in the feel of his hard body solidly pressed against her own.

Ethan feathered kisses across her cheek till he found her ear. Tess moaned softly as he nibbled on her earlobe, then moved to the sensitive flesh just under her ear on her neck. He leaned over her as he caressed her throat with his lips, his tongue. His hand brushed across her breast, the heat of his palm moving slowly across her nipples, sending shivers through her till her body responded.

Tess's stomach chose to protest at that moment, grumbling loudly enough to disturb them. Ethan ceased his heated caress and chuckled against her throat. 'I think we're being told something.'

Tess placed a kiss against Booker's cheek as she laughed with him. 'Like maybe you need to feed me?'

'Don't worry, sweetheart,' he said with a grin as he put his arms around her waist and pulled her to him. 'I plan on feeding you, all right. You're going to need your strength.'

Tess's brows rose and her cheeks warmed at his provocative statement. She said nothing, merely allowed him to take her hand and guide her to the kitchen. They made an unspoken agreement not to discuss the investigation into Harolds' murder or the kidnapping of Janet as they began pulling things from the refrigerator and pantry for their dinner. Tess knew within her heart that the psycho Badger would not hurt Janet, only use her as a pawn in his twisted little game. For some reason he was giving them a brief reprieve, and then the game would start yet again. Probably with renewed vigor.

Tonight she would take that reprieve. Take the brief time to let her mind relax, and her body. She knew without a doubt that once the sun came up in the morning she would probably need both, especially if Badger decided to give them another riddle to solve.

Tonight she would enjoy just being with Ethan. Tess smiled to herself, and she stole a glance in his direction as he worked at the stove. It seemed like ages since she had walked into his office wearing that ridiculous red wig, though in reality it wasn't that long ago at all. Somehow during that short span of time he had gone from being 'Booker' in her mind to something more.

To being Ethan.

A man with a job that dealt with the darker side of humanity day in and day out. Though he investigated death on a chrome table, he vibrated with an energy she envied. His wicked sense of humor, his sensitivity to others. His willingness to just listen.

He turned at that moment to meet her gaze, a knowing smile growing on his lips. Tess looked at her hands where they had stilled as she had been caught simply staring at him. Ethan said nothing, only leaned over and kissed her softly on the lips, then the tip of her nose before he returned to his task at hand.

Still she continued to sit and watch him. She gave up the pretense of acting busy and simply watched him. Tess bit softly at her lip as she watched the movement of his sinewy muscles under his T-shirt. What would it be like to be with him? she wondered. Her body reacted immediately to the thought and Tess knew without a doubt that Ethan would be a wonderful, sensitive and considerate lover.

Still . . .

It was one thing to make love to a man . . . Tess was not a virgin, hadn't been for many years, but she had never been one for easy romance. Her lovers had been men she had cared very strongly about. Had thought she loved. Men she had thought about spending her life with. Fortunately, in both cases, they had realized the limitations of their relationship before they had taken that final step.

They had wanted her to change.

Tess looked away from Ethan, tears welling in her eyes as she remembered. She forced them away, swallowing the burning urge as it lodged in her throat. They had said they were proud of her accomplishments, but she was too independent. Every compliment she had ever received by either of her two suitors had usually been followed by a 'but.' Finally she had got to the point where she no longer believed the compliments, just skipped that part, then waited for the 'but'.

Her two fiancés, though they never really had got that far, had been up-and-coming professionals. Men who'd needed a traditional wife to fit their idea of a traditional world. Looking again at Booker, Tess knew he did not work at a traditional career, but he was still a professional.

With that little Porsche sitting in his garage, she doubted he was looking for a wife anyway.

Tess started at that thought. Damn. Where had that come from?

Tess sighed as she resumed her task of tearing lettuce to add to the salad fixings they had brought with them to the cabin. Ethan finished the ham and cheese sandwiches he had been grilling. He pulled two plates from the cabinet and transferred the sandwiches into them with his spatula.

He turned back toward her. 'Are you finished, sweetheart?'

Tess gave him a small smile. 'Almost. Would you please get the salad dressing for me? I put it in the refrigerator.'

Booker nodded as he headed to the refrigerator and retrieved the salad dressing. He brought it over to the counter and opened the bottle. Quickly they finished the preparations and took their sandwiches and salads to the dining room table.

Tess speared a leaf of lettuce with her fork. Lifting it to her mouth, she took a bite. She looked at Booker out of the corner of her eye as she ate. Did she really know him? she thought to herself. She knew his wild sense of humor, his sensitive touch, but what about *him*? His favorite color? His favorite band? His favorite movie? What about his family? she thought.

Then a thought struck her that stopped her mid-chew. What about the picture of that beautiful woman that held center-stage on his fireplace mantel?

She finished her bite. She toyed with her salad as she glanced occasionally at Booker.

As if sensing her gaze, Booker put his sandwich down. 'What is it, Tess?'

'Nothing. Really,' she said, returning her attention to her food. She picked her sandwich up and quickly took a bite before he could ask her another question.

Booker watched her, his expression showing he didn't believe her. He too picked up his sandwich and began eating. They ate in silence as Tess continued to think about the picture of the woman. She had not thought about the woman once since that time she'd first seen it, but now she couldn't seem to get her out of her mind. Tess finished her meal, though her appetite had diminished considerably since the woman had invaded her thoughts.

Finishing his meal as well, Booker took a sip of his drink as he studied Tess. Setting the glass down, he looked at her. For a moment she thought he was going to prod her again about what was on her mind. Instead he surprised her, by taking their dishes and heading toward the kitchen.

'I'll take care of these,' he said over his shoulder.

Tess sat for a moment, at a loss for anything to say or think. She looked around the room as if it would give her an idea what to do next. Her gaze fell on the fireplace and she smiled. She would build a fire.

A fire was relaxing, she reminded herself. Conducive to not talking, and it would give her something to look at besides hungrily staring at Booker. She pushed back from her chair and moved to the fireplace. Opening the glass doors, she retrieved a trio of good-sized logs and stacked them on the raised grate. Wadding a section of newspaper, she placed it under the grate and lit a match to light the paper. A small finger of yellow curled at the paper's edge, then spread. Tess continued feeding strips of paper to the hungry licking of the fire as it worked on the logs above. Finally a piece of the bark on one of the logs flickered with the flame and began to glow red with the building heat.

Tess sat on the floor with her arm across her knee as she occasionally fed paper to the fire till it had established itself thoroughly with the logs. It grew steadily, and she leaned back to simply watch it.

She took a deep breath and released it on a sigh as she watched the fire. Something about a flickering fire was relaxing, almost hypnotic.

Tess didn't even jump when Booker's voice broke into her thoughts. 'You're pretty good at that, sweetheart.'

She smiled, looking up at him as he stood over her. 'I didn't hear you come in the room.'

'Just call me the Thief of Hearts,' he said smoothly, as he lowered himself to the rug beside her.

Tess gave him a dry look. 'You can forget this heart if you know what's good for you, buster.'

'Oh, I know what's good for me, sugar,' he assured her easily. He studied her with those mischievous sexy eyes and suddenly she realized the fire probably wasn't such a good idea after all.

A fire was romantic. Conducive to touching and caressing. To removing each other's clothes and . . . Tess closed her eyes. For her own good she had to force those thoughts out of her mind. *Now*, she ordered herself.

He pulled one of the end-tables closer to them and placed the two glasses he had brought on top of it. Reaching behind him, he produced with a flourish a container holding a bottle of wine nestled in a bed of ice. 'I want wine with my fire.'

Tess laughed at him. 'Are you ever serious?'

Booker raised a brow as he stopped opening the bottle of wine. He shook his finger at her in warning. 'Remember what happened the last time you said that.'

The problem was Tess could remember it all too well. So well, in fact, that she almost craved the feel of his lips against her own again. She shook those thoughts away. Remember the picture of the gorgeous woman, she reminded herself.

Booker broke into her thoughts by taking her hand and pulling her back till they were both on the thick pile of a rug. She peered below thinking they were resting on a poor little lambskin rug, then breathed a sigh of relief when she realized it was a reproduction and not the real thing.

He had piled the pillows from the couch into a backrest for them, so they could recline in front of the fire. The end-table was beside him, so he could easily fill their glasses with the clear amber liquid. He topped their glasses and handed one to her.

Tess accepted it, then took a small sip. She sighed her appreciation. The wine was a wonderful blend of sweet fruit with a touch of a tangy kick. 'This is nice.'

She closed her eyes, letting the warmth of the wine slip through her to relax her mind as the heat of the fire worked to relax her body. She nestled into the softness of the pillows. Booker touched his knuckle to her cheek, sliding it slowly across her skin in a soft caress. Tess opened her eyes and met his gaze.

He smiled at her. 'I think this is even better.'

She blinked, choosing to say nothing. They both took a drink of their wine. She averted her gaze, instead watching the reflection of the fire within the glass of amber liquid.

'Tess,' he said softly, 'what is it? Something is bothering you, I can tell.'

Tess shook her head as she sipped lightly at her drink. 'Nothing's wrong. Really.'

'Are you afraid of me?' he asked easily.

Tess gave an inelegant snort without even thinking about it. 'I don't think so.'

'Then what is it?' Booker prodded.

She eyed him speculatively for a moment. As if he would really answer her if she asked him, she thought. She shook her head. 'I've just got a lot of things on my mind, that's all.'

'Like what?' he continued.

Tess could see that he was not going to let up on her. She was not about to tell him what was really on her mind. Instead she chose to focus her thoughts, and his, on something else. 'So where did you get your ugly cat?'

Booker laughed out loud. 'I can't believe you are slandering my cat.'

Tess shrugged. 'Hey, you asked.'

Putting his glass on the table, he scooted till he sat next to her. Tess had snuggled down in the pillows till she was almost flat on her back. He stretched out beside her. Lazily he began tracing the contours of her hands as she held the glass of wine.

'I doubt you were wondering about the origins or pedigree of my cat, sweetheart,' he told her with a knowing smile. 'Now, tell the good doctor what's really bothering you.'

Tess giggled at the last part as the wine started to warm her. 'I've already told you that nothing is wrong. Doctor,' she added teasingly.

'Then perhaps you're not feeling well, and you need to be examined,' he said, his hand slipping beneath the sleeve of her shirt to touch the soft skin on the inside of her wrist.

Laughing, she pushed his hand away. 'I don't think so. You're worse than a sixteen-year-old boy.'

'So that's it. I'm too old for you,' Booker said with mock horror.

Tess gave him a dry look. 'I'm just not your style.'

'And what is my style, sugar?' he asked, as he took the opportunity to slide his fingers back under her shirtsleeve and began caressing the smooth skin yet again.

Tess leaned back in the pillows and studied the flames of the fire. 'Your style is drop-dead gorgeous. Like that woman in the picture you have on your fireplace mantel.'

Tess heard the words, then immediately wished she could suck them back into her mouth. Damn it, she hadn't intended saying that. She looked accusingly at the glass of wine she held in her hand and saw that she had indeed drunk it empty. She kept her gaze focused on the dancing flames of the fire, not wanting to see the look on his face at all because of her inappropriate statement.

The circular caressing movements of his fingers stopped. Unwillingly she looked in his direction to find him with his brows furrowed in a frown, his thoughts obviously elsewhere.

'Picture on my mantel?' he finally said quietly. He turned to look at her as he shook his head. 'What picture?'

The warm fuzzy feelings the fire and the wine had created congealed within her. Anger quickly replaced it. He's one of those creeps who's actually going to try to deny the woman's picture, even though he knows I saw it with my own two eyes. She pushed his hand away from her as she sat up. 'Booker, don't even try to give me the line that you don't know what I'm talking about. I saw the picture myself. She's a very beautiful woman.'

He continued to frown. 'What did this picture look like?'

Tess felt like growling at the man. 'It's in a silver frame – a dark-haired woman with gorgeous eyes.'

'Oh,' Booker said with sudden comprehension. He grinned as he began to chuckle. '*That* picture of a beautiful woman. Now we get to the heart of the matter.'

'Yeah, that picture,' Tess said as she narrowed her eyes at him and crossed her arms over her chest. 'How could you forget?'

'Well, it's because when you said "beautiful woman,"' he explained easily as he took her spot against the pillows and retrieved his glass of wine, 'I didn't think of her.'

She blinked in disbelief. 'Didn't think of her? How could you not think of her, Booker? Her picture is prominently displayed on your fireplace mantel. Not to mention the fact that she's drop-dead gorgeous. How could you not think of her?'

He shrugged, then took a sip of his wine. 'I wouldn't exactly call her drop-dead gorgeous myself.'

'I'm sorry,' she snapped, uncrossing her arms to turn back toward him. 'What exactly *would* you call her?'

Booker smiled into his wine as he chuckled softly. 'I'd call her my sister.'

'Oh,' she said. Stunned into silence, she simply stared at him for a few moments. She could hear the fire crackling behind her as her cheeks grew warm with the comprehension of her embarrassment.

'Oh,' she repeated, apparently not able to say anything more.

Where was a big rock to crawl under when you needed one?

CHAPTER 12

'Your sister?' Tess repeated.

She didn't know what to say exactly, if anything. His sister? Now that he said it, there were striking similarities between the two. The woman's eyes were blue, though not as vivid as her brother's. They both had the same dark wavy hair. Picturing the woman's image in her mind, Tess realized that they both had the same mischievously sexy look about them. His sister?

'Yes, my little sister.' Booker continued to grin at the humorous situation. 'Her name is Elisa.'

'Oh,' she said. When she realized she was repeating herself again, she frowned. Rolling her shoulder to ease her tension, she flicked a glance at him to see how he was reacting. She hoped he wouldn't continue to be amused. She tried to smooth over and past her *faux pas* with chit-chat. 'She's very beautiful,' she offered lamely.

'You mentioned that,' he said, his lips lifting up at the corners as he watched her.

Okay, so he was going to continue enjoying this. Tess stared down at her hands. She truly wished she could simply disappear. Instead she took a deep breath to fortify her courage. 'Yes, I did, and I meant it, Booker.'

'Well, I think models are supposed to be drop-dead gorgeous,' he said softly as he took a sip of his wine. He lifted his gaze and suddenly he was once again studying her. 'Now you know where the Porsche came from.'

'Really?' Tess asked. It finally soaked in what he was saying and she raised an eyebrow. 'Your sister gave you the Porsche?'

He nodded as he murmured his agreement. He tilted his head, his heavy-lidded gaze moving lightly over her face. 'Remember I told you a relative had given it to me as a present? Well, it was Elisa. She's been very fortunate in her career, and she said she wanted to do something nice for her big brother. Something about making up for my date ditching me at my senior prom.'

'What?' She laughed, snuggling contentedly into their conversation. 'How did she do that?'

'She jokingly walked up to me at the prom and put her arms around me, then kissed me on the cheek.' Booker chuckled at the simplistic memory, though at the time it had been catastrophic. 'My date went wild, didn't believe a word I said about her being my sister, then stormed off with the captain of the football team. In fact, last I heard, they have three children now.'

At the kids part Tess raised her eyebrows. 'Good thing you got out of it when you did, huh?'

Booker shrugged, his gaze locked on hers, hot and unwavering, then just as quickly he focused back on his drink. He reminded Tess of a shy boy talking to the teacher he desperately had a crush on. 'Maybe. Maybe not. Depends on how you look at it.'

Tess looked away, staring at her clenched hands for a moment. She really had underestimated him, and had jumped to conclusions about the woman without really knowing what the whole story truly was. It was not in her personality to do such things, and the fact that she had disturbed her more than she cared to admit. What was it about this man that made her react so differently? His mere presence in her life had unsettled the security and routine of her day-to-day activities. She was not used to reacting in such a way.

She licked her lips nervously, then cleared her throat as she spoke softly. 'I jumped to conclusions, Booker, and I'm sorry. It's really none of my business to begin with.'

He lifted his gaze to her. She could feel it, though she didn't know if she had the courage to meet it. At least not after making a number one ass out of herself. He said nothing, forcing her to meet his gaze.

He held his hand out to her, waiting for her to take it before he spoke. His voice was soft, velvet, barely above a whisper. 'I kinda like having you jump to conclusions, Quintessa.'

He pulled her toward him and she followed easily. He brought her to rest beside him on the pillows. He situated her in his arms, wrapping them around her to cuddle her to his side. Tess snuggled against the warmth of his chest and breathed in the male scent of him. His aftershave was long gone, but she could still smell the outdoors on him as it mingled with the fragrance of the fire, wrapping its warmth around them like a blanket.

Having him beside her with his arms around her felt natural. Established. As if sitting in front of the roaring fire wrapped in each other's arms was something they did every night. Tess gave in to the urge to nuzzle her cheek against the ridges of his chest, reveling in the feel of the solid strength of him beneath his shirt. Her hand was curled on his chest and she relaxed her grip, stretching out her fingers till she could feel him pressed against the length of her hands.

His hand lifted to caress the long curls of her hair, the stroke of his touch sending warm shivers through her.

Booker shifted beside her, his movement rolling Tess to her back, with him lying beside her, looking over her. He lifted his hand to touch her cheek. He skimmed his finger across the ridge of her cheek as his hooded gaze held hers. Tess simply returned his look, unable to tear herself away. She felt beautiful as he continued to study her. With the shadows of the fire flickering across his handsome features and his heavy-lidded sexy gaze smoldering with his passion as he touched her, every part of her felt vibrantly like a woman. His woman.

'Make love to me, Ethan,' she whispered, reaching to stroke his dark-stubbled chin. It was a request she had never made before. It was not one she made lightly. She didn't allow herself to think of tomorrow, or the day after that. She didn't want to think of what expectations might be made by this one night spent with him. Her heart ached, mourning the loss of him before she'd even had him, but one night would be all that they would ever have together. All that they ever *could* have together.

He tilted his head, his eyes never leaving hers as he placed a kiss on the palm of her hand. 'You've never called me by my first name before.'

Pushing her reservations and doubts away, she relaxed and simply enjoyed being with him. She smiled lazily as her fingers continued to play across the strong ridges of his face. 'You have a wonderful name, I love it.'

His smile lifted as it reached his eyes. 'As long as it pleases you, that's all that matters.'

Ethan held her cheek as he slowly lowered his lips to hers. He touched her, a soft, feathery touch that was filled with adoration and awe as his eyes remained open, watching her. Tess returned his gaze, lifting herself to meet his kiss. He slid his lips in a slow caress over the curves of her lower lip and she sighed with the sensual pleasure. His lips never left hers as his hand moved down her body with deliberate slowness to circle her waist.

Ethan deepened his kiss as he pulled her against his body. He pressed her to him as if he wanted to envelop her within his skin. Tess sighed into his kiss, her hands sliding into his hair as she opened herself to him.

His touch was a slow stroke as he smoothed his hand over her hips to cup her bottom and press her to him. Tess felt the hunger within her spark, then grow as she arched against him, her need matching his own.

Her fingers shook as she reached for his shirt and began pulling it from his jeans. She felt the fabric give, then moaned with pleasure when her hands had access to the corded muscles of his back.

Ethan trailed nipping kisses down her throat till he found the sensitive skin of her chest. He worked the buttons of her shirt till he had unbuttoned them all, giving him complete access to her. He smoothed the material away, his touch moving over her breast as he opened her to his gaze.

Tess helped him remove her shirt, then giggled as he fumbled with the snaps of her bra. 'I thought you were a pro at this?'

'I used to be,' he murmured.

Once the items were gone, he took one peak into his mouth and stroked it with his tongue. The hot moistness of his mouth bathing her nipple sent spikes of pleasure to the core of her belly. Her breath caught in a gasp as he turned his attention to her other breast. She cupped her hands on his head as she let herself get lost in the feel of him. The touch of him.

She slid her hands over his shoulders, frowning when she felt the material of his shirt. She pulled at it, and he obliged her by leaving her just long enough to remove it. Then he was back, touching her, tasting her. Driving her senses wild with something she had never experienced before. Need.

His hand slid across her stomach, his touch causing her to tremble as he found the catch of her jeans and pulled. Tess suddenly wanted no barriers between them. She would allow herself one night with this incredible man and she didn't want one moment of it marred with barriers.

She'd started to reach for her zipper, to hastily remove her jeans so she could feel him against her, when he caught her hands. His lips found hers, bold, hot, demanding as he leaned with her, pressing her back against the pillows. Once she was reclining, he lifted his lips from her, only a whisper above them as he spoke. 'Let me.'

Ethan knelt beside her, his hands cupping her face. Slowly he began his journey down the contours of her body. His eyes followed the path of his hands, his fingers, as he traced the smoothness of her skin with torturous leisure. When his hands moved to her breasts, to hold them within his palms, his thumbs circling her nipples, she sighed, then lifted her arms to rest them on each side of her head as she arched into his touch.

He made her feel bold, beautiful. Sensual and wanton. She moved against his touch without embarrassment or reservations. She simply enjoyed the special magic being made between them.

Ethan traced his hands down her stomach till he reached her jeans. He unzipped them, then took the band and started pulling it slowly down. She lifted herself to help him ease the jeans past her hips. As he pulled the material down her thighs, he leaned over her and kissed her stomach. The feel of his tongue tracing erotic patterns along her navel, and lower, threw her past the ability to think, and she drifted along the pleasures he continued to create and build within her.

She did not know when he had fully removed her jeans, let alone his own, but he had. She only knew that he had moved between her legs, his lips, his tongue, his mouth moving over her lower abdomen and her thighs in teasing, nipping strokes as he worked toward what she wanted him to touch the most.

She moved beneath him, her hips, her breasts, alternately arching against him as she reached for his touch. She wanted him, her body aching on the point of pain for him to touch her. To be with her. To fulfill her.

She slicked her hair back with her hand, her breath coming in short gasps and pants as Ethan eased his mouth over her. He took her aching bud into his mouth and sucked softly on her core. Tess cried out at the pure heat of pleasure that centered through her, radiating from his touch to the rest of her body. The warmth of the fire in the fireplace heated her skin, caressing her nakedness, yet it was nothing compared to the touch of his mouth, his hands as he held her to him.

His tongue moved over her again and again as he drove her higher, hotter. She moaned as the energy created and stoked by him coiled deep within her, pulling tighter and tighter till it exploded and washed over her in wave after wave of her release.

The tremors softened, leaving her pulsing, but still wanting more from him. She slid her hand through his hair, down his neck to grip his shoulders. Ethan moved over her, stopping only to take her nipple in his mouth for a soft moment, then his lips were on hers again. His kiss was demanding, full of need and hunger, matching her own. His tongue plunged into the soft velvet of her mouth as he moved over her. Tess opened herself to him, feeling as if she would die if he didn't come to her soon.

He joined with her, moved in her as he swallowed her cry of pleasure with his kiss. She felt driven, mindless of anything but him. She caressed the slickened contours of his wide shoulders till she found his buttocks. She clutched the hard ridge of his bottom as he moved within her, and she gasped at the strength she felt beneath her fingers. Together they moved as she kissed his neck, tasting the salt of his sweat as he too was driven into ecstasy.

The hard length of him speared through her womanhood and she again felt the energy building within her. She opened herself to him and reveled in the release he gave her. Clutching him to her, her stomach trembled with the gripping of her release. His own hold tightened on her as he arched against her, his cry muffled against her throat.

Ethan relaxed against her, his skin slick and heated like her own. She turned her head to press a kiss to his cheek. She closed her eyes and nuzzled slowly against his skin.

Moving beside her, he pulled her within the circle of his arms. Tess snuggled against him, resting her head in the curve of his neck. She caressed his chest, the thin mat of hair tickling the palm of her hand. Moving lower, she traced the ridges of his stomach, smiling contentedly when she felt him tighten beneath her touch.

Ethan's hand rested on her hip, and he squeezed her to him as he placed a kiss on the top of her head. 'You're so beautiful, sweetheart.'

Tess giggled, her lips resting against the hard ridge of his chest. 'I bet that's what you say to all the girls.'

He playfully swatted her on the behind. 'You are not just one of the girls, Tess.'

'Oh, really?' she murmured, lifting herself to rest on her elbow and look him in the eye. 'Just exactly what am I, if I'm not a girl?'

He drew his fingers across her cheek, his expression becoming serious. 'You're the kind that scares the hell out of me.'

Her body stiffened, her heart feeling as if it had clenched in her chest. She searched his gaze, trying to see what he was feeling, her own doubt and uncertainty filling her at what she saw. The room was bathed in the flickering glow of the fire as it danced over them. His hooded gaze was shadowed, and she was unable to see if he was teasing her. Or, as her heart was too fearful to want, was he serious? Could Ethan Booker ever truly be happy with her? Accept her for the person that she was, not the type of woman he wanted her to be for him?

Tess lifted her finger to slip her hair behind her ear as she looked away. Hadn't she told herself that she would give herself this one night with him? She'd share this night with him, not allowing herself to second-guess her decisions. Or to contemplate what the expectations of her heart might be.

'I'll get us some blankets and pillows,' she offered, swiftly side-stepping any further discussions on the subject.

She stood, and had started to walk away when Ethan called to her. She stopped and turned back toward him. 'Yes?'

His eyes moved over her naked form, silhouetted against the light of the fire. He paused, then gave her a small smile, as if he'd changed his mind about what he was going to say. 'Hurry back before you freeze.'

'Okay,' she said simply, returning his smile. She padded toward the stairs, climbing them slowly to give herself time to gather her scattered thoughts together. Reaching her room, she pulled two pillows from the bed and a couple of blankets for them. She walked to the staircase and paused. Closing her eyes, she took a deep breath and forced all the contemplation of her heart from her thoughts. She had not wanted any physical barriers between them while they were making love, and now she didn't want any mental barriers put in place by her questioning heart. She resolved that there would be no questions, no expectations. And there would be only one barrier.

The one she had built around her own heart.

Barney, the big ape, as Janet called him, had drawn the short straw and had been left to watch over the petite woman. Joe had left the night before, after receiving the boss's call ordering them to watch the security woman and her boyfriend back at the cabin. Barney, of course, had quickly volunteered to go, but Joe had shaken his head. They had argued about which one of them was going to go, till finally Joe had decided they were going to draw straws.

He'd not only drawn the short straw, but he was stuck with the short woman as well.

She'd been quiet since Joe had locked her in the 'guest' bedroom. He'd figured that once she heard the door close after Joe's departure she would start screaming like holy hell, but she hadn't. She hadn't even given him a peep all night long – not that he had stayed up and listened for her every move. No, he'd fallen asleep watching the late show on the old television in the front room. It hadn't come equipped with a remote, and after a while he had gotten tired of getting up and turning the channels every time he wanted to see what else was on. It was definitely close to impossible to channel-surf when you didn't have a remote.

Finally he'd fallen asleep in the old recliner, despite the spring poking out slightly through the warn fabric. Now, stretching his arms above his head, Barney yawned so big he thought his jaws were going to pop open from the effort. He scratched the stubble of his day-old beard and headed to the bathroom to relieve himself.

After leaving the bathroom, he started to walk by the 'guest' bedroom when it suddenly occurred to him that the woman hadn't been let out since the night before. She was probably about to bust herself, he thought, his lips thinning into a grim line. Digging around his pocket, he found the key to the room and slipped it into the doorknob. Barney opened the door and leaned into the room, refusing to even put one foot in the same room as her for fear of what the boss might do if she said something to him. After what the boss had done to her, though, he doubted she would say much of anything to the old man.

'Hey, time to get up, lady,' he called, his gruff morning voice scratching through the stillness of the room.

Barney had started to swing the door shut to give her privacy, in case she had taken her clothes off to sleep, when his gaze stopped on the bed. He frowned as he tried to make out the form lying on the bed in the darkened room. She had closed the thick curtains on the window, leaving the room dark even in the morning light. Slowly his eyes became accustomed to the light, and he was able to make out the outline of her in the bed.

Unconsciously he stepped into the room, before he remembered himself and stopped. He tilted his head as he looked at the sleeping woman. Something was wrong. 'Hey, lady, are you okay?'

Nothing. The woman did not answer, nor did she move. He stepped a little closer, his eyes narrowing as he studied the woman's sleeping form on the bed. The room was silent, except for the sound of his own breathing. Too quiet, he thought to himself as he timidly stepped closer. Maybe she was a heavy sleeper, he thought. As he moved closer to her he realized that she was lying very still. Unmoving.

Barney had started to reach out to touch her shoulder when he drew his hand back sharply. The boss would have his head, or worse, if he touched her again. But he wasn't going to touch her in a mean way. He was only going to shake her shoulder to wake her up so she could go to the bathroom, that was all, he assured himself.

He reached his hand out as far as he could without actually having to get his body all that close to her. He timidly touched the sleeping form of the woman and poked at her.

'Hey, lady, wake up. I thought you might need to go to the bathroom,' he said, his voice barely above a whisper so he wouldn't frighten her.

His finger barely prodded the blanket covering her. Barney frowned when she didn't respond to him in any way. He eased just a little closer, and this time used his hand to shake the woman. Pushing slightly against the blanket to shake the woman's shoulder, his hand encountered little resistance. Almost like a pillow.

'Damn it,' he said. He snatched at the hem of the blanket and yanked it back. He gritted his teeth in anger and in fear when he saw the pillows and sheets wadded into the shape of a sleeping person. He frantically looked around the room, his gaze immediately settling on the window. He strode to it and flung the curtains back. The brilliance of the morning sun instantly blinded him, and he gave a yelp as he looked away. Shielding his eyes better, he turned back to the window and found it still sealed shut.

'Damn it,' he muttered under his breath again. How the hell had she got out? She hadn't escaped out the window. He turned back to the bed and knelt on the floor to look under it. Again, nothing.

Barney stood, balling his hands on his hips as he looked around the room. She hadn't gone out the window; that much he knew. She was too little to pry the window open, not to mention he would have heard her if she had. The door had still been locked from the outside, so she hadn't got out that way either.

His gaze moved over the room, then across the floor. He stopped and looked back at something that had caught his eye. Walking to it, he crouched to see what it was. It was a screw. Barney picked it up with his fingers as he studied it. Frowning, he looked around the floor and found nothing that it might have come from. Then suddenly a thought occurred to him and he looked up.

He found where the screw had come from.

Standing, he then walked to the old-fashioned vent on the wall. A chair had been moved directly beneath it. The grille of the vent looked exactly as it should. Moving closer to look at it, he found that the screws were loose, just barely hanging from the holes and one had apparently fallen when she had put it back in place.

'How the hell did she do that?' he wondered out loud, though there was no longer anyone to hear him. The vent couldn't have been bigger than eighteen inches wide, and it was rectangular. For a large man, like himself, it would be impossible to squeeze into it. But a petite little thing like her would probably have been able to do it. It would have been a tight fit, but if she had worked at it she probably could have inched her way from the room into one of the others that was not locked, then she had probably waited for him to fall asleep before she simply walked out of the house.

Barney looked around him as a cold sweat broke out on his brow. The boss was not going to like this at all. No, sir, he was not going to like it one little bit. And there was not telling how long she had been gone or where she had gone. Though by now he would almost bet she had made it to safety.

A part of him almost felt relieved that she had escaped. He had had a bad feeling that the boss wasn't going to continue providing hospitality to their guest. It had been a possibility that had worried him, and he had tried hard not to think about. He might be a crook, but he was not a murderer.

Barney shook his head, then ran both his hands through his hair. 'Man, he's going to kill me. How the hell am I going to explain this?'

He didn't know whether to laugh or cry about the whole thing. 'No matter what I tell him, he ain't going to believe me. He won't believe me when I tell him that she squeezed her way out through the duct. 'Damn it,' he muttered, then pulled his cellular phone from its usual place on his belt. He stabbed the numbers in with his finger and waited impatiently for the answer at the other end.

'Joe, we have a problem,' he stated without preamble. There was a long moment of silence. Long enough to have his heart tighten with dread. Finally Joe sighed, and asked him what the problem was.

'She's gone.'

Tess opened her eyes, enjoying the sensation of being snuggled within a warm cocoon. There was no moment of disorientation for her when she woke from her slumber. When she had awoken she had known immediately where she was. Had known immediately the source of the warmth wrapped around her. Ethan had proven to be a selfless and tireless lover during the incredible times they had made love through the night. Finally he had pulled her within his embrace and they had both fallen asleep in contented exhaustion.

She stretched her legs, her movement causing him to flex his hands in his sleep, one of which rested snugly over her breast. She'd almost bet he had been a blanket baby. She giggled at the image of a cute, curly-haired little boy, clutching his blanket as he walked around the house in footed pajamas.

'What are you giggling at, little girl,' Ethan asked, his voice rough from sleep.

'Nothing,' she said easily. Finally she couldn't resist asking. 'You didn't by any chance used to sleep with a blanket when you were a child, did you?'

'Yeah, I did,' he answered, his voice cautious against her ear. 'How did you know?'

Tess slid her hand over his where it covered her breast, and gave his fingers a gentle squeeze. 'Just a wild guess.'

Ethan chuckled as he lifted his head to nibble her earlobe. 'There are just some things you never outgrow.'

'Thank goodness,' she laughed, turning in his arms to face him. She wrapped her arms lazily around him as she snuggled closer. 'Good morning.'

'Good morning yourself, sweetheart,' he murmured against the sensitive skin of her throat, then stilled.

Tess waited patiently, then grinned when she realized that he was content to just fall back to sleep. She threw the covers back with a flourish, exposing their warmed flesh to the cold chill of the morning air. Ethan yelped at her as he grabbed for the covers.

Tess dodged his hands as she stood. 'I'm headed to the shower.'

Instead of wrapping himself back in the blanket, Ethan watched her pick up her cellular phone and walk nude toward the staircase. His gaze heated and brow arched as his eyes roamed over her body.

'Sounds like a great idea,' he stated, and he quickly rose to his feet to follow her.

Tess giggled as he headed toward her, and started to run to the stairs. Ethan chased her up the stairs and down the hall to the bathroom. At the door, he grabbed her by the waist and wrapped his arms around her. Spinning her around, he pinned her with his body against the wall.

He ran his hand suggestively down her slim hips. 'I think I've got you covered, sweetheart.'

Tess laughed easily, 'Brute.'

Ethan looked at her, his expression mock horror. 'Me? No, this is being a brute.'

He lifted her over her shoulder, then held onto her legs. He carried her the few steps to the shower and set her down. Holding her hand, so she wouldn't run away from him, he turned the shower on and adjusted the water. Tess placed her phone on the counter beside the shower, safely away from the water. When it was ready, he pulled her into the shower with him.

Tess's hands flew to her face as the water from the shower cascaded down her cheeks. She swiped the wet strands of hair out of her eyes as she blinked through the water at him. 'I can't believe you did that.'

Ethan grinned mischievously as he picked up a bar of soap, and wiggled his eyebrows provocatively. 'I'm not finished with you yet.'

Tess opened her mouth to protest, her words forgotten at the touch of his lips on her own. Ethan kissed her, his hands moving over her slickened skin as he caressed her. He had lathered his hands and was touching her here, then there, as he soaped her body. He found her breasts, his fingers swirling slowly over her nipples till they hardened.

She softly moaned with pleasure, kissing him as she smoothed her hands over the thick muscles of his biceps to the width of his shoulders. He pulled them below the shower of water, rinsing the soap off them, bending his head to find her breast with his mouth. He ran his hand down her stomach, till he found her hot and aching for his touch.

When his finger began moving over her, Tess let her head fall back as she gripped his shoulders to hold on. Hot, radiating pleasure shot through her, and her breath caught as she whispered his name. He drove her till she cried with the release that shook through her.

Tess softened her hold as she slowly became aware that she had been clutching at his thick shoulders as he pushed her on. Ethan's lips found hers, and he kissed her as he leaned against her till her back pressed against the wall of the shower. Pulling her leg up to his hip, he eased himself within her, sheathing himself within the heated velvet of her center.

Her hands slipped into the wet silk of his hair and she moaned with pleasure as he began moving within her. Tess wrapped her arms around his broad back and held on as he drove them both to their release. When his tremors subsided a few moments later, she hugged him to her.

Ethan pulled her away from the wall and lathered his hands to soap them both, this time to actually clean them. Tess giggled as his fingers tickled her ribs.

'What are you laughing about, Tess?' He grinned at her, his hair sleek against his head.

' "Take a shower" has a whole new meaning for me now,' she teased as she took the soap from him and stepped behind him to do his back. 'Coach.'

He turned to face her, his expression soft as he tilted his head to study her. 'I like hearing you laugh.'

She held his gaze for a moment, then lifted her hand to caress his stubbled cheek. 'I like it when you make me laugh.'

Ethan stroked her cheek. 'Tess, when I walked into that lobby and I saw you dressed in that frumpy outfit and that ridiculous red wig I was drawn to you. I don't know what it was about you, but there was something.'

'Ethan, I don't think this is such a good idea –' Tess started.

He put his finger over her lips to quiet her, only the sound of the water showering over them to be heard. 'Tess, I don't know how you feel, but I think you know something special is going on here between us.'

Tears welled in her eyes. How am I supposed to fight this? she asked herself. He was everything she could hope for. She felt incredible, beautiful, vibrant, when she was with him. Like him, when she had first seen him, her soul had told her *There he is*.

Tess shook her head, her tears mingling with the water of the shower. 'Ethan, what we have is special, but I don't know if it can be enough.'

He took her hand and pressed his lips against her knuckles. 'Tess, I'm falling in love with you.'

A sob caught in her throat as she wished desperately that she could forget all the hard lessons she had learned. Throw caution to the wind and pledge her love to him.

When she didn't respond, he dropped her hand. She lifted her eyes to find the hurt in his gaze before it hardened. 'Ethan, please.'

He opened the shower door and got out. Mindless of the water dripping from him, he grabbed a towel and started to walk from the room. She called to him and he paused.

Tess had opened her mouth to explain her feelings when the shrill chirp of her cellular phone broke the silence. She met his gaze, and for a brief moment they simply looked at each other, the same question in both their eyes.

Was the call from the Badger, to give them yet another riddle to solve?

CHAPTER 13

Tess stepped to the counter, where her phone was placed, and picked it up. She punched the button, then lifted it to her ear. 'Hello?'

'Tess,' the woman said, her voice mingling with the static from the cellular line. 'I'm sorry I couldn't return your call sooner. This is Marcy.'

Tess closed her eyes as she gave a sigh of relief. She met Ethan's gaze and she could see that he had figured it out that it was not who they had expected it to be.

'Marcy,' she said, as she pulled a towel from the rack and wrapped it around herself. 'I really appreciate you returning my call. I think we've already found what we needed, but I guess I'll go ahead and ask you anyway. I know it's hard for you to discuss your former relationship with Gare Harolds –'

'Tess, don't worry about it,' Marcy interrupted. 'I made a mistake. I chose to let it strengthen me, not break me. If I can help you with your investigation in any way, I will be more than happy to answer any questions you might have.'

'Thanks, Marcy,' Tess said, avoiding Ethan's gaze. They had already found the underground shelter that Badger had sent them to look for, but it wouldn't hurt to see what else they could come up with while they had her on the phone. 'We're at the cabin right now. I can't really go into the details, but a friend of mine is in trouble and we were wondering if there were any other structures or places around the cabin that we don't know about. The one thing we did find was an underground shelter yesterday.'

'Oh, you found Harolds' badger hole, then,' Marcy said.

Tess froze as a chill spread over her body, causing her skin to dimple with goosebumps. 'What did you say?'

Marcy laughed, completely unaware that her words had caused such a chilling reaction for Tess. 'I only saw it one time, when we'd been out hiking and it had started raining. He took me to this underground shelter that he called his badger hole.'

'Why did he call it that? Do you know?' Tess asked, her voice sounded unusually calm to her, though her thoughts raced frantically through her mind. Her chest felt tight from the disbelief and fear that had wrapped around her.

'Something from when he played high school football, I guess,' she chuckled. 'I guess it was a guy thing. Anyway, his nickname in high school was The Badger.'

Tess's heart began pounding, the sound of it so loud it pulsed in her own ears. Distractedly she thanked Marcy for calling her, then switched off the phone. She blinked, dazed by the implications of the information she had just been given.

'Tess, what is it?' Ethan asked softly, and he stood in front of her and cupped her chin with his fingers.

She lifted her gaze to meet his, which was filled with concern. She shook her head; she still just could not believe it. She looked at him, her body, her mind feeling as if they were were numb.

'That was Marcy,' she said hoarsely. 'She was Gare Harolds' former mistress.'

'I got that much from your end of the conversation,' he said. Though his concern showed in his eyes, Tess could see that he had dropped a mask over his emotions. 'What did she have to say?'

Tess had to take a deep breath before she could speak. Her mind raced frantically. She pressed her hand to her mouth, then let it drop to her side as she nervously licked her lips.

She met Ethan's gaze. 'She said that Gare Harolds' nickname in high school was The Badger.'

Ethan's eyes widened, the implication hitting him with full force. 'Oh, hell.'

Janet bit her lip, trying to make herself slow down her breathing. *You're going to get yourself beat up*, she'd berated herself. *Or worse*. She'd spent most of the night pacing the room, searching it by the light of the moon, trying to find something, anything to help her escape. Joe had not said anything, his manner in dealing with her had not changed, but when he had closed the door behind her she knew he had meant for her to get out of there as best and quickly as she could.

She had seen his face, had turned and looked him in the eye, but even now she could not really describe his features. That was why he'd removed the blindfold, she thought. His face was so ordinary, so non-descript, that he hadn't worried about her seeing him.

Still, he had given her a look, and she had known she had to get out of there. Now.

Though he had reassured her that she would never be harmed, Janet had no doubts in her mind that the cruel man who had kidnapped her did in fact mean her harm. She wasn't a fool. Her kidnapping had been pulled off to use her as bait to maneuver Tess into coming to them. Nothing more. Now that he had Tess where he wanted her, her life wasn't worth a plugged nickel.

Janet was worried about Tess, yet she had worked with her long enough to know that she was very capable of taking care of herself. She also had a feeling that the handsome doctor, Ethan Booker, had accompanied Tess to help her. To protect her.

That thought alone helped her feel better about Tess. Not much, but at least she knew that she wasn't facing the cruel one alone.

Now who was going to take care of her?

After throwing the curtains open to bathe the sparsely furnished room in moonlight, Janet had paced the whole night through. She had poked, prodded, pulled and pushed on everything in the room trying to find a way out. She had even removed the screws from the old-fashioned grate and pulled a chair under it in an effort to escape. Not only was she too short to get up to the duct opening, but she was too big. That was a first for her. Never had she been too big for anything.

Feeling frustrated, verging on panic, Janet had forced herself to calm down and try to think what Tess would have done if she had been locked in a room with the windows painted shut. Tess was taller than she, so Janet knew she would have been able to reach the duct opening, but she wouldn't have been able to squeeze herself into the opening either. Besides, Janet thought to herself, even if she had made it into the opening, with her luck she probably would have got stuck in a bend somewhere in the system and would have been forced to yell to Barney for help. That would have only served to make the big ape mad at her and defeat the whole purpose of escaping.

Then it had come to her.

A slow smile spread over her lips as the idea sparked, then began to grow in her devious little mind. Janet didn't know if it would work, but it was worth a try. Besides, a part of her still wondered why Joe had left her with Barney, when they both knew he was not the brightest of individuals. Maybe that was why she'd felt he had been telling her to get out while the getting was good, by leaving her with Barney, Joe was 'letting' her escape.

Janet had left the chair under the grate. Then she had replaced the grate cover, but left the screws loose, she'd even left one on the floor, where she was sure it would be found. She had pulled the sheets from the bed, then arranged them with the pillows under the comforter to represent her sleeping form. She could only hope this 'Hollywood' trick would work in her favor.

She carefully went over the room again, then pulled the thick curtains shut to throw the room into darkness and resigned herself to waiting through the night. She crawled under the covers with her 'partner' and tried to sleep. She cat-napped through the rest of the night, never worrying about falling into a deep sleep and missing her opportunity. She couldn't have fallen asleep even if she had wanted to with the amount of snoring Barney was doing. The man had sounded like he could shake the plaster from the ceilings with his rattling.

Finally she had heard him snorting awake, and she had jumped out of the bed and rearranged the covers. Janet had then stepped quickly, quietly into the closet of the darkened room. She hid in the corner of the small walk-in closet; it was pitch-black. Janet had left the door to the closet standing wide open, exactly as it had been when they had put her in the room. There were no clothes, no boxes; nothing was in the bare closet for her to hide behind or under. The only thing she could do was to press herself as tightly into the darkest, furthermost corner of the closet and pray that he did not look in it. She also took the precaution of loosening the light bulb so it wouldn't work if he tried to turn it on.

Janet's plan had been simple because she thought that would be the safest. With the curtains closed and the grate loose, she hoped Barney would assume she had crawled out through the ductwork. That kind of thing only worked in the movies, and Barney seemed like the kind of guy who spent a lot of time in front of the television. Janet hoped it would never occur to him to actually think about the reality or plausibility of her escaping through the ductwork.

After what felt like hours, she'd finally heard him leave the bathroom. She'd been terrified that her breathing would give her away, and she had concentrated on taking as quiet breaths as possible. Janet had jumped when the key rattled in the lock. Pressing herself against the corner, she'd felt the sweat bead on her forehead.

She had almost smiled at the timidness she had heard in his voice as he called to her to wake her up. When it was obvious that he had discovered her 'absence' she had to bite her lip to keep from gasping for air in panic. She could hear his muttering and knew it was now or never.

Janet squeezed her eyes shut and swallowed her fear as she said a silent prayer. She left her eyes closed, hoping that the childhood belief of 'if I can't see you, then you can't see me' would work, even as she worried that the incredible pounding of her heart would give her away. At the fear and worry in Barney's voice, she had almost – not quite, but almost – felt sorry for him. He was right, though, he would have a hard time explaining how he let her get away. At the thought of the cruel one and the way he had coldly touched her, she hoped Barney had enough brains to figure out that what he needed to do was get out of there as quickly as he could too.

She heard him make a call on the cellular phone. Apparently he had called Joe to tell him she had escaped. Then he was gone.

Janet let her breath out as she slid quietly down the wall. She ran her hands through her hair, then wrapped her arms around her knees as she almost cried in relief. She couldn't believe it. It had been such a simple plan and it had worked. It had really worked. He thought she had escaped and was leaving.

The metallic twist of the key in the lock jolted Janet where she crouched in the closet. She stiffened as she listened. Was he coming back?

Maybe he had remembered that he hadn't searched the closet and was coming back. Janet strained to listen, to hear anything that might tell her what was going on. A few moments passed, then she heard the closing of the front door. Getting to her feet quickly, Janet carefully stepped out of the closet. Sticking close to the wall, she moved toward the window to see what was going on. A car started outside and she could hear the crunch of gravel as it drove away.

Janet took the risk and peeked out the window. She was in time to see Barney drive around the bend in the road and disappear. It was the first time she had seen where they had brought her in daylight. She leaned over to get a closer look out the window and found that she was in a cabin-like house in what was apparently a pretty remote area.

Her heart pounding wildly with fear, relief, and excitement, Janet spun around and hopped toward the door as she laughed. 'I can't believe it actually worked. I just can't believe it.'

She closed her hand around the doorknob and began to twist. Her smile froze as the door knob remained unmoving in her hand. A chill moved over her as she paused to take a breath. 'Everything's okay. The door is just hard to open. That's all.'

Wiping her hand on her jeans, Janet gripped the knob again and twisted it. Again it remained unmoving. Janet gave a cry of disbelief and fear as she rattled the knob and pulled on it as she tried to open the door.

'No,' she cried, yanking on the doorknob. 'Damn it, Barney.'

Fear turned to anger. Anger turned to rage. Janet cried, then shouted as she banged her fists on the door, not caring who might hear her. Finally, her anger spent, she stepped back, her chest heaving as she gasped for air.

Janet walked away from the door; her hand whipped through her hair and she bit nervously at her thumbnail. She once again paced the now familiar floor as she tried to figure out what to do. Why had he locked the door? she wondered. The only thing she could think of was that he had either done it out of habit or had wanted to 'preserve the scene' to show them that he hadn't just let her escape.

Janet almost laughed at the thought. Such a simple plan would not have worked on anyone with half a brain and yet somehow it had. The simpleton had actually believed she'd escaped. He had told Joe that she'd escaped, then he had locked the door and left. They all thought she was hot-footing it back to the police, when she had actually never had left and was still captive in the very room they had put her in.

Shakespeare would have been proud of the irony of it.

Her chuckle caught with a sob in her throat. She looked back at the door and felt the anger flare again. Yelling, she ran a few short steps and tried a flying kick at the door. Her foot connected squarely with the center, making a loud thump, but nothing more. Pain shot like sharp jolts of electricity through her leg.

Hopping on her good foot, Janet leaned over to grab her leg. 'Damn it.'

She skip-hopped back to the bed and fell on it. She gritted her teeth against the pain throbbing through her leg. Great. Not only was she still locked in a room in a house that probably no one knew about, but she had hurt herself acting like an idiot.

Janet shook her head as her mouth thinned into a grim line. 'Barney, why did you have to be such a conscientious idiot?'

She looked at the room around her. Now what was she going to do?

Tess shook her head in disbelief as she managed to pour herself a cup of coffee despite the shaking of her hands. After Marcy's bombshell she had somehow found her way to the bedroom to put on fresh clothes. Ethan had also taken the time to get dressed, and had met her back in the living room of the cabin. She glanced at him to try to read his expression, and sadly found that she couldn't. Once again she had messed things up.

When it came to personal relationships, she always managed to find a way to screw things up. Now Ethan paced the room, thoughtfully rubbing at his chin lost in his own thoughts. He had been polite to her, painfully so, since what had happened in the shower.

Was he really falling in love with her?

It wasn't that she didn't care for him. On the contrary, she was beginning to care for him entirely too much. And in her line of business feelings could mess things up considerably, not to mention place people in danger. Especially with what they were involved in now, a personal relationship and all its assorted baggage could prove deadly to them all.

Tess rubbed at her brow. She just could not get over it. Gare Harolds was alive. That was the only thing that made sense to her. Or did it? Why would a wealthy man with a family and a top executive position in a successful company want to fake his own death? It was ludicrous, that was what it was, she thought. The only explanation had to be that someone was posing as the deceased.

'I just do not understand it,' she said out loud, though she was talking more to herself than Ethan. 'Why would someone pretend he was Gare Harolds? Surely he didn't think he could take over the company in Harolds' place, or get his money. After all, the man knew too many people who could identify him, both professionally and personally.'

Ethan stopped his pacing. He put his hands in his pockets as he rocked back and in forth in thought, not quite looking at her. 'We don't know if they are trying to impersonate him. What Marcy said was that he called the underground shelter his badger hole. Your computer stalker calls himself Badger; it could be only a coincidence.'

Tess leveled her gaze on him. 'Do you believe in coincidences, Doctor?'

Ethan gave her a lop-sided grin, finally meeting her gaze. 'Not really. But the point is we need something more solid than a nickname before we start jumping to conclusions.'

She let her breath out on a sigh as she placed her hands on the edge of the table and leaned forward, her thoughts distracted. 'You're right, but we still have nothing to go on. I've been investigating this case for months now, Ethan. Every time I think I've found a lead, it disappears or turns out to be a dead end. Now I've got people blowing my truck up, kidnapping someone important to me, and I don't have any idea why. Who the hell are these people?' she demanded, frustration filling her voice with a hiss.

He studied her for a moment, his hooded gaze growing distant as he considered what she'd said. 'Who would want to go to such lengths to get you out here?' he murmured.

'I don't know.' She shrugged, running her hand through her hair in frustration as she started to meander around the room. 'There have been very few leads to go on in Torkelson's and Harolds' kidnappings and deaths, if any. It's been frustrating as hell. Sometimes I felt like I was always one step behind the individuals pulling this off.'

'I wonder if that was because you always were, Tess,' he said, nodding slightly as he stared off into the distance.

She turned to look at him, frowning at his statement. 'Gee, thanks, Ethan. I really appreciate your faith and support during this trying time.'

He shook himself out of his thoughts and returned her frown. 'What?'

'You just said I was always one step behind.' She blinked, feeling slightly irritated at his remark and his obvious lack of attention.

The implication of what he had said suddenly hit him, and he laughed. He shook his head as he lifted his hand to stop her before she said anything else. 'I didn't mean it quite like that, I promise.'

'Then how did you mean it, Ethan?'

Ethan started pacing again. The energy seemed to radiate from him as he walked through his thoughts. 'It's just an idea, but one we can actually test.'

'Ethan!' she cried, wanting to break into his thoughts. Again, she felt he was leading them in the right direction. His energy radiated from him to her, and she felt it move through her, making her antsy and ready to act. 'You're driving me crazy. What's your idea?'

Ethan stopped, and studied her for a moment. 'I think Badger *is* Gare Harolds. Maybe even Torkelson.'

Now it was Tess's turn to laugh. 'Weren't you just the one talking about coincidences?'

He waved his hand, as if sweeping all those thoughts aside. 'Let's just forget about that for a moment, okay.'

Tess walked to the table and pulled a chair out to take a seat. 'Okay, we'll forget all that other stuff for now. What's your idea? Besides thinking that Badger is Harolds or Torkelson and vice-versa?'

'It's a theory, actually,' he said. At Tess's irritated look he chuckled. 'All right. Here it is. When Torkelson and Harolds were kidnapped, the "ladies" visiting them were gone before it happened, right?'

Tess nodded. 'The women followed them to the cabin in their own vehicle, then when they were done with their . . . uh . . . meeting, they drove themselves home.'

'So much for chivalry,' he murmured under his breath.

She leaned back in her chair, giving him a half-smile. 'You don't have to be too chivalrous when you're paying someone a hundred bucks an hour, Ethan.'

'A hundred bucks an hour?' he stated, then raised a brow as he tilted his head. 'Damn. A hundred bucks an hour? I'm obviously in the wrong profession.'

'I wouldn't give up my day job yet, if I were you.'

She crossed her arms over her chest and Ethan continued. 'So, the "ladies" were not witnesses to the kidnapping itself. That's my point. No one was. Then they find Torkelson's body in a shallow grave, but not Harolds; so they assume he is dead also.'

'They identified both bodies, Ethan,' she reminded him. 'In fact, you identified Harolds' body yourself.'

'Not exactly,' he stated, and he rubbed distractedly at his chin.

'What?' Tess shot forward in her chair and leaned her hands on her knees as she watched him intently. 'You had the body, a wallet, and dental records. What more could you need?'

'Well, let's look at it this way,' he started. 'Torkelson's body was . . . for lack of a better word, we'll say "fresh". Torkelson's body was found not too long after death and could be identified visually and physically. I talked to the officers and they said his wife identified the body and that his dental records matched. We need to remember that even in this case, according to the coroner's report, Torkelson's body only "somewhat" resembled the man. Even *his* death could have been faked. The distortion in appearance is a normal occurrence in decomposition, so once the dental records matched, it wouldn't have helped the case more to continue past that.'

'Isn't comparing dental records what you did with Harolds' body?' she asked.

He shook his head. He stood by the table as he paused to figure out how best to explain the difference to her. 'Torkelson was found out in the open, not too long after his death. The fact that it was cold helped preserve his body somewhat. Though there was some decomposition, his face was still recognizable. The hair, his build, the dental records – everything matched the records the investigators had.'

'Harolds' body had been placed in the basement of a building scheduled to be imploded. The blast should have taken care of the evidence, so to speak. When you're clearing the debris of a building away with a bulldozer, who's going to notice a bone fragment? What they hadn't counted on was the walls forming a pocket that protected the condition of the body. In the cool, dry air, the body mummified. This distorted the features, so a visual identification was out of question. Also, the body would naturally appear smaller than what the man did while alive.'

She narrowed her eyes. 'Why go through the elaborate scheme of grooming a body double, then stick him in a building that's going to be imploded and will destroy all the evidence?'

'I don't know,' he said on a sigh as he shoved his hands in his pockets. 'Maybe they made a mistake somewhere along the line.'

'But the dental records?' she asked, waving her hand in question. 'What about those? You said they matched.'

'They matched the records we were given,' he answered simply.

Tess nibbled on her lip as she thought about it. It was elaborate, she had to give him that much, but it sparked a seed of reality in her. She nodded as she continued to process what he had said. If Harolds' was alive, calling himself Badger, then he would have known what she was doing all this time. Probably he still had access to his computers and security system. Might even still have people inside the company reporting to him. All of which would explain how her witnesses disappeared as she started getting closer. Why he'd never seemed too worried about the death threats against himself or his family. Why her search into his paper trial had fizzled to nothing.

Paper trail.

'Oh, hell,' she said without thinking. Her eyes widened and she raised her hand to her mouth as she turned to Ethan.

'What is it, Tess?' he asked, concern filling his gaze.

'Dental receipts,' she murmured, her mind racing frantically. 'It never occurred to me that they were anything more than what they seemed. Everyone goes to the dentist, right?'

'Was there something unusual about them?' he asked, breaking into her thoughts.

She nodded. 'About nine months before he . . . allegedly died, receipts showed that he'd started paying the dentist's bill for one of his employees who apparently had quite a bit of work done. I didn't think anything of it, because it was not unusual for Harolds to pick up the tab for one of his employees now and again.'

'What was so unusual about this one?' he asked.

She met his gaze, her brow lifted in distaste for the man they were discussing. 'The employees Harolds usually "took care of" were women.'

'But this particular employee was a man, I gather?' Ethan finished for her.

She nodded, her voice flat. 'Like I said before, he was one hell of a nice guy.'

'Do you have the name of the dentist he paid for?' Ethan asked.

Tess felt her nerves humming. They were getting close; she could feel it. 'I'll have to call the office and they can give me the information. But where would he have got a person willing to have dental work so he could be a stand-in?'

He walked to the window, propping his arms against the frame, and looked out at the beautiful scenery surrounding them. 'It's really not all that hard. One source that comes to mind is the homeless. Harolds could have looked around till he found a man approximately his age and build, then befriended him. My autopsy of the liver did not show any signs of alcoholism, but of course not all the homeless are alcoholics. However, a few do have mental problems . . .

He pushed away from the lush scenery. Turning, he leaned his hips against the window-sill.

'Because of some of the test results, I tend to believe that the victim could have been suffering from mental problems. This would have made it extremely easy for Harolds to convince the individual to let him "take care" of him. Harolds would have found a place for him to stay, made sure he had food to eat, and that he was healthy. He would have needed time to find a dentist who would cooperate with him, and it would also have taken time to have the dental work altered to resemble Harolds'. Then all he would need to do was switch the records. The records would match, and would also match the memory of those close to him. If I remember right from the autopsy, Harolds had a gold tooth fairly close to the front of his mouth. People would remember that, and that's why it would have been important to get the mouths to match as closely as possible.'

'It all makes a terrible kind of sense, doesn't it?' Tess lifted her gaze to hold his. 'You mentioned earlier that you could test your theory. What did you mean?'

Ethan put his hands in his pockets as he shifted on the window-frame. He looked down and crossed his feet in front of him. Then his eyes were back on hers, the vibrant energy focusing on her, and her body instinctively responded. 'Well, it's actually very simple, but it will take some time.'

Tess leaned her arm on the table-top as she propped her chin on her hand. 'DNA?'

He gave her a smile of approval as he slowly nodded. 'Yes, that's correct.'

'But how?' she asked, lifting her shoulder in a shrug. 'If one or both of these guys faked their death, and the bodies are not that of Gare Harolds or Ken Torkelson, then how can you test their DNA to make sure it's them?'

His smile spread to a grin. 'Now that we have some doubt as to the identity of the corpses, we can conduct the DNA test. But not on them. We test the two men's children. They will have inherited certain traits from both their mother and their father. By looking at their DNA and comparing it to that of the victims, we will be able to tell if the children could have come from that particular man.'

Ethan's eyes lit with energy. 'It's basically a process of elimination.'

'You are so wicked.' Tess returned his smile. 'When can we get started?'

'At this point we need to make a few calls,' he answered. 'My office can go ahead and start the testing.'

'Great,' she said, jumping up to head to Harolds' office. It seemed only appropriate that they use his conveniences to catch him, if indeed he truly was the one 'badgering' them.

She moved quickly to his desk and sat in the chair. Punching in her office number, she put it on speaker phone. The voice of the temporary filling in for Janet bit at her, but Tess pushed those thoughts aside. For Janet's sake she had to keep working at this case.

She let the woman know who she was, and asked for one of her guys. Barely a moment passed before a loud voice boomed across the speaker. 'Tess, where the hell are you?'

'Hi, Tim, nice to hear from you too.' She smiled, thinking of her barrel-chested partner shouting into the phone at his end. Tim was a retired cop and the office father-figure all wrapped up in one. Their contrasts in personality had helped their business grow considerably. 'Is Tom there with you?'

Ethan raised a brow at her as he leaned against the desk. 'Tess, Tim, and Tom?'

She batted her eyes playfully at him as she coyly answered, 'In times of trouble call the three Ts of Securitee,' she said, emphasizing the rhyme.

He shook his head. 'I hope you didn't make that your company slogan.'

Tess chuckled as she pulled a drawer out to retrieve a pen. 'No, just had it cross-stitched on a pillow and put it out in the lobby.'

When he remained quiet she glanced up, then laughed when she saw the look on his face. 'I'm kidding, Ethan.'

'One can never tell with you, sweetheart,' he murmured as he pushed away from the desk. He grabbed one of the wing-back chairs and pulled it over to the desk. Sitting down, he propped his feet against the silky finish of Harolds' expensive and luxurious desk.

It was the least he could do, he thought with a humorous smile.

Tess watched his movements with a playful gleam in her eye. 'Make yourself comfortable.'

'If Harolds is behind this,' he said with icy calm, 'I plan on it.'

Tess studied him. Once again she was taken aback by the conflict of impressions she had of Ethan. He was a coroner, she thought dryly. When she thought of a coroner she always pictured an older man with a paunchy belly, sallow skin and sparse hair. Ethan was anything but that, with his thick dark hair and his sexy hooded gaze that made you wonder what he was thinking and left you wishing he would do it. Her body clinched at the provocative memory of him touching her with his hands, his lips, as he had made love to her.

It was with regret that she remembered the hurt in his eyes when she had not been able to acknowledge his love. She looked away, missing the warmth that the memory of being with him had given her.

Now she was seeing something else in Ethan. She had seen its presence flickering just below the surface before, but now it had come out in full force. It was the dark side of him that she had not expected. A cold, calculated, cunning darkness that hardened his gaze, transforming him into someone she did not recognize.

Tom's voice broke into her thoughts as he announced his presence. He clicked a button to put them on his own speaker phone so that the four of them could talk together.

Tess cleared her throat and focused on the task at hand. There were several things at stake here, the least of which was her heart. 'Okay, guys, we've uncovered what could be a major break in the Torkelson and Harolds murder case. We think we've figured out who Badger might be.'

'What's the bastard's name?' Tim demanded. Tess could almost see his fists clenched, his cheeks red, as she had seen him many times when he became angry.

She smiled affectionately as she answered. 'Gare Harolds. Or Torkelson, his vice-president.'

'What the hell?' both men exclaimed at the same time. She chuckled. At least they hadn't told her she was full of it.

'I didn't stutter, guys,' she said, tapping her pen against her hand as she related what they had found out so far. When she'd finished, and the line remained silent, Tess frowned as she tilted her head. 'Are you guys still with me?'

'Yeah, yeah,' Tom said, then murmured a few things to Tim that she couldn't quite make out. Then he spoke to the speaker. 'It's beginning to make sense, Tess. What's your next step?'

Tess tossed the pen on the table as she leaned back in Harolds' chair. She met Ethan's dark gaze as she spoke with deliberate calm.

'Gentlemen, I think it's time we called this guy's bluff.'

CHAPTER 14

Barney fidgeted in his chair. He kept darting quick glances to Joe, then back to his hands, which were tightly clasped in front of him. Finally he shot up from his chair and began pacing nervously across the floor of the underground shelter.

He ran his hands frantically through his short, sparse hair, then shook his head in disbelief at some notion running around his thick head. 'He ain't going to believe me, man. I know he ain't. I swear I didn't let that girl go, Joe. She just escaped, man. Just disappeared, I'm telling ya.'

'I know,' Joe said calmly from where he sat at the table. Unlike Barney, he was sitting quietly, an arm thrown over the back of the chair as he slouched in front of the table. He fiddled with a stick, running it back and forth through his fingers. He didn't even bother to glance toward the large panicking man pacing behind him. 'There's nothing you can do about it now, Barney. Just relax, and when he gets here we'll explain everything to him, okay?'

'Explain things?' he shrilled, flexing his fists at his sides. 'Yeah, I'll explain how I just happened to lose the girl while he was gone and he'll just smile and shoot me in the head.'

Joe continued tapping the small wand of wood against the table, smoothing his fingers up the sides, then flipping it to slide them back down. His eyes never left the hypnotic movement of his fingers. 'I think you're getting yourself all worked up before you even know what's going to happen, pal.'

Barney, blew his breath out loudly, then sucked it rapidly back in. Joe began to wonder if he was going to hyperventilate on him. Just what he needed was to babysit a kid the size of a small mountain while holding a bag to his mouth. Joe shook his head at the thought, his lip curling up in a hint of a smile.

'He ain't going to believe me, man,' Barney repeated for about the fiftieth time.

Joe tapped the wood one last time with a resounding whack, and immediately caught Barney's frantic attention. 'Take a seat, kid. Too bad we didn't have a couple of beers stashed here, or I'd give you one. You could probably use it.'

Barney skulked to the chair he'd just vacated and perched on the edge. He shook his head, his eyes wide with fear. 'He's gonna kill me. I just know it.'

'Barney, you're starting to get on my nerves,' Joe said calmly as he yawned. He stretched his arms out beside him.

'What do ya think he's gonna do when he finds out she took off like that?' he asked, his gaze skittering around the room to finally settle on Joe.

Joe shrugged his shoulder, 'I have no idea, kid. No sense borrowing trouble, if you know what I mean.'

'He's gonna kill me, that's what he's gonna do.' Barney rubbed his hands back and forth on his jean-legs, rocking slightly in his chair. He stilled suddenly, his gaze flipping back to the older man. His voice dropped to almost a whisper as he leaned toward him. 'Don't you think there's something . . . strange about him?'

Joe's eyes were riveted to his, his body suddenly tense at the unexpected perceptiveness of the kid. 'What do you mean, Barney?'

The kid looked around them, as if someone could overhear their conversation in the underground shelter. 'Like he's psycho, or something?'

Joe blinked. The thought had occurred to him. It had first grown in the back of his mind when the man had paid him to kidnap the guy with the Reynolds woman. When he'd found the coroner's identification, he'd had that punk kid dump the man at his house. Joe had sent the man back his money, with a note stating that he did not kidnap anyone involved with law enforcement. The nameless, faceless individual who had hired him had then called. How the man had found him in the hole-in-the-wall hotel he'd checked into, he did not know. But one thing Joe had known was that he better go along with the individual's plan till he could think of a better one, or he'd find himself with a bullet in his head, just like the image Barney had been spouting a few moments before. He still did not know the man's name, nor did he care to know. They simply called him the boss.

He knew the man wouldn't have any problems killing him, or Barney for that matter. Joe had a distinct feeling that murder was not something new to that man. For a brief moment he thought about telling the kid that the best thing they could do was high-tail it through the forest and get the hell out of there before the man showed back up. Take that unexpected vacation he'd been thinking about.

Joe's lips thinned into a grim line as he brushed past that thought. No, it would be better to see things through a little farther, or otherwise they'd have that guy with his uncanny ability to find people hunting him down.

That was why he'd pretty much let the girl escape. She was a bright one, and he knew she would get the idea to get out of there once he left her with Barney. And he'd been right. She was gone and it was a good thing, because otherwise she would be dead. That he had no doubt of. The man paying them was a cruel son-of-a-bitch, and he looked at people who were not relevant to his plan as being expendable as used chewing gum on a sidewalk. Joe shook his head. People like that were dangerous to be around. He might be a lot of things, but he was not a killer, and he did not plan on becoming one anytime soon.

He returned his attention to Barney. Sweat had started to bead on the kid's wide forehead as the silence lengthened between them. 'Kid, I'd just find other things to worry about.'

Barney blinked at him. He frowned as he leaned against the table to talk to him, his voice an urgent whisper. 'He's crazy, man. I'm telling you that if he don't kill us himself, he's gonna get us killed trying to pull some crazy stunt.'

Joe's gaze hardened. If the kid didn't get a grip on himself, he would get the two of them killed. The simple truth was that Barney was right; the boss was crazy. Not only that, but he was cruel and would enjoy killing the both of them if he thought they were taunting him. He had not known the man that long, nor did he care to know him much longer, but Joe was smart enough to know how to wait things out till they could get away safely.

'Barney, I think you ought to shut up and get a grip on yourself before you get yourself in trouble,' he said, his gaze hard and unwavering as he tried to push the point across to the hard-headed kid.

Barney returned his look, his mouth moving as if he were about to say something, when a voice broke the brief silence, sending a chill through them both.

'I would take his advice if I were you, young man,' the cruel one said, behind them.

Joe stiffened as he watched Barney's face pale with fright. Several moments passed, the silence lengthening till he thought it would break the thin wire of his nerves. Having the boss behind him made him vulnerable. A bead of sweat trickled slowly down his back between his shoulderblades, causing his skin to itch. Joe fought the urge to twist around to confront the man. Instinctively he knew the man would look for any sign of weakness and jump on it.

Instead he picked up the stick of wood and resumed the hypnotic movement of sliding the piece of wood through his nimble fingers. With a slow, quiet breath, he released the tension from his shoulders. 'You're back early.'

He could feel the frustration radiate in waves from the man as he refused to cower in front of him. He heard the slow intake of breath as the man fought his own anger. 'The only schedule you have to worry about is the one I set for you.'

Joe's gaze moved swiftly to Barney's face. He could tell the man's movements by watching the kid's expression. Barney's face was still pale, and now his forehead was beaded with sweat as he followed the man's restless movements.

'You're the boss,' he said simply.

Joe kept his gaze fastened on Barney's eyes as he traced the man's movement around the underground shelter. He could feel the tension build as the boss looked around the quarters.

'Where is she?'

There was no need for Joe to ask who he was referring to. If he had asked, the boss would have used it as an excuse. He'd say he was being mouthy and probably kill him without batting an eye.

There had to be better ways to earn a living, he thought without humor.

Individuals like this guy made him realize that he liked living, and that the only way to ensure that he continued to live was to keep his nose clean. Once he got out of this, he'd very seriously reconsider his priorities in life.

Philosophical thoughts aside, he blandly answered the man's harsh question. 'The woman escaped last night.'

The man did not make a sound. Did not ask how or why, simply took a slow, deep breath. Joe continued sliding the wood through his fingers. If he was going to get it in the back, at least he wouldn't die being a coward in front of this maniac. He had to work to force out the man's building anger behind him, but he did it so he could remain calm and cognizant of the man's movements.

'She's gone?' the boss asked simply, his voice no more than a whisper filled with the tight thread of rage. 'Would you like to explain how she was able to escape?'

In any other circumstance, Barney's frozen expression of fear and horror would have been comical to Joe. His lip curled up in a hint of a smile as he studied the movement of the wood in his hand. 'She's a pretty smart little cookie. She couldn't get out the window so she apparently went out the duct system. It would have been a tight squeeze for her, but she was a tiny little thing anyway.'

The man walked away from them to the wall at the back of the shelter. He lowered his head as he balled his fists on his hips. After several tension filled moments he turned his head slightly to speak over his shoulder at them. 'Have you heard anything?'

Joe took the opportunity to adjust himself to face the man. With the man's back turned to him, he could swivel to face him without it seeming as if he was scared of him. He stopped playing with the wood and shifted to face the boss. 'She was not aware of the route to get to the house where we took her. It's pretty remote, and even though she's a smart little thing, she's also a city girl, so it will take her a while before she can get somewhere to call for help.'

He nodded absently. 'What about the cabin?'

Joe noticed Barney's gaze fixed on the man. The poor kid's eyes were wide with terror and his wide shoulders were beginning to shake slightly. He looked like a deer caught in a truck's headlights on a dark country highway. Frowning, Joe gave a small wave with his hand to catch the kid's attention and shook his head at him. The kid needed to snap out of it or he would be dead. If the maniac caught one whiff of his fear, he'd jump on it like a wolf on a lamb.

Barney held his gaze for a moment, then slowly nodded. He squeezed his eyes tightly shut, then opened them. Joe could see the kid struggle, then finally overcome the fear and allow his gaze to look a little mean. The glint of fear fixed with it added a reckless look to the kid, making him look almost as crazy as the man standing with his back to them.

Joe gave him a small encouraging smile as he gave a nod of approval. 'There hasn't been much of anything going on there. I figure they're holed up talking to their people. Probably trying to find the girl and us at the same time.'

The man whirled toward them. His eyes were gleaming and reckless. Wild like a rabid skunk as he glared first at him, then Barney. 'We don't have any more time. We're going to have to move now.'

He slicked his hair back as he began to pace. 'We'll have to move quickly if we want to avoid any other screw-ups. We'll storm the place, kill them, then tear that place from the roof down till we find what I'm looking for. That bitch has to have it with her or otherwise she wouldn't be here.'

Barney's pale gaze slowly moved to Joe. He sighed, feeling the uncomfortable and definitely unwanted feeling of responsibility for this kid who looked more like a dumb college linebacker on a football team than a crook.

Slowly the poor kid shook his head in disbelief. He turned, unwillingly meeting the cruel one's hard gaze. 'We can't kill them.'

The sounds of Barney's shrill words fell like lead, leaving silence in their wake as the chamber filled with a growing tension. As if suddenly realizing his blunder, the large hulk of a kid started stumbling through several lame excuses for his outburst. 'I mean . . . we can't . . . not to say . . . it wouldn't be . . . I just don't think . . .'

'Don't think,' the cruel one ordered sharply, his feral gaze pinning the kid's large frame. He pulled his gun and cocked it in front of Barney's face. With evil relish he leaned across to prop his hand on the table as he spoke through clenched teeth a breath from the kid's face. 'I'll tell you what I want you to think, got it? Otherwise what I have planned for those two up in the cabin could just happen to you.'

The man let his words sink into Barney's thick skull till he could see the fear growing in the kid's eyes. 'I've already killed two people. Shot both of them in the back of the head, like they used to do in the war. One or two more bodies isn't going to hurt my conscience any.'

Barney's face was pale, almost white. His trembling lips were turning blue as if he were standing in an arctic wind.

'That's enough,' Joe stated quietly.

The boss's eyes darted toward him and his eyes narrowed. Joe cocked his own gun in his hand, his eyes never leaving the man's as he did it.

'You want people watching your back when you go to that cabin, boss,' he said calmly as he lowered his hand to rest the gun nonchalantly across his lap. The barrel of the gun remained unwavering on the man standing in front of Barney. 'Not shooting you in the back.'

The man backed off, his gaze cooling as he studied Joe. After a long moment, he nodded, then walked away from Barney. 'We need to get going. It's going to be dark before too long.'

He walked to the bunk, where he began unpacking a duffel bag to ready his equipment. His back was to them, his movements relaxed and unhurried as he busied himself. Joe watched in fascination as the man's demeanor changed as swiftly as if he'd never pulled a gun on them at all.

The man was crazy, he thought. For the first time his mouth was dry, cottony as he swallowed. It was one thing to speculate that an individual was a lunatic; it was a completely different matter to *know* he was. The realization of his predicament left him unsettled.

The situation was going from bad to worse. For the first time in his career, he didn't know what the hell he was going to do about it.

Tess lifted her gaze from her notes to the window, where Ethan stood. He had his hand resting on the wood frame of the window as he studied the forest surrounding the luxury cabin. Tess's gaze moved over his silent form. His hair was tousled from running his fingers restlessly through it. His shirt was rumpled, yet still sexy as it clung to his wide muscled shoulders. The tail was untucked, but did not quite cover the hard ridges of his backside, where the denim was snug against the corded muscles of his thighs. Each detail she memorized, searing the image of him into her thoughts, though she doubted that she would be able to ever forget him.

Ever.

Her skin dimpled with goosebumps as her body recalled the feel of his touch on her skin. She let her gaze fall back to the papers in front of her and tried to refocus her thoughts on what she had been working on. She found that she couldn't even remember. Soon the case would be over, she could feel it deep down inside her. Then where would they be?

Nowhere, she reminded herself sharply. When, and if, they made it through this ordeal, they would find that the only thing they had had in common was danger. When the smoke cleared they would find themselves facing each other, seeing each other as they really were for the first time. They would be facing each other without any murders, kidnappings or threatening notes to throw them together. It would simply be a man and a woman in the reality of a normal world. Ethan would go back to his normal job and resume his normal routines.

And what would she do then?

Tess's job held some aspects of normality, but not many. Sometimes she had to leave at a moment's notice to fly to some location halfway around the world. Very rarely was her life normal, so how could she expect anyone to understand, let alone accept that in a relationship?

The painful truth was, she couldn't. She'd tried it before and it hadn't worked. She couldn't expect Ethan to change just for her. Not that there was anything she would want to change about him. Nor could *she* change for *him*.

Still her heart clenched whenever she remembered the pain in Ethan's eyes when he had told her he thought he was falling in love with her and she hadn't been able to respond. Never would she have wanted to hurt him. Since that moment Ethan had been quiet, withdrawn, polite as they had talked with her partners, as they'd planned out how they were going to handle things. Once that was done he'd retreated from her. She knew the only reason he didn't completely avoid her was the constant threat threat Badger might try to jump them.

Tess turned her head, her gaze instinctively focusing back on Ethan. It startled her to find him studying her.

His hooded gaze held hers for a tension-filled moment, before his voice finally broke the silence between them. 'You look like you have a lot on your mind.'

She nodded in response. She was glad he had brought it up. They were both in danger, at least till they discovered the identity of the man following them. Until the situation was resolved, they simply could not afford to be distracted by their emotions.

'Ethan, I'm sorry about what happened earlier,' she said quietly. She was thankful her voice did not catch with the pain that was spearing through her. 'We're caught in a very difficult, very dangerous situation, and it can become all too easy to turn to each other for comfort –'

He held his hand up to stop her apology. He walked toward her, then came to a stop in front of Harolds' massive oak desk where she sat. He slid his hands in his pockets as he looked down.

'Tess, you're right,' he said softly. He suddenly looked up, his gaze fastening on hers. Her heart twisted at the distant, flat look he gave her. 'Being in danger can cause people to think funny things. It's been a long time since I faced it, and I guess I put too much into . . . certain things. Thankfully you're more experienced at this than I am. You saved both of us a lot of trouble.'

His gray-blue eyes held hers for a moment longer, the silence taut and expectant between them. Then he was gone.

Ethan turned on his heel and walked casually from the room as if he didn't have a care in the world. As if he hadn't ripped her heart out and left it bleeding on the desk in front of her.

Tears welled in her eyes and her breath caught as a sob choked her throat. She swallowed, closing her eyes against the retreating figure of Ethan's back as her hand flexed unconsciously. She wanted desperately to reach out to him to stop him from leaving.

But she didn't.

Joe stooped as he ran silently toward a clump of bushes. The chill of the evening air cloaked him, chilling the sweat already beaded on his forehead. Damn, he was getting too old for stunts like this, he thought without humor.

He turned to look over his left shoulder and found that Barney was coming up slowly behind him. The kid was scared out of his mind, and not being as quiet as Joe would have liked him to be as he ran through a thicket of trees. The brown curled leaves crunched under his feet, echoing his movements as he advanced toward the remote cabin they had been staking out.

Joe looked down as he shook his head. He had purposely put himself between the boss and the kid so that he could make sure that no unnecessary killing took place while they were advancing on the cabin.

They really did not have much of a plan to work with. The boss had instructed them to make their way to their designated spots and wait for his signal before they headed toward the house. Joe had asked what the signal was, and the boss had assured him with a small smile that he would know it when it came.

Again he shook his head. He had a really bad feeling about this one. He looked over his shoulder to check where Barney was and found that he wasn't too far behind him. Good. He wanted the kid to stick close to him during this.

They moved through a thick stand of trees. The low branches were full of small spiky thorns that grabbed at their clothing and hair as they brushed through. Joe didn't know what kind of trees they were, but they were short, squatty things with gnarled bark. His skin itched where the thorns had poked through his clothing.

He heard a low string of curses and looked back to find Barney swatting at the branches of one of the trees. From the red scrape glaring down his cheek, he had to assume that Barney had gotten a little too close to the thorns. A thin trail of blood showed the extent of the scratch before he swiped it away and continued to follow behind him.

They had only a few more feet before they neared the edge of the thicket, then they would be able to skirt through the trees till they were behind the house. Joe scanned the area around the cabin, looking for a sign of the location of the boss. He saw the man's shirt as he streaked through an opening before he was once again hidden by the corner of the house. Joe's lips thinned into a line of distaste. It wouldn't be much longer, and then they would have some idea what the man had in mind.

He waited for Barney to come up behind him before he broke through the edge of the thicket and trotted in a low slouch to the back of the barn. He peered around the corner of the roughened wood to check the house for movement. There was nothing. The panting wheeze next to him let him know that Barney had made the short distance and was working to catch his breath.

He would let the kid rest a bit before they headed toward the house. He would need the time to try to figure out what the hell the boss was doing behind the house. His answer wasn't long in coming as the loud report of a gun shattered the quiet dusk of the evening.

'Damn it,' he muttered, waving for Barney to follow him as he ran toward the cover of the house.

He heard two more gunshots as he ran to the side of the house. Hitting the siding as he gulped air, Joe let his gaze move frantically around him. He could hear people calling to each other within the house. He twisted back toward the barn and waved for Barney to get ready. The kid hit the house much as he had, his wide shoulder bouncing off the side as he held his gun ready beside him.

'What the hell is going on?' he hissed, his eyes wide and searching as he continually looked around them. Sweat poured in tiny streams down his cheeks and neck, though the evening air held a hint of a chill. 'Sounds like a damn gunfight on TV. I thought we weren't supposed to hurt anybody.'

'We're not,' Joe retorted. He had little patience for the kid now that they were at the house and shots were being returned not that far from them. His fingers ached where he clutched the grip of his gun. He switched hands to loosen his fingers, then returned the gun to his good grip.

The man was a damn lunatic, Joe thought. His mind raced through several scenarios of what might be going on inside the cabin, none of which were good. He almost considered grabbing the kid and running, but there was such a thing as accessory after the fact which caused him to stay where he was at.

He took a deep breath, and nodded with his chin for Barney to follow him. 'Come on. It's time we got this show on the road.'

They ran in a slow jog down the length of the cabin to the back door. His gun raised by his side, Joe gritted his teeth as he peered cautiously around the corner to see what would be waiting for them. He found the boss holed up on the back porch, crouching beside the firewood box, his gun aimed at the inside of the cabin.

As he watched, the man fired off two more rounds before he leaped up from his position and stepped up to the back door. The window of the back door was already shattered from the gunshots, and the boss knocked the rest of the glass out before he reached in and unlocked the door. With manic strength he slammed some makeshift barricade aside and shoved the door open. Joe watched him level his gun at the darkened interior of the house, then watched as the man slowly entered the cabin.

Joe turned to whisper fervently over his shoulder to the kid behind him. 'If you don't want to get killed or spend the rest of your life in prison, listen to me, kid.' He glared at Barney to see if he was listening before he continued. 'When we go in there, do not fire your gun. Do you get that?'

Barney quickly nodded his head, his pale face turning ashen as he licked his lips nervously. 'Okay, I won't shoot no one, Joe. I promise.'

'Good,' he said, then returned his attention back to what was going on around the corner. He pushed away from the side of the cabin and ran to the back porch. Not seeing anything immediately, he quickly climbed the steps and barreled his way to the open back door. He ducked his head as he peered into the doorway. He could see the boss a short distance ahead of him.

Nodding to the kid, he stepped gingerly into the hallway. He pushed himself up against a wall as he waited for his eyes to become accustomed to the darkened interior. Objects become more clear as a few tension-filled moments moved silently past them. He could barely make out the furniture in the kitchen and the living room of the cabin beyond the hallway where they were standing. The boss was crouched beside a large cabinet. The heavy wood of its structure would give him an adequate shield against the woman and her boyfriend, located somewhere inside the cabin.

Joe wished he had some idea where those two were. He didn't know where the boss had got his training, but it was looking more every minute as if he had got it while watching the hard-boiled detective shows on television. The bigger the gun, the more you shoot, the better the plan will go. Joe wiped the sweat from his forehead before he darted across the hallway to the doorway of a small room. He knew the real key to success was less is better. Less violence and less noise. Don't bring attention to your actions and you'll receive less. What the boss was doing was causing unnecessary hassles and, more than likely, unnecessary bloodshed.

Joe knelt low in the doorway as he searched the shadows to try to make out the Reynolds woman's position and that of the guy. He couldn't see them, and figured that the boss must not have got the jump on them quite as he had planned. That small thought gave him enough of a reason to smile a little, then just as quickly it faded.

Now what the hell was he going to do?

CHAPTER 15

Janet paced restlessly within the confines of the room. Her prison, as she was beginning to think of it. She ran her hand distractedly through her hair as she growled. Her gaze furtively scanned the room . . . again.

She was truly sick of being stuck in this room. She had done it. She had actually concocted a half-baked plan, carried it out with surprising success – she still couldn't believe Barney hadn't even tried to use his head and search the room for her – yet she was still trapped in the damn room.

It was driving her crazy.

She was still limping from where she had tried to kick the door down, and her idea of removing the hinges of the door to pull it out of the frame had been a dismal failure. She was down to pacing the room, wondering how long it would take her to scratch her way through the wood floor, then dig a tunnel out to the freedom of the yard taunting her outside the window.

Her gaze fell on the window. The window that was not only painted, but nailed shut. It was the weakest point of the room. It had to be; it was the only thing left in the room she hadn't tried to break or remove. She rubbed at her chin as she continued her movements, her eyes never straying from the window as she paced back and forth.

Janet limped quickly over to the old chair that she had used as a prop in her previous fake escape, and ran with it at the window. When she neared it, she yelled as she swung the chair at the window pane as hard as she could manage. The wood smacked against the surface of the glass with an impressive explosion, and pieces rained clumsily around her shoulders

She had squeezed her eyes shut to protect them from the shards, and now timidly opened them as she staggered backwards from the momentum of her swing. Her eyes widened at what she saw. The pane of glass remained unbroken, but the rickety old chair had splintered into a dozen pieces. Her gaze moved to the only section of the chair that remained intact: the two legs she held.

She tossed them angrily aside, causing them to thud noisily against the wall. Janet spun on her heel as she moved around the room like a caged animal. She was beginning to *feel* like a caged animal, and if she didn't get out of there soon, she would turn into a foaming rabid animal.

'Damn,' she muttered, rubbing her arms briskly while lost in her devious plotting.

Janet moved quickly to the closet and studied the wooden bar that spanned the width of the interior. Standing with her hands on her hips, she studied the placement of the rod. A slow smile spread across her lips as she found that it could be removed quite easily. It looked as if all she had to do was lift it out.

It took several minutes of grunting and straining to get the old fixture out of the frame, which had probably held it for a couple of decades, but she was finally able to pop the rod out of the bracket. Janet lifted it triumphantly out of the closet and giggled as she took a few practice swings with it.

It would work nicely, she thought.

She could practically taste her freedom as she trotted to the window. She stood beside it, then lined her 'bat' up to the frame. Pulling back, she swung the rod at the center of the glass, hoping that was its weakest point. She put her full force behind the swing as she brought it against the pane.

Nothing.

Janet blinked. She couldn't believe it. Half of America had experienced broken windows from kids playing baseball in the front yard, amateur golfers shanking a ball, even hailstorms, but she couldn't even break one lousy window.

Her anger turned to fury. It was no longer the situation of a woman trying to escape from her prison. It was a conquest. Woman against the inanimate existence of a window pane. The fixture was supposed to be a window to the world, not a barrier to keep her from it.

Pursing her lips, Janet vowed that she was going to win.

She resumed her stance in front of the window and focused not only her weapon, but her mental energy as well as she faced her opponent. She waved the tip of the rod in small circles as she wound up for her shot. Once again, she swung the rod at the window, the force so strong her hands bore the reverberations of the blow. Forced to drop the rod, she muttered a string of curses, then lifted her gaze back to the window almost reluctantly. This time she was rewarded with a webbed circle of cracks from the hit.

Janet smiled, the heat of it evil and joyous.

Two more whacks proved only to widen the circled web; it did not give her her freedom from her prison. Janet walked to the bed and fell on it as she caught her breath. She turned to face the window from her perch on the covers and studied her foe. As her breathing returned to normal, she realized that she was making some headway. She only needed one good whack and she would be free.

Slowly she rose and returned to the window. She studied the cracked glass as she stiffened her resolve. Shouldering the rod for another swing at the window, she focused her thoughts on the glass. She pushed the image of another adversary over that of the window. She pictured the cruel one's image standing in the middle. Janet did not know what his face looked like, didn't need to know. She only knew that the thing she needed was her dislike for that man.

She drew back and centered all her anger, her humiliation, her will to live behind that one swing.

The rod hit dead center in the webbed circle. The glass shattered explosively. Though most of it projected outwards, Janet was forced to shield her face with her arms as she twisted away from the flying debris. She shook her head, dislodging glass, then looked back to the window.

It was broken and she was free. The cruel one had lost.

Janet prayed that both Tess and Ethan would be able to beat him wherever they might be facing him.

She knocked out the remaining glass as best as she could, then very gingerly climbed out of the window.

She jumped from her precarious perch on the window-sill to land somewhat painfully on her feet. She straightened, and for the first time was really able to scan her surroundings.

She didn't know where she was, but she was almost certain that Tess and Ethan were at Harolds' cabin, where she had been held first. Looking around her, Janet did not recognize anything. She really had no idea how far she would need to go to reach someone. But one way or another she *would* find someone and get help.

For Tess's sake, she hoped she wasn't too late. She had to let her know she was okay, so the cruel one couldn't use her life to try to trick Tess into doing something that would place her in danger.

But, more than anything, she wanted to help Tess catch the guy and make him pay.

Tess walked across the rug to the bookshelves, picked through a couple of volumes before she randomly selected one, then headed back toward the couch, where she had been sitting only a moment before. She had watched Ethan walk out of the library after their very brief conversation earlier and her heart had felt heavy, sad as she'd watched him go. She was not anywhere near being an expert in love, and she had no idea how to fix the fissure between them.

Nor she did she think she wanted to fix it.

Her eyes moved over the text of the book, but saw nothing. Her mind still tortured her with the sound of Ethan's voice, the image of his face and the memory of his touch. She took a slow, deep breath. No, it was better this way, she reminded herself. Eventually he would have been disappointed with her. Disappointed with what she was. What she did for a career. The men in her life always were after they realized that she would never be their concept of the 'little woman'.

Tess flipped absently through several pages before she realized what a waste of time it was for her to be holding a book when her attention was lost elsewhere. They had decided to hole up in the library while they waited for Badger to show up. Her anxiety continued to grow with each passing moment, because she knew within her that it wouldn't be long before he came. At least in the library they weren't as exposed as they would have been in the living room, with its huge windows that revealed them too easily to the view of someone hidden in the bushes outside.

She rose again to take the book back to the shelf. Her mind was too tense, whirling with too many thoughts to concentrate on printed words. Instead, she stuffed her hands in her pockets and walked in a slow circle around the room as she studied the decor of Harolds' library. Every once in a while she could see a movement from Ethan out of the corner of her eye, now sitting back at the desk, but she would not allow herself to turn to look at him. One look and she was afraid that her resolve to protect him from her would be dissolved. She wouldn't allow herself to do that to him. She cared too much for him to hurt him.

Tess didn't want to stop and analyze why it was so important to her that she should take care of Ethan. She paused to look out the window, though her gaze did not see the beauty that was outside. She saw only Ethan. His smile, his wit, his charm, all that made him irresistible to her. She brushed her hair behind her ear with her finger as she recalled his teasing manner, his humor, something he had seemed to lose since their conversation earlier.

Looking away from the scenic wonder beyond the window, that she was oblivious to anyway, she focused her gaze on a crystal figurine on the shelf by the window. She studied the glass figure of two lovers dancing, their bodies perfectly twined together to unheard music. What she felt for Ethan was like that crystal figurine, she realized. Beautiful, ethereal, almost magic, but something that should be put on a shelf to protect its fragility. Something to admire, but never to touch. One blow and the magic, the beauty, would be destroyed.

Now Ethan wasn't even talking to her. Not that he was that petty an individual, but she was sure he was feeling just as uncomfortable as she was. Neither one of them was the kind of person to be good at idle chit-chat. Occasionally she would sneak a glance at him just to look at him. To drink in the sight of him. Then she would look away before he could see the longing in her eyes. Her need for him.

Really it was just as well;' it would save them both time and trouble. And considerable heartache from a relationship gone sour. More than anything, Tess wanted to keep the memories of the good things between them. She didn't want the beauty of what had happened between them to be tarnished by what would eventually come between them. She didn't want to have any bitterness or anger between them.

Tess had come to realize and accept a long time ago that her professional life would be all that she would ever have. It didn't mean she liked it, or that she didn't still wish for a fulfilling love to share with someone. She had just come to accept that she would never have it.

She'd started to turn away from the window when a muffled sound form the back of the cabin froze her. Tess tilted her head as she strained to hear what might have caused the noise. Her gaze moved instinctively to Ethan's and she found that he too was still. His eyes met hers and his gaze reflected her recognition that the time had come.

Badger had arrived.

Now they would know what the man behind the cruelty looked like. Was it Harolds? His vice-president Torkelson? Or was it someone close to him who had developed an intricate plan to profit from his death?

There was another sound from the back, and both of them pulled their guns from their holsters. Holding her gun ready by her side, Tess moved swiftly to the doorway. She pressed against the doorframe, then peered cautiously into the hallway as she tried to locate the source behind the noise.

Ethan moved behind her, his voice low and soft in her ear as he spoke. 'Remember what Janet said. We have to assume that there are three of them, and they may not all be at the back of the cabin.'

Tess nodded in silent agreement. Ethan was right, and she had to admire his observations. She twisted her head to whisper to him over her shoulder. 'We have to try to stay together. If they are at both the front and back, we could accidentally shoot each other in a crossfire if we split up.'

He gave her shoulder a gentle squeeze, his body so close to her own that she could feel the heat of him. Then it was gone as he moved quickly away. 'Come on, Tess.'

She gasped in reaction, anger filling her. His boldness could get him killed. He ducked low in the hallway and headed toward the entrance of the living room. She was forced to follow him and she mimicked his movements. She had to smile in admiration when she realized where he was headed. Ethan had apparently come up with the same plan of action she had. They would head to the mud room, where a side door was located. The proximity of the room would give them close access to both the front door and the side door of the mud room, while providing them with some protection.

They knelt at the end of the hall as they both scanned the living room and the windows to the side. Tess let her gaze roam to the tall windows again, but from her low vantage point she was not able to tell if anyone was standing outside. She looked over at Ethan and shook her head, then motioned with her chin for him to go.

He grinned mischievously before he bolted from his position and moved quickly, quietly across the length of the front room. At the kitchen he stayed close to the wall, then he turned back to cover her as she darted after him.

Tess ran up beside him, pushing herself to the other side of the doorway they were hiding behind. Two gunshots rang after her, splintering the wood a scant twelve inches above Ethan's head.

He looked up at the scar of splintered wood on the

doorframe, his gaze then moving to meet hers. 'I think my life just flashed before my eyes.'

Another shot drew their attention back to the intruders and they flattened themselves against the wall. She turned her head to glare at him. 'This isn't the time for wisecracks, Ethan. We do happen to have people shooting at us at the moment.'

He ducked back when another shot sliced through the air between them and shattered the glass of the window in front of them. Ethan looked at the window, then back to her, his brow furrowed with his irritation. 'Who says I was kidding?'

Tess scanned the mud room. The side door of the cabin was located to her right, about ten feet away. She could reach it somewhat easily, but Ethan would have to cross in front of the door. He would have to cross directly in the line of fire. Though the exposure would be brief, it would still make him a vulnerable target.

Tess shook her head. She could not risk Ethan's life like that. If he made it to the door safely, there was still no guarantee that there wasn't one of Badger's men waiting outside for them.

The breath tightened in her chest when she realized the gunfire had stopped. Silence enveloped them. Tess's eyes widened as she strained to hear the intruders' movements. Anything that might tell her what was going on in the room behind them.

'Tess.' A man's voice called to her from the living room. 'We don't want to hurt you. We only want to talk to you.'

Her eyes widened and she turned to stare blankly at Ethan. His expression was filled with concern as his gaze searched her face. 'Tess, what is it? Do you recognize who it is?'

She nodded slowly. She licked her lips, her mouth dry and cottony as a chill moved through her. Hearing the man's voice was like hearing the murmuring of the dead. She just could not believe it.

'Tess, I know you can hear me,' the man called again. 'Come out so we can talk.'

She shook her head as she fought to snap out of her shock. Her skin still prickled with goosebumps, but the iciness that had filled her was fading away. They were in terrible danger.

'It's Gare Harolds.' She swallowed as she looked back to Ethan. 'You were right. Somehow he faked his own death.'

'Come on, sweetie,' Harolds called softly. 'Let's stop this foolishness and talk.'

Tess pressed herself flat against the wall, then turned her head to peer slowly past the frame. She could see Harolds crouched in front of the couch. He raised himself slightly till he could see her. Her eyes met his and held them for a moment. Then the tension flowed from his to her, stiffening her body in reaction. His eyes were brown, so dark that she could not quite make out the black iris. It made him look like a man without a soul.

His eyes locked with hers. The look he passed to her was cold, hard, as a smile spread slowly across his face. The smile never reached his eyes, but instead made him look evil. Menacing.

'Tess, we're friends, remember?' he said softly as he started to rise slowly. 'I always respected you professionally. Didn't I always treat you like an equal?'

Tess felt like a deer caught in the middle of the night in the high beams of a car on a darkened deserted highway. Her gaze seemed frozen to his as she watched him stand. He lifted his gun in the air, to his side, his hands up where she could see them as he never removed his gaze from hers.

Out of the corner of her eye she could see Ethan's gaze dart from the man standing in the living room to her, as she remained unmoving where she stood.

'Tess,' he called softly to her. She could feel his gaze bore into her. He continued to talk softly to her, pulling her from the shock and the fear of finding that he was still alive.

Gare Harolds wasn't dead. She had not killed him. The weight of the guilt that had been burdening her for the past several months lifted from her weary shoulders, only to be replaced with anger. How could the man fake his own death like that? What about the few people who had actually mourned for him? Not that Tess could remember that many, but how could he be so thoughtless of those he had hurt?

Her anger mingled with her shock, numbing her against the chill her realization had enveloped her with. Harolds' dark gaze mesmerized her, and as she stared into his eyes she tried to rationalize within her mind the fact that she was *not* seeing a dead man before her.

She didn't see him raise his gun till it was too late. She sucked in her breath, the scream catching in her throat. Ethan's voice boomed beside her, his anger deepening his voice like a roar. Harolds lifted his gun, swift as lightning, and leveled it on her. His eyes were hard and malicious as he smiled with evil pleasure.

Harolds pulled the trigger and the bullet shot from it in an explosion of fire as Ethan yelled her name and dove towards her. Feeling caught, as if in slow motion, Tess turned her head, lifting her hand to try to stop Ethan even as she opened her mouth to call to him. She screamed and shook her head wildly. She was too late.

Ethan flew across the opening of the doorway at her. His outstretched hands connected with her, roughly sending her flying backwards. She hit the ground hard, her head connecting with a thud to the floor. The wood floor and Ethan's chest pushed the wind out of her and she struggled for air as sharp pain filled her chest. Ethan lay sprawled across her, unmoving.

Panic filled her and she grabbed him, then began to shake him wildly. 'Ethan?'

He groaned, trying to lift himself off her. 'Sorry about that.'

His voice mingled with shouted orders from the living room. It was Harolds, barking orders to one of his men. Though he shouted, she only caught a few words as her gaze moved frantically over Ethan. They were coming in.

Her gaze had just reached his shoulder, finding the blood that seeped through his shirt in a growing stain, when a movement in her peripheral vision caught her attention. A man walked into the kitchen with a gun held ready in front of him. Fighting through the shroud of the fear enveloping her, Tess realized that the man was not Harolds, but one of his henchmen.

At the sound of Ethan's groan of pain, the man swiveled toward them, his gun leveled on them. The end of the black barrel wavered slightly, but was firmly targeted on Ethan's back.

Tess pulled her trigger and fired.

His eyes registered his shock, then reflected the sharp bite of pain as the bullet tore through his shoulder. The momentum of the bullet twisted his body under him and the large man fell with heavy thud on his back. Tess struggled under Ethan's large body and shoved him unceremoniously off her. She breathed a small apology to him as her eyes tracked the movements of the man sprawled on his back only a few feet away from them. His breath was coming in quick gasps as he tried to lift a hand to his injured shoulder before it dropped limply to the floor. His eyes remained open as he stared at the ceiling, but the rise and fall of his chest let her know that he was still alive.

Tess heard a voice call sharply to the man lying on the floor in front of them. It was Harolds, and he was barking orders at the injured man as if his anger alone would spur the kid into rising to his feet and capturing them. Harolds continued to yell at the kid until another deep voice boomed from the other room, telling him to knock it off.

Tess rolled to her feet and moved quickly to Ethan's side. She knelt beside him as she gingerly examined his bleeding shoulder. Ethan was now up on his hands and knees, his ashen face covered with sweat as he panted.

'Ethan, baby, are you okay?' she whispered quietly as her gaze searched the familiar contours of his face.

At her unexpected term of endearment, his mouth twisted up in the ghost of a smile, and he turned his face slightly toward her to meet her gaze. He started to open his mouth to talk, then nodded instead, the effort to speak apparently too hard for him.

Tess chewed her lip as ice-cold fear mingled with the strong will for her own survival. She searched his gaze. 'We need to get out of here now, Ethan. Can you make it?'

His dark head bobbed up and down in an unsteady answer. He forced himself shakily to his feet. 'We don't really have a choice, do we?'

'You're right. We don't.' She offered him an encouraging smile, even though every part of her had nothing to smile about.

He was pale. Deathly pale as he stood stiffly. When he wobbled slightly she immediately grabbed hold of his arm to steady him. Ethan was forced to lean heavily against her as she guided him to the side door of the mud room. Tess gritted her teeth as his weight pushed down on her, forcing her to struggle with the knob of the door with the same hand that held her gun. Ethan finally shifted his weight, and she was able to switch her gun to her other hand, holding him up, then twist the door open.

As they shuffled out onto the porch she heard Harolds and the other man make their way into the mud room behind them. The door slammed behind them, and Tess whispered her encouragement to Ethan as she pushed them as quickly as she could toward the steps of the wide porch.

Somehow Ethan found the strength to push himself into a lurching trot as they made their way to the barn. It was the only place she could think of to take him. Harolds yelled angrily as he came to the door of the mud room. They were quickly closing the distance between themselves and the barn when he fired his first shot at them.

Out of the corner of her eye, Tess saw the clods of dirt kick up from the bullet bouncing off the ground close beside them. She muttered a few oaths as she turned to glance frantically over her shoulder. Tess twisted just enough to turn toward Harolds as she fired her own gun at him. She had not really been able to take aim, but the wayward bullet still produced the desired effect. Harolds dived back into the door way of the house to take cover, giving them the small amount of time they needed to make it to the barn.

Tess's lungs gulped for air as sweat rolled down the side of her face. Ethan's weight was considerable, and made her legs feel like chunks of cement as she helped him make his way toward the barn. She glanced at the lock of the barn door and was relieved to see that they had not slipped it back into its clasp. She ripped the large metal lock from the loop and tossed it without a glance into the grass somewhere beside them.

Propping Ethan against the side of the old barn, she gripped the door handle and yanked it open just enough for them to squeeze through. She'd be damned if she would make things any easier for them; they'd have to struggle with the door to open it wider.

Tess swiveled quickly on her feet as she looked back toward the house, furtively searching for signs of Harolds and his men. She had shot one of them, wounding him, but that still left two of them against her and Ethan.

Turning back to him, she felt her breath catch in her chest as fear gripped her. He was still breathing heavily from their trot across the uneven yard. His eyes were half open and dark circles had already appeared under them. Slowly he lifted his unsteady gaze to hers. Without a word he lifted his arm out to her for help to move himself inside the safety of the barn.

Tess gently pushed him through the small opening, apologizing softly as the door pushed against his wound, causing him to groan with pain. 'I'm sorry, baby. It's not much further, I promise. Please stay with me, Ethan. Please don't give up on me now.'

He didn't make an attempt to talk, only nodded his head slightly as he allowed her to pull him behind her. Ducking her head to look into his face, Tess could see she was losing him quickly. His strength was fading fast, and she needed to get him somewhere where she could stash him safely.

Once inside the darkened interior of the barn, she scanned around her, searching frantically for something, anything, she could use to help them. Her gaze fell on the thick metal tack shed where they had found the snapshot of Janet tied to the chair. She suppressed the faint twinge of anger that surged through her at that memory as she shuffled Ethan toward the door. Again, they had left the lock hanging loosely from its ring.

It only seemed right that they use one of Harolds' little tools of manipulation against him.

Tess swung the door open, the thick metal creaking slightly as she pushed it to the side. She said soft words of encouragement to Ethan, as asking him to lean against the wall for a moment. Stepping quickly to the opposite wall, she removed several horse blankets and spread them haphazardly in the farthest corner of the small room. At least there he would be more protected if any bullets were to make it through the metal. Judging by its thickness, Harolds would have to be crazy to fire at the metal and endanger himself with a ricochet.

She paused for a moment. Crazy? They were talking about a man who had faked his own death. He was more than crazy; he was a lunatic.

Tess ran back to Ethan's side, gripping his good arm gently. 'Sweetie, I need you to walk a few more steps with me. That's it, Ethan, you're doing good. I'm putting you in the tack shed. It's metal, remember. You'll be safe there, I promise.'

Worriedly she watched his ashen face pale to a deathly white as he bent to lower himself to the blankets. His knees buckled under him and he fell onto the makeshift bed she had made for him. Tess cried out to him, kneeling quickly beside him as tears welled in her eyes at the incredible pain she witnessed in his gaze.

'Ethan, baby,' she murmured softly. 'Stay with me, please. Don't –'

Tess left her plea unfinished as she swallowed the burning knot caught in her throat. Ethan's eyes were already floating closed as he struggled visibly to talk to her.

Slowly he lifted his good hand, and it unsteadily reached her face. 'Stay with me, Tess.'

She leaned down to him. Closing her eyes, she placed her lips gently, lovingly against the already overly warm skin of his forehead. She lifted her head just enough to glance into his eyes. Already he was fading into unconsciousness.

A tear made a hot trail down her cheek. His eyelids flew open and he forced himself to look at her gaze. His head was unsteady as he swallowed, trying to get the words out.

Tess shook her head as she touched his cheek. 'Ethan, don't try to talk.'

He tried to shake his head, but ended up tilting his face up toward hers. His voice was weak, hoarse with the pain from his wound. Ethan took a shaky breath as he held her gaze.

'I love you, Tess.'

Damn it.

Joe's brow had furrowed into a deep frown as he'd watched the boss's movements ahead of him. He and Barney were still hunkered down behind large pieces of furniture in the hallway. The boss had moved ahead of them and was hiding behind the big couch in the living room.

He had watched in amazement as the man stood while he was talking to the woman. Joe had literally shaken his head in disbelief as the man tried to talk his way into the room with the Reynolds woman.

The exchange of gunfire had been quick and intense. He had watched the man with Reynolds save her life as he took a bullet for her. At the silence, the boss had turned dark vicious eyes on

Barney, and had barked at him to get in there to see what had happened. The poor kid had turned a frightened gaze on him questioningly, until the boss yelled at him again, spurring him into action.

When Barney had advanced into the room, Joe had stood to back him up. Things had gone too far as it was, and he just wanted to get the kid the hell out of there. They needed to leave the whole mess behind them as quickly as possible.

Then the shot had hit the kid, knocking him like a rag doll onto his back.

The next few moments were a blur, but Joe had finally been able to get into the room. He'd scanned the room and found that the Reynolds woman had taken the injured man to escape out the side door. Joe had ignored the boss's continued yelling and rushed to Barney's side.

'You okay, kid?' he asked, peeling back Barney's jacket to look at the wound.

Barney's brow was creased in pain, and he took short breaths because of it. Slowly he nodded, though he didn't try to move his arms or his body. 'I think so.'

Joe's lips thinned into a grim line at the sight of the nasty little hole that had penetrated the kid's shoulder. Barney had been fortunate; the bullet had hit a dead spot, missing anything that would cause serious problems. The bleeding could be a problem, though.

He glanced up to meet the kid's gaze and gave him a small encouraging smile. 'You're going to be okay, kid. Don't you worry about a thing. I'm just going to grab a towel over here and stuff it in your shirt. That will take care of that bleeding for you. You're going to be okay.'

Barney searched his gaze, as if looking for any signs of falsehood. He really wanted to believe this older man he had grown to trust. Finally he nodded his head weakly. 'Okay.'

Joe quickly thumped over to the kitchen to search for a handtowel. He found one hanging from a loop on the wall beside the kitchen sink and grabbed it. Making his way back to Barney, he stopped short when the boss pushed into the room.

'What the hell are you doing?' he snapped as he glared at him.

Joe clenched his jaws together as he spoke in a tight voice. 'Barney's been shot. I'm stopping the bleeding.'

The man didn't even turn to look at the gasping kid, sprawled on the floor. He advanced on Joe till he stood nose to nose with him. His voice was a low threat as he leaned toward him, his stance intimidating.

'Forget the kid,' he breathed, his dark eyes leveled on his. 'Get yourself out there *now*. We've got to find those two before that bitch you idiots let escape has a chance to call the cops on us.'

Joe raised his gun between them, his eyes hardening to match those of the man standing in front of him. 'Go to hell. You can dig your own grave.'

The cruel one's gaze never wavered. Never once looked at the gun less than three inches from his chin. His voice dropped to a menacing growl. 'You'll pay for this.'

'Not half as much as you will if you don't get out of my face,' Joe replied quietly. The thin, icy calm of his voice pushed through the boss's anger. He shouldered past Joe and headed swiftly out the side door.

Without a backward glance, Joe returned his attention to the kid. He knelt beside him and quickly stanched the flow of blood with the towel. 'See, I told you everything was going to be all right.'

Barney looked up at him, his fear strong in his eyes. 'You aren't going to let him kill those people, are you, Joe?'

Hell of a time to develop a conscience, kid, he thought to himself. Instead he busied himself adjusting the makeshift bandage on Barney's wound. He flicked his gaze to the kid's as he went through his motions.

'No, I'm not about to let us become accessories to murder,' he answered quietly. He gripped the kid's good arm. 'Do you think you can stand up?'

Barney nodded, his face visibly paling as he rolled to his side to push himself to his knees. Joe hauled the kid's large frame up as easily as he could, but the movement still caused him to groan with the pain that shot through him.

'Let's get you out of here,' he said. 'Then we'll get those people some help if we can.'

He didn't voice his doubts to the kid because he didn't want to upset him. Unfortunately, at the moment there wasn't much they could do. The Reynolds woman and the injured man with her were pretty much on their own.

CHAPTER 16

Tess closed the door of the tack shed. She pressed her hand against the cool metal of the door as the image of Ethan lying unconscious on the horse blankets swam in her mind. Leaning her forehead against its solid sturdiness, she squeezed her eyes shut, trying to get rid of the shimmering memory. She had left the cellular phone lying beside him. Just in case.

If anything was to happen to her, he would surely die in the locked shed without a phone to call for help to rescue him. Before she had locked the door she had checked, and had been relieved to see that the small face of the phone had showed the signal would be all right in the enclosed area. It had not made leaving him behind any easier.

A sob tore deep within her throat. Her eyes swam with tears and she sniffed. Turning away from the door, she wiped the trail of a tear away with her hand. She had to be strong, she reminded herself. She had to be strong for the both of them.

Tess checked Ethan's gun, which she had put in her holster, then retrieved her own from the top of a crate. She cocked it with a click and walked away from the shed, not allowing herself to turn back for one last look.

She had to lead Harolds away from the barn and Ethan. The last thing she wanted was for him to find Ethan. If she allowed him any time, she knew Harolds would try to kill him. He would be an easy target to take care of, with his injuries pushing him into unconsciousness. If Harolds realized that Ethan was locked in the tack shed, unconscious and defenseless, the quickest way for him to take care of that problem and come after her would be to set the old barn on fire.

Her heart lurched at the thought.

Tess would not allow Harolds to hurt Ethan. She skirted quickly to the wide door of the barn and pushed it open slightly. Harolds was walking calmly, nonchalantly toward the barn, with his gun swinging easily in his hand. The smile on his face was friendly yet maniacal as he strolled toward the barn where she hid.

Tess edged the barrel of the gun through the small opening of the door and fired at him. The bullet whistled across the yard, nicking Harolds on the shoulder. His body jerked backwards as the bullet tore through the fabric of his shirt and broke the skin.

He stopped in his tracks and looked with disbelief at the blood seeping from the flesh wound. Tess cursed silently at her miss. Her luck just wasn't with her today. She had been aiming at his heart, but nerves and his rolling movements had thrown her shot off slightly.

Taking action, she shoved the heavy door of the barn back on its track, sending the large wooden frame creaking back to its place on the wall. Tess fired another round at Harolds, sending him for cover as she bolted out the door to the closest corner of the barn.

Once around the edge of the old structure, she stopped to catch her breath as she pressed herself against the rough grain of the wooden planks. She leaned to her side to peer around the edge to check Harolds' position.

He wasn't there.

Her eyes widened in shock. Where is he? she thought, and her thoughts were frantic as she began to scan the area for a sign of the man.

'Looking for me, Tess?'

Tess swiveled around to face the eerie calm of Harolds' voice. He was smiling amicably at her as he walked slowly. He moved one foot in front of the other as he closed the distance between them. His posture was relaxed, his hands swinging low, though one held a gun. The barrel remained fixed unwaveringly on her as he moved closer.

'Tess, can't we stop this nonsense already?' he asked.

She held her gun with both hands as she faced him. 'Harolds, I will kill you if I have to.'

'Sweetheart, is that any way to talk to one of your best clients?' he offered, holding his hand out in front of him as he tilted his head. He smiled at her, full of charm. His gaze moved over hers in a sensual caress. 'I can take good care of you, if you would only let me.'

Bile rose in her throat at the term 'sweetheart'. Her heart remembered the times Ethan had called her that affectionately; her mind remembered his charm and wit.

Her lip curled in distaste and her gaze hardened. 'You *were* a client, Harolds. Remember that? To the world you are already dead and buried. I can shoot you right now and no one would ever know the difference. I could let your corpse rot in the wild like you let Torkelson's.'

It was his turn to smile. Harolds' lips lifted slightly as he chuckled. 'The difference is, sweetheart, that *you* would know that you had killed me. And we both know you don't have the taste for murder like I do.'

'You bastard,' she spat at him.

'Too bad you won't cooperate with me, Tess,' he said soothingly. With lightning speed, he leveled the barrel of his gun at her and fired.

Tess jumped in a flying leap toward the brush. She landed in a roll, then continued with the momentum to her feet and crouched low as she ran. A bullet whistled past her head, nicking a tree, sending the bark splintering as it exposed the pale flesh hidden underneath. She ran to a stand of trees. Positioning herself behind the largest one, she twisted cautiously around to find Harolds.

Her heart raced, thumping in her chest so hard she thought that surely the sound of it alone would give her away. Tess tried to school her breathing as she searched the surrounding forest for Harolds. She forced herself to calm down, then strained her ears to listen.

The forest had become unusually quiet. No crickets or birds calling, only the wind as it whistled through the long needles of the pine trees. The wind was picking up, she noted, the roar of it moving around her. Tess bit at her lip. With the noise of the wind, she wouldn't be able to hear Harolds as he approached.

Turning back to study the area in front of her, she looked for something that could help her. Her gaze moved over the ground beneath the canopy of the treetops. Her search stopped when she spotted a fallen tree about forty feet in front of her. It would be a risk to get to the log, but once there she could use it as cover. It would also provide her with an excellent vantage point. Harolds would have to circle a long way around before he could sneak up behind her.

She twisted back one last time to try to spot Harolds. Seeing nothing, she pushed away from the tree and ran. The leaves crunched below Tess's feet as she sprinted through the underbrush, snaking between the trees and an occasional bush. Adrenaline and fear pulsed through her as she ran. She half expected Harolds to try to put a bullet in her back as she headed for the log.

Tess leaped over the fallen tree and kneeled quickly behind it. She closed her eyes as she caught her breath. No bullets. He hadn't even tried to fire at her once. Though she was glad that he hadn't, at least if he had shot at her she might be able to determine his location.

Opening her eyes, she pushed up just enough to look over the edge of the log. Immediately a bullet whizzed past her. Okay, she thought, he was not that far behind her, and to her right.

'Must be a better way to figure these things out,' she muttered to herself.

What was she going to do? Tess licked her lips nervously as she pushed several scenarios through her mind. She whipped up to her knees and squeezed a shot in the direction he had fired from. Instantly he returned it, and she noted that he had moved. Tess could tell from the position of his fire that he was indeed trying to circle around behind her.

'Want to play games, Harolds?' she said softly. A blanket of calm settled over her as a plan formed in her mind. As long as he had had her on the run, her nerves had been humming, forcing her mind to not only deal with that, but with survival as well. But now she had a plan.

If Harolds wanted to play a twisted little game, she would give it to him. But this time she would turn the tables in her favor. Not his.

'Tess, aren't you tired of this yet?' he called to her, his voice coming to her in a sing-song appeal.

His voice showed that he had moved again. She moved, keeping low as she headed down the hill to an outcropping of boulders. She ignored his question as she skidded in loose dirt, slipping to her knees. Pushing herself back up, Tess continued cautiously toward the boulders.

'Come on, Tess,' he said. His voice was beginning to show the strain of his building anger. Tess smiled. His movements were parallel to her own as they separately worked their way down the hill. 'Talk to me.'

Her smile turned to a frown at his words. The bastard actually thought he could talk her into giving herself up to him. She shook her head. She'd use that ego against him.

'Why did you do it, Harolds?' she called to him. 'You had everything. You had a position of importance and power, wealth, and a family. What about your wife and kids, Harolds? They think you're dead.'

His low chuckle washed over her with a chill. The humor within it was a stark contrast to the enormity of the situation. 'Yeah, I had everything, didn't I?'

Tess slid through a blanket of leaves. Righting herself, she stopped just long enough to search the trees again to look for him.

'Don't worry about my family, Tess,' he said amicably. She heard him push his way through tree branches and was glad to see that he was heading where she wanted him to go. 'They are being well taken care of. Very well taken care of, believe me.'

'So why did you do it?' Tess pushed him on as she knelt in a stand of trees. She studied the boulders to acquaint herself with the layout.

'I hate to disappoint you,' he answered, 'but I did it because of that old cliché about greed, sweetheart. Yes, my company *made* millions in a year, and the industrial espionage *cost* us millions. But it made me a fortune. I was able to pocket the difference.'

'You're right, Harolds,' she said, letting the disgust she felt about him fill her voice. 'I am disappointed. But I guess I shouldn't have expected too much from you anyway.'

He laughed, and she heard a twig snap as he pushed through the trees. 'You were too good at your job, Tess. I knew the noose was slipping around my neck. When the opportunity to escape my troubles presented itself, I took it. You know, Tess, the sun in

South America is wonderful. And the women . . . ah, yes the women. I get almost as much pleasure out of making a woman climax as I do from my own.'

'How noble of you to sacrifice yourself,' Tess retorted sarcastically. Anger filled her at his condescending attitude. The bastard. What about love or loyalty?

Tess finished her inspection of the boulders and quickly scanned around her. She took a deep breath and pushed from her position to run to the outcropping. She jumped over the small drop and landed with a thump at the bottom. Fighting a groan from the pain of having the wind knocked out of her, she held her rib as she stood.

Looking within the darkened crevice of the large boulders, she smiled. It looked perfect, she thought. She could only hope her hare-brained plan would work.

Gare Harolds stepped cautiously through the woods. He wasn't in a hurry; in fact he was savoring every step of the hunt. How appropriate it should be a woman. Quintessa Reynolds, no less.

He had been intrigued by her from the moment he had hired her firm. It had surprised him that she had been so immune to his considerable charm. He would have loved to get her in bed, make her lose herself in the pleasure he could create in her body. The thought of her naked and submitting in his bed had been the fuel for more than one fantasy for him.

Unfortunately he had also not expected her to be quite so good at her job.

At first he had continually put obstacles in her way, to keep her off the right track. To keep her from following the trail to him. After a while, as the pressure continued to grow, he'd realized it was time to end the game. But how? Things were starting to get a little too hot.

Then the opportunity had presented itself. It had been too golden to be true, but it would wrap up all his loose ends with one little blow. His death. If everyone thought he was dead, he could take the money he had made by selling his company secrets and simply disappear.

It had all been planned so perfectly, except that Tess Reynolds would not let his death alone. She still continued to haunt him even after his 'death.' Now he was left with no choice but to get rid of her.

Harolds stopped short at the sight of Tess running toward an outcropping of boulders. A slow smile spread across his face. He'd had only an idea of where she was headed, but now he knew where she was going to hole up. What better to get something out of a hole than a badger?

He chuckled at his own wit as he headed quietly toward the large rocks. Harolds didn't go over the edge as she had, but skirted around to cautiously peer over the boulder. The space created by the outcropping was large, almost a small cave. He grinned as he realized that she had cornered herself by hiding in this huge crevice cut into the mountainside.

Harolds stayed close to the wall of the rocks as he stepped inside. After pausing long enough to allow his eyes to adjust, he moved slowly forward as he searched the shadows for the Reynolds woman.

The crevice was approximately twenty feet long, a lot longer than he would have imagined from the outside. As he moved slowly within, the interior became steadily darker. The shadows darkened, and Harolds relied more on his hearing than his sight to locate her. Listening for movement, it wasn't too long before he was rewarded with a scraping sound only a few feet ahead of him.

He could just barely make out a ghost of white as something moved quickly further back into the crevice. By the size of it, he had to assume it was her shoes. He grinned as he advanced on her. He heard pebbles skittering ahead of him; he was close now. Harolds leaped forward and grabbed at Tess.

His arms swung, batting only at air. The shock and confusion was instant and icy. 'What the hell?' he snapped in surprise.

A blow to his head caused bursts of colored lights. Though he was surrounded in almost total blackness, he was conscious enough to be aware of his surroundings, and of her grunting and groaning as she dragged him out of the crevice . . .

Apparently he had briefly lost consciousness, because now, when he had awoken, he found himself tied and handcuffed to a large tree.

Harolds stared stupidly up at Tess as he frowned with dazed bewilderment, his head still throbbing from the blow. 'I saw you. The white of your shoes. How did you get behind me?'

'That's always been your problem, Harolds. You never gave women the respect they deserved.' Tess smirked as she tossed her bra at him, the white lace hitting him in the face. 'And you always underestimated them.'

At the sound of the helicopter, Tess ran back to the cabin, leaving Harolds screaming behind her. Never had she been so glad to see her partners in her life than when they whisked in on propellered wings.

'You're late, but I am so glad to see you guys,' she shouted over the roar of the helicopter's engine. She hugged them both, then pointed them to the barn. 'Ethan's been shot and I think he's hurt pretty bad. We need to get him to the hospital.'

She ran to the barn with her partners close behind her. Throwing the barn door open as far as it would go, she rushed to the tack shed. She pulled the key from the nail on the wall and frantically opened the door.

A cry escaped her throat when her gaze fell on Ethan's ashen face. Caressing his skin, she found that he was cold to the touch. Tess turned a terrified gaze to the two men. 'He's not doing well, is he?'

'It doesn't look like it.' Tim met her gaze, his expression grave. 'We don't have time to worry about fixing him a stretcher. Come on, Tom, help me get him in the helicopter.'

They carried him to their roaring transport. Tom stayed behind to stand guard over Harolds till the police came while Tim left with Tess.

The flight to the hospital felt like hours, but could only have been minutes. Once they arrived, Tess refused to leave Ethan's side until the very moment they wheeled him into surgery.

As she watched the gurney disappear behind the swinging doors, she realized she had a decision to make, and there could only be one answer. Tears welled in her eyes as the pain burned in her heart. Never had doing the right thing hurt so bad.

Ethan's wound had required surgery. When he had fully regained consciousness, a memory had floated through the fog. He was not sure whether it actually was a memory or a dream, but either way he had savored it. Still savored it. It had been of Tess, standing beside his bed talking to him softly. Though he could not remember her gentle words, he knew his heart had responded to her touch. She had stroked his brow and held his hand as her voice, soft as silk, flowed over him.

When he had become fully awake, he had asked one of the nurses if he had had a visitor, trying to act as casually as he could. At her knowing look of understanding and sympathy, he felt fortunate that he was not in a hospital where people might recognize him.

The nurse had nodded and told him that a woman with auburn hair had arrived with him, never leaving him till they wheeled him to surgery. Even then she had remained in the waiting room during the long hours of the operation to remove the bullet and stitch his torn muscles together. The nurse had checked on her several times and had found her alternately pacing or sitting with her head in her hands. When he had been wheeled into the recovery room, the nurse told him that she had remained with him till they had upgraded him to stable condition.

Then she had left.

That had been several weeks ago, and he had not seen nor heard from her since.

Ethan had remained in the hospital for a couple of more days, then had been well enough to go back home. When he had finally been able to get out of bed without his head swimming too badly, he had retrieved Sylvester from his neighbor Polly, giving her his eternal thanks. She had only smiled and patted his hand before she shoed him back home. Even though she'd continually scolded him as she walked him back to his house, Ethan had been able to find out that Tess had picked up her cat several days earlier. And again she had gone without a word.

Because his arm was limited by his wound, the office had called in help to cover for him as he recuperated. First he had had to build up his strength. In the beginning just taking a shower had exhausted him. Barely toweling off, he would crawl back into bed and sleep for a couple of hours till he could muster enough strength to put on his clothes. After a week or so, he'd been relieved to realize that he could actually stay awake for more than a couple of hours, and sometimes even walk around the house. Friends, co-workers, and even his family had dropped in on him to check and make sure that he was doing okay. Never had he had so many visitors. It had gotten to the point that the numerous visits had begun to wear him out, instead of helping build up his morale.

Still, it had warmed him to see the faces of the people who cared about him. Julie had brought him a couple of books to read, Doris had even brought him a basket of her famous blueberry muffins, and Roger

Skinner had brought him a video tape to watch. Though he'd enjoyed seeing his friends, and was touched by their concern, there was one person whom he yearned to see, but who never showed.

Tess.

As the days passed and his strength grew, Ethan felt his emotions slump. He was physically feeling more and more like himself with every passing day, as long as he didn't overdo it. Several of his friends, however, eyed him speculatively whenever he answered their question of 'What's wrong?' with a simple 'Nothing.' Even Roger was giving him funny looks. By the hooded gaze of the detective, Ethan figured that even Roger must have a pretty good idea of what was wrong with him. He missed Tess. Still, he did not feel like sharing that with anyone in particular.

As his strength improved, Ethan was able to convince most of his friends and family of his improvement, and the rate of visits was now beginning to decline. He was glad that his life was starting to get back to normal, but as the visits slowed it gave him more time alone. Time alone that let him think. And remember.

His mood had become so blue that even Sylvester wouldn't have anything to do with him. And after a couple of days of this low mood, Ethan decided enough was enough. He got up one morning, shaved, and fixed his breakfast, with a little something extra for his furry friend.

After a couple of weeks at home, he had learned to identify the sound of the mail truck by its constant stopping and starting as the carrier delivered his neighborhood's mail. He headed out the front door to see what the mailman had brought to him today. He waved to his neighbor Polly as she too came out to retrieve her mail.

'How are you feeling today, Ethan?' she called to him as they both strolled to their mailboxes.

'Feeling much better, thank you.' He smiled at her, enjoying the warmth of the sunshine on his face. 'Looks like it is going to be a beautiful day, don't you think?'

She nodded. They both reached their mailboxes at the same time and opened the lids. Ethan pulled out his letters and began to shuffle them as he scanned to see what he had. Never would he admit it, but unconsciously he always hoped he would find a letter from a certain woman who had decided to disappear from his life.

He knew why she had let him. Well, at least he thought he knew. He had seen a flicker of it occasionally in her expression, when he'd found her looking at him. He'd seen the uncertainty and the doubt. Tess was an unusual woman. Because of that he wondered if she felt uncertain about a relationship with him.

Or maybe she simply did not love him.

A movement out of the corner of his eye caught his attention. Ethan turned to find Polly sitting on her curb, staring open-mouthed with a dazed expression on her face. Ethan immediately ran to her side, pointedly ignoring the sharp pain in his shoulder that the run caused him.

'Polly, are you all right?' he asked, concern filling his voice. He automatically took her wrist in his hand and began taking her pulse. 'What is it?'

She turned slowly toward him, her wide eyes focusing on his own. 'I cannot believe it.'

'What is it, Polly? Is something wrong?' he asked as he kneeled beside her. He looked at the mail scattered beside her and assumed she must have received bad news.

She shook her head slightly, her lips alternately lifting in a grin, then falling in a frown. 'Is it real? Is it a joke?'

'Is what a joke?' he asked.

'I sold it,' she murmured, the dazed look returning as she absently handed him the letter she held in her hand.

Ethan sat down beside her, then took the letter she offered, realizing that she had handed it to him to read. Scanning the letter, he was halfway through the body of it when he smiled and was forced to start back at the top. In his excitement, his lips began to move as he read the letter. When he was finished with it he looked up to meet Polly's gaze.

'You wrote a book?' he asked in awe.

'I've written two so far.' Polly nodded numbly. After a moment she started to giggle. When Ethan's deep chuckle mingled with hers, she could no longer contain it and she began to laugh. Ethan joined her as he grabbed her in a fierce hug.

He groaned as the pain shot through his shoulder. At the sound of his discomfort, Polly immediately drew back. 'I'm sorry, Ethan. I didn't mean to hurt you.'

'I'm fine, Polly,' he assured her with a broad smile. 'A book. I can't believe it. I've had an author for a neighbor all this time and never knew it.'

'A writer,' Polly explained automatically, fixing a maternal gaze on him. 'An individual does not become an author till that individual has published a book. I *was* a writer and now I'm an author.'

Her hand flew to her mouth as her eyes widened. 'Oh, my gosh, Ethan. I am an author. I can't tell you what this means to me. It truly is a dream come true.'

'A book,' he laughed. He let the shared joy of Polly's good fortune wash over him and help drive away the blue mood that had been with him too long. He shook his head. He didn't know who was more dumbfounded. Polly or himself. 'What kind of book did you write, Polly?'

She blinked a couple of times, his question forcing the wheels of her mind to work past the fog of her excitement. 'Uh, I wrote a romance mystery.'

Ethan's brows rose as he took in his elderly neighbor's petite frame. 'Romance mystery, huh? Has old Mr Gardner from the next block over been giving you fodder for fiction?' he asked teasingly.

'No.' She shook her head distractedly as her gaze returned to the letter she'd retrieved from him. 'You have.'

'What?' Ethan asked. He was astounded. It wasn't as if he had that much of a love life. Hell, his love life was almost as dead as his patients. He had not even been seeing a woman . . . till Tess. He stopped his mental thoughts in their tracks. He had never had the opportunity to have a normal moment with Tess. A normal date, let alone a normal evening. They had always been on the run, on the chase, and now she was gone.

He narrowed his eyes as he studied his neighbor. 'What do you mean?'

Polly's eyes twinkled mischievously. 'Well, you were sort of my inspiration for the second book I wrote, young man. You and that gorgeous redhead that snuck into your house that night after I found you sprawled on your lawn. The first one – the one they've bought – was also based on you, but loosely.'

'You saw her breaking into my house?' he exclaimed, skipping back to the earlier part of her explanation. Ethan didn't know whether to laugh or fume at Polly. He shifted his feet as he tried to come to terms with the fact that he had unknowingly been made into a character in a book.

Polly eyed him. She started to fidget nervously as she watched the different emotions flicker across his face. 'I knew she wasn't there to hurt you, Ethan. Or I would have called the police. Really I would have.'

He leveled his gaze on her. 'How did you know she wasn't going to hurt me?'

She simply smiled, her face transformed into the ancient mask women expertly wear whenever they want to tell you that they *just know*. Some people called it women's intuition. Ethan did not know what he wanted to call it at the moment.

'I just knew,' she answered easily.

'I can't believe it.' He started to laugh. 'Me, a character in a book. Am I a bad guy or a good guy?'

Polly pursed her lips together as she tried to suppress her smile. 'A good guy, of course. I mean, in the first book I based the physical description of the hero on you, but the plot was my own. The one I just finished is the one that you and your girl inspired, and I think they are interested in it too. You aren't mad at me, are you?'

Ethan shook his head. He waved her question away with his hand. 'Mad? I think it's great.' He stopped, tilting his head to study her. 'Are you using my name?'

Polly's cheeks tinged red as she started twisting her hands coyly. 'Well, your name does have a certain ring to it, you have to admit, Ethan.'

'Wow. My name as a character in a book,' he said. He ran his hand through his hair. 'When is it going to be published?'

She shrugged. 'I don't know. The letter only says they want to buy it. The submission process alone took months to go through – the query, then the request, and now the acceptance. I've never done this kind of thing before, but from what I've heard from my writers' group, it could be anywhere from a year to two years.'

'Writers' group?' He frowned. 'They actually have groups for . . . writers?'

Polly chuckled. 'Yeah, I just started. They even have them for different types of writing. Romance, mystery, science fiction, horror; you name it.'

'I never knew my life was so exciting,' Ethan murmured. He truly found it humorous that his neighbor thought his life was so 'inspiring' as to use it to create a plot for a book. He shook his head. Little did she know. Though the career of a medical examiner was never routine, and was full of intriguing cases, it was not what most people would consider 'exciting.' As for a love life – well, he didn't have one. A spark of romance had flared briefly for him. That was till she walked out of his life.

'Ethan?' Polly called his name.

He was startled out of his thoughts as he turned back to meet her gaze. 'Yes?'

His elderly neighbor chuckled at his distraction, a knowing smile on her face. Ethan was beginning to really dislike 'knowing' smiles.

'I asked how your girlfriend was doing?' she said.

Ethan frowned for a moment as her question caused him to hesitate. Girlfriend? Oh, she meant Tess. Funny, he thought to himself, he had never quite considered Tess as a girlfriend. His heart considered the term an underestimate.

Turning away, he avoided Polly's gaze as he stammered through a few responses. Finally he cleared his throat and gave her an answer. 'She is not my girlfriend, Polly.'

She paused for a moment, almost causing him to glance back to her to see what her expression was. He could imagine what his answer might conjure up for an individual of her generation. His neighbor was probably wondering what the younger generation was coming to.

'Of course not, dear,' she soothed, patting his arm gently.

Ethan rested his arms on his knees as he sat on the curb. He met Polly's gaze and was surprised to find understanding in her eyes.

'What happened?' she asked.

He glanced away. He had always been on good terms with his neighbor, but it wasn't as if they knew each other well. Yet now it seemed perfectly natural to be discussing his love life with her.

He shrugged. After a moment he shook his head, 'I wish I knew. You know we had to go out of state to find the people who kidnapped her friend? Between the kidnapping, and them trying to kill us, it didn't really provide an atmosphere conducive to a relationship, but somehow it happened.'

'You were attracted?' Polly asked quietly.

Ethan nodded. 'I think we both were attracted to each other. I know I was to her. I couldn't seem to keep her out of my mind, and even though she could take care of herself, probably better than I could, I still wanted to be there to make sure she was all right. Everything about her was so incredible. I couldn't believe that I was on such a roller coaster ride with her.'

Polly pursed her lips together, her gaze taking on a faraway look as she remembered her own rocky beginning with her husband. 'You fell in love.'

It wasn't a question, but a statement. Ethan leaned forward and picked up a few pebbles. He began skipping them across the surface of the road. After a moment, he flicked his gaze to her. 'Yes, I did.'

After a moment of silence, Polly held her hands up in front of her in question. 'Well, what happened? You didn't tell her about your feelings for her, did you?'

Ethan shook his head as he chuckled. His voice was threaded with irony. 'As a matter of fact, I did tell her that I was beginning to fall in love with her. I just didn't get the reaction I quite expected.'

'Oh,' she said simply. 'Scared her off, then?'

Leveling his gaze on her, Ethan gave her a lopsided smile. 'Make up your mind, Polly. Was I supposed to tell her, or not?'

Pursing her lips, Polly gave it some thought. 'I think you did the right thing. Besides, it's too late to change the past now, isn't it?'

'Boy, you're cheering me up quick, Polly,' he said.

She chuckled. 'What did she say when you told her you were falling in love with her?'

Ethan's lips thinned into a line of sadness as the memory washed through him. 'Nothing really. We didn't have time to discuss it because things started gaining momentum. Then I was shot. The nurse told me she stayed with me up till the moment when she found out that I was going to be okay.'

'That's good.' Polly smiled widely as her head bobbed up and down. 'That's very good.'

'What?' Ethan twisted on the curb to face her. 'She left, Polly. She didn't even stay long enough to tell me why. How the hell is that supposed to be good?'

'And you haven't gone too much out of your way to find out, have you?' The all-knowing look slipped on her face again as she beamed at him. 'Maybe it's because she loves you.'

'If she loved me why would she leave?' he snapped, though there wasn't much sting to his words.

'I don't know.' She giggled sweetly as she shrugged. 'Cold feet, I would guess.'

Polly's smile dimmed as she leaned closer to peer into his eyes. 'Do you love her, Ethan?'

He frowned at the question. The expression reminded Polly of the ornery little boy that he always reminded her of. 'Yes, I do.'

'Then what are you going to do about it?' she demanded, as she held his gaze.

Ethan looked away. 'There is nothing I can do about it, Polly. She left. Hell, I don't even know where she is. I've tried her house a couple of times and no one is there.'

'That's all?' Polly snorted. 'Seems like you could have tried a little harder.'

His back stiffened and he met Polly's protective glare with one of his own. 'What do you mean, try harder? What else could I have done?'

'Ye of little faith,' she stated, patting his hand as she rose to her feet.

Ethan shielded his eyes with his hand as he peered up at her. 'Well?'

Polly grinned, her shoulders swelling with pride. 'I'm an author, remember? We'll improvise.'

Mr Sturgeon, their neighbor from across the street, called to them from his mailbox. 'You two doing all right out here? Or are we starting a new neighborhood group?'

Polly laughed, and waved his joking question away. She'd started to walk back to her house when she stopped.

Turning back to Ethan, she let out her breath. 'Come on, Ethan.'

Ethan's brows rose at her order. Seeing the determination in his neighbor's eyes, he grinned. If she could write a book, who knew what else she could do?

CHAPTER 17

'So Harolds killed Torkelson,' Janet said, lounging in a chair in Tess's office, 'because Torkelson found out that he was robbing the company of millions of dollars by selling off vital trade secrets.'

'That's pretty much it,' Tess murmured as she doodled absently on the notepad at her desk. It had been a couple of months since she had last seen Ethan. She had thought, had hoped, that time would make the pain of his loss easier. To her dismay, and that of her concerned friends, she had been wrong. Keeping her thoughts on track, on her job, had been hard. Harder than she ever would have thought. Even now, as she talked with her friend, she had to force herself back to the conversation. 'Faking his own death while at the same time killing Torkelson gave him a way out all the way around. The world would think he was dead, clearing him of industrial espionage, kidnapping, and murder. It would also eliminate his ties to his family and he would be free to do whatever he wanted to do.'

'Until you brought him down.' Janet smirked happily. She crossed her legs and bounced her foot with delight. 'That almost makes up for having to walk ten miles till I found a house to call for help.'

Tess's gaze flicked up to meet her friend's, and a smile twitched at the corner of her lips. 'Now that you mention it, how are your legs doing?'

Janet narrowed her eyes at Tess as she folded her arms over her chest. She arched a brow as she haughtily answered, 'They are doing much better, thank you. The scratches are gone and the rash has just about disappeared.'

Tess could not suppress the giggle that fought for escape. When her friend had told her about having to climb a tree to try to get a better look at her surroundings, so she could determine her location somewhat, she had found it amusing. Hearing about how she had slid back down the trunk, catching splinters on the inside of her thighs and clutching at the vines snaking up the tree for support, had caused her to laugh. Janet's minor injuries had not been the source of her amusement, though. No, it was the fact that she had picked a tree loaded with poison ivy that had struck her funny. Janet had told her that climbing the tree had seemed like a Daniel Boone sort of thing to do at the time.

'Yeah, but,' Tess had delightedly pointed out, 'Daniel Boone would not have picked a tree covered with poison ivy.'

Janet tried to act mad, but her own sense of humor won out. 'At least I learned my lesson and I will not be climbing any more trees,' she giggled. She suddenly became serious, her eyes hardening with the change of subject. 'What's happening with Harolds?'

Like Janet's Tess's smile froze, and her good humor slipped away at the mention of the man's name. 'They're searching all of Harolds' hidden accounts, and they've found where he had been staying. They're looking for any information that might lead them to our one-and-only lead, who has disappeared. The woman, remember?' At Janet's nod, she continued. 'If they find he killed her too, then they will add that charge to the other two counts of first degree murder. Since he killed the two men in two different states, both of which have the death penalty, the district attorneys are negotiating to see who gets the first try at him. I imagine Colorado will get the first day in court with him, because Torkelson's murder occurred before the homeless man's death. If he's found guilty he'll be sentenced to death and it ends there. If he gets off on a lesser charge, and doesn't get the death penalty, Kansas plans on extraditing him to charge him here. Either way he loses.'

'Were they able to identify the poor man?' Janet asked.

Her friend's *non sequiturs* no longer often jolted Tess's normally systematic thinking, but this one did. Immediately Janet's cheeks stained red at the implication of her question. The man's death had occurred in Ethan Booker's jurisdiction. The only way Tess would have been able to find out if they had been able to identify him would be to talk to his office. Something she had not done since the day she had walked out of the Colorado hospital.

Tess looked away, her voice quiet. 'I don't know. I guess Ethan knows.'

'Well, I hope Harolds burns in hell for what he did to all of us,' Janet said heatedly, quickly changing the subject. She did not try to apologize, she had learned a long time ago that the best way to handle the situation with Tess was to gloss over it and ignore it.

'With the appeal process the way it is, it will be a long time before he's put to death, if ever,' Tess said quietly. The mere mention of Ethan's name renewed the pain she felt, and caused tears to swell within her throat. She cleared her throat uneasily, leaving the rest of what she was going to say unfinished, unable to trust the steadiness of her voice.

'You're right,' Janet quickly agreed. She shifted uncomfortably in her chair. Remembering the folder sitting on her desk, she jumped up from her seat. 'A new case came in, and since Tim and Tom are still working on the MacPherson case they wondered if you wouldn't mind handling it for them?'

Tess nodded. 'I've pretty much wrapped the RexComp case up.'

'Great,' Janet said, heading out the door. 'I'll be back in a minute.'

Tess rubbed distractedly at the pain growing behind her forehead, thankful for a few moments alone. She had not spoken nor heard Ethan's name in weeks, and the strength of the impact it had caused her surprised her. She rose slowly from her chair, the weight of her emotions pulling at her as she stepped over to look out the window. The summer day was a beautiful one, already promising to be a scorcher, and she watched the people walking on the sidewalk below her office building. She pushed all the pain and the exquisite memories of him from her thoughts, forcing her mind to go blank. She concentrated so hard on the rolling movement of a flag across the street in an effort to push him from her mind, that she did not hear Janet walk back into the room.

'Tess?' she called to her quietly.

'Hmm?' Tess murmured as turned away from the window. 'I'm sorry, did you say something?'

Janet smiled gently. 'I have the folder for the case the guys wanted you to handle. It's a new client.'

'Where are they located?' Tess asked, thankful for the case to keep her busy. Too busy to think of wildly handsome men with mischievous smiles and boyish charm. Taking the folder from Janet, she returned to her chair and opened it. Scanning the information, she frowned.

'New York,' Janet answered. 'It shouldn't take you long. The client would like to have the current security program for his company reviewed. He's apparently already lost something invaluable to him, and he doesn't want it to happen again.'

'Thanks,' Tess sighed. 'I'll head out right away.'

When the door opened, Harolds stood. A slow smile full of charm spread across his handsome features as his wife Elaine strode into the room.

He held his arms out to her, his eyes meeting his wife's. 'Sweetheart, I knew you would come for me.'

Mrs Gare Harolds froze him with an icy glare. He let his arms fall to his sides as he saw the anger and distaste in her expression. 'The only reason I am here, Gare, is to give you this.'

She slapped a folded set of papers against his chest. Harolds took it, opening it to read the contents. His eyes widened in bewilderment. Lifting his gaze, he looked at his wife of twenty-five years. 'What is this?'

'I had to talk my lawyer into it, but I wanted to deliver these to you personally,' she spat, relishing the look on his face. The bastard had taken her for granted for far too long. It sickened her to think of the years she had wasted on this man. 'They are divorce papers.'

Anger flickered in his expression, before he controlled it and smoothed on the charm that had served him well. 'I need you, baby. How can you do this to me?'

'You're dead, remember?' Elaine retorted. 'A divorce should be nothing to you.'

Frustration filled him, mingling with the rage. He viciously crumpled the papers in his hands. The movement caused Elaine's lawyer, a former linebacker, to step forward.

Harolds walked away from the man hovering protectively by his wife and began to pace at the other end of the room. He ran his hands through his hair, mussing it up. 'I can't believe you're doing this to me, bitch. After everything I've done for you.'

Fury rose within Elaine Harolds as she remembered the years of enduring his affairs and his detached treatment of her and the children. Then it dissipated. She realized that he no longer had any control over her. He no longer had the power to upset her. The new-found freedom caused her to smile.

'Goodbye, Gare,' she said simply. Elaine turned. Her lawyer was already holding the door open for her, and together they strode out of the room. As her heels clicked along the hallway of the jail, she could hear the frantic screams of her soon-to-be-ex-husband.

The flight to the 'Big Apple' was uneventful, but long. Long enough to allow her time to think. To be taunted by memories. Her only reprieve was when the multitude of sleepless nights finally caught up with her, the steady drone of the plane's engines luring her into slumber. Sleep continued its own form of torture by filling her dreams with Ethan's presence.

When the plane skidded to a bumpy halt in New York, Tess woke with a start, sweating, her heart pounding with the remnants of a dream she could not remember. It took a couple of hours to make her way through the airport, collect her luggage and hail a taxi to the company's apartment it kept in New York. Opening the door, she deposited her luggage and headed straight for a chair.

Propping her feet up, she closed her eyes against the throbbing of her headache. The phone rang and she groaned. Without looking, she blindly reached for the receiver beside her.

'Hello?' she said.

'Tess, you made it,' Janet stated cheerfully.

'I literally just walked in the door,' she said on a sigh. 'What is it?'

'So much for chit-chat,' Janet giggled. At Tess's pointed silence, she hurried on. 'Your clients just called, and the meeting has been moved up to tonight. They want you to meet them for dinner at seven o'clock.'

Tess tiredly lifted her arm to glance at her watch. It was already late afternoon; she would have just enough time to shower and change before she made the trip across town to meet them. 'Great, I'll just be able to get there.'

Who needed rest anyway? she thought without humor.

'That's the spirit,' Janet offered with a chuckle before she hung up.

Groaning again, Tess pushed herself from her chair, then headed to the bathroom to start her shower. 'To hell with the spirit,' she murmured.

Tess's blue mood had robbed of her any interest in dressing up to impress her clients. When she realized that she was wallowing in her own self-pity, she forced herself to take pains in picking out a conservative but elegant evening outfit. She even spent a few more minutes than usual on her hair and appearance, to make up for her mood.

The doorman rang her room when her taxi arrived, and Tess grabbed her purse. The ride across town gave her time to work at pushing her mellow thoughts out so she could talk business with her clients.

When they arrived at the hotel where her clients were staying, Tess got out of the taxi and paid the unusually friendly man before she headed inside. At the front desk, she gave the clerk her clients' name, as Janet told her she should do, and asked if they were waiting in the restaurant.

The clerk looked through his book, then met her gaze with an appreciative gleam. 'No, they are not. I just received a message that they would like to dine with you in their suite. Allow me to write down the number for you.'

Tess felt the irritation rise within her, but the only sign she would allow was a slow release of her breath. These clients was determined to push things. As a rule, she refused to meet potential clients in hotel rooms. The bedroom atmosphere was not conducive to business.

The clerk handed her a slip a paper with the room number on it. She managed a smile for him as she thanked him. She moved across the wide lobby to the elevator bank and pushed a button. It was only a moment before she heard a soft ding and a door slid open. Tess stepped in and pushed the number of the floor she needed.

Once the doors slid open at her floor, Tess read the signs and made her way to the suite. She knocked softly on the door, noting that her clients had shifted the lever to hold the door open for her. A muffled voice called to her to come in, and that the door was open.

Stepping into the hotel suite, Tess felt a growing sense of foreboding. The lights were dimmed and soft; unobtrusive but romantic music filled the room. She frowned at the beautifully decorated table set for two.

Tess's shoulders stiffened as she groaned inwardly. She had been forced to deal with clients like this before. Hardening her resolve, she called out.

'Tess.'

She froze, her heart not believing what her ears heard. It was Ethan's voice. Slowly Tess turned around to face him.

Ethan stood in the darkened shadows of the room. As he stepped into the lighted area of the dining room her gaze moved over him, as if to confirm he was real, not an illusion from her deepest need. The last time she had seen him he'd been unconscious, seriously wounded, suffering from loss of blood, and oh, so pale. Now, as her gaze caressed him, she was happy to see he had recovered remarkably well.

'Ethan?' she said, her brain unable to move past that one thought.

He put his hands in the pockets of his pants as he walked toward her. His gaze was on the floor as he slowly closed the distance between them. His eyes flicked up to meet hers and he gave her a lop-sided smile that showed he was as nervous as she was.

Tess shook her head, unsure whether to laugh or cry. 'I don't understand,' she was finally able to manage.

'After you left without saying anything . . .' he started, then hesitated. He lifted his hand to touch her cheek, but stopped before he reached her, letting it fall back to his side. 'After you left without saying goodbye, I didn't know if you would see me if I called you. For the first time in my life I didn't know what to do.'

Ethan cleared his throat, his voice husky when he continued. 'I only knew that I was miserable. After moping around for a long time, a friend finally jerked me back to reality.'

'So you came up with this crazy stunt?' she said, tears welling in her eyes.

'Yes,' he answered sheepishly.

Tess sobbed as she wrapped her arms around him. Ethan returned her hug just as fiercely, and placed gentle kisses on her cheek, her hair, and finally the tip of her nose. He held her close to him as his voice became rough with emotion.

'Oh, Tess, sweetheart,' he murmured as he stroked her hair. 'I've missed you.'

Tess pulled back just enough to tilt her face up to his. 'Ethan, I'm so sorry.'

'Shh,' he soothed. 'I'm just thankful to have you in my arms again.'

Standing on her tiptoes, Tess kissed Ethan, hungrily tasting him. The fear, the pain, the doubt began to slip away, and the tone of their kiss changed from hunger to cherished exploration. Slowly his lips moved over hers as he reacquainted himself with the silky contours of her mouth. His hands caressed her arms, her back and her bottom, though he continued to press their bodies to each other.

Ethan's lips left hers as he met her eyes. Tess felt the hunger of her desire spark with renewed vigor at his hooded gaze. How she'd missed those sexy eyes of his.

'Tess, it finally occurred to me why you left,' he said, his voice low. 'At first I thought it was because I'd scared you off, then I realized that it was something more than that.'

'What?' she asked, swallowing nervously.

'It took me a while, but I realized you were trying to protect me from your wild and woolly lifestyle. That element of danger,' he said with teasing softness. He smiled tenderly as he stroked her cheek with his fingertip. 'Problem is I had already developed a taste for that. For you.'

Tess shook her head and pursed her lips together. She started to pull away from Ethan's embrace, but he kept her safely snuggled within his arms. 'Ethan, it was that "element of danger" that almost got you killed. It was my fault. I should never have allowed you to come with me.'

Ethan placed his finger over her lips to quiet her. 'Sweetheart, Harolds was the one responsible for shooting me. Not you. You did not pull the trigger.'

A tear slipped down Tess's cheek. 'Ethan, I can't change who I am.'

He chuckled as he hugged her to him. 'Remember the first time I saw you?'

Tess was forced to giggle as she recalled the dowdy outfit and the ridiculous red wig. She snuggled into his embrace, her voice muffled against his wide shoulder. 'I was hoping you would eventually forget that little escapade.'

He hooked his finger under her chin and gently tilted her face up to his, so he could look into her eyes. 'The moment you turned around and I looked into those beautiful green eyes of yours, I knew there was something special about you. It was like my heart said, "There she is." Why would I want to change that?'

Tess's heart thumped wildly. She remembered her own feelings, which had mirrored his. Her eyes filled with tears, this time for joy, as she smiled at him. 'I felt the same way about you too, when I met you.'

'Ethan?' she said softly, reaching up to caress his handsome jaw. 'I love you.'

He found her lips with his and kissed her. After several cherished movements, she pulled back to look at him, her eyes narrowed playfully.

'This was a pretty elaborate scheme for you to come up with all by yourself,' she said, running her hand through his hair as she spoke. 'Just to see me.'

He smiled wickedly. 'Well, I did have some help.'

Tess nodded as she pulled lightly at his hair. 'You plotted with my partners, didn't you?'

'Polly actually came up with the plot,' Ethan supplied as he moved to nip seductively at her neck. 'Then we pulled your office in on the deal.'

'I can't believe they sold me out like that,' she laughed, opening her neck to his lips.

'They love you almost as much as I do,' he murmured against the silk of her throat.

'Really?' Tess's voice became husky as Ethan's touch worked its magic on her. 'I'm glad you did it. It saves me from having to file a paternity suit.'

Ethan stiffened. Slowly he lifted his gaze to meet hers, his eyes wide with surprise and joy. 'Paternity?'

She giggled. Her turn to be wicked. Ethan deserved it. 'Yes, Sabrina had five kittens. Four of them are gorgeous, and look just like her, but guess who the fifth one looks like?'

'Sylvester,' he supplied. He shook his head as he studied her. 'That was truly wicked, Quintessa.'

'I know,' she said happily, 'but you love me anyway.'

'Yes, I do.'

Tess became serious as she looked into the eyes of the man she loved. 'Ethan, I had given up hope a long time ago that I would ever have happiness. A relationship that fulfilled me completely. Then I met you. What if you get to know me, really know me, and you don't like what you find?'

'Sweetheart, we've been blown up, beat up, kidnapped and shot at.' His soft laughter brushed away her fear. 'I think getting to know each other will be a lot easier.'

Rarely were people given their dreams. Professional success had always been easy for her. Determination and hard work had helped her achieve what she had set out to do. Love had always seemed like a distant and foggy dream that would always elude her. Now that her dream was within her fingertips, Tess was not going to let it go.

 THE EXCITING NEW NAME IN WOMEN'S FICTION!

PLEASE HELP ME TO HELP YOU!

Dear *Scarlet* Reader,

As Editor of *Scarlet* Books I want to make sure that the books I offer you every month are up to the high standards *Scarlet* readers expect. And to do that I need to know a little more about you and your reading likes and dislikes. So please spare a few minutes to fill in the short questionnaire on the following pages and send it to me.

Looking forward to hearing from you,

Sally Cooper

Editor-in-Chief, *Scarlet*

Note: further offers which might be of interest may be sent to you by other, carefully selected, companies. If you do not want to receive them, please write to Robinson Publishing Ltd, 7 Kensington Church Court, London W8 4SP, UK.

QUESTIONNAIRE

Please tick the appropriate boxes to indicate your answers

1 Where did you get this Scarlet title?
Bought in supermarket ☐
Bought at my local bookstore ☐ Bought at chain bookstore ☐
Bought at book exchange or used bookstore ☐
Borrowed from a friend ☐
Other (please indicate) _____

2 Did you enjoy reading it?
A lot ☐   A little ☐   Not at all ☐

3 What did you particularly like about this book?
Believable characters ☐   Easy to read ☐
Good value for money ☐   Enjoyable locations ☐
Interesting story ☐   Modern setting ☐
Other _____

4 What did you particularly dislike about this book?
_____

5 Would you buy another Scarlet book?
Yes ☐   No ☐

6 What other kinds of book do you enjoy reading?
Horror ☐   Puzzle books ☐   Historical fiction ☐
General fiction ☐   Crime/Detective ☐   Cookery ☐
Other (please indicate) _____

7 Which magazines do you enjoy reading?
1. _____
2. _____
3. _____

And now a little about you –

8 How old are you?
Under 25 ☐   25–34 ☐   35–44 ☐
45–54 ☐   55–64 ☐   over 65 ☐

cont.

9 What is your marital status?
   Single ☐   Married/living with partner ☐
   Widowed ☐   Separated/divorced ☐

10 What is your current occupation?
   Employed full-time ☐   Employed part-time ☐
   Student ☐   Housewife full-time ☐
   Unemployed ☐   Retired ☐

11 Do you have children? If so, how many and how old are they?
   _____
   _____

12 What is your annual household income?
   under $15,000   ☐   or   £10,000   ☐
   $15–25,000   ☐   or   £10–20,000   ☐
   $25–35,000   ☐   or   £20–30,000   ☐
   $35–50,000   ☐   or   £30–40,000   ☐
   over $50,000   ☐   or   £40,000   ☐

Miss/Mrs/Ms _____
Address _____
_____
_____

Thank you for completing this questionnaire. Now tear it out – put it in an envelope and send it, before 31 March 1999, to:

Sally Cooper, Editor-in-Chief

USA/Can. address
SCARLET c/o London Bridge
85 River Rock Drive
Suite 202
Buffalo
NY 14207
USA

UK address/No stamp required
SCARLET
FREEPOST LON 3335
LONDON W8 4BR
Please use block capitals for address

SESAT/9/98

 *Scarlet* titles coming next month:

FIND HER, KEEP HER   Judy Jackson
Daniel St Clair is everything Jess Phillips should avoid. She's a career woman – fighting to make a living in a man's world. Daniel, she tries to convince herself, is a pompous university intellect with a pretty face and a nice body! When Jess accepts Daniel's help, she gives in to the physical attraction between them. Why not? They're both unattached, intelligent adults . . . but Jess should have remembered that romance plays by its own rules and it plays to win!

THE TROUBLE WITH TAMSIN   Julie Garratt
Tamsin runs away from love but soon discovers that 'out of sight' doesn't necessarily mean 'out of mind.' She likes men – she might even be in love with one of them: cheating Patric Faulkner, lost love Vaughn Herrick, and the attractively menacing Craig Andrews. Then there is Mark Langham - the one person Tam can always rely on to be there for her. But Mark's patience is wearing thin, and it is only when she begins to lose him that Tam realises just where her true happiness lies. But is she too late for love?

JOIN THE CLUB!

Why not join the *Scarlet* Readers' Club – you can have four exciting new reads delivered to your door every other month for only £9.99, plus TWO FREE BOOKS WITH YOUR FIRST MONTH'S ORDER!

Fill in the form below and tick your two first books from those listed:

1. *Never Say Never* by Tina Leonard ☐
2. *The Sins of Sarah* by Anne Styles ☐
3. *Wicked in Silk* by Andrea Young ☐
4. *Wild Lady* by Liz Fielding ☐
5. *Starstruck* by Lianne Conway ☐
6. *This Time Forever* by Vickie Moore ☐
7. *It Takes Two* by Tina Leonard ☐
8. *The Mistress* by Angela Drake ☐
9. *Come Home Forever* by Jan McDaniel ☐
10. *Deception* by Sophie Weston ☐
11. *Fire and Ice* by Maxine Barry ☐
12. *Caribbean Flame* by Maxine Barry ☐

ORDER FORM

SEND NO MONEY NOW. Just complete and send to **SCARLET READERS' CLUB, FREEPOST, LON 3335, Salisbury SP5 5YW**

Yes, I want to join the *SCARLET* READERS' CLUB* and have the convenience of 4 exciting new novels delivered directly to my door every other month! Please send me my first shipment now for the unbelievable price of £9.99, plus my TWO special offer books absolutely free. I understand that I will be invoiced for this shipment and FOUR further *Scarlet* titles at £9.99 (including postage and packing) every other month unless I cancel my order in writing. I am over 18.

Signed ....

Name (IN BLOCK CAPITALS)...

Address (IN BLOCK CAPITALS)...

....

Town .... **Post Code** ....

Phone Number ....

As a result of this offer your name and address may be passed on to other carefully selected companies. If you do not wish this, please tick this box ☐.

Did You Know?

There are over 120 NEW romance novels published each month in the US & Canada?

♥ *Romantic Times Magazine* is **THE ONLY SOURCE** that tells you what they are and where to find them—even if you live abroad!

♥ *Each issue* reviews **ALL** 120 titles, saving you time and money at the bookstores!

♥ *Lists mail-order* book stores who service international customers!

ROMANTIC TIMES MAGAZINE
~ Established 1981 ~

Order a <u>SAMPLE COPY</u> Now!

FOR UNITED STATES & CANADA ORDERS:
$2.00 United States & Canada (U.S FUNDS ONLY)
CALL 1-800-989-8816*

* 800 NUMBER FOR US CREDIT CARD ORDERS ONLY
♥ **BY MAIL:** Send <u>US funds Only</u>. Make check payable to:
Romantic Times Magazine, 55 Bergen Street, Brooklyn, NY 11201 USA
♥ **TEL.:** 718-237-1097 ♥ **FAX:** 718-624-4231

VISA • M/C • AMEX • DISCOVER ACCEPTED FOR US, CANADA & UK ORDERS!

FOR UNITED KINGDOM ORDERS: (Credit Card Orders Accepted!)
£2.00 Sterling—Check made payable to Robinson Publishing Ltd.
♥ **BY MAIL:** Check to above **DRAWN ON A UK BANK** to: Robinson Publishing Ltd., 7 Kensington Church Court, London W8 4SP England

♥ E-MAIL CREDIT CARD ORDERS: RTmag1@aol.com
♥ VISIT OUR WEB SITE: http://www.rt-online.com